W9-AQX-188

foxfire

OTHER NOVELS BY JOYCE CAROL OATES

Black Water

Because It Is Bitter, and Because It Is My Heart

American Appetites

You Must Remember This

Marya: A Life

Solstice

Mysteries of Winterthurn

A Bloodsmoor Romance

Angel of Light

Bellefleur

Unholy Loves

Cybele

Son of the Morning

Childwold

The Assassins

Do With Me What You Will

Wonderland

them

Expensive People

A Garden of Earthly Delights

With Shuddering Fall

JOYCE CAROL OATES

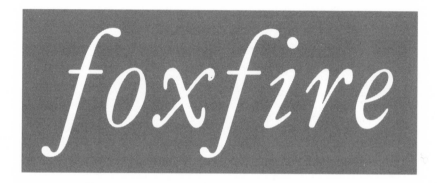

Confessions of a Girl Gang

A WILLIAM ABRAHAMS BOOK

DUTTON

DUTTON
Published by the Penguin Group
Penguin Books USA Inc., 375 Hudson Street,
New York, New York 10014, U.S.A.
Penguin Books Ltd, 27 Wrights Lane,
London W8 5TZ, England
Penguin Books Australia Ltd, Ringwood,
Victoria, Australia
Penguin Books Canada Ltd, 10 Alcorn Avenue,
Toronto, Ontario, Canada M4V 3B2
Penguin Books (N.Z.) Ltd, 182-190 Wairau Road,
Auckland 10, New Zealand

Penguin Books Ltd, Registered Offices:
Harmondsworth, Middlesex, England

Published by Dutton, an imprint of New American Library,
a division of Penguin Books USA Inc.
Distributed in Canada by McClelland & Stewart Inc.

First Dutton Printing, August, 1993

REGISTERED TRADEMARK—MARCA REGISTRADA

LIBRARY OF CONGRESS CATALOGING-IN-PUBLICATION DATA:
Oates, Joyce, Carol, 1938–
    Foxfire: confessions of a girl gang / Joyce Carol Oates.
        p. cm.
    ISBN 0-525-93632-7
    I. Title.
PS3565.A8F69 1993
813'.54—dc20   92-43858
                                                                                          CIP

Printed in the United States of America
Set in Garamond Light

In Memoriam
Marilyn, Rose Ann, Jean, Marian, Goldie, Beatrice—

Part

one

FOXFIRE:
An Outlaw Gang

Never never tell, Maddy-Monkey, they warned me, it's Death if you tell any of Them but now after so many years I am going to tell, for who's to stop me?

I was one who helped make the original rules after all, that very warning. I was FOXFIRE's official chronicler in fact.

Thus the sole person trusted to cast what we did into words, into a permanent record for us. Typed on a typewriter. Kept in neat dated entries, in a loose-leaf binder. A secret document and yet as it was hoped a "historical" document in which Truth would reside forever. *Thus distortions and misunderstandings and outright lies could be refuted.*

Like we did evil for evil's sake, and for revenge.

Of all lies pertaining to FOXFIRE surely that was the worst!

It was between the ages of thirteen and seventeen that I belonged to FOXFIRE and FOXFIRE made sacred those years. Till the last months at least.

Living there. In Hammond, New York. Upstate New York

near Lake Ontario where we'd all been born, all of us FOXFIRE blood-sisters, and could not then have imagined ever leaving, the way a dream, while you are dreaming it, feels like infinity out of which you can never wake.

FOXFIRE NEVER LOOKS BACK! was one of our secret proverbs. Also FOXFIRE BURNS & BURNS and FOXFIRE NEVER SAYS SORRY! but such pertained to regret and remorse and guilt and sin and repentance such as weaker people might feel, not to memory. And such predated, I guess I should state clearly, the nightmare events of FOXFIRE's final days of May–June 1956 which I believe no one of us did not regret.

For FOXFIRE was a true outlaw gang, yes . . .

But FOXFIRE was a true blood-sisterhood, our bond forged in loyalty, fidelity, trust, *love.*

Yes we committed what you would call *crimes.* And most of these went not only unpunished but unacknowledged—our victims, all male, were too ashamed, or too cowardly, to come forward to complain.

It's hard to feel sorry for them! You'll see!

Don't think though that by the end FOXFIRE had no hurt to bear, or that those of us still living aren't bearing it to this very hour.

FOXFIRE IS YOUR HEART!

—was a way for us to declare such truths 'cause you would never utter them in your own voice.

Except Legs Sadovsky who could murmur *Maddy-Monkey you're my heart* in that way of hers I wouldn't know how to interpret, was it serious, was it mock-serious, was it just plain teasing, was it all these things at once?—and she'd give me one of her jungle-cat love-bites knowing that Legs Sadovsky who was FOXFIRE's First-in-Command was the only one of us confident enough of her special power, yes and perceived by others as so privileged, entitled, to words grander and more reckless than ours. So you couldn't be jealous of her, you just couldn't. Like everything she did especially as time passed was magnified onto a giant movie screen, in Technicolor, not fading away like the things most people do, and dying.

And this is one reason: because the way Legs wasn't fearful of heights or swimming in rough water or Death itself she wasn't afraid to risk making a fool of herself. Maybe you think that's something of no consequence but it isn't—for making a fool of yourself, offering yourself to others to laugh at, to jeer, that takes guts.

Things Maddy would have cringed to contemplate, such exposure of the self, Legs Sadovsky did with no hesitation. No doubt that you could observe.

I was, I still am, Madeleine Faith Wirtz. In those days, I was sometimes Maddy-Monkey; sometimes just Maddy, and sometimes (because of my skinny wiry frame, my crimped-kinky dark-brown hair lifting like a crest from my forehead, something sly-shy, simian and pushed-together in my narrow face) just Monkey. Sometimes, less frequently, I was called "Killer"—by Legs mainly—because of my purported razor tongue, cutting and cruel.

Rightly or wrongly, Maddy Wirtz was the one perceived as having the power of words. Thus of intelligence, cunning. The gang took pride in me because I received high grades in school for written work, also I could "talk fast"—that's to say, without hesitating, stammering—most of the time—but there were categories of words, sentiments, I could never say, they'd have stuck in my throat. The embarrassment of it even whispering-teasing to Legs for instance *Yeah you're my heart too!* or *I love you* or *I would die for you,* nobody in my family ever talked that way, mostly there was just my mother and me and we hardly talked at all. Because it would be such weakness. Because it would be such exposure. So crude and raw in our girls' voices, not like the glamor movies we saw at the Century Theater those mile-high flawless faces and plaster-

Egyptian architecture framing them, music welling up like a secret sound of God gazing upon His special creation.

Because: you don't have to believe in God to believe
there's a special creation. Anybody tries to convince you otherwise he's a hypocrite and a liar. Or a politician like this
Congressman X from Uptown Hammond, he was a guest at
assembly one Friday when I was a freshman in high school,
face like a fat fish's and oily eyes up there behind the podium
like a preacher showing us his big happy-smug smile, Good
morning boys and girls, so happy to be here blah blah blah
at CAPTAIN OLIVER HAZARD PERRY HIGH SCHOOL so you
could tell he'd made sure he'd memorized that name, he'd attended a rival school and remembered well his high school
days a fullback on the football team president of his senior
class Class of '33 so proud such an honor American way of
life free enterprise blah blah those of us who served our
country in the War this God-ordained sovereign nation THE
UNITED STATES OF AMERICA as our patriot Commodore
Stephen Decatur said *Our country!—may she always be in
the right, and always successful, right or wrong!* this land of
opportunity of life liberty and the pursuit of happiness tri-
umphing against all enemies because ordained by God
where anyone *yes I mean anyone boys and girls in this very
auditorium this morning* can aspire to the Presidency itself
you can aspire to the head of General Motors—General
Mills—AT&T—U.S. Steel—a Nobel Prize–winning scientist a
famous inventor only have faith, work hard study hard never
be discouraged have faith! and some of us especially the guys
and the rowdier girls like Goldie Siefried who was in our
gang got visibly restless, muttering and laughing behind their
hands, Maddy Wirtz too in her sneakier way, we so resented
that asshole up there talking talking talking taking up the entire assembly expecting us to believe there isn't a special
creation of God, or of man, to which we didn't belong, here
at the shabby south end of Hammond in the worst damn

public school in the district, we didn't belong and never would.

And what the hell?—such truths, FOXFIRE made softer.

I'm looking through my old battered loose-leaf notebook from those years. Wondering how to begin.

Like when you know the long history of Time, going back to—the beginning?—but how's there a beginning, exactly?—how can you say Now, now we start, now we start clocks ticking?—it's like that, so difficult. Because there has got to be a beginning logically yet you always ask yourself—O.K. but what came before?

Maybe I'll just type out the names of the five founding members?—to establish certain irrefutable facts like the skeleton inside the history, the bones that will last.

FOXFIRE's founding members were:

> Legs, sometimes called "Sheena": Margaret Ann Sadovsky. Our First-in-Command.
>
> Goldie, sometimes called "Boom-Boom": Betty Siefried. Our First Lieutenant.
>
> Lana: Loretta Maguire.
>
> Rita, sometimes called "Red" and "Fireball": Elizabeth O'Hagan.
>
> Maddy, sometimes called "Monkey" and "Killer": Madeleine Faith Wirtz.

Yes, FOXFIRE afterward became larger, things loosened. Things wobbled out of control and there were too many of us.

For instance: there was initiated into FOXFIRE a certain protégé of Goldie Siefried's, "V.V.", or "The Enforcer," whose name I refuse to record.

Most of us attended the same elementary school—

Rutherford Hayes. Then on to Perry where a few of us graduated but most flunked out or were expelled. We all lived in the same neighborhood in the south end of what's still called Lowertown, in Hammond, New York, meaning more or less what it says, or describes, on lower ground than Uptown, a long steep hill cutting approximately half the city off from the other half though there was U.S. 33 running north and south through the city, High Street it was called Uptown and Fairfax Avenue in Lowertown, intersecting with U.S. 104 to the north and U.S. 20 to the south—these highways that went the full width of New York State. As a girl I loved to study maps, maps of the solar system, and the Earth, but maps too of local regions tracing how a street familiar as Fairfax where my mother and I lived connected outward to other streets less well known to me and these in turn to other streets—roads—highways—connecting to the nation, the continent, the Earth. There was the geographical Earth, that mankind (I guess I mean *men*) had mapped and given names to, and political designations; and there was the geological Earth, also mapped, but predating maps. It fascinated me that starting *here* you could move, eventually, to *there;* from any point in the Universe you could travel to any other point—if you had the power.

Like Legs Sadovsky that day in the museum when we saw the Tree of Life, how it connected things, like underground roots connecting all things living and dead, and she bit at her thumbnail brooding saying finally, "—You'd think our species would count for more than *that,*" in surprise and disgust for how small *Homo sapiens* was revealed after all.

Such truths, FOXFIRE made softer.

Another thing Legs said I don't believe is recorded anywhere in the notebook, only just in my memory—she had this crazy love of heights, of diving from a high riverbank in Cassadaga Park and into the water, like the most reckless of the older guys, and as a young kid she'd loved to climb almost anything, a tree, a wall, a roof, she told me she had a happy dream over and over of climbing climbing climbing right up into the sky, she said it wasn't the climbing she craved but the chance of falling!—saying in that dreamy way of hers that contained a shivery sort of excitement underneath, "—Like you're falling, Maddy, I mean really seriously falling like through the sky, for a long long time, you wouldn't feel *heavy* would you?—you wouldn't feel your weight any more than if it was a feather. There wouldn't be any *gravity* for you."

Why this meant so much to her she'd dream of it, I didn't know.

I'm not sure if I know, even now.

Thinking of this though, leafing through Maddy Wirtz's notebook, wondering how to proceed—so many entries! so many dates!—I realized that there were deep unarticulated connections among the FOXFIRE sisters we couldn't know at the time. Because we were too close to our origins. Because we spoke in the identical reedy-nasal upstate New York accent, that we couldn't hear. Because different as we were—how different Maddy Wirtz felt herself from Goldie Siefried, from Rita O'Hagan, from Lana Maguire!—how special, how superior she'd needed to be!—we were like family members proud of their distinctions while always *always* confused with one another by outside, neutral observers.

The things that link us deepest, we can't feel.

Except if they're taken from us.

two

How Legs Escaped
Back to Fairfax Avenue

Maddy?—let me in.

Hey Maddy: I'm coming in.

Night. A hard bone-bright moon, a sky fissured with clouds. And she's been running for hours—hundreds of miles!

She hears sirens. Pursuing *her*.

But nobody's going to lay their hands on *her*: she's too smart, and she's too fast.

From Plattsburgh up north near the Canadian border where by order of the State Department of Human Welfare Services she'd been sent eighteen days previous to live with her grandmother because the Sadovsky household had been officially designated as "unsuitable for a minor" to Hammond and lower Fairfax Avenue she's been running and who's to stop her? even to call out her name? as she's running now, leaping and flying effortlessly across the rooftops of the brownstone row houses descending the street toward the invisible river, she's a horse, a powerful stallion all hooves, flying mane, tail, snorting and steamy-breathed and where there's a space between one roof and the next she doesn't break her stride doesn't hesitate simply tenses her long muscle-hard legs knowing she isn't going to fall, leaping from one side to the other her hair whipping in the wind baring her pale angular face and her teeth bared too as if in anger but it's happiness because she's free, she has escaped the place they believed they could send her as if they had power over *her.*

Such happiness Maddy sometimes I can't swallow it, it's like the whole sky shoved into my mouth and I'm gonna choke and below on the street there's an illuminated clock in the window of the shoe repair shop reading twenty minutes past twelve, a slinky sexy black cat with one paw upraised bearing the clock's revolving hands Legs is flying past too fast to see except to know it's there.

Not that clock-time has anything to do with Legs Sadovsky, "Sheena" flying through the jungle.

And the sparely spaced streetlights below on Fairfax with that sharp look of light in freezing air. And the cracked and uneven sidewalks, the steeply descending street, facades of row houses dropping drunk and dizzy toward the Cassadaga River a mile away, the smell of the river lifting, its pull. *Maddy?—hey let me in! Don't be scared, it's me!* Like a blind creature with an unfailing spatial memory Legs knows the houses whose roofs she crosses, family by family she can identify the tenants, yes and the tenants of the houses on the facing side of Fairfax too, their downstairs rooms darkened at this hour but here and there an upstairs room still lit, blinds discreetly drawn, the occasional shadow of intimate movements within from which Legs turns her head swiftly, she's chaste, intolerant, teeth bared in a horse's grimace, *Maddy-Monkey you damn well better let me in!* hunching now so she can't be seen from the street where there's a car passing with jolting headlights, behind it a souped-up Oldsmobile Rocket 98 she recognizes driven by Vinnie Roper and crammed front and back with his gang-buddies The Viscounts who'd recognize Legs Sadovsky could they catch a glimpse of her and who'd let out a collective hyena-whoop of predatory sexual excitement realizing how close how tantalizingly close she is if two storeys above the street and how utterly alone trotting in her dirty jeans, shabby sneakers, thin canvas jacket just like Legs who's so wild and crazy as everybody who knows her knows but *Thank God the fuckers didn't see: just drove on, assholes tires screeching and we're gonna get ourselves a car someday* but suddenly she's cold, nothing on her head in this November wind off the river smelling of snow razor-sharp like snow and oh Christ what happened to her gloves?—those fur-lined gloves she'd picked up at Norben's slipping off the discount counter and into her pocket, must be she'd lost them, left them in one of the cars she'd hitched a ride in skirting the eastern shore of dark somber Lake Ontario in her need to get back here to Fairfax Avenue to home?

Maddy?—wake up!

Don'tcha know who I am?

Her fingers are stiff like exposed bone but fuck it, Legs is almost at her destination.

Chiding herself: you don't feel extremes of temperature when you're on a mission and your very life's at stake, those hateful bastards wanting to put their hands on *you* wanting to impose their plans on *you,* you'd rather die than surrender.

Neon-lit windows up the block at Fairfax and Tideman, the Shamrock Tavern, Buffalo's Café, Acey-Deucy's which Legs has memorized having been brought to these beer joints by her parents for years and then, after her mother's death, by her father, and probably at this very moment Ab Sadovsky is standing at the bar of, say, Acey-Deucy's, drinking in the company of Muriel and their friends but Legs won't think of him, or of Muriel, any of that, "unsuitable" environment but fuck that she's too smart to be going right home, not right now, not tonight, catching hell from the old man who'd thought he'd gotten rid of her for a while but mainly why risk being picked up again by the Welfare Services people and this time, who knows, dumped at Juvenile Hall where she'd been once before and wanted to die, the county shelter for children they'll have to drag her to in handcuffs and beaten comatose with cops' nightsticks *she is not going not ever again* and she knows her official residence is the first place they'll look if Gramma reports her missing which maybe the old lady will out of spite but maybe the old lady won't out of spite washing her hands of Legs forever—but Legs isn't thinking of any of this, now she's where instinct has guided her, breath steaming, heartbeat fast as if she's been sniffing Cutex nail polish remover, fast and kicky but, to her, that's a sign of something good to come as now she's climbing down over the edge of the roof at 388 Fairfax, gawky-graceful and shrewd-muscled as her comic book heroine "Sheena the Jungle Girl" she's lowering herself onto the rusted fire escape, and down, and down, now crouching outside a window (the room darkened within) thinking there's nothing so powerful as the feeling you get turning up in a place nobody expects you, a million million ways of saving your life like Ab Sadovsky says the world's a cesspool so you better keep your head well up out of it and you fucking better learn how to *swim.*

"Maddy?—let me in."

But already she's tugging at the window, grunting to get it raised.

Waking me from my thin shaky sleep that's like ice just beginning to form on the surface of water, and through it I can hear something scratching then tapping on the window pane close by my head, then a voice calling my name I can't recognize at first, it's half pleading half bullying, I wake up paralyzed with fear for a moment my bladder pinching with the need to pee, too surprised even to scream and I see there's a figure on the fire escape outside my window only three or four feet away, I hear my name, chiding, mocking, a low throaty impatient voice, and before I can move to prevent the window being yanked up, or to assist in yanking it up, it's up, and Legs Sadovsky climbs into my room breathless and laughing.

"Maddy, sweetheart: don't look so *scared!*"
Which is how FOXFIRE will come to be born.

Not officially that night, which was November 12, 1952, but that was the night Legs was inspired, in my bed, after I'd crept downstairs to get her some food and something to drink, to talk in her dreamy head-on plunging way of how we must always be loyal to each other, how we must trust and help each other, "—like f'rinstance if one of us is in trouble she goes to the other, and that one takes her in, right?—like you did?—no questions asked, right?" and I'm nodding, murmuring, "Yes, oh yes," a little dazed still and flattered that Legs had chosen *me*, of the half-dozen girls in the neighborhood she might have chosen she'd chosen *me*. Meaning she trusted me even more than Goldie Siefried whom most of us would have named as her closest girl friend, and there was Lana Maguire too, both of them a year older than I was, more mature, with more defined personalities—and much better-looking. So I was flattered as hell not wanting to think that Legs had come to me because she knew I had a room entirely to myself (unlike Goldie, unlike Lana) and because no one else was at our place except Momma who was too ailing and dosed-up with drugs to know what was going on, or to care. It was enough for me just to be singled out for such a privilege and such an adventure anticipating how it would be told and retold around the neighborhood and at school *Did'ya hear how Legs escaped back home, climbed in Maddy Wirtz's window in the middle of the night and nobody caught them—wild!* watching Legs eating like she hadn't eaten in days, eyes leaking tears she was so grateful for the hunk of meatloaf I'd found in the refrigerator coagulated with a lacy film of grease, some cold mashed potatoes in a Tupperware bowl, slices of Kraft's American cheese and Wonder Bread and a Hostess cupcake we shared and a bottle of Pabst Blue Ribbon beer we shared too, as Legs chewed, and swallowed, and smiled, and talked, "—the thing is, Maddy, say you're the one the cops are after and you come to my place, right?—and *I let you in*—" emphasizing these words by squeezing my upper arm so I couldn't help wincing. I asked if the cops had really been after her but she didn't hear, talking in her quick excited but dreamy way, the tiny sickle scar on her chin like a dimple in the gauzy light of my bedside lamp, and her eyes I'd always thought so beautiful, so penetrating and alert filming over slightly with what must have been fatigue but still she talked, words bottled up inside her she'd come all this way to utter, "—my grandmother's so *weird,* man I mean *certifiable,* staring at me all the time saying I look like my mother, my hair like hers, my eyes, that kind of embarrassing crap, so I tell her shut up and walk out of the room and she starts in bawling, then she's trying to get me to pray with her, not just at Mass I mean, that's bad enough, but in the house, y'know, like we're crazy or something, like nuns or something, kneeling on the rug in her bedroom, 'Margaret, we're going to say the rosary together,' the old girl announces, then she's shocked when I tell her the hell with that: I can't sit still, let alone *kneel,* for any goddamn rosary. Also she was try-ing to get me to do these crap things around the house, the dishes, and cleaning up in the bathroom, tried to give me a lesson making my bed, 'There's a right way, Margaret, and a wrong way to do things,' she says, so I laugh in her face and tell her this thought that came to me one day in math class, 'No there's only one *right* way, Gramma,' I says, 'but there's a million million *wrong* ways which is why things get fucked up constantly.' And the old gal stares at me like I'd slapped her or something. Like I'd invented the word *fuck* just to insult her."

Legs talked, I listened, always I was mesmerized listening to her, always and forever. It seemed she wanted me to hide her from the cops?—no it seemed she only wanted to stay the night, in the morning she'd be leaving. Or: she'd come all the way from Plattsburgh on foot, or had she maybe hitched a ride or two; maybe she'd even had to swim . . . Legs Sadovsky *was* a wonderful swimmer but could this be true? swimming across a river, a canal? upstate? and some guys whooping and shouting after her?

Nah probably she'd be going to move back in with her old man, provided there was room. Provided his "girl friend" (uttered with fastidious contempt) didn't take up too much space.

I listened. I wasn't hoping to analyze Legs' accounts of what had befallen her, I never tried, those early years. I wouldn't have granted Maddy Wirtz such authority!—thinking how for as long as I could remember I guess I'd been watching Legs Sadovsky, the long-limbed ashy-blond strong-willed girl the teachers insisted upon calling "Margaret" like they could make her into "Margaret" simply by saying the name repeatedly, I'd been watching her envying her but not mean-jealous or resentful just hopeful of learning from her a certain manner of *being*.

By age sixteen she'd be a beautiful girl, hard and cold and assured, now she was halfway homely: her face thin and bony, her nose somehow wrong, mouth unformed and eyes jerky and suspicious like the eyes of a nerved-up cat. Her skin was grainy-pale; her hair that was so striking a shade of blond always in a tangle as if she hadn't dragged a brush or comb through it in weeks. And there was that sickle-scar on her chin she claimed she'd gotten in a knife fight at age ten (or was it when her father slapped her, years ago, knocked her flying across a room and against the sharp edge of a table), my eye repeatedly drawn to it so sometimes when I was alone or day-dreaming in school I'd catch myself running my finger over my own chin seeking out that scar.

Legs: the Sadovsky girl: the one my mother didn't like, cutting her eyes at Legs in the street saying that girl's bad news, that girl's a bitch you can see it in her face, don't mess with *her*. Legs I'd seen jump from a railroad trestle to the ground twelve feet below, and a hard-packed dirt ground, the boys who were with her and who'd dared her and boasted of not being afraid either had jumped only after hesitating—the visible sweat of fear. I'd watched her striding across the asphalt school yard, I'd seen her running in the street, solitary in running, she was happiest running, in my memory once a few years before leaping over a dangerous pit of an opening in a sidewalk on Fairfax where coal thundered down a sliding chute from a truck, and the delivery man shook his fist at her, swore at her, and Legs ran on not hearing, you wouldn't have known except for the wild bushy ashy hair that she was a girl thus especially forbidden to take such risks.

Legs whispered, "What's that?" narrowing her cat's eyes thinking she'd heard something close by, but it was only a car out in the street, voices lifting, some drunks leaving Acey-Deucy's probably, still she'd leapt out of my bed (where she'd been lying sleepy and twitchy in her jeans, shirt, orlorn cardigan sweater, stocking feet, propped up against my single pillow: I'd been sitting on the edge of the bed facing her) and stood crouched at the window, her extended hand warning me back, fingers outspread as if truly there might be danger. Then the noise faded, and Legs squinted up at the sky, the moon so bright you'd never think it could be merely rock like the earth's common rock and lifeless, merely reflected light from an invisible sun and not a powerful living light of its own, and Legs said, "Y'know what I'm gonna miss, Maddy?— after I'm dead? Nights like this and everything clear and cold and sharp, like up in the sky, so you don't mind you're the only one, y'know what I mean?"

It was one-thirty in the morning. Legs who'd claimed to have come on foot more than three hundred miles that day now swayed with tiredness. She took up the bottle of beer, swallowed another large mouthful and I extracted the bottle from her fingers so she wouldn't drop it and helped her settle back into bed, my pillow beneath her head and the two of us beneath the covers crowded and giggly-shy, my bed was just a damned kid's bed I'd outgrown, and I switched off the light and Legs shivered and sighed and giggled again and whispered, "You're my heart, Maddy, y'know? Taking me in like this?" then making a joke of it, "—You won't tell the cops, will you?"

That night our hair tangled together, we must have wakened each other a dozen times, restless in sleep, kicking, tripping, trying to turn over dragging at the covers. I was barefoot but wearing a baggy sweater I'd put on over my pajamas when Legs first climbed into my room and Legs was still in her clothes, her jeans with items in her pockets including her switchblade with its several blades. She boasted she always slept prepared for a quick getaway.

three

They, Them . . . Others

Once FOXFIRE was born and our blood intermingled there was a way of saying They, Them, the Others, and immediately you'd know what was meant, but before FOXFIRE came into being things weren't clear and mistakes could be made, even Legs must not have known exactly what was coming. The way, groping in the dark, even if it's a familiar dark, a place you believe you've memorized, the distances between objects are distorted by the very fact of the dark and you're losing your way even as you're convinced you know where you're going.

This time I'm thinking of, I never recorded it in my original FOXFIRE notebook but it belongs here now, as I try to trace the coming-into-being of FOXFIRE and its hold on our hearts. We'd come from the Century Theater downtown, Legs, Lana Maguire, and me, Legs had three new five-dollar bills she'd gotten from somewhere she wouldn't say where ("Ask me no questions," she said teasing, "—and I'll tell you no lies") and she'd treated us, showing up at my house Saturday afternoon saying Hey Maddy-Monkey let's go downtown, you and me and Lana, but not saying why, not saying she had money, it was like Legs in one of her good moods to be generous even careless with money, taking pleasure in surprising her friends, seeing the warm startled smiling look on your face when you were surprised, and happy. We'd seen a double feature at the Century, we were coming home at dusk, crossing the Sixth Street bridge and shivering in the wind, there were flying bits of icy snow and grit hitting us in the face. It was just after Thanksgiving and already there were colored Christmas lights strung up along the fronts of some of the stores, some of them meager, even shabby, but festive nonetheless, and we passed a corner lot at Sixth and Randolph that was just a vacant lot ordinarily but now CHRISTMAS TREES—YOUR PICK were being sold there hundreds of firs, spruces, tall fragrant evergreens snow crusted on their boughs and I thought of how we wouldn't have a Christmas tree at home of course, we had not had one in a long long time but truly I wasn't thinking of that, or of Momma, she wasn't a thought I allowed myself to think, as in this notebook (as you'll notice) adults are never spoken of except in specific terms of FOXFIRE, but I was staring at the trees, like woods in the midst of the city it was, except the trees had been sawed down, they were still living and green but already dying maybe but still very beautiful and I watched a plump loud-laughing man who seemed to be the proprietor of the lot, a big-bellied man with a flushed face, cigar, wide-rimmed cowboy-looking hat, he was clapping his bare hands together to keep them warm, smoke curled from his mouth, talking with a man in a nice camel's-hair coat with two little girls hand in hand, you knew they were his daughters, one wore a red coat bright as a dab of paint, she must have been about ten years old, the other was a little younger wearing a yellow plaid coat, and both had leggings on, I had not worn leggings in a long long time and smiled to see them, and there were other customers buying trees, a young couple, arms around each other's waist, and a well-to-do woman in a silvery fur coat mincing through the snow in shoe-boots and I was staring I don't know why, Legs and Lana walking fast and Legs talking in her rapid jeering way of the movie we'd just seen, a musical, Esther Williams, gorgeous sequinned swimming routines, synchronized movements of dozens of female bodies, and I was stumbling behind looking over into the Christmas tree lot until Legs reached back to poke me and asked what was wrong and I said nothing, I said I didn't know, then went on vague and rambling and wondering the way I sometimes did in those days when no idea was articulated to me except by being voiced, most of all voiced in the presence of Legs Sadovsky, "—There's something about other people isn't there?—you'd like to know who they are?—you'd like to *be* them, maybe? People you never saw before and"—my voice lifting in excitement, "it's so strange how they're different from you, isn't it?—or like if somebody had the power, say somebody said to you, 'Would you change places with the next person you see, a stranger just turning a corner,' I'd say, 'Hell *yes.*' "

Such wild ideas that came to me, swept through my head and left me weak and moony-eyed. A shy girl who, once talking, doesn't know when to shut up.

And when you're older you keep these flights of fancy to yourself. You've learned.

Well I didn't think anything of it, Legs quiet and Lana just shrugging like she thought I was crazy, then twenty minutes later on Fairfax when we were almost home Legs turned suddenly to me, no warning, her mouth pale and working, her eyes showing anger, hurt, "What kind of crap were you saying back there, Maddy, you'd trade places with anybody?—just anybody? *Is that what you said?*" advancing upon me as if we'd been quarreling, as if I'd challenged her, she didn't give me a chance to reply, both Lana and I were taken by surprise by her ferocity, "—You'd betray your friends, huh, not giving a shit about anybody who knows *you* and is *your* true friend not some fucking stranger, huh?" her voice rising, I couldn't follow her words, she was shoving me backward with the flat of her hand, I couldn't believe this quicksilver change of mood you never really believed these moods in Legs though they happened frequently, I stumbled backward into the gutter, "Legs don't, hey Legs that *hurts,*" but she kept on, the wrath was in her face, her eyes weirdly beautiful and dilated showing a rim of white above the dark iris, "Traitor!—you love *them* so much, go suck up to *them,* get out of my sight and away from *me!*" and I didn't see her arm swinging, her fist cracking me in the face, my nose began to bleed, icy-eyed and furious Legs would not relent even when I burst into tears, just pulled Lana away with her, the two of them walking quickly away leaving me standing there in the street dazed and uncomprehending as headlights glared up and swung past, dangerously close, a horn or two sounded, in warning, but in warning of what, I didn't know.

four

FOXFIRE: First Victory!

Poor fat little Elizabeth O'Hagan, the ninth child in the O'Hagan family, the second daughter, why did everybody torment her?—her brothers for the amusement of the neighborhood boys, those loud raucous jeering boys, once when she was seven years old they'd torn off her panties and tossed them high up into a tree in the Rutherford Hayes school yard, once they'd draped a stunned, wounded garter snake around her neck so she ran screaming in mad hysteria a spectacle of much hilarity, another time yet more cruel (to this, Maddy Wirtz who'd tried to stop them had been an unwilling witness: so vividly she remembers it to this day, this moment) they'd drowned Elizabeth's calico kitten in a ditch in front of her terror-filled eyes, this too construed as hilarious, the consequent weeping, the girl-hysteria, so plumply cute a child as Elizabeth, with her strawberry-blond curls that looked as if someone had set a match to her hair, those warm moist brown eyes of perpetual wonderment and hurt, by age eleven and certainly by age twelve she'd begun to take on the contours and proportions of a woman, soft fist-sized breasts not very adequately contained by the cotton undershirt she wore, jellyish hips and thighs, pale knees that were both dimpled and scarred from childhood mishaps since of course Elizabeth, Rita as she came to be called, was famously clumsy. If not shoved to the ground, she was likely to fall. If her lunch bag or school books were not snatched from her fingers, she might well drop them herself. Cries of *Slowpoke!* and *Dumbo!* and *Fattie!* and even *Half-wit!* attended her well up into junior high school and though these cries were mostly male they were not exclusively male, and though they were mostly jeering they were not exclusively jeering but had a tone sometimes of what might be called excited affection, feverish interest—for inside Rita O'Hagan's plump pale face, as inside her childish terror, there shone, discernible to even the crudest eye, an American prettiness of the kind commonly exhibited on the covers of *Screen World, Women's Day, Collier's* and in advertisements of household products manufactured by Procter & Gamble and General Foods. And Rita's tears—those quick fat globules of tears of utter helplessness—no defense—were unfailingly gratifying: her tormentors' reward.

So when Rita murmured to Maddy Wirtz, "—I don't want these things to happen, they just do," Maddy Wirtz shrugged impatiently, not wanting to hear, not wanting to be associated with this luckless neighborhood girl who was in fact her friend or could claim friendship of a tenuous kind when those jeering others were not near, "Oh Maddy don't look so disgusted I don't *want* these things to happen, they just *do*,"—a repeated lament as if the embarrassing and shameful and occasionally alarming and even painful things that happened to Rita occurred outside her, beyond her, like weather, with no specific reference to her: her physicality, her female being.

"It's because you cry, they like to see you cry," Maddy Wirtz told Rita O'Hagan, not once but numerous times, those years the girls were neighbors, "—if you just wouldn't *cry*," and Rita, typically walking fast to keep pace with Maddy, would say, breathless, nodding so her soft pale chins jiggled,

"Oh I know, I know—I don't know I'm doing it, it just *happens.*"

Rita's childish teeth were slightly crooked and discolored so she had a habit of hiding her mouth behind her hand when she laughed or smiled, a habit she would never outgrow, yet more annoyingly she had a tendency to squint and blink in her sweetly cowering way as if the fact of another's intimate gaze, another's consciousness, were daunting. Rita was not truly fat but only plump and even delicately boned inside her plumpness nor was she slow-witted, Maddy believed her as smart as the majority of their classmates, perhaps smarter, whether or not this manifested itself in school work and grades as usually it did not. Maddy felt sorry for Rita of course she felt sorry for Rita (whom in fact she was slow to call "Rita" since the name had some mocking-teasing reference to Rita Hayworth whose hair was also a brilliant flamey red) yet she resented Rita too, yes probably she despised Rita too, and feared her, so strangely she feared her as if both the girl's conspicuous female helplessness and the attraction this helplessness bore for others might be somehow contagious: as, she'd heard, you could get your period at a younger age if you had older sisters especially if you shared a bed with one.

There came then the summer before seventh grade when the story was of how Rita O'Hagan's own brothers, the two youngest, talked her into coming with them to a clubhouse of sorts built by a gang of older boys, the Viscounts as they called themselves, somewhere beyond the railroad tracks beyond a hilly trash-littered wasteland of billboards on giant stilts, and of how, captive there, Rita O'Hagan, twelve years old, was the object of certain acts performed upon her, or to her, or with her, for most of a long August afternoon; and when, disheveled and weeping, and leaking menstrual blood, Rita was released to make her way home, alone, her mother screamed at her and slapped her and did not then, or subsequently, inquire of her what had happened that afternoon—whether anything had happened at all. (Mrs. O'Hagan's primary concern was that her husband know nothing since Mr. O'Hagan, a machine-shop worker, was inclined to melancholic binges of drinking and sporadic acts of violence, most of them domestic, when things troubled him.) Nor did Rita ever tell Maddy Wirtz what had happened that afternoon though Maddy was prepared to say, in disdain and contempt and even loathing of her friend, these things don't just happen to you, you let them happen.

You'd have thought, wouldn't you, that Rita O'Hagan's teachers would have been protective of her, and maybe some of them were, but there was Mrs. Donnehower in eighth grade English who spoke in a bemused patient voice to Rita when it was her turn to read aloud (we were reading Marjorie Kinnan Rawlings' *The Yearling*—we'd been reading it for weeks) and Rita stammered and blushed and lost her way though moving her forefinger with fanatic precision beneath the lines of print; and there were numerous episodes of humiliation in gym class from which that teacher did not trouble to spare her, poor Rita with jiggling breasts and hips amid a little group of overweight or myopic or illcoordinated girls barely tolerated by the rest; and worst of all was ninth grade math where Mr. Buttinger's drawling nasal voice rang out repeatedly, "Rita! Ri-ta! Go to the blackboard please and show us how it's done!" and the class sniggered in anticipation as Rita fumbled even taking the piece of chalk from Mr. Buttinger's fingers and went to the board in a daze of incomprehension and mute physical shame. Not that Rita O'Hagan was the slowest and stupidest pupil in Mr. Buttinger's class (though for amusement's sake she could be made to appear so) but rather that she was the pupil most humbled by her mistakes, most apologetic, most likely to burst into tears. And what big jewel-like tears, streaming down her face! So Mr. Buttinger might at last take pity on her, as her chalk-scribblings came to so little, for even if Rita knew the correct answer she could not reproduce it in front of so many scornful eyes, nor did he really expect it of her, sending her back to her seat with flurried waves of his hands as you might drive along a dog or a sheep, shaking his head, smiling, winking out at the class, "That's enough, Rita—you've exposed yourself enough."

His eyes glowering oyster-pale behind the lenses of his glasses. Close up, you could see the fingerprints smudged on those lenses.

Many days he disciplined Rita after school—carefully enunciating the word *"dis*-ci-pline"—by having her make up her errors of the day, at the blackboard. Sometimes other slow or unprepared students were present, most often not.

So he could give Rita, as he sourly said, the attention her ignorance required.

Mr. Buttinger was himself a fattish man, short, squat, with a head of spiky ginger-grizzled hair and a face that looked many-layered as if stitched together, like an elephant's skin in creases and folds; his lips were thick and perpetually moist— "Nigger Lips" he was called behind his back. His first name was Lloyd and he was forty-seven years old as we would learn afterward from newspaper accounts of his retirement. Every math formula and problem and page of our textbook he knew by rote, he could teach us while staring out the window at the sky or staring half smiling and glowering at the rear of the room as if it were the earth's horizon or at one or another of us, Rita O'Hagan for instance, clearly she fascinated him, a baby-woman, a female budding ripe to blossom, cringing meekly in her desk only a few feet from Mr. Buttinger's own in the first row, first desk at the far right. Where so naturally slow and ignorant a student would be seated, for practicality's sake; where without leaving his desk he could keep an eye on her.

I have to say though I wouldn't have known to say it then that I learned from Mr. Buttinger. Or through him, or despite him. I hated him and he hated me for sitting there like Legs staring refusing to laugh at his nasty jokes refusing to grin at the spectacle of Rita of whom, yes it's true we were ashamed yes but she was our friend, she was our friend and we were stuck with her, but still I learned the textbook lessons week following week, maybe my grades didn't always show it (Mr. Buttinger like others in the school graded severely ·if homework was what's called messy, you could have a perfect paper downgraded to, say, 85% for reasons of "messiness") but I saw the excitement of a Universe of numbers invisible and inviolate never to be contaminated nor even touched by their human practitioners, and this fact Mr. Buttinger must have known as well, he with his comical loud sigh, his soiled handkerchief mopping his forehead, the way he'd interrupt a stumbling student to pronounce the correct answer, the correct steps leading to the correct answer, always there *was* a correct answer in the Universe of numbers.

And he'd heave himself to his feet and go to the blackboard panting and perspiring, there was a happy violence in the way he wielded his piece of chalk, "You see?—like this!" His lips shone with spittle. Was he furious with us, or laughing at us—we couldn't tell.

Shrewdly Mr. Buttinger confined his teasing persecutions to the weaker students, like Rita O'Hagan. He knew not to invite confrontations with others, those overgrown boys for instance with names like Bocci, Rinaldi, Wolwicz, Korenjak slouching in their seats at the rear of the room, nor even with certain independent-minded girls like "Margaret Sadovsky" who could not be drawn into smiling and who was likely to hand in homework that was nothing more than a blank sheet of paper with her name scrawled on it sloppily torn from her notebook.

(Boasted Legs, "Let him fail me during the year, if I pass the final he's got to pass me," and this was correct except like some of the other older teachers at the school Mr. Buttinger failed almost no one, duly passed students along whether they'd learned anything or not. This was his way of sweeping house, exacting a subtle sort of revenge.)

Through the fall and into the winter of that year, our ninth grade year, Rita came to dread the "disciplinary" sessions after

school because, she said, Mr. Buttinger stared at her so hard!—
made her do math problems at the blackboard while he sat on
his chair pulled out from behind his desk and facing her close
beside her uncomfortably close beside her so she could hear
his breathing and she could smell the slightly sweetish-stale
odor of his body permeating his clothes and now and then
he'd grunt approval, or was it disapproval, now and then he'd
sigh as if it were a paternal sort of task, a chore, heaving himself onto his shortish legs to take the piece of chalk from Rita's
fingers to show her how the problem should be executed,
now and then even squeezing her plump shoulder in empha-
sis, "No Rita, like *this,* please pay attention it's like *this,"*
frowning and breathing harshly and if Rita shrank from him he
might advance upon her nudging against her even sometimes
drawing his thick beefy hands against her breasts quickly and
seemingly accidentally so she didn't know what was happening or how she might be to blame for it happening if it was.

That terrible afternoon back in August, Rita had tried to
run away from the boys—they'd made her scream with pain.
Mr. Buttinger never hurt her exactly. Nor threatened her. So
she never ran away, wouldn't have had the courage to run
away just walked home after the "disciplinary" session
numbed and sobbing quietly to herself hoping that her mother
wouldn't look at her and immediately see something in her
face she didn't know was there and like that time in August
slap her, hard.

Except: one afternoon in late January 1953 there comes
out of the rear door of Captain Oliver Hazard Perry Junior-
Senior High School the ninth grade math teacher Buttinger,
alone, briefcase in hand, clearly in a hurry clearly hoping not
to see any of his fellow teachers nor to be seen by them, he
glances swiftly from right to left then crosses to his car, a non-
descript Ford parked in its usual position in the faculty lot, he
clears his throat vigorously and coughs up phlegm and spits it

onto the ground unlocking his car, getting in, awkwardly, he's a short squat fattish man with a face that looks heated, nervous eyes but in truth he's excited, even gleeful, his trousers too tight in the crotch and waist but baggy at the knee but he isn't thinking of this he's thinking of something that makes him smile sly and lewd quick as a snake's tongue then he's backing out of the lot he's out on the street headed north on Erdman. Then east on Church, then north again on Fairfax. He takes his usual route home to Second Street where he lives in an apartment building near a small park, it's ideal for a bachelor and in a decent neighborhood where people know him and respect him as a school teacher thus a professional man, being respected means a good deal to Lloyd Buttinger which is why, he thinks, he's successful as a teacher, feared and admired and never lets any of his students get out of line, you must command respect says Lloyd Buttinger or you've lost your authority and nothing is so precious as authority.

On Fairfax near Sixth there's a railroad crossing and a train is passing, freight cars rattling endlessly and it's four-thirty and traffic is backed up for nearly a block which is when Lloyd Buttinger begins to be uneasily aware of people staring in his direction: at his car? at the sides and rear of his car? and then at him, behind the wheel? He swallows, frowns, shifts his weight clumsily in his seat, looks resolutely away and then can't resist looking back and as in a nightmare it's so, a man he has never seen before in a denim jacket is standing on the sidewalk staring incredulously at his car, blinking and squinting, and two teenaged boys break their stride to pause, to stare gaping, to break into whoops of laughter pointing at him, he's desperate now for the traffic to move to release him into motion but the freight trains continue to rattle by and now a young woman in a coat with a stylish fur collar pauses in the act of getting into her parked car at the curb staring frowning at something at the rear of his car then she stares at him pursed-lipped in disapproval and isn't she someone whom he knows?

the mother of one of his pupils, worse yet the wife of a colleague?

Lloyd Buttinger knows he should get out of his car to investigate but he dreads what he might see, he wants only to get home, desperately to get home to make things right, to become invisible. But it's a nightmare half-hour along Fairfax running the gauntlet of witnesses, some of them students, faces he would recognize if he dared look, he's aware of being a spectacle yet cannot guess why for the expressions he sees are all different, expressions of startled disapproval, of disgust, of mirth, most upsetting is rude ribald hilarity, men grinning and wagging their fists at him, boys making obscene gestures, a few horns sounding and at a busy intersection a young man trots out to pound on the hood of his car calling out words Buttinger can't make out: he has rolled his window up tight, he is not listening. Turning into the parking lot beside his building he must endure two or three more witnesses, fellow tenants also parking their cars, people who know Lloyd Buttinger by name and by reputation and these, seeing his car, seeing him, stare for no more than a few seconds then look resolutely away and walk away without greeting him thus no one appears to be watching (unless of course someone *is* watching, in secret) when at last he gets out of his car to walk dazedly about it not once but twice, not twice but three times, himself staring at the tall lurid red letters painted on the dull finish of his 1949 Ford: I AM NIGGER LIPS BUTTINGER IM A DIRTY OLD MAN MMMMMM GIRLS!!! I TEACH MATH & TICKLE TITS IM BUTTINGER I EAT PUSSY.

And most riddlesome of all perhaps is FOXFIRE REVENGE! painted on the rear bumper not once but twice FOXFIRE REVENGE!

So there Lloyd Buttinger stands staring at the terrible words painted on his car, not on the left side of his car where he would have seen them when he'd unlocked it but at the rear and along the right side, he's dazed, sickened, literally nauseous as a roaring rises in his ears, compulsively licking his lips, trying to comprehend who has done this and why and is his secret now revealed, he can't think but yes it is revealed it can never be secret again now it's revealed staring blinking through his smudged eyeglasses FOXFIRE REVENGE! FOXFIRE REVENGE! even as a disgusted man calls over to him, "Hey you better wash that stuff off, that's pretty nasty stuff, man!"

five

Tattoo

Says Legs, Whatever passes between the five of us tonight must forever remain unspoken to the world. Under penalty of death.

Says Goldie, Yes. Right.

Says Lana, Yes.

Says Rita, Oh *yes!*

And Maddy, after a pause, swallowing, *Yes.*

I was thirteen years old *Oh yes I would have sworn anything I would have stuck the ice pick deep into my flesh to bless such a Sacrament had my hand not faltered* on New Year's Day 1953 the day of the birth of FOXFIRE.

Dusk came early. A sunless day smelling of something acrid and yeasty borne on the wind from the chemical plants across the Cassadaga, you wouldn't believe such a day would change your life you wouldn't want to hope such a day would change your life would you?—as one by one they arrived at the rear of the Sadovsky house feeling shy, uneasy though Legs had assured them that her father and her fa-

ther's current woman friend would be gone, Mr. Sadovsky
had a mean temper and a way of looking at you that discouraged visits to the Sadovsky house even if Legs were to invite
you which wasn't often: Legs was fond of saying *I keep myself to myself* but maybe she was fearful of Mr. Sadovsky too?

Already excited they came secretly to the back door
where Legs in black slacks, black shirt, handcarved mahogany-
dark cross around her neck greeted them in an undertone and
hurried them inside so no one (yet who would it have been
across the weedy rubbly space of the rear yard behind the row
houses sloping downhill to a warehouse and a lot where used
cars and trucks were sold) would see them. So these were
Legs' dearest friends! So these were the girls of her gang-to-be!
Maddy smiled weakly at big-boned Goldie Siefried standing
five foot ten aged fifteen, meat compact and sinewy on those
bones and that lopsided cool-goofy grin with the ungiving
stare behind, Goldie had been kept back in school or had begun school late so she was in Maddy's class towering above
everyone except the tallest boys and famous for her hyena
laugh which had the unnerving power to draw your laughter
with it whether it was your wish to laugh or not or whether
there was logic to such laughter or not and she and Maddy
Wirtz were respectful of each other if wary of each other:
Maddy feared Goldie's quick exuberant temper, Goldie feared
Maddy's intelligence, the presumed judgment in her watchful
brown eyes. And there was Lana Maguire tall too, and lean,
platinum blond hair at odds with the girl's somewhat coarse
skin, she was good-looking except for the fact that her left eye
was weak-muscled and in times of upset or excitement the iris
came unmoored so if you were talking to Lana sometimes suddenly weirdly you wouldn't know which eye to regard, which
eye, deep behind the iris, contained *her.* Sporadically Maddy
and Lana had been friends, even for a while (but this was
years ago now) their mothers having been friendly having
gone to the same neighborhood school having been newly
married at about the same time with infant daughters and hus-

bands away in (and never to return from) the War, thus there was a dim sisterly regard between Lana and Maddy, uneasy and unresolved.

And there was Rita O'Hagan, the mild pang of disappointment of Rita O'Hagan, seeing fat little hapless little Rita at Legs', thinking, Oh why *her?* Maddy knew that Legs felt sorry for Rita angry at the way Rita was bullied ridiculed teased in the neighborhood and most of all tormented in math class, Maddy knew that Legs felt "sympathy" (at this time "sympathy" was one of Legs' favored words) for Rita and planned some sort of revenge on Mr. Buttinger yet still it pricked her pride, seeing Rita in Legs' room as welcome there as Maddy Wirtz herself.

What was it, what would be the instrument of their revenge, or was it to be something more significant more lasting more deeply binding?—Maddy'd heard from murmured words exchanged between Goldie and Lana that a "gang" was possibly to be formed, the very sound of the word sent her blood racing, "gang," there were gangs in Hammond in Lowertown in the Fairfax neighborhood but they were all boys or young men in their late teens, early twenties, there were no girl gangs nor were there stories of or memories of "girl gangs" Oh Jesus the very sound "girl gang" had the power to send the blood racing!

Legs' imagination had been stirred by much that was current in the newspapers and on radio having to do with espionage, accusations of Communist spies here at home and glorified American spies in wartime, almost in retrospect it began to seem that the massive historical event "World War II" itself had been but the mere outward consequence of ideas in a few men's heads, a very few devious men holding power over the lives and deaths of billions. There were two moralities: two ways of being: what you did because you were empowered to do it regardless of the cost to others innocent or otherwise, and what you acknowledged you did because such actions were criminal or sinful or scandalous. And Legs was one who knew by heart the sagas of Jesse James and of Billy the Kid and closer to home in upstate New York the Mafia tales of Buffalo and Rochester and even Hammond, there were names uttered with respect yet dryly, suggestively, Mafioso warlords living at this time yet as mythic as Al Capone and John Dillinger and in fact one of Legs' stories was about a relative of her father's living on the East Side in Chicago when news spread through the neighborhood that John Dillinger, Public Enemy Number One had been shot down by Federal officers outside a sleazy movie house, the date was July 22, 1934, Legs knew the actual date Legs boasted of facts not commonly known Legs claimed she'd held in her fingers the very handkerchief stiff, stained, filthy yet priceless her father's cousin had dipped in the pool of blood on that sidewalk outside the Biograph after Dillinger's body had been carried away.

Legs said that her father's cousin had been offered money for that souvenir—"But you wouldn't ever sell anything like *that.*"

Yet who would have anticipated the solemnity with which Legs greeted them that night her eyes shining her hair not in its usual tangle but newly shampooed and brushed lifting pale as broom sage from her shoulders as one by one she led them to her room at the top of narrow steep stairs her fingers hot and tight clasped in theirs, how unlike Legs Sadovsky to be so quiet, so seemingly reverent as if knowing this evening, this hour would change their lives forever. Maddy had prepared a casual witticism of some kind but it flew out of her head at once, her heart was beating quickly as if she were about to swoon and quickly her eyes darted about *So this is where she lives!* in a rhapsody of seeing the ordinary shabby interior of the house only a few doors from her own, sparsely and haphazardly furnished as her own, yet so profoundly different from her own because it was Legs' house and not Maddy's and therein lay the mystery: the most degraded images of God would have aroused her adulation had Legs commanded it thus.

So she was smiling. In fear. Eyes widened, damp seeing the blurred passage of soiled wallpaper, doorways, dim-lit rooms, rug remnants laid upon unpainted floorboards and gauzy curtain panels from Woolworth's or Grant's affixed at the windows with thumbtacks, there was an odor of cooking grease, there was an odor of cigarette smoke, there was an odor of mice that sweet-rancid odor saturating the walls that was home, the very smell of home, and Maddy had a glimpse of an unmade bed, a doorless closet spilling clothes or rags, a man's work shoes tossed onto the floor and a woman's single high-heeled pump beside them, evidence of Mr. Sadovsky and his girl friend Muriel that pig as Legs spoke contemptuously of her those pigs as Legs spoke of them both but never saying more and naturally Maddy did not ask. And there was a crucifix, white plastic and stainless steel and Maddy stared wondering was the crucifix a sign? for Legs as for herself? of all that you didn't, and did, believe? Or was the inexpensive object forgotten in the Sadovsky household like certain plaques and grubby little monuments in Lowertown at which no one ever consciously looked any longer, now merely decorative, or not even decorative but simply . . . *there?* nailed up on the hallway wall between Ab Sadovsky's bedroom and Legs' bedroom by the woman who'd been Legs' mother who had died of what illness or accident Legs refused to say nor would she so much as speak of her lost mother even to confirm grudgingly yes she'd *had* a mother, once.

Shit. That's ancient history.

The five of them, crowded into Legs' narrow room with its single window overlooking the rear yard.

The five of them, oddly breathless, shy.

Each was wearing a cross around her neck as Legs had instructed. They'd asked why and Legs had said never mind why, just do it, you'll see, so of course they obeyed.

Rita's cross was silver, or silver plate, lightweight but pretty winking between her plump breasts snug in her tight red orlon sweater, new at Christmas. Maddy's was smaller, the kind of "silver" that left stains on her skin if she wore it overnight. Goldie's cross was chunky and glittery with a brassy tarnished cast taking light from her brassy tarnished hair that lifted like steel wool from her head, and her eyes too, sly and amber, deep-set, restless—"Boom-Boom" was the kind of girl needful of joking, solemnity discomforted her. Lana's cross was ornamental gold, a cross in the form of a locket, nervously she fingered it between her pokey conical breasts in a black cardigan sweater. Legs' cross the most unusual, Maddy had never seen it before, in fact she'd never seen anything quite like it before—a carved wooden cross, very finely carved, deep russet, from Poland Legs had mentioned, and Maddy admiring it wondered if this too might have something to do with Legs' mother but she didn't dare ask.

Allusions to the past annoyed Legs, like fingers plucking at her as she ran. Ran and ran and ran.

This, New Year's Day 1953. What else mattered?

Like Maddy's room, Legs' room had a single window. But its ceiling sloped severely downward on one side, against which her bed had been shoved.

A drafty space that would have been dark except for the candles Legs had lit: five white candles placed about the room like votive candles so the girls' pulses quickened at the sight, the scent too of hot melting wax of heat itself and the kind of fire-radiance that's hypnotizing. *So this is her room! her bed! the place in which she dreams!*

When she first came inside, Goldie, seeing the candles, snickered in surprise. "Christ—like in church!"

Lana nudged her daringly in the ribs. "Shhhh, hunky."

Legs had disappeared, now she returned carrying shot glasses and a bottle of whiskey and with priestly decorum she poured whiskey in the glasses—proper shot glasses of the kind Maddy had only seen previously in taverns, and then rarely—and gave them to the girls one by one. And to each, one by one, she said, "Happy New Year."

They were seated, crowded on Legs' bed and on the floor and Legs stood over them lean as a knifeblade in her black clothes, a satiny sheen to her blouse, shiny black buttons too and the beautiful dark-carved cross on its chain hanging heavily around her neck. Legs smiled lifting her glass and the others lifted their glasses and all drank hesitantly, Maddy had never swallowed hard liquor before, her hand shook as the fire of it burnt her throat, ran up like white-hot wires through her nasal passages and into her brain.

And down into her groin too, warm and liquidy. Oh unmistakable.

Legs began to speak, standing over them. Her voice was incantatory, you could feel how she held it back, how she forced herself to speak slowly and calmly. And the feverish excitement rippling beneath. And how beautiful she became, the beauty of her sharp-chiseled features emerging. And how strange that the room's verticals shifted and planes of light eased together and deepened. From somewhere came a glow like a candled egg enveloping them as if the veins of one coursed into the veins of the others as if the spontaneous startled tug of a smile tugged at the others' lips as well. And the lovely warm liquidy sensation, shared.

Do you solemnly swear to consecrate yourself to your sisters in FOXFIRE yes I swear *to consecrate yourself to the vision of FOXFIRE* I do, I swear *to think always of your sisters as you would they would think of you* I do *in the Revolution of the Proletariat that is imminent in the Apocalypse that is imminent in the Valley of the Shadow of Death and under torture physical or spiritual* I do, I do *never to betray your FOXFIRE sisters in thought word or deed never to reveal FOXFIRE secrets never to deny FOXFIRE in this world or the next above all to pledge yourself to FOXFIRE offering up all fidelity and courage and heart and soul and all future happiness to FOXFIRE* yes I swear *under penalty of death* I swear *so help you God* I swear *forever and ever until the end of time* Yes I will: I swear.

Like a magician laughing in delight at his own sleight-of-hand Legs produced the ice pick, sterilized the sharp sharp point by holding it in fire. An elegant silver ice pick this too of a quality and a type Maddy, eyes misting over in wonderment and dread, had never previously seen.

"I will."

"*I* will!"

"Legs—here!"

Maddy watched. She was not frightened though a roaring sounded in her ears: the great Niagara Falls: to which she'd been brought long ago by someone now dead.

Certainly she was not frightened for how could she be frightened of Legs Sadovsky who was her friend who'd slept beside her in her bed six weeks before as no one had ever done and as no one ever would *so help me God*. But seeing that Legs' eyes were dilated round as pinwheels, and spinning. But still she insisted: "Yes. I will." And then when it came her turn, and she was the last of the five, she heard her voice pleading softly, "Legs do it to me," her hand trembled so badly, she was in terror of dropping the silver ice pick to the floor.

Legs drew her lips back from her teeth and smiled, hard.

That smile of triumph. As if, of the four, it was Maddy who *was* her heart.

Whispering, "Hold still, baby, O.K.?"

And so Maddy did. As the others craned their necks watching the sweet glisten of blood.

So Maddy was tattooed in FOXFIRE as, in a dream, Legs had envisioned their sacred emblem, red-stippled dots defining themselves into the shape of a tall erect flame

At first it was a tattoo of blood, oozing blood-droplets, points of pain, needle-stabs of pain on the pale tender flesh of Maddy's left shoulder. So she clamped her jaws shut so she would not cry or whimper or even grunt half comically as Goldie had, sweat shining on her face, nor would she wince giggling as Lana had, or tremble visibly biting her lower lip as Rita had, she knew this was pain this was madness to mutilate her flesh yet in truth it was sweetness she felt. *So happy my heart swelled to bursting.*

Later, when the bleeding stopped, they would rub alcohol into their little wounds and tap in red dye to form the flame-tattoo, vegetable dye of the kind used for Easter eggs, but, now, while the bleeding was fresh, they pressed together eagerly to mingle their blood their separate bloods as Legs instructed so that from that hour onward they were blood-sisters in FOXFIRE all five were one in FOXFIRE and FOXFIRE was one in all.

Partly undressed, giddy and excited, they clutched at one another: the crosses around their necks collided, clattered. A single swooning fall gripped them. A ringing of distant church bells grew louder. There was a drunken joy to the flickering candle flames. So long restrained by the gravity of the strange ritual through which Legs had led them Goldie who was "Boom-Boom" now broke loose, hugging the others one by one to smear her blood against theirs her braying laughter rising and contagious so suddenly they were all laughing shrilly breathlessly even Legs even Rita who was white-faced even Maddy who was not only white-faced but sickish, swaying dazed by the sight of her friends' bleeding shoulders and her own and the smell of blood *like the blood of a headless feath-*

erless chicken brought home and tossed into the sink but it turns out Momma's too sick to clean it then Goldie seized Legs in a bear hug tugging Legs' black shirt completely off both her shoulders tugging down too the straps of Legs' little-girl cotton undershirt so her small pale breasts were exposed, Legs laughed angrily but Goldie wasn't to be dissuaded shaking and shimmying smearing blood onto Legs' chest, their crosses flying together and tangling and Lana giggled trying to embrace them both, Lana had had more whiskey than any of the others suddenly she was drunk giggly-squealing drunk and desperate to be included in the horseplay so Goldie dragged her in Goldie gave her a jungle-cat bite of a kiss the two of them careening back against a bureau so one of the little candles went flying its flame extinguished in mid-air though no one noticed for now Lana was tearing at Goldie's shirt to pull it completely off, tugging at her brassiere that was sweaty and stained with blood and Rita and Maddy were frantic crowding near laughing wildly grappling with the others and who was it dragging Maddy's shirt off not giving a damn that buttons flew off tossing the shirt itself gaily up into the air, someone's hair was in Maddy's face, she was spitting laughing to get free but she didn't want to get free her lean little muscle-hard arms closed tight around one of her friends as they turned, reeled, staggered, nearly fell in a perspiring tangle to the floor but managed to right themselves in time squealing with laughter and there was the surprise of Rita shrieking smearing blood on Goldie pressing her grapefruit-sized bare breasts against Goldie's smaller taut breasts and someone dribbled whiskey on Rita's breasts and licked it off, whiskey and blood and Rita was in a fever her hair in her face red-flaming and electric and Maddy's chest was bare her tiny breasts bare and the tiny nipples frightened and erect, Maddy and Legs had torsos like boys lean and angular and the bones prominent beneath the skin but there was Lana grabbing at them both wriggling herself against them both in a frenzy of giggles so Maddy slung her arm around Lana to wrestle her still her other arm was around

Legs Maddy clung Maddy pawed Maddy burrowed her face against someone's neck Maddy's eyes were shut tight in ec-stasy *So happy my heart swelled to bursting, my heart did BURST.*

Afterward they asked Legs how had she thought of the name FOXFIRE that lovely perfect name FOXFIRE of which they were already proud FOXFIRE FOXFIRE and Legs said that the initial name for the gang she'd thought of had been "Foxes of Fairfax Avenue" but then in a dream she heard "FOX-FIRE"—"So FOXFIRE is a code for the other, and the other is a code for *us.*"

six

FOXFIRE: *Early Days*

What is memory but the repository of things doomed to be forgotten, so you must have History. You must labor to invent History. Being faithful to all that happens to you of significance, recording days, dates, events, names, sights not relying merely upon memory which fades like a Polaroid print where you see the memory fading before your eyes like time itself retreating.

Five of us walking abreast along the sidewalk in bright windy air each of us wearing a flamey-orange scarf around her neck, genuine silk, knock-your-eye-out quality, gifts from Legs who'd found some money somewhere as smilingly she said she bought them for us at one of the good Uptown stores. *And the way They looked at us. The way They regarded us guardedly and respectfully having to wonder who we were, why we were. What bound us together excluding Them.*

For ours was a gang like no other, like none of the crude boys' gangs, the Viscounts, the Aces, the Hawks. Ours was a true sisterhood not a mere mirror of the boys whom Legs urged us to mistrust beyond even the degree of mistrust we naturally felt for them, or for most of them.

There were girls' sub-deb sororities as they called themselves, at school. But they were nothing like FOXFIRE as the world was quickly to learn.

"Secret" organizations were forbidden by the school but FOXFIRE granted no authority to school nor any allegiance to a power higher than FOXFIRE. Legs said, "A rule can only apply to something already in existence, it can't apply to a thing so new it's only been named." This was a thought I would not have known to think until, hearing it so expressed, I saw the logic of it: and how They, from whom FOXFIRE was to be forever secret, therefore could never know of FOXFIRE.

Therefore could hardly "forbid" it!

Knowing now I would never be alone again never lonely again as in those years God allowed me to be thus as if He did not exist forcing onto me the bitter knowledge that He did not exist in truth or if He did His existence touched in no way upon my own.

Even before FOXFIRE meted out perfect justice to Rita's persecutor and revealed the name FOXFIRE to the world there was the sense you could almost feel you could almost taste that people were beginning to be aware of us, or of something new about us. For if we were observed in the neighborhood or at school exchanging our special glances or laughing together talking together then growing quiet when an outsider approached, and if it began to be observed that we five were suddenly in each other's company often where previously we hadn't been or in unlikely combinations—Goldie and me for instance, Lana and Rita—and if we wore our scarves, or gold-stud earrings of an identical kind, or behaved with a certain measure of dignity and aloofness, then people began to know or to suspect, people were curious, one of our neighbors calling out to me one afternoon when I returned from school

"Maddy?—I see you running with that overgrown Siefried girl, what does your mother think about that?" and I felt my face heat as if I'd been slapped by the bitch but politely I said, making an effort to be polite not sarcastic I said, "Well my mother doesn't choose my friends. I choose my friends myself."

And she looks at me, and blinks. Mumbles, "Oh!"

That was the look from Them we began to notice we were drawing, and there was a fearful sort of pleasure in it. Because though we'd pledged our secrecy this secrecy in itself was palpable to those it excluded. As if we were no longer individual girls as we'd been before but walking FOXFIRE-flames like our tattoos and, seeing us, people registered FOXFIRE when they believed they were seeing just an individual. As if a special glass had been slipped between us and the world so the world was changed to our eyes and we were changed to the world's eyes yet the glass was invisible.

Then at the end of January there came FOXFIRE-revenge and the start of our fame.

Before FOXFIRE some of us had felt sorry for Rita O'Hagan when Mr. Buttinger tormented her and some of us had felt disgust and derision yes and maybe even laughed that mean twisty laughter that's always a sign of evil. Thinking *Thank God, not me! She's crying not me!* But after FOXFIRE there was no doubt which way to feel.

Legs said, "When that sonuvabitch picks on Rita you better tell yourself he's picking on you 'cause the fucker sure *would* if he *could.*" And right away I could see the logic of that, so clear and so final it about took my breath away.

Legs looking at us, the three of us—Rita wasn't there: she'd been humiliated in math class that day, she was staying late for "discipline"—with her eyes that had that quality of spinning motion to them though they were icy-cool, calm.

Goldie squirmed and objected, whining, *"She's* the asshole, letting him get away with it."

Legs said, *"You're* the asshole, letting him get away with it."

Nobody talked like that to Boom-Boom did they?—Goldie stared blinking at Legs her tawny eyes going flat then brightening again, she too understood.

For Legs had that gift, or was it that power—not just her words but *her.*

And there was Lana nodding, grim and nodding, she with her weak left eye who'd endured years of school yard abuse *Cross-Eye! Freak!* and who dreamt of having an eye operation one day to make her perfect, sure Lana like Maddy-Monkey often felt relief in Rita's presence, an angry sort of gratitude *She's crying not me!* but now Lana was shamed by Legs' words so you'd think, seeing her, the steely resolve in her, she'd had such convictions all along. "Legs is right. If Rita wasn't there he'd pick on someone else and if that person wasn't there he'd pick on someone else till it got down finally to one of *us."*

I said, "—And then we'd want to stop him."

Goldie said, grinning, "—*Kill* 'im!"

So Legs outlined her plan. The red paint, the brushes. The things we'd write on Buttinger's car. The revelation of FOXFIRE to the world: not *what* or *who* but just *that*—that FOXFIRE existed, thus all were warned.

Legs said she'd got the idea in a dream she'd been thinking of it for some time turning the tables on that fucker so people laughed at *him* so the object of derision was *him* but also he'd be exposed having the hots for Rita (or any other girl: sure there must be others) and he'd be made to know all the world knew and he could never not know. "That's the thing," Legs said, "—he can run, he can hide, but he can't ever *not know."* She was flexing her fingers, she was coiled and restless as a young snake ready to spring.

When we told Rita of our plans it was typical Rita: jamming her fingers into her mouth, looking frightened, even guilty. Saying, "Oh—what if we get in *trouble? Expelled?"* But the crucial word was *we.*

Said Legs, "Before that's gonna happen we got to get *caught.*"

And we didn't: we didn't get caught.

FOXFIRE being too smart, and too precision-coordinated.

FOXFIRE being blessed with the grace of Rightness.

It was only two days later that Rita was kept in after school for "discipline" by Buttinger so we were prepared, red paint and brushes in a big shopping bag stuffed in my locker ("Madeleine Faith Wirtz" was the FOXFIRE girl least likely to be suspected by anyone in authority of anything criminal) and while Lana kept watch at the rear door of the school, Legs, Goldie, and I got to work on Buttinger's dun-colored old Ford, hunching low, working fast—I mean *fast:* Legs had made us practice beforehand getting the words right and the size of the letters large enough—so it was finished in less than ten minutes and no one saw and then we were gone, choking with laughter waiting for Buttinger to come out and drive away and we were positioned in a bus stop shelter on Erdman he'd have to pass and sure enough thirty minutes later there he drives by, his car that's just an ordinary-looking car bearing such astonishing messages your eye just naturally flew to it and stuck in disbelief I AM NIGGER LIPS BUTTINGER IM A DIRTY OLD MAN MMMMMM GIRLS!!! I TEACH MATH & TICKLE TITS IM BUTTINGER I EAT PUSSY and most curious most proud most provocative of debate in the days following FOXFIRE REVENGE! FOXFIRE REVENGE!

"Now all of Hammond's gonna know," said Legs, "—but what it is exactly, they won't *know.*"

Next morning Buttinger tried to play it cool coming to school in a taxi. Hoping to behave, the hypocrite, the son of a bitch, as if nothing had happened. As if everyone at Perry wasn't talking about him, not just students but teachers even the cafeteria workers even the Negro custodians, some of them laughing and some of them jeering and some of them angry and disgusted, naturally FOXFIRE pretended ignorance of FOXFIRE which was on everyone's lips too: what it *was,* what it *meant?*

A gang? A new gang rivaling the Viscounts, the Aces, the Hawks?—but none of the guys admitted being involved, none of them claimed to know.

About mid-morning it became known that our principal Mr. Wall had called Buttinger in to speak with him and following that, according to Lana—she had Buttinger for study hall, fourth period—things went kind of crazy. "He walks in the door and my God you almost wouldn't know who it is, old Nigger Lips like he's drunk or dazed or walking in his sleep his eyes all bloodshot and his face this weird color of puke but with red blotches like measles, he was sweating hard, he was scared shitless walking in that door and y'know that study hall's got fifty kids at least, guys from three grades he'd always had a hard time controlling anyway, they hated him like poison and he sure hated them so he walks in and there's IM BUTTINGER I EAT PUSSY on the blackboard and right away everybody's whistling, hooting, laughing like hell and stamping our feet and he tries to erase the blackboard but gets dizzy or something and drops the eraser and one of the Viscounts, that Rinaldi kid, runs up and takes it and tosses it, and Buttinger tries to get another eraser and Potato Head Heine snatches *that,* by this time we're all laughing and screaming like crazy and out in the hall there's Mr. Wall peeking in wondering what the commotion is and—oh God I like to wet my pants, laughing—Wall opens the door and starts in and Buttinger's running out and they hit like bumper cars—" dissolving into peals of laughter so the rest of us joined in, laughing and laughing so we felt weak.

Like we'd been hit over the head.

Never did Lloyd Buttinger return to Perry, he had to retire from teaching altogether. Moved away from Hammond. He was *gone.*

The rest of the school year we had substitute teachers for math. Nobody missed Buttinger except to talk about what'd happened to him, to tell the story again, again, again, to marvel at FOXFIRE's secret power.

Because, even in FOXFIRE's earliest days, when we were just young kids, we came to realize we had power. Only just not how much.

"It's weird Maddy, it's almost scary, like Goldie said it's like, y'know, we *killed* Buttinger," Legs said.

That windy February day, the two of us leaning over the railing of the Sixth Street bridge, shivering, our hair flying, not looking at each other as if suddenly we're shy of each other, shy of what we might see in each other's eyes. Legs examining her hands that are chafed and reddened as usual, her fingernails ridged with dirt, and I'm looking at her hands too, we're both smiling, "—He's walking around in the world but he's *dead*," Legs says and I murmur, "Oh yes," and the shivering gets worse but we don't want to move off the bridge, not just yet.

Part

two

one

Happy?

There was this elderly ex-priest who lived by himself above the Goodyear Tire store on Tideman, some sort of Frenchy name like Theriault but Legs cautioned you had to be polite you had to call him "Father" otherwise he'd be insulted and there were times he had a quick temper too, it was funny almost like a toothless dog trying to bite. A wizened little hairless man with rummy-eyes, an ulcerated nose, wheezy breathing and both hands palsied but every afternoon in decent weather there he'd be in the park, I'm talking about Memorial Park above the river, he had his bench, his particular bench and we'd see him there with his quart bottle of Thunderbird hidden in a paper bag clasped tight between his skinny thighs or raised to his mouth in a motion repetitious as clockwork yet contemplative, even with a kind of dignity. "Father" Theriault: you could see that in him. And always when you approached on the path it seemed he was brooding over the World War II tank that was a monument to Hammond's war dead, the big hulk of the tank and its long gun on the other side of the path, it looked as if the old priest might be praying at least for the poor souls in Purgatory—the souls in Hell are permanently damned, we were taught, the souls in Heaven naturally require no prayers from the living no assistance of any kind—but if you passed between him and the tank you'd see how his eyes stared through you, ghost-eyes fixed on nothing steady. Some of the boys hanging out in the park taunted him, they taunted the older men the solitary drinkers and rummies in the park if they were bored and feeling mean and there was a nasty incident around the time I'm writing of when some Aces gang members torched a Negro man asleep under newspapers, but Father Theriault seemed unafraid, always he was there on his park bench sometimes even in the cold or a fine light drizzle. Legs boasted he was her friend and confided in her all sorts of things he wouldn't tell anyone else.

"What kind of things?" we asked.

"Secret things," Legs said vaguely, evasively, "—that only a priest knows. Like about the Eucharist how it's really sometimes, I mean *really* the body and blood of you-know-who. So if it was desecrated it would bleed. And things about the confessional, things priests hear. And certain Popes and their bastard children. And how Hitler was a guest of the Vatican. And the Revolution," Legs said, nodding, "—the one that's on its way."

Legs took me with her to the park to talk with Father Theriault, to listen to him I mean, I never talked to *him*. It was strange and unnerving to me to be in the presence of a man an old alcoholic with a ruined face, a hoarse sandpaper voice, those eyes, who'd once been a Roman Catholic priest but wasn't a priest any longer. I wondered had he been not only defrocked but excommunicated. Or had he elected to leave the Church himself. (There was a distant uncle of mine in Troy, New York, who'd been a parish priest and who'd left the priesthood to marry his housekeeper: but no one ever spoke of him.) I feared such a person gave off an aura of danger like daring God to strike with lightning and each second God holds back is like the TICK TICK TICK of an invisible clock.

Father Theriault peered at me asking what was my name

and I told him Madeleine, he couldn't hear so Legs said in a louder voice "Madeleine" and Father Theriault said yes that was a nice name, I looked like a nice girl. Then he forgot me entirely.

Legs asked him something and he answered and rambled on talking quietly and purposefully the way a priest might do, not in the pulpit but in the confessional, stretching his mouth in a twitchy smile squinting up at Legs from time to time seeing how she stared at him so you'd think there was some connection between them, some urgency, some secret. So you'd think almost the two of them were related which maybe in fact they *were*.

Legs Sadovsky who was "Sheena" for laughs who said she despised all priests and nuns but there in Memorial Park she'd be standing shifting her weight from one leg to the other for long minutes listening with a strange sort of eagerness even anxiety to this aged alcoholic ex-priest ramble on about Revolution, so many Revolutions!—1848, 1798, 1917, 1776!—and the Revolution-to-come!—and by degrees his eyes lost their ghost-lustre shining with feeling and conviction.

Did we know, Father Theriault went on, growing excited now, of the Church's betrayal of the faithful? of the Church's betrayal of Christ? of the Church's wealth, the Church's militancy, the Church's fear of truth? Did we know of the pitiless inquisitions through history continuing to this very day? this hour? The burning of the ancient Gnostic gospels as "heresy," the invention and promulgation of "sin"? The tyranny of the Bishops, the Popes?—the murderers?

In 1909 as a young seminarian of twenty-four, Father Theriault told us, he'd attended a Socialist party congress in New York City where with thousands of men and women his brothers and sisters his comrades he'd stood to sing the "Internationale," and in an instant he'd known God as every heart in that gathering beat in unison with every other, yes he'd known God then and understood perfect happiness: the liberation from God: the ascension of mankind collectively to God and the oblivion then of God, yes it can be achieved he knew since he'd achieved it himself but could it be sustained?— "That's the question! *That's* the question!"

And to our astonishment Father Theriault collapsed into a fit of wheezy derisive laughter, then into a fit of coughing, we realized suddenly he was a very sick old man he was a filthy doomed old man a toothless rummy the very image of God's exclusion, terrible to look upon.

"O.K. he's crazy. But he's a saint too."

"He scares me, I don't like him."

"He scares *me*. What the hell—he *knows*."

"Yeah? Why? What does he know?"

"—Things most people'd have to die and go to Hell for, to know."

This talk of *happiness,* so much talk in the United States of happiness. *Happy, unhappy*—what does it mean?

I look back now to that first year that was FOXFIRE's supreme happiest time but we didn't know it then, you never know at the time. Living's immediacy, you go full sail, you're in a fever of motion. Until it's safe and past and done and *dead* and you can say, like waking from a dream, "Yes I was happy then, yes now it's all over I can see I was happy then." Maybe that's the advantage of dying?

two

Black Eye

And there suddenly was Momma in the bathroom doorway. Murmuring something that was just sound, startled, an exhalation of breath *Hhhhhhh!* unless the sound came from me. And quickly clumsily I snatched up a washcloth to cover myself, to hide the FOXFIRE tattoo on the inside of my left shoulder I'd been staring at, as so often I did mesmerized for long long forgetful minutes, you could say I'd gone into a zombie trance staring at that lovely bloodburst flameburst tattoo mostly healed now months after Legs had stabbed it into my flesh. *Hold still baby, O.K.?* and I'd held still. I was fourteen years old and I stood before this mirror naked from the waist up I was astonished and mortified to be growing tough little muscle-breasts that shamed me as I believe Legs' shamed her, each of us in secret grimly punching pummeling squeezing those doughy little tits to discourage their growth for our lean hard boy-bodies were one sure measure of superiority over Rita, Goldie, Lana and numerous others though never *never* did we speak of such matters, Legs and me: "Sheena" and "Killer" didn't give a damn for such matters, only for FOXFIRE standing firm and united against our enemies.

It was six forty-five that morning. Early summer, sun rising like a tarnished disk.

I had not known for certain Momma was even home. Or, if home, wouldn't she be flat out on her back in bed her eyes rolled up into her head her breath rasping and gurgling like a bad drain.

The bathroom door's lock was broken, broken for years but who'd expect Momma to shove it open half-naked herself, we were cautious about intruding into each other's territory. Like creatures of different species forced to inhabit a small space together we'd learned to avoid each other by instinct so I'd been careless that morning exhibiting myself to myself contemplating my beautiful FOXFIRE tattoo that at least partway redeemed my monkey-ugliness, my tattoo so lurid and flamey-red exposed for Momma to see: and surely she saw: how could she not have seen as in that same instant I saw in the mirror incredulous Momma's big purplish-orangish black eye as if a giant's fist had walloped her good on the right side of her face so the eye was swollen almost shut and her nose, her nose that was fine-boned and thin now had a pink-poached look to it and the right half of her mouth looked like a sponge soaked in blood, oh Momma I squinted at you, I shrank seeing and not seeing just as you saw my FOXFIRE birthmark and didn't see shrinking away too fumbling with the doorknob murmuring something vague, apologetic, inaudible and slipping away.

The two of us. By instinct.

three

How Maddy Acquired Her Underwood: How FOXFIRE HISTORY Began

Oh. My God.

   A typewriter?

A Saturday morning in early summer, sheets of bright sunny heat, and there on Seneca Street just off Fairfax was Uncle Wimpy Wirtz cleaning out trash from the rear of WIRTZ'S MEN'S CLOTHES, sweating puffing hauling cartons of things he'd been lazily accumulating for years: and prominent amid the trash set on the curb to be picked up by the Hammond sanitation crew was a typewriter.

The sight of which, so astonishing, stopped Maddy Wirtz in her tracks.

   A typewriter? To be thrown away like trash?

Enchanted, Maddy paused to examine it. It was an Underwood office model. Antiquated and battered-looking; tall, upright, heavy; black, but so coated with dust it appeared gauzy. Its keys were worn so smooth by years of use that Maddy could barely distinguish certain of the letters *a, s, e, t, o, u,* the ribbon was worn nearly transparent and was partly tangled in the machine's intricate interior. But how elegant it looked! How noble! Maddy, who wasn't above prowling the streets

Saturday mornings on the lookout for treasure, had never in her life found anything like this.

Of all things, Maddy most wanted a typewriter.

Long before FOXFIRE, and her solemn duty as FOXFIRE's chronicler, Maddy had wanted a typewriter.

As a small child Maddy had believed that a certain talismanic power resided in handwriting: *in knowing how to write.* Now she believed that power of this sort might reside in owning a typewriter: *in knowing how to type.*

Maddy was squatting at the curb examining the typewriter when Wimpy Wirtz appeared, a slovenly stack of old newspapers in his arms which, grunting, he let fall to the pavement. He was a fattish man in his mid-forties who dressed in starched white shirt, necktie, trousers with a modicum of a crease: being the owner of a men's clothing store, even a modest store like WIRTZ's, he felt obliged to look the part. Maddy squinted up at him, and smiled. Tried to smile. And maybe that was her mistake—the smile. Or the pleading in her voice. "—You're going to throw this typewriter away? Could I have it, instead? Please?"

Wimpy Wirtz, whose true name was Walt (for "Walton") Wirtz, wiped his face with a rumpled handkerchief and regarded Maddy with shrewd piggish eyes. He was no uncle of hers really but an uncle of her dead father's: for as long as Maddy could remember there had been virtually no connection between the Wirtzes of Seneca Street and the Wirtzes, Maddy and her mother, of Fairfax Avenue. Wimpy Wirtz smiled his thin sly smile and said, "Eh? You want my typewriter? I'll sell it to you—for five dollars."

Maddy stared at him in dismay. "But you're throwing it away, aren't you? It isn't anything but junk to you, is it?"

Wimpy laughed. "If it's junk, why d'you want it?"

"Oh, but it wouldn't be junk to me," Maddy said naively, "—I could type on it."

"Then it's worth five dollars."

"But you're going to throw it away—"

"You got five dollars? I won't throw it away: I'll sell it to you."

"But—"

"I'm a businessman, sweetie. I'm not in the goddamned Salvation Army."

And Wimpy Wirtz laughed heartily, a cartoon sort of laugh as he was a cartoon sort of man: with small bright eyes and pink-flushed skin, big belly straining at his shirt front, he seemed to Maddy a sinister mix of Porky Pig and Gestapo. She could not make out how to interpret his words. Was he teasing? Was he serious? In the neighborhood Wimpy Wirtz had the reputation of being a practical joker, a "character." He was a man's man, a back-slapper, good-hearted and funny and generous; unless he was a steely-eyed son of a bitch notorious for his stinginess and, in his worst moods, insulting his wife in front of others and refusing to allow Negroes, "niggras" as he called them, to enter his store. Maddy feared and disliked him yet was oddly drawn to him as we're drawn to those who believe themselves superior to us and who seem to be sitting in judgment on us. And he *was* a blood relation after all.

But she didn't call him "Uncle Wimpy" to his face. She didn't call him anything.

Now, amused at her distress, he let fall one of his ham-hands on her shoulder. Repeating his proposition: she could have the Underwood for five dollars, "cash and carry," which was a "real bargain." You couldn't find a second-hand typewriter anywhere in Hammond for that price, let alone an Underwood office model.

Maddy saw the purposelessness of trying to reason with this man yet couldn't resist. She cocked her head Legs style, an edge of belligerence in her voice. "I don't have five dollars exactly. I mean, to put my hands on. Right away."

"Then borrow it from your mother."

"I—can't."

"Eh? Why not?"

When Maddy didn't answer Wimpy Wirtz said, sneering,

"Your momma shouldn't oughta get fired from her jobs, then. She shouldn't oughta let go of her pride."

There was ill feeling between Maddy's mother and her in-laws that had something to do with Maddy's mother's behavior during Maddy's father's absence as a soldier. Maybe it had something to do too with Maddy's mother's behavior as a young widow in the days immediately following the Armistice.

Of these matters, Maddy knew nothing. Or very little. Nor did she have any curiosity.

Quickly Maddy said, "I have about three dollars saved up at home. I can work for the rest, I'm promised a babysitting job this weekend"—which was true, or possibly true: the offer had been ambiguous, and contingent upon circumstances. There were very few jobs in Hammond for girls of Maddy's age. "Could I bring you three dollars now, and the rest on Monday? Please?"

Uncle Wimpy leaned his hand heavier on Maddy's shoulder, and expelled a warm breath in Maddy's face. All sighing mock sympathy, ripe with the odors of tobacco and meat. "Shucks honey, Walton Wirtz is a *business*man not some kinda damn dopey charity."

"Oh—please!"

"Just get the five dollars right now, before the niggras come and haul this stuff away, and the typewriter's yours. Seems to me that's a real bargain." Leaning toward her so Maddy could see his eyes, the meanness in them intended to be transparent, Uncle Wimpy added, "Like you said, honey, you could *type*. Chrissake you could be some kinda *writer!*"

So Maddy pleaded a bit more, and Uncle Wimpy teased a bit more, like allowing a gullible fish to take out line, and finally, as if doing her a favor, he relented somewhat—she could have until the afternoon to get the five dollars provided she acted "in good faith."

"Oh thank you," Maddy cried, "—Uncle W-Walt!"

* * *

You son of a bitch. You selfish tight-fisted mean-hearted son of a bitch.

Trotting off with the urgency and myopic desperation of a child who can imagine only a single obstacle between himself and absolute happiness. As, running, she glanced repeatedly up the street and back over her shoulder in dread of seeing one of the Hammond city sanitation trucks on its way to Seneca Street: the vehicles were battleship gray and thunderous, clattering through the streets reeking of raw garbage and diesel exhaust. A surly white man behind the wheel, a crew of brawny black men, shirtless in summer, hanging from the rear, leaping down to fetch trash cans and dump their contents into the truck. The black men shouted to one another, laughed with manic glee that penetrated windows, walls, doors, white residents couldn't judge were they happy were they furious were they murderous were they simply doing their job as efficiently as possible? The thought of them snatching up Uncle Wimpy's typewriter, *her* typewriter, and tossing it away with garbage, made Maddy feel faint.

But he won't let them take it, she thought.

He'd promised. The son of a bitch was mean but not that mean.

Most days, those years, Maddy avoided Wimpy Wirtz's territory. If he happened to be lounging in the doorway of his store smoking a cigar, chatting with another man, as she passed by he'd whistle thinly through his teeth, not recognizing her apparently, as he'd whistle at other girls and young women in the neighborhood: not jeeringly exactly, in fact rather softly, but not in a way to make you feel proud. Maddy guessed that, at such times, Uncle Wimpy didn't see *her*—she was just something female to him, bare-legged in summer, bare-armed, young. But if she was in the company of her FOXFIRE sisters, especially Lana, or Legs, or even Rita, Wimpy Wirtz wouldn't waste time looking at her, in any case.

Not often, but occasionally, unavoidably, the Wirtzes of Seneca Street and the Wirtzes of Fairfax Avenue encountered one another in the neighborhood, at Mass for instance, at St. Anthony's—Maddy and her mother didn't go to church very often but they *did* go sometimes; out of superstition, Maddy guessed—and Wimpy Wirtz and his bulldog-faced wife would mumble "H'lo" staring at them and unsmiling as if smiling might cost them money, and Maddy's mother mumbled something cool and inaudible in reply, turning stiffly away. So once, but this was years ago, Maddy tugged impatiently at her mother's arm asking what was wrong, why didn't Uncle Wimpy and Aunt Edna like them, and Maddy's mother frowned, she'd long had a habit of frowning severely, as if even mild light hurt her eyes, and said, easing her arm out of her daughter's grasp, "You want to know?—ask *them.*"

Like hell I'm gonna ask them. Nor *you*, ever again.

This sentimental business about the past. Years ago. What somebody did or didn't do or said or didn't say, that crap. What had any of it to do with *her.*

What had anything not of her own doing to do with *her.*

Legs would say, "Drop it," if anyone asked questions too personal, just "Drop it" with a warning look, a pinch maybe or a light punch on the arm to show she meant business. Legs' mother had died suddenly when Legs was a young girl, there were stories whispered of her in the neighborhood but none of these stories ever came from Legs so you'd almost think Legs was ashamed if you didn't know her and know *Legs was always proud even before FOXFIRE, that's the primary fact about Legs Sadovsky: pride.* And Maddy Wirtz had her pride too. You bet.

Maddy's father's name was_____, no it wasn't a name she allowed herself to think like her mother's name_____she'd never articulate, it was enough to think "Mother." (Since FOXFIRE was making her stronger Maddy was growing away

from "Momma"—that silly baby-name.) For why be curious
about a man who was dead, why give a damn when she'd
scarcely known him except as someone in a uniform, breath
smelling of whiskey, quarrels in the house and there weren't
even any snapshots of him so far as she knew. The fact was,
Maddy's father was dead. The fact was, the man who'd been
Maddy's father was dead. But not buried properly, not identified, his "remains" never located, thus diffuse and scattered as
milkweed seed, irretrievable. Somewhere in Belgium. Somewhere in Europe. Maddy thought, *I hate them all* not knowing
exactly who they were but knowing, goddamn, how she felt.
 FOXFIRE BURNS & BURNS!
 FOXFIRE IS NOW!

"I have it! I have it! Five dollars *even!*"
 Maddy carried the money clutched in her hand, sweaty-
smelling bills and coins, the copper pennies the most
distinct—three dollars and twenty-seven cents from her glass
piggy bank she'd been shrewd enough to smash inside a sock,
one dollar and seventy-three cents borrowed from a
neighbor—and there stood Uncle Wimpy smiling-glowering as
if not knowing whether to be pleased, or annoyed, she'd returned so quickly and in such childlike excitement. The trash
men, the "niggras" as Wimpy called them, had come and gone
but out of the kindness of his heart he'd lugged the typewriter
back inside, it was in his office at the rear waiting for her. So
Maddy thanked him, and trotted back. A customer had just
come in whom Wimpy had to wait on—and how suddenly genial the man had become, how loud-laughing, garrulous: transformed at once by the presence of another white adult male
with money, just possibly, to spend—so Maddy went back
alone, not pausing to wonder why if he knew she'd be returning to get it, he'd carried the typewriter so far.
 WIRTZ'S MEN'S CLOTHES: a man's place, a place for
men: counters of men's underwear, socks, shirts, coats and

such hanging on racks, crowded together on racks, a stale mildewy odor to the air mixed with a smell of cigar smoke and perspiration and hair oil, Wimpy Wirtz's unmistakable odor that made Maddy's nostrils pinch. But there, on the floor, in a corner of Wimpy's cubbyhole of an office, was the Underwood typewriter . . . *her* typewriter.

She was thinking how she'd surprise Legs with it. *Now FOXFIRE's going to have a true formal chronicle. Now our history begins!*

Squatting over the typewriter shyly touching the keys. Her heart beating as if the Underwood were a living thing.

Uncle Wimpy's office had a single window overlooking the back alley, a cracked shade partway drawn. There was a battered metal desk heaped with papers, ashtrays, candy wrappers, and in the center a new typewriter (Wimpy's wife Rose was the one who used it, doing accounts, sending out invoices and so forth) smaller and sleeker than the Underwood. The smell back here was intensified, Maddy would remember it all her life.

Awkwardly she inserted a sheet of paper into the typewriter and began to type, using two fingers only. Of course, she had no idea how to type: she'd never used a typewriter before. MADELEINE FAITH WIRTZ. JUNE 22, 1953. HAMMOND, NEW YORK. Then: FOXFIRE. FOXFIRE FOXFIRE in red ink. Several keys stuck and had to be forcibly unstuck. Part of the "e" was missing. The ribbon was worn so thin it had torn and there seemed to be something wrong with the carriage return but the Underwood *worked,* it could be made to *work.* There was magic to it.

When, after some minutes, Wimpy's customer left, Wimpy approached the back room and Maddy hastily x'd out FOXFIRE—what had she been thinking of! What a dope she was! Going next door to ask their neighbor could she borrow one dollar and seventy-three cents was a capitulation to Them, an acknowledgment of how dependent she was upon Them, and yes the woman had peered at Maddy oddly as if guessing there was a secret here, something Maddy wouldn't want to talk about as, months before, she hadn't wanted to talk about her new friendship with Goldie Siefried. *Boom-Boom's none of your business. Yours, or Momma's.* The woman had asked Maddy if something was wrong, seeing, maybe, a feverish look in Maddy's face, but Maddy had said no, no, nothing was wrong, she just needed one dollar and seventy-three cents and she needed it right away.

"So, honey, you been messing with that typewriter? You like it pretty well, eh?"

Maddy stood. She counted out her money so Wimpy could see she had it all, every penny.

Except, lounging in the doorway, gazing at her with his small damp piggy eyes: "What's that—*five* dollars? Ain't you missing some?"

"What? What do you mean?"

"I asked for eight dollars, didn't I?"

"Eight—?"

"I asked for eight dollars for that typewriter, that's a damn good typewriter, you're trying to give me *five* dollars? What kinda trick is that?"

Maddy said, dismayed, "But you said five dollars. You did. I went to get—"

"Hell no, I said eight dollars. I must've said eight 'cause I'm expecting eight. Also, I had to lug the damn thing all the way back here—that's labor." Uncle Wimpy grinned, wiping his forehead and the nape of his neck with a handkerchief; his little eyes gleamed merrily.

Was he joking?—teasing? Maddy tried to keep calm, she tried not to show the outrage she felt. She said, "Oh Uncle W-Wimpy!"

Uncle Wimpy laughed sharply, as if she'd reached out and touched him. As if he'd never heard that fool name before.

"Hey—who you calling *what!*"

* * *

There followed then an hour, and more than an hour, of bargaining: of teasing cajoling bullying bargaining: and afterward Maddy would realize that no customer interrupted because Wimpy had shrewdly locked the front door and hung a CLOSED sign in the window.

Several times he seemed about to relent, then he'd change his mind—"At eight dollars it's a bargain, and you know it," he said. "Try to find a decent typewriter that cheap."

"But you promised."

"I did not."

"You did. You promised."

"I did *not*. You heard me wrong."

"Oh I did not! You *know* I did not."

Wimpy shrugged, hitching up his trousers. He had a big bloated stomach: like a load in a wheelbarrel that gave him trouble pushing. He said, "Honey, you want this typewriter, or not?"

"No."

"You don't want it?"

"No."

"Sure you do. 'I could type on it,' you said."

They fell silent, they were running out of things to say.

Maddy's mind worked quickly but she could not understand what Wimpy wanted; what logic lay behind his behavior. *He's an adult isn't he. He's a blood relation isn't he.* She made as if to pass him, he was blocking the doorway, his pink-flushed skin glowing, his lips stretched in a smile. Seeing she was serious he sighed, and said, in a flat voice, a voice meant to be sincere, "All right, then, you can have it. I was just kidding."

"I can have it? I can?"

"Not for eight dollars but for five. If—"

"If what?"

Wimpy didn't answer. Something seemed to crinkle, to constrict, painfully, in his face.

Maddy repeated doubtfully, "If—if *what?*"

Staring at Maddy, licking his lips, Wimpy groped for her hand, closed his fat moist fingers around it to shake it? as adults shook hands? but why, now, with *her?* *why?* and she acquiesced, unthinking, not fearful but merely wondering, as he drew her to him almost gently, urging her off balance so she had no choice but to step toward him, her eyes wide and fixed on his.

"If you're a good girl."

The words were unnaturally slow, spaced. All the while he was staring at her never once glancing down where, as if inadvertently, he brought her hand against the front of his trousers: against his bulging crotch.

Maddy screamed. Maddy shrieked.

As if she were being not attacked but tickled—pushing at Wimpy as a small child might, laughing, frightened and a bit hysterical pushing at the fat man who blocked her way through the door, and Wimpy was laughing too, grunting, trying to catch hold of both Maddy's wrists as if this were a game of some kind or might be renegotiated as a game; and Maddy butted her head against his chest so the air was knocked out of him.

She was running to the front of the store, she'd had presence of mind enough to scoop up her money from the desk where she'd counted it out. Wimpy Wirtz called after her, "I ain't going to keep the damn fucking thing past next Saturday— you want it, come get it."

Maddy couldn't catch her breath, trying to unlock the door. Laughter bubbled up in her like fizz in soda tickling her nose. She whispered, "Let me out of here, oh let me out of here I hate you, I hate hate you goddamn you," as Wimpy, hitching up his trousers, breathing hard, came up behind her in a stealthy sort of haste. For a fat man, he could move almost gracefully. His face was a greasy boiled red and strands of his no-color hair hung in his eyes. He was sweating so profusely a true stink lifted from him but he managed to calm himself so that, unlocking the door for Maddy, even opening it for her to slip through, he repeated, "I ain't going to keep that typewriter past next Saturday, you understand? So you want it, you come get it. The price is eight dollars. *No trying to cheat me next time.*"

"You're serious? Wimpy Wirtz? Isn't he your own uncle, or something?"

"When I got home I washed my hand. Both my hands. Oh God!"

"But you didn't touch *it.*"

"He wasn't unzipped. He didn't have time."

"Long as you didn't touch *it.*"

"Oh no. Oh no I didn't. I didn't touch *it.*"

Hardly could Maddy bring herself to look up at Legs' face. She feared disgust, contempt. She feared her friend's chaste icepick eyes. But Legs was sympathetic: nearly as upset, it seemed, as Maddy herself. In recounting the episode Maddy had abbreviated her own role considerably—you wouldn't know how naive she'd been, how childish and trusting, how *hopeful.* What an asshole letting Wimpy Wirtz close his fat hot fingers around her own.

Legs said speculatively, "That man is a capitalist, that's one thing about him. The fucker!"

"A capitalist?"

"He wants to *profit* by selling goods for more money than they're worth."

Maddy recalled Father Theriault's words and the contempt that underlay them but she could not see their application here.

Maddy said hesitantly, "Well—but he'd have to make some profit, wouldn't he? Or how could he pay rent? buy food? Or—"

"Are you defending him? That lecher?"

"I—"

"Y'know what he is?—a pervert. Like Buttinger."

Maddy stared in dismay. A wave of heat washed over her. "But—I'm not Rita."

This while Legs had been pacing restlessly back and forth, striking the palm of her left hand with her right fist, how fierce she was in her male clothing—long-sleeved plaid shirt, jeans, ankle-high black sneakers worn without socks—how passion fired her with authority, her tangled matted lovely ashy hair bristling on her shoulders and the sickle-scar prominent on her chin, dead-white against even her pale skin. She cast Maddy a pitying look, bit her lower lip as if to keep from laughing, and said, with a dismissive gesture, "Oh Maddy-Monkey, shit— *we're all Rita.*"

So FOXFIRE convened.

An emergency meeting in one of Legs' secret places, an upper floor of an abandoned warehouse on Pitt Street above the river. And Goldie said, flexing her fingers, "Let's just go *get* it," meaning the Underwood typewriter Maddy so coveted, she'd fixed upon the typewriter as an *object,* a *possession,* of which FOXFIRE had been outrageously cheated. And Lana shivered, hugging herself, and said, "Hey I'm not gonna go near *him:* that Wimpy Wirtz scares me, the way he looks at me, one time when I was just a kid he sort of winked at me, y'know?—and I was so damn dumb I guess I stood there and smiled, y'know?—and the sonuvabitch made his eyes roll, sort of, like he was making fun of me the bastard, and since then I'm afraid of him like if he knows you're afraid, if he catches you looking back at him, the two of you knowing what's in his nasty mind, he makes you feel—" Lana was talking rapidly, al- most stammering, her agitated left eye veering out of focus, "—*disgusted.* I mean like deep in your soul in your *guts.*" And Rita shivered too, but not in dread, in excitement, and said, her eyes flaring bravely up, "Oh let's go take it from him—let's *kill* the son of a bitch!"

There was a moment's pause, then Legs said, "O.K.

sweetie-Fireball, you got the right idea," and the others laughed a little startled, at Rita's words which were not words you would have expected from Rita O'Hagan.

Now that FOXFIRE had come into her life, however, Rita was changing. Conspicuously changing. Still a plump little but-terball with wiggly breasts and hips but not *fat,* still shorter than most of the neighborhood girls and boys her age but not *short,* no longer so crippling-shy, nor so meek: not even the crudest boy would have called her "Dumbo" or "Half-wit" any longer. Rita's gang names were "Red" and "Fireball" and she thrilled to be called one or the other, such names were like ca-resses, new and amazing in her life.

Seeing how she'd surprised her sisters, even Legs, Rita cried, pounding her fists on her knees, "Oh *let's!* Goddamn it *let's!* Let's kill him! *Let's kill all of them!*"

So they laughed. Even Maddy who'd been feeling so sickened-ashamed. She laughed, all of FOXFIRE laughed, a wild incandescent laughter, and the misery of it, that man touching her as he had, oh Christ her touching *him,* was eased from her as if it had never been.

WIRTZ'S MEN'S CLOTHES on Seneca Street, late Monday afternoon near closing time, and there's Wimpy Wirtz lounging beneath his awning smoking a cigar and complaining about the heat with the butcher from GUNTER'S MEATS next door, the two of them beefy big-bodied men with smallish heads, fleshy faces and restless eyes, old friends in the neighborhood, or if not friends exactly old acquaintances, fellow merchants but not competitors, and Wimpy Wirtz in his starched white shirt, necktie, snug-fitting trousers is clearly feeling the heat, wiping repeatedly at his forehead and the back of his neck with a damp handkerchief, he's cursing, he's unhappy, nearly five o'clock and not much business that day he's blaming the weather: this muggy moist inert heat hanging over the city that's scarcely disturbed by any breeze from the river, in fact the river gives off a brackish smell as of floating garbage, the rotting corpses of fish, untreated sewage—"Like living in a niggra neighborhood, for Chrissake," Wimpy observes, and his friend the butcher yawning and spitting is inclined to agree.

The butcher returns to his store to close for the night, Wimpy remains under his awning irritably smoking his cigar, he's crinkle-browed, gives the impression to passersby of thinking hard but what's he thinking *of?*—rocking slightly on the balls of his feet, blinking, frowning, sweating. Maybe contemplating how old Harry Truman gave the order to drop the A-bombs on the Japs and what a good feeling that must have been, how *he'd* love to do it maybe push the button himself or whatever you do, turn a lever and the bombs slip out of the plane like a big sleek eagle laying eggs. God yes. Except old Harry started too late and quit too soon.

Still, all your life afterward, no matter what, you'd be able to look back at that, those fucking A-bombs, and say, At least I did *that,* and nobody's gonna undo it.

And in the midst of Wimpy Wirtz's cigar-reverie comes Maddy Wirtz out of nowhere, unexpectedly crossing the street heading in his direction.

Maddy who's fourteen years old. In her slapdash summer clothes, shapeless T-shirt, loose-fitting khaki shorts, rubber thong sandals bought out of a heap of discount shoes in a sidewalk sale in front of Woolworth's uptown. She's a skinny flat-chested little thing with dark watchful eyes, except now they're shiny innocent eyes, and there's a childlike bounce to her step and an elation in her voice Wimpy can't quite, for the moment, decipher, except he feels a stab of guilt seeing her but deeper than that a stab of excitement in his groin, now the cigar's gripped between forefinger and thumb still clamped between his teeth now he's awake he's alert he's *at attention.*

Maddy calls out, trotting toward him, "Oh Uncle Wimpy, I have the money! The eight dollars!"

Wimpy says, staring at her, this girl he can't figure out except for Chrissake she's come back, and clearly he hadn't expected her, "—What d'ya mean 'Wimpy'? My name's Walt, goddamn it."

Maddy giggles. "Well. 'Walt.' 'Uncle Walt,' then. O.K.?"

Wimpy glowers, staring. Not knowing what in hell to think. Has she forgotten exactly what happened between them? Has she *not* forgotten, and she's come back for more?

She's come back to make a deal?

Guardedly he says, his tongue poking against the inside of his mouth, "Uh honey—I told you didn't I, you could maybe have the typewriter for nothing? Maybe?"

"You said eight dollars. 'Cash and carry.' "

She's clutching the money in her hand, opens it to show him, proudly, somewhat nervously: two crumpled dollar bills and the rest coins. Quite a few pennies.

"That's one thing I said but I also said another thing," Wimpy says, smiling as it occurs to him that the terms of the game have been entirely renegotiated, they're back at zero and *he's* in charge. He flips his cigar out into the gutter mumbling, "Well—let's see. That damn old thing taking up space in my office, somebody better buy it soon. No reason why not you."

So Wimpy Wirtz leads Maddy inside his store. He's a bit distracted but not at all suspicious; with enough presence of mind to note that, so far as he can see, nobody on the street is watching them, and to lock the door and slip the CLOSED sign in the window. Hitching up his trousers, saying half chiding, as if they'd been arguing about this, "—Walton Wirtz never goes back on *his* word."

In the dim-lit little cubbyhole of an office at the rear of the store there's the Underwood typewriter amid the dustballs on the floor, exactly as it had been on Saturday. Nothing seems to have changed.

Moving with that odd fat-man's stealth Wimpy yanks down the blind to the bottom of the windowsill and even a little beyond. He shuts the door. Which makes two doors firmly shut against the street.

Saying, vaguely grumbling, for the sake of filling the silence, "Uh-huh: there's still some folks don't go back on *their* word. No matter what."

Maddy is squatting over the typewriter, *her* typewriter, as if it's a lovely toy. That heavy old-fashioned machine, *hers.* She seems unaware of Wimpy Wirtz hovering above her gazing at her slender back at the delicate little vertebrae of her spine prominent beneath the thin white material of her T-shirt, gazing too at her buttocks, so small so smooth so perfectly shaped, two hand-size melons, inside the khaki shorts.

Wimpy says, bending near, "How old are you anyway?"

Maddy who's fussing with the ribbon spools doesn't glance up. "Old enough."

"Yeah? For what?"

"For typing."

"Typing?"

Wimpy laughs nervously but Maddy isn't laughing with him. She's so damned *serious* examining that typewriter he's beginning to wonder if maybe she's a bit simple-minded; just slightly off in the head.

Which is fine with him. Oh yes it's fine with him.

He says, "Honey you don't need to fool with that, that's guaranteed to work. It sure does work. Maybe it needs oiling or a new ribbon or whatever, any damn thing I'll fix it up for you, O.K.? Long as we understand each other? O.K.?"

Maddy peers up at him. Her expression is quizzical, hopeful. He says, "So, uh—you gonna pay cash or you maybe gonna negotiate it for nothing? 'Cause if it's cash it's ten dollars, honey. But if it's nothing it's *nothing.*"

Maddy says, "What? Ten dollars? But—"

"Except if it's nothing then it's *nothing.*"

"You said eight dollars, you promised—"

"That was Saturday. This is Monday. Our kind of rapid-growth economy, prices steadily rise. There's inflation. There's interest. A genuine Underwood office-model typewriter, ten dollars is a bargain." He pauses, his tongue poking slyly between his lips. " 'Course paying nothing is a better bargain yet. Right?"

"I don't have but eight dollars. I—"

"Oh for Chrissake honey, stop playing dumb. Long as you're here you might as well accept the damn thing for *nothing.*"

All the while, Wimpy has been nudging Maddy with his knee. He's beginning to lose patience but he's smiling, there's almost a kindly look to his face, slowly he's undoing his trousers, very slowly unzipping his fly, murmuring, no one more reasonable, "—You be considerate with me, you won't need to *do* anything much just be, y'know, considerate, we'll see what we'll see honey, O.K.? I guess we understand each other, maybe?"

Maddy's crouched before him, squinting up at him, her pale lips drawn back tight from her teeth so it looks— almost—as if she's smiling at him. As with a whimpery little sigh he takes out of his trousers *a red-boiled sausage, ugly vein-raddled blood-swollen thing* showing it like a prize he's proud of, his big body tremulous on tiptoe and the pupils of his eyes blackly dilated, he's whispering, "C'mon honey, stop kidding around, you and I both know why you're here—"

Maddy cries, "Oh yes? You know?"

She scrambles to her feet, tugs at the blind to release it so it flies up to the ceiling, gives a cry and at once the girls in the alley launch their attack as planned: they have a board they're using as a battering ram, within seconds the window is broken, shards of glass go flying, it's an explosion, it's festive, the girls of FOXFIRE piling through the window like young dogs eager for the kill, there's Legs, there's Goldie, there's Lana, there's fierce little hot-eyed Fireball, and Maddy's one of them, five girls springing on Wimpy Wirtz caught frozen in astonishment and disbelief, gaping, pants open and penis exposed, big as a club but already it's beginning to wilt, and retreat.

And they're on him.

* * *

How long the skirmish lasted Maddy wouldn't know precisely, she'd log it in the FOXFIRE notebook as truthfully as possible—probably not more than three or four minutes. But it seemed longer. Surely to Wimpy Wirtz, thrashing about on the floor desperate as a big beached fish, it must have seemed like an eternity.

FOXFIRE REVENGE!

FOXFIRE NEVER SAYS SORRY!

They pummel him. They tear at him—clothes, and flesh. They kick him. There is a point early on when Maddy Wirtz herself breathless and frenzied pulls feebly at the others' hands suddenly worried Wimpy Wirtz might have a heart attack or a stroke but her FOXFIRE sisters rightly ignore her, little high-pitched cries and yelps, skeins of wild giggling, and Boom-Boom's hyena laugh, Boom-Boom that husky gal straddling Wimpy who's now trouserless bouncing up and down on his cushiony belly slapping and punching and squeezing cruelly, "Giddyup fatso! Giddyup you prick!" and Legs in a transport of bliss her eyes afire has hold of Wimpy's hair so she can bang his head *thump! thump! thump!* rhythmically against the floorboards—Uncle Wimpy's hair was thinning but out of vanity he wore it long, combed it over the crown of his head: more than enough for Legs to grasp—and Lana the quietest of all nonetheless breaks several manicured fingernails clawing at Wimpy's shirt, then at his bare oily-gleaming chest, she's smiling, she's truly happy both eyes in perfect alignment but the wildest of all is Fireball whose curly red hair's alive with static electricity though her face is clammy-pale, she's that intense as she tugs Wimpy's trousers off, manages to get the man's boxer shorts down past his thrashing naked thighs, knees, ankles, feet, and off, in singleminded fury kicking him as he kicks, or tries to kick, to protect himself *but there is no protection against FOXFIRE.*

Poor Uncle Wimpy!—he must fear being found out since

he isn't yelling loudly, doesn't in fact call for help at all only this whimpering begging choking, "—girls!— *no!*—oh please!—stop!—*no!—girls—*"

Legs bangs his head against the floor so hard his eyes shimmer out of focus, she's laughing, savage, infuriated, "Who are you calling 'girls,' you old lecher! Filthy old lecher! *What do you know!*"

There's Lana clawing like a tiger at the man's exposed flesh however and wherever she can so trickles of blood run freely, there's the red-haired Fireball O'Hagan pounding and squeezing the man's heavy thighs, belly, genitals as you'd knead bread dough in a wicked mood, most flamboyant of all is Boom-Boom squealing in delight rising up high on her knees to come down hard, which is to say *hard,* on the man's chest so the breath is knocked completely out of him, he groans, "Oh— *oh*—" and his eyes roll up into his head.

And he's suddenly unresisting. No more struggle, no more thrashing about.

Not dead though since he's still breathing, labored arhythmic gulps like a bellows and there's a wet snuffling noise so very likely his nose is broken, certainly his nose is bleeding, blood splattered everywhere, on himself, on his assailants' bare legs, arms, soaking into their clothes, and Maddy is really worried now so she begs her FOXFIRE sisters to stop, they don't want him to die after all do they?—and reluctantly they rise from him, a final cruel kick at his shriveled penis from Fireball and the attack is over.

Legs declares, brushing her hair out of her face with both hands, "O.K.—enough." She smiles at her sisters across Uncle Wimpy's inert body. "It's wrong to keep after somebody once he's fallen. Y'know—once he's *out."*

Boom-Boom's in her glory, laughing, wiping blood from her hands onto Wimpy's torn white shirt, she's the one to carry away FOXFIRE's prize, the Underwood typewriter, doesn't require any help from her sisters. And Maddy too has her moment, a final glorious moment—but too bad: Uncle Wimpy isn't conscious to see—taking up the money she'd laid on his desk, dollar bills, coins, not a penny less than eight dollars and in a histrionic gesture she lets the money fall through her fingers onto Wimpy's bare nail-raked chest.

" 'Cash and carry'!"

And that was how Maddy Wirtz acquired her Underwood typewriter, and how the FOXFIRE CONFESSIONS came to be formally, meticulously, *typed*.

four

FOXFIRE *Fear & Respect!*

Never never tell, it's Death if you tell any of Them we swore many times in the most solemn oaths of FOXFIRE. Yet there gradually emerged in Hammond, both Uptown and Lower-town, in the first year of FOXFIRE's existence, certain mystery-signs of which the ignorant world had no choice but to take note.

At first it was our secret flame-tattoo in red crayon or ink or nail polish just a few inches high on a locker or a desk or a window at school, then in paint on a sidewalk or a door, so people began to take notice, wondering what it was, who had done it, and why, and then one morning it was a giant flame five feet in height in bright red-blood paint on these surfaces: the eastern side of the railroad viaduct above Mohawk Street; the southern side of the Sixth Street bridge; the wall facing Fairfax Avenue of the boarded-up Tuller Bros. warehouse; the brick wall facing Ninth Street of the high school; the tattered billboard high on stilts overlooking the Northern Pacific rail-road yard! So people gaping in ignorance were forced to *see* though not knowing what it was they were *seeing*, saying, "What *is* that?—it looks like fire, like a torch," and saying, "Is it supposed to mean something?—what's it supposed to *mean?"* but most of all, and most gratifying to hear, "How on earth did they get it up *there?"*

Like spies then we of FOXFIRE mingled with the unsuspecting on all sides, overheard their quizzical commentary to report back to FOXFIRE breathless with hilarity. And if in the midst of Them there happened to be two or more of FOXFIRE we scarcely dared glance at one another for fear of revealing the exultation shining in our faces.

For instance, contemplating our gorgeous flame painted on the wall of the high school (it was dull beige brick, that wall, begging to be defaced) the morning after FOXFIRE had painted it there, a guy named Ned Sullivan who belonged to the Hawks said he thought it was a gang from Oldwick High that must have done it, and it burned his ass, and called for retribution, but a girl named Linda Fearing who was a senior and a popular girl, a cheerleader, said, *"I* think it's some sort of religious sign to give us warning, 'the coming of the End' like the world's in danger of going up in fire, y'know?" And Lana Maguire standing on Linda Fearing's other side cast me a look that went through me like an electric shock, like the two of us Lana and Maddy were secret lovers, and Lana said in a strange high-pitched voice I'd never heard from her before, "Yes. That *is* what it is: 'the coming of the End.' It *is*. I just *know."*

And turned to run off as if the thought terrified her so the rest of us stood staring amazed and terrified too staring after *her*.

In such remarkable ways FOXFIRE's proud red flame (which was also FOXFIRE's secret tattoo) became known to the world, and began to cause unrest.

You're wondering about our FOXFIRE tattoos. How we could hide them from the eyes of Others for instance our families or in the summer when we went swimming well we didn't go swimming that first summer except at dusk or even in the dark and undressing in the presence of Others we kept our tattoos hidden as best we could.

My tattoo healed slowly, the skin was tender and inflamed for weeks but I wasn't worried about infection, none of us were. A homemade tattoo is likely to be blurry, which mine was, and is still, the red dye bleeding under the skin but you could see it was surely a flame or a torch, hot enough looking so it might *burn* if touched.

(That time Momma barged into the bathroom and saw it she never said a word afterward, thus it came to seem Momma hadn't seen it, or explained to herself exactly what she saw, any more than I'd seen her blackened eye or wondered who had done it to her. Just as, forever afterward, for years after we'd carried off our Underwood typewriter in victory, if any of our gang ran into fat-ass Wimpy Wirtz in the neighborhood there was blank stiff silence all around—just NOTHING. Like he didn't know who we were and we surely didn't know who he was, not even me, Maddy Wirtz, related to the old bastard by some remote entanglement of "blood.")

It's true, a few times in school in the girls' locker room changing my clothes for gym I'd notice someone watching me just a little too closely but only one time, back in January, did a girl actually inquire. Her name was Sonia Wilentz, she had a sweet soft voice, "What's that on your shoulder, Maddy?—is it a *tattoo?*" her eyes widening as I pulled my T-shirt over my head, not quickly, but decisively, then looking her calmly in the eye I said, "It's a birthmark." Sonia said, "But—you never had it before, did you?" perplexed, slow to catch on and I said, "Only just since I was born." And staring her in the eye so she had to back away, blinking, hurt, and never did Sonia Wilentz ask me about my tattoo again, nor even speak to me if it could be avoided.

A few weeks later Legs herself was asked about her tattoo, called into the gym teacher's office to explain it but all Legs said was, "It is what it *is.*" Of the five of us Legs was the one who most insisted upon secrecy yet the one who was the most careless about hiding her tattoo, or maybe defiant, why should I hide it, it's beautiful Legs would say so rumors were spreading and Miss Diggs tried to interrogate her without success saying, "You know the school has a rigid policy forbidding secret societies, don't you Margaret?"—she was sharp-eyed and inclined to sarcasm like many other teachers but instinctively cautious in the presence of certain students, "Margaret Sadovsky" for instance, you couldn't predict what this lanky ice-eyed girl might say or even do, her pale mouth working, her expression steely and deadpan so when Legs mumbled, "That's got nothing to do with *me,*" Miss Diggs regarded her in silence for a beat or two then decided not to pursue the issue. Nor did she report it to the principal Mr. Wall. For certain of Them even in their confusion and ignorance were beginning to perceive how things fitted mysteriously together, like pieces of a jigsaw puzzle, these rumors of tattoos, a new secret gang, vivid blood-red flames painted around town and those words painted, also in red, on Lloyd Buttinger's car: FOXFIRE REVENGE!

Most of all the fate that befell Lloyd Buttinger.

Says Lana, "You get the feeling They're afraid of us?" licking her lips 'cause it's such a nice feeling, and Goldie smiles saying, "Huh! They better be," and Legs says, smiling but serious too, " 'First comes fear, then respect' as Father Theriault says. 'The oppressed of the Earth, rising, make their own law.' "

five

FOXFIRE Adventures, Missions, Triumphs

ITEM. The prize is seventy-five dollars—or is it a cruel collective bet that no one there is agile enough or strong enough or brave enough or crazy enough or drunk enough to climb the Memorial Park watertower using not the skinny rusty ladder which would be dangerous itself at this time of night (past midnight: and no moon) and in these circumstances (the high hilarity and rowdy unraveling end of the UAW-CIO Annual Labor Day Picnic) but the mere side of the tower that's shingled and serrated, crossbars every few feet so the logic is it *could* be climbed, maybe. Now the families have gone home and only the drinkers remain, mostly men, some young women and girls, teenagers too at the periphery of the action and these high too on beer they aren't supposed to be drinking 'cause they're under age, or are they high, some of them, on what they've been passing among themselves smoking shrieking and giggling back in the shadows, so the atmosphere of the picnic has changed, every year this happens and there'll be complaints in the days following possibly even arrests and certainly quarrels to last for lifetimes in certain cases but no one is thinking of that now: now's not the time. The prize is seventy-five dollars if you can climb the side of the watertower *to the very top* which means not slipping halfway and falling thirty feet to your death or such severe injuries you'll be crippled for life but naturally no one's thinking of that: now's not the time: six or seven volunteers push forward eager to take up the challenge for the money or possibly for the hell of it such an opportunity to show off, among them Potato Head Heine pulling off his shirt so he's in his undershirt showing bulging sweaty muscles in his back and shoulders but Potato Head is too drunk to be allowed to climb, another who does climb at least for a few shaky yards is Vinnie Roper president of the outlaw gang the Viscounts that causes so much trouble at Perry High, another is Jake Korenjak's older brother Steve who's already been in, and discharged from, the U.S. Navy, still another is an older guy must be in his late thirties so you'd expect him to have better sense but, this time of night, beyond the beer tent at the Labor Day picnic, there's no accounting for crazy behavior and hopes.

Among the men though there's a girl, it turns out, a young girl possibly fourteen or fifteen years old, so there's a brief noisy debate about whether she should be "allowed" to compete and she's "allowed" at least provisionally, a tomboy sort of girl in T-shirt, jeans, sneakers, ashy-blond hair in a ponytail hanging halfway down her back, she starts her climb agile as a monkey unhesitating as if she's climbed the side of this tower before and everyone watches mesmerized as she pulls away from her competition as one by one they drop back, give up, lose their grip or their audacity and clamber back down chagrined at being so defeated but most of all defeated so publicly by a mere girl, and so young and thin a girl, Ab Sadovsky's daughter it turns out and where's Ab?—he'd be astonished and madder than hell seeing his daughter displaying herself in this fashion risking her neck for seventy-five dollars poor bastard has troubles enough these days women trouble and job trouble and drinking trouble and now this, someone says Ab was in the beer tent a short while ago but must be he's drifted off, gone home, or off with some of his buddies to a tavern on Fairfax. So there's no one to insist that the Sadovsky girl come back down though a few people in the crowd, mainly women, are calling up *Be careful hon, hey—be careful!* and now the last of the men is giving up, blond kid with sideburns and a cigarette jaunty behind his ear but one of the crossbars twenty feet up is rotted or termite-ridden and nearly breaks off in his hand and he's panicked and sober suddenly hastily backing down crab-fashion while his buddies hoot and jeer and clap he jumps down to the ground safe and cursing laughing to disguise the fact that he's nearly pissed his pants oh man and his stomach is queasy, he's had enough of playing the fool for one night.

But the girl, Ab Sadovsky's daughter, the one they call Legs, keeps climbing. No awareness that her rivals have dropped away or possibly no interest in them just climbing a little slower now as if the first feverish adrenaline rush has subsided and she's getting smarter with each foot of elevation climbing the vertical surface up into the sky forty, fifty feet above the ground as some in the gaping crowd that's primarily men fall worriedly quiet and others continue to cheer to shout to whistle in a raucous chorus and there's a small group of her girl friends screaming *Legs! C'mon Legs! Almost there Legs!* in dread and exultation beating their fists against their thighs their faces contorted with the strain of willing their friend not to slip and fall, not to topple down before their eyes and die *Oh God Legs—c'mon!* Now unbelievably she's sixty feet above the ground approaching the walkway from beneath and climbing more hesitantly now, or is it more thoughtfully as if the weight of that very height lies heavily upon her narrow shoulders and the wonder is almost audible—is she? isn't she? is she? *is* she? going to make it to the top of the watertower and win the seventy-five dollars? going to fall, and die? and where are the police? and where is her father? and isn't anyone going to call her back down? but Legs climbs on heedless of the crowd of mostly drunken Others beneath her giving no sign of hearing even her FOXFIRE sisters calling to her, now she has managed to grip the edge of the walkway from beneath she has hold of the ledge with fingers that must be hard as steel and unerring and there's a moment's panic below and a palpable intake of breath as, unbelievably, the girl swings herself out into space in a flamboyant audacious utterly unnecessary gesture like an acrobat, it looks as if she's going to fall but she has sufficient momentum to bring her back to the tower's side and safety and now she's pulling herself up carefully onto the walkway in the practiced manner of a swimmer pulling herself up out of a pool, she's safe.

We on the ground clutched at one another faint and delirious moaning *Oh! oh oh!*—Lana and Goldie and weak-kneed Maddy, just the three of us that night, Rita'd had to stay home. Staring up at Legs so high above us we almost couldn't see her except someone on the ground was shining a flashlight to where now she was strolling on the ledge lithe and graceful and assured as a cat oblivious of the cheers, whistles, shouts, drunken applause—high above the crowd of mostly drunken Others she scorned in her heart.

Why'd I do it?—for FOXFIRE.

No I was never scared not for a second, I'm used to climbing.

This selfish idea people have of wanting to live forever, their 'immortal souls' and that kind of shit, that's not for me. Like they want the Earth for themselves and nobody else—that's not for me.

Half the money's for FOXFIRE any crazy damn thing we want to wear, or to own, or to eat, the other half I'm gonna send to my grandmother up in Plattsburgh that I feel sort of guilty about treating her last year like I did.

Up there on the walkway flexing her arms and legs not glancing down you could see it wasn't the seventy-five dollars that was the true prize nor even the challenge of beating out those Others in public, so ever afterward they'd have to acknowledge Legs Sadovsky, it was Legs herself balanced against Death, and she'd won.

ITEM. TYNE PETS & SUPPLIES on Tyne Street, a narrow dim-lit cave, parakeets, goldfish, puppies for sale and the first whiff hits you in the face when you step inside out of the fresh air, smells of ammonia, disinfectant, rancid food and dust and animal bowels and Goldie who's the most upset we've ever seen her is saying, "—These poor dogs! their cages have got so small for them they can hardly turn around, they're gonna maybe be *crippled,*" leading the four of us to the rear of the shop where there's a dozen cages against a wall stacked three deep, only half the cages occupied by these sick-looking dogs so your heart just goes out to them, poor things. Goldie is talking loud and excited and righteous the way she does, not caring, maybe not noticing, that the proprietor is watching us and isn't looking very friendly, "—It's wrong! It's a crime! I been in here before, and I told them! What happens to a poor innocent puppy that gets too big and nobody buys him and nobody *cares!*" There's a golden-haired cocker spaniel in a cage at eye-level sprawled listless against the wire mesh of the cage scarcely aware of us, there's a wire terrier lying in his food and water dishes like he's comatose, there's a dachshund with a stubby tail trying to wag but his eyes are dull, there's Goldie's favorite, the dog she'd buy if she could buy a dog, a silvery-haired raccoon-faced husky whose eyes flare up briefly when she pokes her fingers through the wire mesh and speaks to him but he doesn't make any effort to get to his feet—maybe can't, his cage is so cramped. Goldie says, "He doesn't look like a puppy, the breed's so big, but he *is.* He's only four months old."

"How much does he cost?" Lana asks. "You could buy him, hon. *We* could buy him, for you."

"That isn't the *point,*" Goldie says almost in despair,

"—the point *is* all the dogs in this dump, in these cages, need to be *freed.*"

So we're talking like this, the five of us, and pretty soon the man comes over to us and says in this cold flat nasty voice, "You want to look, or to buy?—loitering's forbidden in this shop." He and Goldie know each other, there's animosity between them so Legs cuts in quick before Goldie can speak, "You need to take better care of these dogs, mister," and he says—he's a guy in his fifties maybe, not tall, shorter than Goldie, with a slight hunch to his shoulders, near-bald and horn-rimmed glasses and a gray-grizzled look around his lower face like an old dog's muzzle—in this sour voice he says, "You feel sorry for 'em, buy 'em," and Goldie says, "There's laws about cruelty to animals! You could get into trouble, mister!" and Rita says, standing on her tiptoes, her voice quavering, "I bet you don't let them out of those cages, ever—I bet you don't take them outside to exercise!" and suddenly we're all arguing with him and he's telling us to get out and right then the door opens at the front of the shop and a customer steps inside but, hearing the commotion, backs right out. So this really pisses off the proprietor, he's saying, "Get out! You're troublemakers, get *out!* I'll call the police—" so Legs gives us a sign we'd better leave, and we do.

Those early times, before FOXFIRE was known, we'd never ask for trouble if trouble could be avoided. Like Legs said, there's always other ways to make people do what you want them to do.

But we couldn't stay away of course. Now it wasn't only Goldie sickened and disgusted to think of those wretched dogs (maybe the parakeets were sickly too, even the goldfish, for all we knew) but all of us. I believe I must have dreamt of the dogs in the cages because one night in the middle of the night I woke frightened and breathless, I was being suffocated I was being shut in tight inside something getting tighter like bars or that story of Edgar Allan Poe that'd made such a deep impression on me, "The Pit and the Pendulum"—nowhere to go that isn't Death.

Legs said she'd dreamt of the dogs too. Or something, in cages. Maybe *her.*

"I never had any pet, a dog or a cat, anything," I told my friends, giving my mouth a sarcastic twist—a Monkey-twist, I guess you'd define it, "—my mother says, 'They eat too much, they get in the way, then they die on you.' "

My friends laughed. I could always count on them, to laugh.

Legs said thoughtfully, "It isn't just that he's a petty capitalist out to make a buck—his name's Gifford, by the way: I found out—but he's *mean.* Selling living creatures you don't give a damn for is the meanest of *mean.*"

Goldie said, "He's a fucking Nazi. FOXFIRE's gonna show him."

So we plot our strategy which, as Legs says, has got to be reasonable, and a few days later we return to TYNE PETS & SUPPLIES, it's a sun-warmed September afternoon and there's a customer in the shop, and Gifford's wife is there too, you can tell this squat froggish woman with her hair in the hairnet is Gifford's wife because they look alike, like twins, especially in the eyes and mouth. It's as if Mrs. Gifford is lying in wait for us 'cause immediately we walk in she tries to cut us off saying sharply, "Yes? What do you want?" while Gifford's staring at us outraged so he almost drops the twenty-pound bag of dog food he's lifting onto a counter, "—you girls," she says, "—you're not wanted in this establishment," and Goldie sticks out her lower lip and pushes past saying, "We're just gonna *look,* lady, nothing's gonna get hurt by us *looking,*" so Goldie, and Legs, and Lana, and Rita, and Maddy march right back to the rear of the store where nothing appears to have changed, the cages as they were, the smells a little stronger, the golden-haired cocker spaniel, the little terrier, the dachshund, the beautiful silvery husky all in their cages cramped as before, and we're saying calmly to Gifford who's come up behind us that we just feel sorry for his dogs, isn't there a more humane way of keeping them, and Gifford says, as if it's some old Biblical injunction or a famous quotation, "You feel sorry for 'em, buy 'em."

Goldie says, "How much is this husky?"

"Forty dollars."

"How much for all the dogs?"

There's a shrewd glint like mica in this old fart's eyes behind his glasses, he says, quick, "I'd have to add that up," then, sort of sneering, "—You girls don't look like *you* could afford them."

Goldie says, excited and nervous, "How *much?*" but Legs lays her hand on Goldie's arm, Legs says, "Say we did buy all these dogs, you got to know he'd just bring in more—say we bought *them* he'd bring in *more*. Also it would be collusion with the enemy, to pay his price."

So there's this scene: Mrs. Gifford comes over and she and Gifford start shouting at us, telling us to leave they're going to call the police, we're trespassing, we're disturbing the peace, we're interfering with their business, and some of the dogs start in barking, the first we've heard a peep out of them, the little terrier splashing his water dish, the husky the loudest, and there's Maddy saying, raising her voice to be heard so the Giffords have no choice but to hear—and by this time there's another customer come in, and she's listening too—"It isn't the individual dogs, it's the principle: if you don't respect living life you don't deserve to live yourself." And this is such a shocking statement, just popping out of Maddy's mouth, it stops things cold for a beat or two.

But FOXFIRE has its strategy, only we'd planned to give the Giffords another chance first. So we leave the shop and take up our picket signs we'd hidden in the alley outside: white sheets of cardboard with neat red letters TYNE PETS IS CRUEL TO ANIMALS and IF YOU LOVE ANIMALS DON'T SHOP HERE and SHAME SHAME SHAME and two signs with

"HAVE MERCY ON ME" and "HELP ME PLEASE" above drawings of dogs squeezed in such small cages their noses and tails are poking through the bars. And we put on Hallowe'en masks: Legs has a crafty fox mask, Goldie has a snarling wolf mask, Lana has a snooty cat mask, Rita has a panda mask, and Maddy, naturally, has a puckish monkey mask.

You wouldn't believe, how quickly we get results.

Not even Legs would have guessed, how quickly!

The Giffords are horrified, they're the kind of people who most dread public exposure so first they order us to get away they'll call the police but we tell them they don't own the sidewalk, then they pull down the blind over their front door and lock up and turn out the lights hiding in there fearful of what might happen, but we don't quit picketing, we've just begun, chanting "Justice for animals! Mercy for animals!" and sometimes, daringly, under our breaths, "FOXFIRE REVENGE!" as people on the street stare at us, gather around to stare and make inquiries. It's amazing to us how much attention we draw and how quickly, and it seems too there's sympathy on our side—other people in the neighborhood tell us they've noticed how badly the Giffords treat their pets but they never thought to do anything about it. All our lives we've been seeing men (and some women) in picket lines, Hammond is a union town so most people here will refuse to cross a picket line and will respect it, and they respect us, but the real surprise is how a little later that afternoon a photographer from the Hammond *Chronicle* comes by to take our picture!—so next day there we are, on page three, the blood-sisters of FOXFIRE in Hallowe'en masks carrying picket signs, unidentified, above a caption reading "Young animal lovers protest 'inhumane' conditions in local pet shop."

When I saw the photograph I thought how the animal masks gave an eerie authority to what we did. I couldn't remember whose idea the masks had been, Legs' or mine.

* * *

We couldn't have guessed how quickly things would happen, or how they would turn out: how by the following Tuesday, after so much publicity, and a visit from the S.P.C.A., the Giffords decide they will discontinue selling pets; how they price their dogs low to get rid of them; how Toby comes to live with Goldie and to be FOXFIRE's mascot—Toby the four-month-old silvery-haired raccoon-faced husky, acquired by FOXFIRE for twenty-five dollars.

The oppressed of the Earth, rising, make their own law.

ITEM. Hallowe'en: the sisters of FOXFIRE in disguise as gypsies in long black skirts, exotic scarves and jewelry, wearing black domino masks travel miles away to uptown Hammond to go trick-or-treating in the affluent residential neighborhoods, they're amused at the expressions on home-owners' faces when they open their doors to see such apparently mature trick-or-treaters—Goldie, for one, looms nearly six feet tall, menacing in her wolf mask, and wordless—and they're gleeful acquiring such a cornucopia of treats, candies, fruits, coins, dollar bills; but their real mission as Legs envisions it is to familiarize themselves with this alien territory—the world of the "propertied bourgeoisie."

Rita asks, worried, "You mean we're gonna come back sometime and break into these houses? *rob* them?" and Legs says laughing, "Hell, no, FOXFIRE is above petty thievery," giving Rita a chastising little pinch on the arm, "—But we should know who our enemies are."

Maddy thinks, The more you see of the world the more enemies you discover. She's mildly disoriented; giddy. The evening's trick-or-treating in these remote Hammond neighborhoods, the hurried glimpses of domestic interiors resplendent to her eyes as Hollywood sets designed to dazzle, have left her permanently impressed. It's with a queer high-pitched laugh that she says, *"Why* 'above petty thievery'? Who says?"

Goldie, Lana, even Rita join her, laughing. Legs just stares.

Later that night, tireless, exhilarated, they shed their bulky gypsy costumes but retain their masks and gaily yet assiduously apply wax, soap, and vivid red crayon to the plate glass windows of certain pre-selected business establishments in the Main Street area. SATAN LIVES! Lana writes boldly on the window of Van Leer Jewelry, BEWARE THE CAT! Maddy prints in foot-high letters on the window of Worthington Furs, NO ESCAPE NO MERCY $$$$ IS SHIT ABOMINATION DEATH Legs scrawls in three-foot-high letters on the window of Empire State Finance and Loan Inc. Goldie reveals a true talent for cartoon art, she's enraptured drawing monstrous male genitalia on any available surface, upright penises with cartoon faces, whiskers, top hats and canes, priestly collars so the others shriek with laughter, and Rita who's likely to misspell words draws swastikas in red crayon on whatever surfaces she can—

"Christ, Red, you got it backward," says Legs, laughing, and the others join in, girlish-giddy laughter and no cruelty to it, "—just like Red, isn't it, to get a thing *backward.*"

Rita giggles happily. How she loves Legs calling her "Red."

Protesting, "Well, getting it backward's a one hundred percent better than nothing."

Which sets them off laughing again, the logic of such a statement, the truth. Even Maddy whose father died as a result of swastika war laughs, tears stinging her eyes beneath her cheap-glamorous black domino mask.

Over the years, well into adulthood, recalling that insight of Rita's: whatever you do, with whom you do it or whether you do it alone, and when, and how, and why, to what mysterious end—it's balanced against nothing, against Death and forgetting. *You* balanced against oblivion.

Says Legs, as if she's just now thought of it, "Be careful

where you put the FOXFIRE flame, O.K.?—it's got to have dignity. Not mixed up with this Hallowe'en crap."

They get the idea then, and it's a terrific idea, to transcribe the heraldic symbol, the torch, onto solid brick surfaces mainly: the fronts of the First Presbyterian Church, and St. John's Roman Catholic Church, and All Saints' Episcopal Church, and Prince of Peace Lutheran.

Careful!—for what if they get caught?

As the hour gets later, the wind rises and it's a wild scary-giddy time, the FOXFIRE sisters scrambling for cover as police patrol cars cruise past, and there's the danger, a great danger, of being sighted by other Hallowe'en pranksters, carloads of drunken young men and boys out to make trouble. Near two in the morning in a fine light freezing drizzle Legs and Goldie and Lana and Rita and Maddy are at last headed home down Fairfax when a souped-up car approaches from the rear, unmistakable the sound of its mufflerless roaring, unmistakable the sight of its weird-bright canary-yellow chassis streaked with black zigzag bars, Vinnie Roper's Oldsmobile Rocket 98 roars past and a brick goes flying and glass in the front window of Angelo's Pizzeria shatters and a sliver of glass strikes Maddy in the lower part of her face and she isn't even clearly conscious of bleeding as she and Legs and Goldie and Rita run, run run down an alley panting and giggling and frightened, not until minutes later beneath a street light do they notice the blood on Maddy's face and she discovers it glistening on her fingers, pokes and pries and manages to get the glass out of her flesh and there's a crazy thought I've been hit, I'm dead, it's nothing.

So to the amazement and alarm of her FOXFIRE sisters Maddy-Monkey is laughing, her grin wide as a jack o'lantern's as Legs fusses over her, most tenderly wipes away the blood with her shirt sleeve, half chiding, "God, Maddy! you could've let us know you were hit," and Maddy can hardly catch her breath it's so late she's so cold so exhausted so close to tears hearing her voice so oddly lifting, "Oh I don't mind, maybe it'll turn out like yours," touching her finger to the scar on Legs' chin, "—why should I *mind?*"

ITEM. Says Legs somberly, almost pedantically, "The basis of human life is *charity,* which means love for people you don't always know," it's one of her notions picked up from wizened little Father Theriault probably but she takes it seriously, Legs takes everything seriously thus when she has "loose change" as she calls it (in fact, Legs often mysteriously has money in bills in denominations of five, ten, even twenty dollars) she'll ask her FOXFIRE sisters to add to it, anything they can spare no matter how modest a sum say a dollar, even fifty cents, fifty cents is enough, and this fund she'll designate as FOXFIRE CHARITY and wrapped sometimes in an orange-red silk scarf of the kind that by now is identified with the secret girl-gang FOXFIRE about which so many rumors and whispers circulate it will be given to someone "deserving" in the neighborhood: seventy-year-old Mrs. Paxton for instance whose half-crazy daughter beats her and steals her Social Security check . . . sixteen-year-old Wilma Lundt who had to drop out of Perry High because she's pregnant, and now she's living by herself away from her family . . . a crippled U.S. Army veteran named Fensted about whose sad plight Lana had heard by way of her father . . . a woman in her thirties named Kathleen, or Katherine, who'd once been a girl friend of Ab Sadovsky (at which time Legs had violently resented her) now a precariously reformed alcoholic recently released from Milena State Psychiatric Hospital up north. And, unofficially, there's the elderly ex-priest to whom Legs evidently gives, not cash, you don't give a man with his habits cash, but food, warm clothing, if he'll accept her charity. But this Legs won't discuss, not even with Maddy Wirtz who's her closest friend.

Says Legs, her eyes shining, "Someday, y'know, nobody'll

be dependent on other people giving them things. 'Charity's' gonna go extinct."

In her frayed Navy jacket, jeans, scuffed boots, her hair in her face and her nostrils reddened from a bad cold, thin cheeks waxy-pale.

Goldie says thoughtfully, "It's the wildest thing, I mean— *weird.* Anybody told me I'd be giving money away a year ago, even a dime I'd of laughed in their face, but y'know once you get doing it, especially if you can't exactly afford it yourself it's kind of a, a good feeling . . ." her voice trailing off as if she's baffled, not knowing how to express what she wants to say. It's Goldie and Maddy in the Siefrieds' kitchen with little Toby the silvery-haired raccoon-faced husky cavorting on the lino-leum floor, a white-blizzardy January morning and Goldie and Maddy happen to be alone together 'cause Maddy has come to live temporarily with the Siefrieds 'cause there's a problem with her mother she'd rather not talk about even with her blood-sisters, and Maddy's shaky, Maddy's feeling vulnerable as if the outermost layer of her skin has been peeled off so she says only, "Yes," in a voice so faint Goldie can barely hear above the puppy's happy clamor.

ITEM. *What is it you have? Is it a secret? How can I join? What can I do, to be allowed to join? I'll do anything . . .*

There's Violet Kahn, there's Toni LeFeber, there's Marsha Lauffenberg . . . one by one approaching the FOXFIRE sisters with their wistful questions their hopeful eyes *Oh please please tell me what to do, don't turn me away oh please* and after the first stab of satisfaction when you know you're envied there comes a feeling of something like remorse and generosity combined and now the problem is, by New Year's Day 1954 a year following the formation of FOXFIRE, should FOXFIRE be expanded? should new members be initiated? and how to have them prove themselves worthy?

FOXFIRE has become a public fact.

FOXFIRE is *famous.*

six

Homo Sapiens

For every fact transcribed in these CONFESSIONS there are a dozen facts, a hundred facts, my God maybe a thousand left out.

For writing a memoir is like pulling your own guts out inch by slow inch. I didn't know this when I started but I know it now.

Can you tell the truth if it isn't the *entire* truth?—and what *is* truth?

Some things, I can't fit into these CONFESSIONS. Nor can I calculate how truly I should explain any incident. Because one thing rises out of something that came before it, or many things that came before it, so it's like a big spiderweb in Time going back forever and ever, no true beginning nor any promise of an end the way in those years it was believed the Universe was, a steady mostly unchanging pool of galaxies and gases and emptiness going on and on like a dream to no purpose in all directions and forward and back too in Time. The kind of Time that, if you tried to show your place in it, not even the snap of your fingers could count for it. Not even the *idea* of snapping your fingers.

One nasty-blowy winter day, a Saturday it must have been, Legs and Maddy visited the natural history museum Uptown on Van Buren Boulevard, why Legs wanted to go I don't recall, or maybe it was Maddy who'd had the idea, scientific-minded Maddy Wirtz who never forgot some vision or understanding she'd had one day in Buttinger's math class, the world of Numbers that doesn't change, immutable facts, celestial bodies. Legs and Maddy in an ellipsis of Time after FOXFIRE was taking its form so unexpected and with a kind of power like a tough city weed forcing its way through concrete, but Legs had something on her mind that wasn't FOXFIRE, she'd gotten worked up about some things that'd happened in the past few months, not to us nor even to anyone we knew but to girls and women in the area, it was a time of violence against girls and women but we didn't have the language to talk about it then. For instance a nineteen-year-old nursing student from Hammond was raped and strangled and her body left in a drainage ditch outside town and the guy that did it, or maybe there was more than one, had never been caught. For instance a pregnant woman, a young wife in Sandusky (Sandusky is a small town outside Hammond, not exactly a suburb) was stabbed to death in her house by an intruder it was believed, and her unborn baby killed too, and eventually it was revealed that the "intruder" was her own husband!—and nobody talked of anything else for weeks. And the year before there'd been this guy in Buffalo the "Black Scarf Killer" (so-called 'cause he wore a black silk scarf over the lower part of his face) who was charged with killing eight girls and women over a period of fifteen months, the oldest woman in her eighties, and in a neighborhood in Port Oriskany where Lana Maguire had cousins there was this poor little six-year-old girl slashed by some madman with a razor, her face "cut to ribbons" it said in the newspaper and her belly and even her little vagina slashed and she'd have bled to death except a motorist saw her crawling in a vacant lot, said he thought it was a rat at first . . . these terrible things that don't have any place in the

CONFESSIONS exactly and none of us wanted to talk about them much, or think about them, except Legs of course, saying, "—They hate us, y'know?—the sons of bitches! This is proof they hate us, they don't even know it probably, most of them, but they hate us, they'd kill us all if they could and get away with it like in a dream, like this 'Jekyll-and-Hyde' in the movie!" excited, words tumbling out, the pupils of her eyes dilated, so one of us would try to calm her down saying these were just special cases, these maniacs and murderers, and Legs would interrupt saying angrily, "No it's all of them: men. It's a state of undeclared war, them hating us, men hating us no matter our age or who the hell we are but nobody wants to admit it, not even *us*," she'd get so worked up there was no reasoning with her and it made us nervous 'cause like I said (and this is true right up to the present time in America) there are things you don't want to think about if you're female, say you're a young girl or a woman you're *female* and that isn't going to change, right?—so Legs and Maddy are in that ellipsis of Time after FOXFIRE was coming into shape but before Maddy's mother had her breakdown (as it was called) and had to be carried out of their house on a stretcher with the neighbors on the sidewalk staring, Maddy's mother sobbing whimpering soiling herself like an infant, this too was before Legs got into the famous fight at the high school that caused Wall to expel her thus altering the course of her life forever: the two girls wandering gum-chewing and hands in their pockets through the cavernous corridors of the old museum, only a handful of other visitors that Saturday and the few guards watch Legs and Maddy closely giving them the fish-eye 'cause these girls are dressed in jeans and jackets and boots and wearing matching red-orange scarves around their necks that are maybe gang-colors?—both of them thin, watchful, peering at the exhibits, each dust-stippled display of leathery dinosaurs, mannequin American Indians phony as papier-mâché, fossils like plastic, a smell of grime, disinfectant, wet wool, rubber boots, and Time, and it's as if the girls are hunting something that eludes them, always around the corner, up a flight of worn marble stairs, the secret heart of the museum, the core of all adult knowledge where mere words, mysterious tangles of sound, have an uncanny power:

MESOPOTAMIA XOCHIPILLI NESTORIAN

AUSTRALOPITHECINE NEANDERTHAL

PITHECANTHROPUS CRUSTACEA

TRILOBITA PALEOZOIC BRACHIOSAURUS

TYRANNOSAURUS REX MIOCENE ZINJANTHROPUS

RAMAPITHECUS

Staring at simian glassy-eyed jut-jawed *Ramapithecus* a "probable human ancestor" then contemplating THE TREE OF LIFE: EVOLUTION a many-tendriled bas-relief inside a dimly lit glass display case, Maddy is fascinated by how *complex* the tree is, how multiple its branches, and probably the diagram itself is a simplification, how scary to be told that so many more animal species existed in the deep past than exist at the present time and scariest of all that ninety-nine percent of all animal species have become extinct across the vast oceans of Time for why's that? to what purpose, such losses? if a species is born, why should it die, why be born if only to die, why come into being if it must become extinct? *what is God's purpose?*

The girls locate *Homo sapiens* represented by a small human figure perched atop one of the tendrils lifting from a slender branch floating precariously in air, other figures on the tendril and on the branch are humanoid, apelike, in fact apes, they succumb to a fit of giggling, seeing *Homo sapiens* is no big deal! and it doesn't look as if there's any logic to it, the TREE OF LIFE, man's position on the tree, *Homo sapiens: thinking man:* created by what humanoid God in His own image?—they're laughing derisively, Legs sniffs and wipes her nose on her sleeve, "Christ you'd think our hot-shit species

would count for more than *that!*" and Maddy not to be out-
done in coolness (though her heart's broken? she can't take
God seriously ever again?) laughs her sharp nasal laugh that's
the very sound of adolescent cynicism, "Yeah? Wouldn't you?"

seven

Wild Wild Ride

This episode, I'm laughing as I transcribe.

I remember it so vividly: the ending most of all.

FOXFIRE DEFIES DEATH!

There are only two sloppily typed pages in the original notebook dated March 25, 1954, which was the date of FOXFIRE's famous car-kidnapping and flight out into the country that made us so talked-of in Hammond, even kids from other parts of the city who didn't know *us* knew about *it* and probably remember to this day.

Of course, you'd have had to be a witness or at least you'd have had to be there with us in Hammond in Lowertown in our old neighborhood to fully understand.

The car Legs kidnapped was Acey Holman's brand new 1954 Buick DeLuxe sedan with the white wall tires, gleaming turquoise and chrome polished to a high sheen and that black leather interior smelling of newness, the car seats front and back made of some special wool fabric unlike the car seats most of us knew, cheap vinyl that stuck to your bare legs in summer or sweated under your rear end, but Acey Holman's got money, he's known in Lowertown as a smart operator a gambler and the story is he'd left the keys to the Buick in his ignition so he could duck into Eddie's Smoke Shop on Ninth Street to collect a bet on a boxing match then three minutes later when he comes back out—*the Buick is gone!*

How this happened, I'll have to go back a step or two to explain.

"Snow White" was her secret FOXFIRE name, her name to Others was Violet Kahn.

Of our FOXFIRE initiates of January 1954 "Snow White" was the *prize,* I guess you'd say.

Fifteen years old, a sophomore in high school and not a good student 'cause she had trouble concentrating she said, she was Lana's good friend living just across the street from the Maguires and we all knew her of course, Violet had had boy friends in sixth grade, boys fighting over her and I mean actually *fighting* with their fists, but she was sweet-natured, unnervingly beautiful with skin doughy dead-white as Wonderbread you think you could poke your finger into, and eyes black as if the pupils had bled out into the irises and her hair jet-black too and straight as an Indian's falling to her waist. Like Lana she wore bright crimson lipstick, her mouth was fleshy and moist. When we initiated her I guess we were hard on her, at least two of us, cold and cruel in our commands reducing the naked girl on her hands and knees to a state akin to terror though she was whispering *Oh thank you oh I love you all!*

Like Maddy, Violet Kahn was too shaky to tattoo her own flesh. It had to be done for her.

Of the four "Snow White" was the only one who fainted from the blood, or the pain, or the excitement—who knows?

Crying in long gulping sobs but the tears were tears of elation like some crazy Protestant witnessing for Christ and in her nakedness there was *so much* of her, handfuls of her it seemed, a big fleshy pulpy baby with no bones we could knead, squeeze, pinch, slap, Goldie slapping the hardest her face contorted her lips drawn back from her teeth, and panting so, so seeing Goldie Maddy felt sickened, a pang of dizzy self-loathing, *Why am I doing this, I'm not like this I'm not cruel like this I don't want to hurt another human being do I?* and she turned her attention to another of the quivering scared naked initiates but did not knead, squeeze, pinch, slap to evoke pain, not that anyone noticed, this wild wild scene in the candlelit FOXFIRE chamber hidden from Others' eyes in a third-floor room in a boarded-up warehouse out beyond Fairfax near the railroad yard, the FOXFIRE sisters were in a delirium of ecstasy worked up to a higher and higher and higher pitch on whiskey and those skinny parchment cigarettes the black guys called reefer and sold, anywhere you could find them, for a quarter apiece, the sight of blood made them more feverish so Maddy had the terrible thought, *What if we lick blood?—what will stop us, then?*—but in fact they did not, they merely mingled blood, their separate bloods, the five original FOXFIRE sisters and the new initiates Violet and Toni and Marsha weeping together hugging one another staggering and swaying and *Oh I love you! love love love you all!* it was Violet/"Snow White" sobbing the hardest grateful for all we'd done whatever it was, exactly, we'd remember afterward we had done.

Those FOXFIRE members skeptical of the wisdom of bringing Violet Kahn into the gang were two: Goldie and Maddy: not that they were jealous were they?—of Violet's startling good looks or of the disturbing fact that Legs so favored her, argued impatiently on her behalf? (As Goldie complained, Legs was flattered by Violet Kahn's sucking up to *her*. Those dewy-moony eyes and moist smiles cast in Legs' direction you'd have to be a saint to ignore and Legs, for all her pretensions, was no saint.)

Not that they were jealous, they were simply being cautious arguing wasn't it asking for trouble? becoming blood-sisters with Violet Kahn who was known to be emotional, unstable? like all the Kahns? Violet was plagued by boys interested in her, older guys too in their twenties chasing after her cruising past her house or through the parking lot behind the school whistling and calling *Hey baby, hey Vi'let honey, hey hot stuff how's about a ride?* and except for the quietest shyest most tongue-tied boys Violet never went out with them, claimed to be "repulsed" by them and "disgusted" and "scared to death" and yet: what could you make of her Liz Taylor–Debra Paget look, the white-powdered face, long silky-slinky black hair, those crimson lips?

Goldie made a gagging gesture, as if the very thought of Violet Kahn made her sick. If Toby was in her lap squirming and kissing the way he did, in a frenzy of affection most times we saw him, she'd pretend that Toby was poor Violet lapping-kissing with her tongue and push him away. "I *know* she's sweet, I *know* she's desperate to belong, but I don't give a damn—she's just gonna be trouble, all those fuckfaces after her."

Maddy made an effort to keep the hurt out of her voice (she *was not* thinking of Legs spending time with Violet Kahn instead of with FOXFIRE or better yet with her) echoing a stray remark of her mother's she'd heard years ago that must have lodged deep, it's so lurid, ugly, graphic, "What Violet Kahn *is* is honey left out in the open, in a saucer for *flies.*"

Goldie laughed hard, Goldie liked that. "Honey!—*flies!*"

Legs' logic when Legs argued was: "Then we need to help her. FOXFIRE's gonna be Violet Kahn's *redemption.*"

Immediately Lana piped up, "Yeah. Right. Violet Kahn's a good sweet kid, she's easy to handle. 'Redemption'—whatever that is, that's right."

And Rita who was in a fever of charity those days since she'd lost twelve pounds by scrupulous dieting, will power, FOXFIRE encouragement, no need now to be jealous of Violet Kahn, naturally Rita said, "Oh yeah, right! Like you guys

helped *me!*" so passionate in her speech the others were embarrassed, "—Like you saved my *life!*"

So Goldie and Maddy gave in, finally.

Decided not to exercise their veto power.

Goldie and Maddy and Toby the silvery-haired raccoon-
faced husky pup ravenous for LOVE.

When they told Violet Kahn the news she burst into tears.

Clutching their hands as if in desperation, embracing them
fumbling and blind, sobbing what sounded like, "Oh oh *oh*—
you want *me?* My God I'd d-die for *you*—" so even Maddy was
moved to think, *Maybe* this isn't a mistake after all.

And at the initiation ceremony Violet was the most passionate of the girls, the most vehement *Do you solemnly swear
to consecrate yourself to your sisters in FOXFIRE yes I swear to
consecrate yourself to the vision of FOXFIRE I do, I swear to
think always of your sisters as you would they would think of
you I do in the Revolution of the Proletariat that is imminent
in the Apocalypse in the Valley of the Shadow of Death and
under torture physical or spiritual I do, I do never to betray
your FOXFIRE sisters in thought word or deed never to reveal
FOXFIRE secrets never to deny FOXFIRE in this world or the
next above all to pledge yourself to FOXFIRE offering up all fidelity and courage and heart and soul and all future happiness to FOXFIRE yes I swear under penalty of death I swear so
help you God I swear forever and ever until the end of time*
Yes I will: I swear.

Looking back on Violet Kahn/"Snow White" I have this
thought, one of the odd slant thoughts I can't fit into the Confessions but don't want to discard: she was one of those ripe
fleshy baffled girls already blown up to maturity in their early
teens, thus cheated of true maturity. Your eye snagged in the
jiggly body, breasts hips buttocks, even a sisterly and kindly

eye so you found yourself staring at her, Marilyn Monroe was the same way, guessing that inside all that warm mammalian flesh there was a *person,* a *being,* trapped and breathless. And her eyes might catch at yours for just a moment so you knew, and she knew. But the moment never held.

In their new FOXFIRE sister's very presence Goldie couldn't resist muttering to Maddy out of the side of her mouth, " 'Honey—*flies.*' " And both girls would laugh meanly.

No one except Maddy had any idea what Goldie meant, or what logic there was to the pun on "flies."

"Hey Vi'let baby, how's about goin' for a ride?"

"Hey sweetie-tits! 'Snow White'! How's about a—"

"Mmmmmmmmmm 'Snow *White'!*"

A blinding-bright March day, snowfall the night before, slick curvy patches of ice gleaming on the pavement behind the high school and the sun like a burnished coin in the blue blue sky so everybody is feeling good—livened up, nervy, reckless. It's about twelve forty-five but nobody's ready to go back inside. As usual at this time of day, in clear weather especially, there are a half-dozen groups of students standing about talking and laughing and calling to one another and jeering and rocked by unaccountable spasms of high crude hilarity and now and then there's the scratching of a match, quick smoke-puffs of a forbidden cigarette . . . but these Perry students, the ones most eager to get out of the cafeteria and into the parking lot are such a scruffy lot, "disciplinary problems," certain of the girls as well as the majority of the boys, the school authorities don't try to monitor once they're outside the walls of the school.

So Violet Kahn is there with three FOXFIRE sisters including Goldie who has skipped school that morning but who, being Goldie Siefried, that's to say "Boom-Boom," thus perverse, has wandered over to the school for the hell of it in jeans and cowboy boots, brassy hair wind-whipped and Toby the husky pup cavorting and yipping at her heels—everybody at Perry loves this dog who's so sweet-tempered and grateful for affection, everybody wants to pet Toby, it's a way too of placating quick-tempered "Boom-Boom" as well. Beside her there's Lana Maguire bare-headed so her eye-catching white-blond hair is stirred by the wind, she's glamorously made up like her friend Violet, and smoking a cigarette she shares with Violet, the two of them taking long giggly drags doing their best to ignore the Viscounts' crude shouted teasing; and there's little fox-faced Toni LeFeber ignoring it too. Legs Sadovsky who's generally with them out in the parking lot at noon isn't there at the moment nor is skinny Maddy Wirtz—where *is* Maddy when the fight breaks out?—in an empty restroom tormenting herself with her reflection in one of the unflattering mirrors? These FOXFIRE blood-sisters are blatantly sporting their outlaw gang insignia for all to see, not only the familiar orange-red silky FOXFIRE scarf knotted around their necks in identical fashion (which no other girl at Perry dares emulate, that could cause trouble) but, since last fall, oversized black zip-up corduroy jackets with their initials elegantly stitched in orange-red thread on their left breasts and the mysterious word, or abbreviation, "FXFR," on the right.

(Asked naively does she belong to an outlaw gang, one of these girls will turn absolutely blank innocent eyes to her questioner, saying, " 'Outlaw gang'? *'Gang'?* I don't know what you're talking about.")

The self-assured FOXFIRE girls in their silky scarves and black corduroy jackets evoke strong feelings among the boys at Perry High School, especially among the gangs: the Viscounts, the Hawks, the Aces, the Dukes . . . each of these all-male gangs has its "female auxiliary," an ever-shifting pool of steady girl friends and available, or promiscuous, girls, but FOXFIRE's no "auxiliary," FOXFIRE can't be appropriated. FOXFIRE can't even be *approached*.

Today, this icy-bright March 19, 1954, there's the pretense that that new FOXFIRE sister Violet Kahn gave Moon Muller, one of the Viscounts, a "false signal" the other day—about which there's naturally vehement disagreement: Violet swears *no* she hadn't even looked at Moon, Moon swears *yes*—and the guys are buoyant and teasing edging closer to the girls, as always there's an undercurrent of something angry in their raw young male voices, an undercurrent of bafflement, wonderment, their high-pitched hoots of laughter, their flaring-up eyes, steps springy as if, like a wolf pack, they're about to dart in for the kill. Why is their behavior any different today? Is it because Legs Sadovsky isn't there?—and where *is* Legs? In their brown cracked-leather brass-studded jackets, terrycloth silver "V's" on the backs, these boys seem to mean business even as they're playful, clowning, crooning, "Hey Viiii'let! Mmmmmm 'Snow White'!" cat-calling, "Lookit *here,* honey, Moon's got something for ya!" as poor Violet Kahn tries not to hear, murmuring as she takes a drag from Lana's Chesterfield, "Oh shit, I could just *die,"* and Lana says, raising her voice so Vinnie Roper, Moon Muller, Bud Petko can hear, should they wish to hear, "Just ignore those assholes, hon, that's all they *are."*

At once the boys step closer, grinning. It's as if Lana, unknowing, has reached out and tugged them forward.

Vinnie Roper makes a playful swoop at Lana's scarf, he's a tall ox-size nineteen-year-old with bulging mock-wild eyes, oiled black hair combed back from his forehead in spiky quills, he's a charmer, yes but he's foul-mouthed, whistling, saying, "Hey who're you calling asshole, *cunt?"* Moon Muller's lewdly zipping and unzipping his jacket, falsetto-voiced, "Hey cross-eyes, wanna *fuck?"* and Bud Petko's convulsed with laughter and Goldie Siefried's standing there suddenly blocking them saying, tall, furious, *"You* fuck off, cocksuckers," and Toby begins to bark frantically, and it happens, that suddenly, as if a match had been tossed into a pool of gasoline, that these several Viscounts and these several FOXFIRE girls begin to trade insults . . . there are raised voices . . . some scuffling . . . Violet's breathless screams . . . a quickened sense among the scattered groups behind the school that trouble is imminent, it's what everybody has been waiting for and now it's *arrived*.

And suddenly out of nowhere there's Legs Sadovsky, a six-inch switchblade in her hand.

As Legs is running from the rear door of the school building, before even she's sighted, this happens: two of the Viscounts rush Goldie so, agile as if she's practiced this acrobatic move many times, the big brassy-haired girl swivels, brings her knee up swiftly into an undefended groin, and in nearly the same instant drives her right fist square into an astonished face loosening and bloodying three teeth before the victim, who's Bud Petko, is even aware she's about to swing. And Legs, swift and silent, ducking beneath someone's arm, springs up in front of Vinnie Roper to bring the tip of her knife close, very close, tremulously close, to the boy's Adam's apple.

"Freeze!" says Legs.

And there's a full stop, for a long long moment.

And everybody's watching, quieted suddenly, standing on tiptoe and jostling one another to see.

Moon Muller and Bud Petko on their hands and knees dazed in the snow, Bud Petko dripping blood, and Vinnie Roper standing there at the tip of a six-inch knifeblade that's glittering like a smile, he's paralyzed, blood drained out of his face, *Is that Roper? Vinnie? A girl's got him with a knife?* Legs says calmly, in a bell-clear voice, "You heard her, asshole— *fuck off*. All of you."

Legs Sadovsky!—her breath is fierce and steaming, her ashy-blond hair coarse as a horse's mane blows about her face. She's wearing her black corduroy FOXFIRE jacket, her bright silk neckerchief, black wool slacks with a sharp crease and pegged tight like a guy's at the cuffs. Of all the FOXFIRE girls Legs is the most reckless, the most extravagant, thinking now, Damn lucky she stayed inside watching since if she'd appeared too soon there might not have been any confrontation at all. *Coward Viscounts might've backed down.*

Legs gestures with her knife allowing Vinnie Roper to back off, that big hulking Viscount in his gang jacket, sleek oiled hair, reduced to such humiliation and you can see clearly he's scared, animal-scared, brought up close with the possibility of dying. He's three years older than Legs, must be more than one hundred pounds heavier but he carries himself fragile as fine-spun glass . . . the gathered crowd expels a collective breath part of relief and part of disappointment. Such a public victory and Legs is magnanimous, not gloating as any guy would do, not even smiling, knife still upraised and gleaming at throat level she's exchanging a long measured look with Vinnie Roper, it's a cool erotic look, deeply sexual as only Legs Sadovsky who's a beautiful sharp-cheeked girl can manage in such circumstances.

Never will Vinnie Roper be able to expunge this look from his memory, never will he be able to expunge this public shame, he'll bear it the remainder of his life.

All this while Toby has been barking, deep guttural sobbing sounds as if he's in a frenzy to attack, this sweet-tempered dog no one has ever seen in such a state. Both Goldie and Lana are required to restrain him, fingers looped through his collar. Goldie laughs breathless, "Toby *hush!* It's O.K. boy, everything's under *control!"*

Now out of a rear door comes Mr. Zwicky the vocational arts teacher who's also the boys' football coach, seeing Legs and her knife and Vinnie and Bud Petko swaying on his feet wiping blood from his mouth he pauses for just a moment then plunges forward calling, hands cupped to his mouth, "You! I see you! Throw that knife down!" and the guys are shrinking away, everybody shrinks back hoping not to be seen or identified except Legs who stands unmoving, eyeing Zwicky who she sees is scared of her too and she's thinking should she simply shut up her knife, slip it in a pocket, turn, run run run away, should she toss it into a snowbank, beneath a parked car?—and now Morton Wall the school principal is pushing his way forward, shouting, "What's going on! What's going on!" he's a man of recent griefs and publicized embarrassments, much-disliked by Perry students and it's this man's enormous fear that someone soon will be seriously injured or even killed at Perry and as principal he'll be the one to blame, maybe he'll be personally sued, so he's in a state of near-hysteria before even he sees Legs and the others, hears a dog barking wildly, for months and even years he's been aware of these outlaw gangs but hasn't been able to deal with them hasn't been able even to approach dealing with them so now he sees that Sadovsky girl who's rumored to be the head of a girl-gang as tough and troublesome as any of the male gangs, a foul-mouthed slut isn't she? that one? Sadovsky? one of the school disciplinary problems, and what has she in her hand? a knife? a switchblade *knife?* raised against *him?*

Shakily he commands, "Put down that knife! Is it—Margaret? Sadovsky? Put down that knife at once," and his voice retains something of his usual authority though he's terrified to the point of hyperventilating.

Legs says coolly, "You want it?—come get it."

"I'll have you arrested, young lady."

"Oh fuck off. You don't know *shit.*"

Legs' FOXFIRE sisters try to explain the situation, Violet Kahn is crying saying Legs was just protecting *her,* but Morton Wall is too upset to hear, there's Toby barking and so many people crowding around gawking staring what if these adolescents get out of hand suddenly? rise up against him? a mob? a mob riot? so Wall isn't listening to anyone he's saying, "Call the police, somebody call the police," he's saying, "You—Margaret—you're suspended until further notice," he's within six feet of Legs now doubtful of the wisdom of coming any closer but still commanding, "Put down that knife! That knife, put it down! This is outrageous! This is against the law! A concealed weapon! A felony! I'll have you all arrested! Expelled! *You're* expelled, young lady! And you—Roper! You, and you, and you!—is it Petko?—Siefried? And you, what's your name—"

Now Toby slips free of Goldie and Lana, he's a young healthy husky must weigh thirty pounds rushing at Wall and tearing at his pant legs so Wall's begging, "Help! Stop him! Call off your dog!" and Goldie takes her time sauntering over, Goldie's mock-chiding, tugging at Toby's collar to get his teeth loose from Wall's trousers, "O.K., Toby-Tiger, let the asshole alone. *He* ain't any danger."

By now Legs has shut up her knife, languidly slipped it into her pocket. She confers briefly with her FOXFIRE sisters she's observed hugging Violet Kahn and being hugged by Violet passionately in return, then Legs is off, the crowd parts for her, running lithe and graceful as a cat through the snow and the treacherous patches of ice behind the school yet with no suggestion of haste as if running, now, breath steaming, hair flying in the bright cold sunshine, is just something her young legs are urging, by now too the guys involved in the fight have slipped away, walking fast desperate to be gone and Goldie's trotting off too snapping her fingers so Toby rushes with her, for them too the crowd obligingly parts, and Morton Wall's left there half-sobbing in frustration, outrage, fear, both his pant legs torn, his voice quavering, "D'you hear me? Expelled! You're all expelled! You're all expelled! *Never return to school property!*"

Morton Wall's an unpopular principal: along with three members of the board of education he was investigated the previous year for possible "misuse of public funds" and though no formal charges were ever brought against him or his friends it's generally perceived he's a crook, he has no ethical basis for disciplining or even scolding any of the students under his jurisdiction and there's muffled laughter now at the spectacle of him, slack-bellied mottle-faced man in his fifties, hair disheveled, necktie blown back over his shoulder, Wall's staring after the girls, he's panting can't seem to catch his breath then suddenly he's pressing the flat of his hand hard

against his chest *Is it a heart attack?* so most attentively we're
watching, all of us watching, most attentively very likely two
hundred of us by this time including Maddy Wirtz staring transfixed at Morton Wall and there's the collective prayer you can
almost hear, *No not now—not Wall, now* 'cause so much that's
wonderful has happened in so small a space of time, anything
more would simply be wasted.

Off they're running, those two girls in their FOXFIRE jackets and scarves, bare-headed, wild, shrieking in the street slip-
sliding on ice like small children so high it's beyond alcohol
it's beyond marijuana it's beyond sniffing nail polish and contagious so Toby the silvery-haired raccoon-faced husky races
past them barking crazily then doubling back as a dog will do
to race by another time, there's a sound of horns, a sound of
brakes in the street and Legs and Goldie are on a rampage
their blood so stirred they aren't even required to glance at
each other as at the corner of Holland and Seventh Street they
stoop to pick up chunks of ice from the gutter to propel them
for sheer malicious pleasure at traffic, tossing ice as they run
convulsed with laughter as a man in a fancy hearse-black Lincoln Continental gapes at them through his web-cracked windshield and glass goes flying startled as a sneeze from the front
window of SCHOOR'S UPHOLSTERY but already the girls are
cutting through an alley, Toby racing up behind them his long
tongue lolling, panting steam, on Fairfax they turn right and
there's the Cassadaga a half-mile below ice-locked chill and
unsparing as bare bone, Legs gives Goldie a poke in the ribs
having sighted the turquoise Buick DeLuxe parked in front of
Eddy's Smoke Shop waiting for them, naturally the motor is
running, exhaust spewing out the rear so the keys are in the
ignition, naturally, Legs doesn't hesitate, it's Acey Holman's
Buick recognized everywhere in Lowertown as Acey's recognized, yes and respected and feared in certain quarters but
Legs and Goldie aren't thinking of Acey Holman, no time to

think of Acey Holman any more than there's time to think of Morton Wall, or Vinnie Roper scared shitless at the point of Leg Sadovsky's knife or what it might mean to be expelled from high school who gives a damn for high school?—"Get in, man! Move your ass!" Legs commands, already climbing inside the Buick that's wide and low-slung like a yacht and Goldie unthinkingly obeys, Goldie will do anything Legs instructs climbing into the passenger's seat with a high-pitched yodel and Toby clambering after her his snow-cold pads all over the girls and his warm wet tongue on their faces so Legs has to elbow the pup aside, rapidly she checks out the dash of this amazing car, the stick shift with its elegant leather handle, Legs knows how to drive a car, she's been taught but *this* car?—new 1954 Buick DeLuxe four-door with white wall tires just rolled out of the dealer's showroom all gleaming turquoise like a robin's egg, and so much chrome, bumpers, trim, fins all chrome and this black-leather interior that's mouthwatering it's so luscious all awaiting FOXFIRE, it's the logic of dreams, *Who's gonna stop us?*

So Legs shifts into first, presses down on the gas pedal, presses harder and they're speeding along the street, skidding a bit before the tires take hold then they're out in traffic, easiest thing in the world, *Who's gonna stop us?*—Legs' eyes opened wide transfixed by movement and Goldie's going *Oh-oh-oh!* 'cause Legs is coming close to sideswiping parked cars, there's a red light she bursts through not seeing it until she's gone pressing down on the gas pedal and gripping the steering wheel tight, and there's hardly any surprise, in this logic of dreams how sighted trailing along Holland Street, in the street moving like dazed wondering abandoned cattle there's Lana, there's Violet, there's Toni, there's Maddy in their FOXFIRE jackets and orange-red scarves, they've gone out looking for Legs and Goldie, is that it?—no idea where Legs and Goldie are except somewhere in this direction but in any case these FOXFIRE girls can't possibly remain in school that afternoon they're too highly charged chattering and laughing shrilly and interrupting one another walking four abreast in the street, the eye-witnesses to the episode in the parking lot are telling Maddy what happened and Maddy's exclaiming *Oh no! oh no!* buoyed by hilarity and by something beyond hilarity so she isn't thinking what it might mean for Legs, the switchblade, the public exposure, did she really threaten Vinnie Roper? did she really threaten Mr. Wall? and she's expelled, and Goldie's expelled?—forever? Maddy's shivering laughing incredulously, they're all laughing except Violet Kahn whining it's all her fault she hates herself wishes she was dead bringing her nails down hard against her cheeks, crazy "Snow White" actually meaning to draw blood so Lana slaps her hands away, tells her sharply quit talking so crazy—"What good's it gonna do Legs, your crazy talk?" And walking four abreast bare-headed in the wind they're watching this car approaching them fast on Holland, turquoise car with flashing chrome speeding in their direction, it's wild, it's fantastic staring at this stranger's car and seeing the face behind the windshield in the driver's seat materializing into the face of their First-in-Command, Legs Sadovsky?—and beside her is Goldie? and there's Toby too, three dream-faces and the FOXFIRE girls trailing along Holland Street are struck dumb as *as if by dream logic* Legs brakes the Buick skittering to a stop near the intersection with Fifth, opens her door, yells, "C'mon get in, don't just stand there like dopes!"

So they do. They get in.

Pile into Acey Holman's kidnapped car, shrieking high school girls wholly unquestioning and credulous, prepared to do anything Legs Sadovsky commands, follow Legs anywhere she requires *and nobody's gonna stop us,* Lana and Violet and Toni and Maddy squeezing into the cushioned back seat of the Buick, hardly are the doors shut when Legs presses down on the gas pedal bearing them off, that gut-cry of tires on pavement that's a summons to your wildest blood and amid the breathless cries and chatter and Toby's commotion (he's leaning over the back of the front seat trying to kiss the girls' faces) someone has switched on the radio loud, there's Rosemary

Clooney singing in her happy unreflective voice *If you loved me half as much as I love you* and as Legs bears them now along Fourth Street veering around slow-moving traffic Maddy grips the edge of the seat trying to control her pounding heart thinking how close she came to having missed this, to having been excluded from this, if for instance she'd ignored the disturbances outside the school building, the sounds of running feet in the corridor outside the room she was in, the raised voice of one of her teachers and another in reply in adult alarm and fearfulness that is the most disorienting sound *You wouldn't stay away half as much as you do* and there's the jolt of the car's wheels passing over railroad tracks, a brief skid along trolley tracks hidden in the tight-packed snow so the girls cry in a single voice *Oh!* as if they're being tickled deep deep inside and again as Legs turns the steering wheel sharply to swerve around a parked bakery truck *Oh!—oh—* but the Buick flies effortlessly past, no one can stop them, along Fourth to Mercer, along Mercer to Dwyer, Holland Cement Co., Mohawk Light & Power, the long curving slope of Fairfax Avenue descending into the countryside past old factories, warehouses, a water tower, turning into a country highway bound for Lake Ontario, patches of ice raw and ribbed and treacherous, powdery snow loosed in nervous skeins along the side of the road and Lana is thrown giggling against Maddy, and Maddy is thrown against Violet (what's that perfume Violet wears?—in all this agitation, it retains its fragrance), and Violet is thrown squealing against Toni, the doll-size little Toni thrown breathless against the arm rest, they're outside the Hammond city limits now, speeding into a blinding sun passing in a mile or so the Oldwick Race Track, its tattered flapping banners, its tin signs advertising Camel Cigarettes, Sunoco Motor Oil, Mail Pouch Tobacco pocked with .22-rifle shots, and there's the Hammond County Fairground with its look of winter dereliction and it's here that, suddenly, a siren begins behind them faint initially then high, urgent, angry, unmistakable so Legs squints into the rear view mirror murmuring "Oh!—oh shit" though she can't at first see the patrol car (it's a State Highway Patrol officer, he's clocking the speed of the kidnapped Buick at between eighty and eighty-five miles an hour in a fifty-five mile zone), at once, as unthinking as at the moment she'd climbed into the car, or switched open her knife to bring its point up against the throat of her enemy, she hunches forward gripping her small chafed strong hands against the steering wheel gripping them high, at the positions of eleven o'clock and one o'clock, her face is set in an expression of adult purposefulness and determination, she presses the gas pedal to the floorboards so her FOXFIRE sisters shriek as if they're in a roller-coaster car dipping deliciously dangerously downward, this wild wild ride plunging where?

"Legs—don't let him get us!"

"—the fucker!"

"I'm never gonna go back!"

"What we need's a gun!"

"Blow out his tires!"

"He's gaining!"

"No he isn't!"

"He *isn't!*"

" 'FOXFIRE NEVER LOOKS BACK'!"

"Oh—Legs—"

"Jesus!—"

There's a diesel truck entering an intersection, flashing yellow lights but Legs isn't going to stop even if she's able to stop she's traveling too fast she's leaning hard on the horn and the Buick's filled with screams as Legs swings blind into the left lane and plunges past and the truck driver's face is a balloon suspended astonished in his windshield as Goldie choking with high hyena laughter gives him the finger, Legs swings the Buick back into the right lane avoiding a head-on collision with some old fucker in a rattletrap pickup truck and the car's tires skid but only briefly, as if teasingly, they're descending gradually into the deep country into farmland unfamiliar to their city-bred eyes, U.S. 104, a two-lane highway bounded by fields of glittering snow, rows of desiccated cornstalks above which large black birds—crows?—are lazily circling, behind them the cop's been slowed down but they can still hear his siren and one of the girls in the back seat leans over to turn up the radio high to drown the sound out, it's "The Song from Moulin Rouge" blasting their ears so plaintive and yearning, shameless in yearning and Maddy in a state of exquisite terror is crouching close against the rear of the front seat curved to Legs' shape like an infant dumbly curved to her mother's sleeping shape and her eyes are shut, the eyeballs jerking behind the lids but her eyes are shut, *Oh God, oh dear God don't let*—it isn't a prayer since Maddy-Monkey who's "Killer" 'cause of her sharp shrewd wit and refusal to be suckered by Others' crap doesn't believe in God, surely she's too wise to believe in any old God-the-Father up there in the sky *(where* in the sky would He be?—she's been reading astronomy books these past few months, she's been staring perplexed and fascinated at the night sky which isn't very clear above the industrial city of Hammond but at least it's *there)* but her lips are moving independently of sense and of volition and she's thinking of how long long ago she'd slept with Momma, that woman now lost who was Momma, *her* Momma, no need to determine where one body begins and another leaves off in such warmth in such intimacy in such love but then suddenly she's seeing Momma's face upside down, puffy groggy face upside down and Momma's badly bruised arms are strapped to her sides, where she'd hurt herself on the stairs bruised and bleeding, it's for her own good: the ambulance, the stretcher: mouth distended like a fish's mouth in mute anguish and Maddy's hearing *I must break the spell this cloud that I'm under* but beneath the words and rearing up behind them there's the cop's siren, the fucker *is* gaining but Legs isn't going to surrender FOXFIRE NEVER SAYS SORRY! FOXFIRE DEFIES DEATH! trees are flying past, mailboxes tilting up out of banks of snow, a bluish sheen to the air curving close to snow, ice-shafts, ice-needles, the

whining wind buffeting the car rocking the car filled with cries
Oh! oh oh! and Toby's urgent yipping, Maddy crouching in
Legs' shape her eyes shut believes she can feel at last the spin
of the Earth, the invisible current bearing you forward unde-
tected until your speed surpasses its speed and at last you're
free of gravity FOXFIRE NEVER SAYS NEVER!

By the time the kidnapped turquoise-and-chrome car
overturns—turns and turns and turns!—in a snow-drifted field
north of Tydeman's Corners Legs Sadovsky will have driven
eleven miles from Eddy's Smoke Shop on Fairfax Avenue, six
wild miles with the Highway Patrol cop in pursuit bearing up
swiftly when the highway is clear and the girls are hysterical
with excitement squealing and clutching one another thrown
from side to side as Legs grimaces sighting the bridge ahead,
it's one of those old-fashioned nightmare bridges with a steep
narrow ramp, narrow floor made of planks but there's no time
for hesitation Legs isn't going to use the brakes, she's shrewd,
reasoning too that the cop will have to slow down, the
fucker'll be cautious thus she'll have several seconds advantage won't she?—several seconds can make quite a difference
in a contest like this so the Buick's rushing up the ramp, onto
the bridge, the front wheels strike and spin and seem at first to
be lifting in decorous surprise *Oh! oh* but astonishingly the car
holds, it's a heavy machine of power that seems almost intelligent until flying off the bridge hitting a patch of slick part-
melted ice the car swerves, now the rear wheels appear to be
lifting, there's a moment when all effort ceases, all gravity
ceases, the Buick a vessel of screams as it lifts, floats, it's being
flung into space how weightless! Maddy's eyes are open now,
she'll remember all her life this *Now, now* how without consequence! as the car hits earth again, yet rebounds as if still
weightless, turning, spinning, a machine bearing flesh, bones,
girls' breaths plunging and sliding and rolling and skittering
like a giant hard-shelled insect on its back, now righting itself
again, now again on its back, crunching hard, snow shooting
through the broken windows and the roof collapsing inward

as if crushed by a giant hand upside-down and the motor still gunning as if frantic to escape, they're buried in a cocoon of bluish white and there's a sound of whimpering, panting, sobbing, a dog's puppyish yipping and a strong smell of urine and Legs is crying breathlessly half in anger half in exultation, caught there behind the wheel unable to turn, to look around, to *see,* "Nobody's dead—right?"

Nobody's dead.

Part

three

one

Red Bank

One.   *Two.*
Three.
       Four.   *Five.*   *Six.*
   Seven.   *Eight.*
Nine.
    Ten.   *Eleven.*

She counted: eleven hawks slow-circling in the sky.

Smiling she counted: eleven sparrow hawks that morning, a hazy sky incandescing, mid-summer, sometime in July, a day without a name.

One of the guard's thumbs had all but gouged out her eye but she counted: as if her life, the life of her soul, depended upon it: eleven sparrow hawks rising . . . spiraling downward, so graceful . . . then rising . . . then again slow-spiraling, downward. Dun-colored feathers, shrewd camouflage. Wide-stretched wings so powerful they bore the hawks' weight while scarcely moving.

Hunters. Masters of the air.

Am I one of you? Take me with you.

Here in The Room measuring (she knew well: she'd counted in the past) nine foot-lengths by eight foot-lengths, in "isolation" as it was called, wakeful at all times yet yearning for day and now straining on her toes determined to see out the grimy little window so like an eye grudgingly opened and cruelly positioned in the cinderblock wall (and Legs Sadovsky's a tall girl: five feet eight inches barefoot) but she had to stand on her toes, the muscles of her calves trembling, she craned her neck desperate to see, not to be cheated of seeing, the blue of morning, the pale vaporous sky, and these hawks, her heart was stirred seeing them, sparrow hawks she'd been told, out here in the country in Red Bank fifteen miles north and west of Hammond and Legs was a city girl, Christ she didn't believe she'd ever seen an actual hawk before, birds of such astonishing size and strength, early morning, very early, and at dusk they appeared suddenly high in the air like unexpected music witnessed only from this window, this cell, not visible from her room in the "cottage" with the other girls, only here, rising seemingly without exerting any effort, as if borne solely by the wind, their wide wings, wide feathered-muscled wings, graceful wings lifting them to the top of the spiral then there's a moment's pause . . . a heartbeat . . . then they spiral downward again, slowly circling . . . dipping, descending . . . riding the air currents beyond the twelve-foot cinderblock wall that bounded the property of the RED BANK STATE CORRECTIONAL FACILITY FOR GIRLS topped with concertina wire like a wicked necklace you wouldn't want around your neck.

I am one of you.

Banging her forehead against the sweaty wall, her forehead that's already bruised, sore, and her eye inflamed from the guard's thumb, and she can't remember how many days she's in for this time, or if they'd even told her.

I am one of you oh God oh sweet Jesus-God let me out.

two

"Justice"

Now They took their revenge on us, it was Their turn. Those Others we'd scorned thinking we could fly past them, they'd never catch *us* in their nets.

FOXFIRE BURNS & BURNS! we'd come to sort of *believe,* I guess—like in a dream you can't tell what's askew and what's normal, it's all braided together.

Probably you're among those Others . . . you safe and smug and self-righteous thinking *juvenile delinquents—gang girls—little bitches*—right?

Yeah I don't blame you. That's how most people in Hammond were thinking when the news of what we'd done got around, us FOXFIRE girls in real trouble, arrested by the police, some of us charged with real crimes.

Brought by ambulance to Hammond General, to the emergency room, then taken into custody at juvenile hall, lucky we weren't dead, or crippled for life, except for some of our relatives (and not *all* our relatives that's for sure) everybody was saying not just Legs Sadovsky but all of us should be sent to Red Bank instead of just put on probation.

There was even an editorial in the Hammond *Chronicle* about the menace of "outlaw gangs" in the public schools!

But six of us (Lana, Violet, Toni, Rita, Marsha, Maddy) were lucky, given five months probation, and talk talk talk by the judge, especially he warned us about consorting with "dangerous companions"; Goldie was sentenced to twelve months probation—*really* lucky since it looked for a while as if she might end up at Red Bank with Legs, charged as Legs' accomplice in an act of grand larceny (taking Acey Holman's car!—that was just a *lark*) and with some serious charges herself such as assault and malicious destruction of property. Legs drew what's called an indeterminate sentence, five months *minimum,* no stated *maximum,* so the inmate never knows how the hell long she's going to be what they call incarcerated, always under the thumb of her jailers, meaning the facility staff but also the trusties, the prisoner-trusties, the very kind of inmate you couldn't *trust.* (As Legs would discover.) One of the things we learned was how, in New York State, minors in correctional facilities had to be released at age eighteen, regardless of when they went in; but, with indeterminate sentences, they might not be released *until* they were eighteen. So you could be kept in Red Bank for years charged with some negligible "crime" no adult could be charged with, like being a *runaway,* or a *truant,* or *incorrigible*—"What's 'incorrigible,'" Legs said, "except some adult objects to your attitude?"—or *promiscuous.* (Only girls could be *promiscuous:* never guys.)

You quickly caught on how these charges could be made to mean almost anything police and "juvenile authorities" wanted them to mean, yeah and parents too, there's plenty of parents hopeful of getting rid of their kids, so Legs tried to argue with the juvenile court people, with the judge himself, pointing out how it's crazy, it's just plain unfair, that, say, a thirteen-year-old kid could be sentenced to Red Bank as a runaway, and, if the staff didn't like her attitude, she could wind up serving *five full years*—as long a sentence as some adult men got for armed robbery, even manslaughter!

Legs actually said to the judge, a guy named Oldacker, "—I bet it's *unconstitutional*—treating kids like that. Like, 'cause we're 'minors,' we aren't human!'"

Oldacker was the same guy who ruled on all of us, at different hearings, prune-faced son of a bitch regarding us FOXFIRE girls (but most of all Legs Sadovsky) as if we're the scum of the earth, of actual danger to *him*.

Legs had guts but it was pretty reckless talking like that, insisting on her rights, repeating a dozen times how she'd only been protecting one of her girl friends who was being harassed by some guys; she'd had to use her knife 'cause that's the only kind of persuasion the gang-guys take seriously. And Wall expelled her and her friend Betty Siefried from school without giving them a chance to defend themselves so they'd gone off for a ride—"We weren't *stealing* the car," Legs said, "—we were just *riding* in it, we were gonna bring it right back except that cop started chasing us, I was fearful he'd shoot out our tires, I guess I panicked and—kept on going."

All of us who were charged had the same social worker, a woman named Siskin, appointed by the court: she'd talked Legs into brushing her hair neatly, and tamping it down with barrettes; but some of Legs' hair came loose springing up frizzy and kinky as Legs shook her head. It was the left side of her face that was the most bruised and swollen so she looked lopsided, defiant. Desperate. Saying, in a voice suddenly thin, doubtful, "—This court doesn't have any jurisdiction over *me*."

Oldacker smiled a mean little smile contemplating this wild-haired gang-girl Sadovksy over the shiny surface of his big raised desk.

"Oh yes? It doesn't?"

Here's a sheet of yellowed tablet paper folded up in Maddy's notebook, scribbled in haste, worry, dread. I open it and smooth it out and discover it's a list of the formal charges brought against MARGARET ANN SADOVSKY on 8 April 1954, Juvenile Court, Hammond County, New York State.

I can't remember writing this yet I must have. For the "historical record."

My God they charged Legs with: grand larceny; driving without a license; reckless driving; speeding; endangerment of life; refusing to obey a police officer; malicious destruction of property; disorderly conduct; possession of a concealed weapon; possession of an illegal weapon; attempted felonious assault with a deadly weapon; habitual truancy; being a "disciplinary problem" in school; being an "incorrigible minor"; being a "promiscuous minor"—!

It was Legs' own father who came to Juvenile Court, to betray her. Testifying even worse lies and exaggerations than Morton Wall (who gave false testimony against all of us). Can you believe it?

Ab Sadovsky!—with his reputation everywhere in Lowertown for his bad temper, crazy-quick temper, propensity for fighting, drinking drinking drinking and problems with women and employers, the very look to this man like one of his legs is shorter than the other so he veered along the sidewalk at a dangerous angle, scowling—a good-looking man, or had been, though dark, thick-bodied, nothing like Legs—so he shows up in Juvenile Court with Legs but hardly looking at her like he's wounded with shame and hurt, he's stone cold sober and clean-shaven and even wearing a suit and tie Legs said she hadn't seen on him since one of his drinking buddies died five years before and he'd gone to the funeral in that suit and disappeared for three days winding up finally in the county drunk tank so she had to go down and bail him out, and he's talking quiet-like to Oldacker "admitting" he can't handle his daughter any longer she's out of control like so many kids these days and maybe if he'd remarried after her mother had died things would be different . . . and Legs said she couldn't believe what she was hearing, just couldn't believe it, they fought a lot and avoided each other when they could but she'd never thought he would betray her in such a way, to strangers—"Oh Maddy my heart's broken, I'll never forgive him."

They asked Ab Sadovsky was his daughter involved with drugs?—was she a gang member?—was she "promiscuous"?— and that traitor stood silent chin creased against his neck as he stared at his shoes like he couldn't bring himself to answer.

Legs Sadovsky—"promiscuous"!—Legs who'd have killed any guy who laid a hand on her *that way*.

So Oldacker took possibly ten minutes to deliberate with the prosecuting officer and Mrs. Siskin, then sentenced Legs to the place we'd all been scared to hell we'd be sent, Red Bank State Correctional Facility for Girls. (There was a separate facility for boys, twice as big, closer to the town of Red Bank itself.) In Lowertown, most people knew of kids or were in fact related to kids who were in Red Bank, just as most people were well acquainted with Maywood (State Prison for Men) and Milena (State Psychiatric Hospital), so there were jokes about those places, jokes you heard all your life, not that they were funny jokes because they weren't, like making jokes about Death. And hearing names like those actually spoken in court, pronounced by some son of a bitch who had no idea what they meant so they got transcribed and made real, is about the most terrible thing you can imagine.

Right away Legs said, " 'Five months minimum'—what's the *maximum?*" and Oldacker said, "That's up to you, young lady."

While the police matron looked on, watchful lest we slip our FOXFIRE sister some contraband, Legs hugged us one by one: Goldie, and Lana, and Rita, and Violet, and Toni, and Marsha, and Maddy: and all of us (except Legs) crying like our hearts are broken. Maddy, Legs hugged extra hard, knocked the breath out of her and wincing herself 'cause of her hurt collarbone, and whispered in Maddy's ear, a sweet-searing sound, "Monkey-baby c'mon don't look so *melancholy,* I'm gonna be back in five months," squeezing Maddy close, murmuring secret in her ear so no one else could hear, "—Maybe sooner."

Meaning?—Legs had a hope of escaping Red Bank?

three

A Short History
of the Heavens

Some *somewhere* you can't know.

In 1594 in Rouen, France, a shower of "fiery stones" falls out of an empty sky into a hillside, killing an elderly man and injuring several bystanders and some cattle: when the man is cut open by a doctor, it's discovered that one of the stones, a livid pink in color, had passed cleanly through his chest in fact *through his heart* causing instantaneous death. In 1701 in Cheswick, England, an "avalanche" of similar stones penetrates the roof of a church during Easter services, throwing the priest against the altar; causing flames to consume most of the building; but sparing, seemingly by divine intervention, the fleeing worshippers. In 1889 in Lima, Ohio, the caboose of a passenger train is riddled with rocks, stones, and "needles" pitching from a seemingly clear sky, nine thousand of these objects raining down, the smallest no larger than grapes and the largest weighing seventy-five pounds. "—We thought it was the end of the world, the Apocalypse!" the railroad men said.

And then in Salem Falls, Connecticut, in 1923, a gala outdoor wedding reception of several hundred people is interrupted by "raining-burning rocks" making a sound like artillery so it's believed at first, by the panicked guests, that the party is being attacked by gunfire. More than fourteen thousand of these "raining-burning rocks" will fall.

And in 1931, in Wurmwell, South Dakota, an end-of-season softball game in its ninth inning is suddenly interrupted by a thunderous volley of small rocks raining down for several minutes: terrified eye-witnesses report that the earth for miles in all directions is pocked with dust-explosions. In a nearby farmhouse the McNamara family, mother and father and six children, are just sitting down to supper when a single round object crashes through the ceiling, rolls swiftly across the kitchen floor as if directed, and disappears bouncing noisily down the cellar stairs. Mr. McNamara exclaims, "My God— somebody threw a bowling ball through our roof!" and one of his grown sons says, "That wasn't any bowling ball, that was a *fire*ball." When it burns out it's seen to be a shiny chunk of rock, almost perfectly round, weighing thirty-two pounds.

And in 1952, in Puce, Ontario, a display like crazed Christmas lights illuminates the southern sky one summer day at sunset, and an object shaped like a "pineapple with wings" plummets to earth and explodes, digging a crater thirty feet deep and fifty-three feet in circumference. For miles surrounding this crater a gritty salty black dust settles on everything, animate and inanimate, seeps into scalps, beneath fingernails, into crevices in skin.

They thought for sure it was the United States hit by the H-bomb from the Russians, Puce residents say.

No. It's rock-debris from somewhere out beyond Mars.

What *is* a meteorite?—it's the metallic substance of a meteoroid that has survived its swift, violent passage to earth through the earth's atmosphere. A meteoroid?—small planets or chunks of planets that, passing into the earth's atmosphere, become incandescent; sometimes trail flame.

And there are asteroids . . . comets . . . "shooting stars" . . . "earth-crossers."

Rock falling from the sky. From some somewhere you can't name.

These were notes, mainly, taken in the Hammond Public Library, Maddy Wirtz so desperate to *learn* to *memorize* things she believed to be permanent, she'd sit for hours after school dutifully copying information out of books, one of them with the title *A Short History of the Heavens,* now long forgotten. (I've forgotten all of this. Only coming across the notes so neatly folded and inserted into the original notebook brings it back.) So staring at people especially adults she'd be like a dreamer distracted by a scrim of information or illustrations/ diagrams superimposed upon their faces, their (unknowing) eyes fixed on hers. This strange girl presenting one side of herself to adults, one side of herself to her FOXFIRE sisters, but another side, or maybe it's the innermost core, she kept to herself.

Nobody knows me. Nobody can hurt me.

Except once Maddy read a passage out of a book, probably *A Short History of the Heavens,* to Legs, about "earth-crossers" as they're called, which means chunks of rock-debris that can be all sizes and can do considerable damage to the earth if they hit, so Legs was amazed, Legs made a joke of it expressing amazement and worry—"So some damn thing like that, any time, can wallop you on the head?—take your head off?" and Maddy said, "Well—it's pretty rare actually. It isn't anything that's really gonna *happen,*" but Legs didn't want to let it go, she'd take some idea like that and play with it, suck on it like a piece of hard candy, "—Shit Maddy: just when you get it figured out, about God, and that crap, that He ain't gonna hurt you 'cause He ain't even there, some new fucking thing comes along to be scared of!"

It's so. But you can't spend your life in terror of something falling out of the sky, can you?

* * *

So: there's Legs Sadovsky brandishing her switchblade knife that she'd always been a little too proud of, and showy with, for her own good. And there's Legs running hot and nerved-up down the street just happening to see Acey Holman's turquoise Buick parked where it is. And the keys left in the ignition—which Acey Holman swore he'd never done before in his life. And the accident of us four trailing after Legs in the street not knowing what we were doing either but knowing *something's gonna happen.*

FOXFIRE BURNS & BURNS!

But the sad end of it is Legs in Red Bank, out there in the country in such desolation, stuck away with three hundred other girls—"juvenile delinquents"—behind twelve-foot cinderblock walls topped with loops of concertina wire. The very person who should never be locked up, locked *in.* "—I wish, I wish—" I was saying to Goldie, "—*I* could go in Legs' place," and Goldie gives me a look, she's hugging Toby tight to her chest and he gives me the look too, I could see, yes, why wasn't Maddy the one to be sentenced to the reformatory, so Legs could remain free.

four

Insult

In a trance she moved through the hours, the days waking with the others when the deafening buzzer sounded at five-thirty in the morning in the dark not knowing *where I am, what this means* herded into the bathroom into the dank stinking showers into the dining hall not knowing *what must I do, to make things right again* as a person who has been struck on the head or has suffered oxygen deprivation to the brain is capable often of standing erect, of walking normally, even of speaking normally with others seemingly lucid in full consciousness yet uncomprehending *how to avenge this insult* and the insult itself not comprehended: not named.

Waking a half-dozen times, that first month at Red Bank, to the jeering laughter of others as stupidly she tried a door: turned a knob and pulled, pulled as if the fact that it was locked against her was a misunderstanding mere childlike persistence could make right.

Until one of the guards (usually Lovell) or one of the trusties (usually Dutchgirl) came over to reprimand her. Gripping her by the shoulder, sometimes slapping her in the face, amused, playing for laughs but fearful too of that look in her eyes like light coming off broken glass.

Daring her to strike back. As of course, from time to time, she did.

And so could be punished. Her specific violations of the rules duly noted, recorded, passed on to the superintendent's staff along with notations of the specific punishment exacted: loss of dayroom privileges, loss of shower privileges, meal reduction (it was customarily lunch that was eliminated), extra work (kitchen? laundry? lavatories? showers? floors? grounds?— Red Bank State Correctional Facility for Girls was a perpetual motion machine ceaselessly breeding new elements of disorder and filth that naturally had to be dealt with); and, most dreaded punishment of all, time in The Room—meaning, in isolation.

Wincing in pain she didn't want to reveal, when they laid hands on her. Fucking collarbone's slow to heal.

Says Dutchgirl, smiling-sly with her greenish inward-slanting teeth, "You're real tough shit, eh? 'Legs Sadovsky. FOXFIRE.' Yeah, I been hearing about *you*. Hoping I was gonna see *you*."

Pride demands *walk: don't let the sons of bitches drag you* but there she was being dragged whimpering to The Room, hyperventilating *Jesus God what's happening to me, who am I turning into* the joke was this new girl Sadovsky so loathed her roommate (Bobbie Meldon who *was* a problem—slow sullen weak-brained farm girl whose smell was famously virulent though she claimed she washed "just like everybody else") she preferred solitary confinement. Yet not seeming to know dragged stiff-legged eyes leaking tears *where I am, who I am* alert and muscle-quick with reflexes yet not seeming to comprehend *what this is: doors swung shut, locked? windows cov-*

ered in wire mesh? so her knees buckling beneath her she fell or was pushed face down on the filthy mattress laid flat on the floor cockroaches scurrying for cover inside the wall where the exposed pipes loomed so Legs slept, and woke, and slept her head heavy as crockery then woke again alert and terrified in the dark her heart beating frantic to escape as she came to rapid consciousness twisted on her side on that thin smelly mattress stained with stale menstrual blood, aged grief, vomit, others' tears. *Maddy I want to die, I'm scared I'm going crazy. Screaming and screaming and there's nobody here.*

The Room was the place of terminal gravitation, when you fell you fell fast and you fell *there.*

Stiff-walked out of the day room, that was the first time she'd lost control only a few days after being admitted suddenly pulling screaming at the (locked) door then ramming an elbow into the trustie's meaty side then all hell broke loose, stiff-walked another time out of the dining room, six A.M. and the sun scarcely up and first she'd demonstrated "silent disrespect" in the cafeteria line when a half-dozen girls (Sadovsky included) were being yelled at by a guard named Lovell for pushing but who the fuck *was* pushing, it had just sort of happened like a landslide and this scared little black girl (Marigold: from south Fairfax Avenue, Lowertown Hammond) was getting the worst of it so Legs stood in the way shielding her so Lovell pulled her out of the line so a few minutes later Lovell said something with "nigger-lover" attached so Legs lost her cool not remembering afterward what in Christ she'd done only remembering it was something that had to be done.

FOXFIRE HONOR!

FOXFIRE JUSTICE!

Says Lon Lovell, swollen-faced, sweaty with pleasure, "You little *shit!* You little *cunt!* Oh baby are you gonna be sorry for *this!*" grinning as if somebody has just handed her a gift, all unexpected. And there's emergency authority for such episodes, Lovell and two other guards immediately "segregate" the inmate, dragging her with both arms twisted up behind her back, such pain Legs is starting to vomit starting to faint, these big husky women in their navy-blue starched uniforms and stockings thick-textured as nurses' stockings take no notice, this is their job they're hired to do by Christ they're going to do it.

Dragging Legs Sadovksy white-faced in pain out of the now silent dining room, past the kitchen with its doors open onto the corridor pulsing steamy heat, powerful odors of scorched oatmeal, sickish-sour milk, grease, detergent, past F-Cottage past G-Cottage past H-Cottage (none of these squat little single-storey buildings are cottages, just storage spaces, like sheds or coops, cinderblock and concrete, small square windows of grimy glass protected by wire mesh—H-Cottage is Legs Sadovsky's but she isn't going to be back for several days), past the twilit airless cave that's the infirmary, six beds perpetually occupied, and a brief crossing outdoors so the chill early-morning air's a shock, the sudden curved openness of the sky disorienting as if the earth underfoot has dropped away but the sensation is fleeting for here in a narrow alcove adjoining a maintenance equipment shed there is The Room.

Lucky for Lon Lovell and the other guard The Room's unoccupied this morning, they hadn't thought to check ahead.

Or to check if it's clean, prepared for human occupation— the toilet not stopped up again, for instance; roaches teeming in full view.

"O.K. hot-shit nigger-lover, here y'are—" propelling her inward flinging her down trifling as a rag doll.

So scared I'm going crazy Maddy. Scared I'm not strong like I thought I was.

The lidless stained toilet, the mattress flat on the floor. No sheet and no pillow and the single window set cruelly high in the wall measuring approximately twelve inches by fifteen. A pane of grimy glass and the usual wire mesh except the wire mesh, here, was on the inside of the glass.

So you couldn't smash it and cut your wrists.

Through the long day a rectangle of grudging light inched across the floor. Illuminating the fine fuzzy layer of dust, dirt, hairs covering the floor like cottonwood seed.

Father Theriault said her name: Margaret.

He didn't love her, that old man, 'cause he didn't know her. But she always listened when he spoke. It was fate, she knew. She *listened.*

Repeating what he'd told her once in the park, about Death.

The older you get the more times you've rehearsed dying. So you aren't so scared, that way. Not Death itself but the approach to Death, your thoughts, *you,* in Death's presence.

Legs said laughing, Shit I'm prob'ly a coward, it comes down to it.

Father Theriault laughed too. Wizened little man, his precious pint of whiskey hidden in a paper bag. Saying, Oh no no no you're not, my dear. No.

Skeptically Legs said, Yeh? How do you know?

Father Theriault said, Blessed are the pure in heart, Margaret. For you shall see God.

It was at the precinct where they booked her, and interrogated her, that the insult started. So she'd tasted the first panic sensing how things were shifting out of control.

Sure she'd been scared, that highway cop chasing her. Scared shitless in fact. But hiding it from her FOXFIRE sisters who needed her, trusted her. FOXFIRE's First-in-Command.

Once the cops had her, she accepted she'd be treated rough; maybe even slapped around the way her old man did, sometimes. Not to hurt (she thought) but just to make a point. Like punctuating a sentence. Diagramming a sentence on the blackboard. But the insult the cops laid on her was their way

of looking at her like she was some kind of slut; cheap whore;
asking repeatedly who her boy friends were, what kinds of
things she did for them, which gang was it?—Viscounts,
Hawks, Dukes?—or some older guys?

Afterward Legs said she was sort of shocked hearing
adults saying these names; names of Lowertown gangs you'd
expect only kids to know, or to care about. But these cops
were from the neighborhood themselves so probably it figured. One of them, the rudest, staring at her running his eyes
up and down her calling her "Legs" and "Legs honey," was a
McGahan: lived just up the street from Legs and her father.

Whether they had the right or not, or whether Legs' rights
as a juvenile were suspended 'cause she'd committed some
pretty serious crimes—so they said—trying to scare her,
maybe—they kept her in custody at the Fourth Street precinct
for five hours into the night, asking repeatedly which gang she
and her girl friends "ran with"—hid weapons for, and stolen
goods? Each time Legs said, "My girl friends and me, we're just
us, we stand alone," the cops nodded not listening or giving
her knowing little smirks asking Which gang? which guys? or
were they older guys? Like Acey Holman?

Cops barging in and out of the airless bright-lit room, not
always a police matron present, the longer they interrogated
her the nastier it got so Legs protested almost screaming, "—I
told you. You don't *listen.* FOXFIRE is just us, not some auxiliary for some sons of bitch high school punks." So they eyed
her close, liking it they'd got her excited, reckless in her
speech. As if, so doing, she'd given them a sign they could get
reckless too.

Brushing against her, accidentally-on-purpose touching
her arm, her breast. Saying, "Sweetheart you can tell a better
story than *that.*" Saying, "Sweetheart which of them 'punks'
d'you put out for?—or is it all of them?"

So Legs was feeling scared, helpless, these guys supposed
to be *police officers* coming on to her like they were, using
words blunt and smirking like "put out," even "screw," even

"fuck" and she was all alone—she'd given the cops her telephone number at home but they hadn't been able to contact Ab
Sadovsky or hadn't tried very hard. She could see she wasn't
providing these bastards with the answers they wanted, the
names of gangs and of specific guys. So it wasn't FOXFIRE they
cared about in the slightest—but only male gangs—*males*.

The deepest deepest insult. Lodged so deep, she wouldn't
be able to consider it right away.

Eventually the cops at the Fourth Precinct lost interest in
Legs, maybe she didn't have any valuable information after all,
just a poor scared-shitless girl aged fifteen who doesn't know
the trouble she's gotten herself into so they signed her over to
the juvenile detention people just across the street, and, later,
when Mrs. Siskin asked had those cops done anything more
than interrogate her when the matron wasn't in the room, Legs
flew almost into a rage, she said, glaring, "Huh! I'd kill any
bastard that laid his hands on me."

Already forgetting, maybe, who had.

From then on the dreaminess set in, a waking trance interrupted by sudden spasmodic episodes of anger, frustration, violence *where am I, why can't I walk out that door* though
knowing with one part of her mind why she was in custody,
accepting her fate she nonetheless resisted finding herself
locked in a reception-observation room with padding in vertical strips on the walls like the mats laid on the floor in gym
class at Perry because, and Legs didn't remember this, refused
to believe it, she'd been acting "combative."

What's the proof of it?—*it was written down on some report.*

Finding herself forcibly stripped, it's a "narco search" and
she's sobbing humiliated never never is she going to survive
such insult, fingers in greasy rubber gloves poking into her
body, into the most secret most hidden-away parts of her body
and they inquired too about her tattoo, so crudely done it's a

homemade tattoo, honey, isn't it?—your boy friend done it to you, huh?—damn lucky you didn't get an infection. And they felt through her hair, her straggly snarly hair, used a small flashlight to examine her scalp, her ears, even her nostrils, even her mouth, Legs Sadovsky who's just a body to them now, a name and a number too exhausted to protest.

And the first of how many baths, showers. With female officers looking close. *Why am I here, what has happened to change me so* like a dull-witted child actually instructed how to wash herself how to scrub don't forget between your toes honey y'know you aren't the cleanest you can be, shampooing her hair with QUICK CLEAN SHAMPOO strong as lye, sometimes her overseers were amused by her physical shyness, sometimes derisive, jeering, You ain't the only one born with tits and ass, honey, depending upon whether they felt sorry for her or not; or if there'd been too many juvenile girls processed through the center that day, not enough sorrow to go around.

After that initial bath in the detention center Legs had had to scrub the tub, this enormous old stained battered white tub with claw feet, she'd had to do it naked, panting and sobbing so exhausted so ashamed naked, insult lodging in her throat like a clot of phlegm. And then: they sprayed her with disinfectant like you'd spray an animal, QUICK CLEAN LOTION in a ten gallon tank, a hose and a spray nozzle spraying this stinging liquid under her arms, under her breasts, into her pubic area to kill lice.

Leg said, "—I *told* you, I don't have lice, you can see I don't have lice," and they said, "Sure honey that's what they all say," and one of them added, watching Legs put back on her underwear and a cotton smock several times too large for her, "—Where you're headed, honey, who you're gonna be with, you might get them. Even with these precautions."

At first at Red Bank holding herself stiff from the others, they were Others, not just the guards and the trusties but the other inmates not to be trusted, Legs Sadovsky was prickly with pride and bafflement, hurt, rage, worry so her muscles were aching to run to run to run, muscles twitching and jerking and even her scalp shivering like a shoal of tiny fish sensing danger and the need to flee, the strain was near-ceaseless especially when she wasn't exhausting herself in work, several times she woke out of a thin nervous sleep grinding her teeth so hard her back molars were actually *hot.*

And Bobbie Meldon her roommate whose only happiness was eating and sleep, but especially sleep, was begging in a childlike despairing voice *Why won't you let us sleep?—why're you so* hesitating trying to think of the right word, groggy, sleep-dazed . . . *so hateful?*

There's John Dillinger lying in the street riddled with bullets bleeding to death, shot in the back by cowards till he's transformed to meat, Legs stoops over him touching him her finger in his blood then both her hands, the palms of her hands, covered in blood.

The danger was *she* might be next: shot down too in a hail of bullets, thrashing and dying on the pavement.

Standing there erect, purposeful: waiting?

Another dream and she's back at Perry in the parking lot running with her switchblade knife in her hand, blade gleaming bold in the sun and her FOXFIRE sisters awaiting her and this time she plunges the blade into Vinnie Roper's throat, doesn't spare him 'cause nobody's sparing *her.*

In H-Cottage was a trusty named Dutchgirl, big meaty clumsy girl reminding Legs of Goldie except this Dutchgirl had no inclination to be subordinate to *her.*

Early on, Dutchgirl singled Legs out for attention, crowding her in the shower line, or at meals, muttering, "C'mon you, *move,*" so Legs would wake from her dreamy state looking at Dutchgirl more in surprise than anger, saying, "What the hell I can't just walk over them, can I"—meaning the girls in front of her in line. So Dutchgirl would smile her sly sliding smile saying, "Don't talk fresh, baby. You know what's good for you."

Dutchgirl, seventeen years old, scheduled for release on her eighteenth birthday in January 1955, was a favorite of the guards 'cause she'd cultivated the bullying-suspicious manner of the guards, a zest for trouble gleaming in her eyes so she could declare her authority, lay hands on weaker girls, challenge and connive with the stronger. She'd been in Red Bank for two years for having helped her twenty-nine-year-old boy friend rob a gas station and hiding his gun after he'd shot a man. Her face was brutal as a boot, dented, scabbed, scarred; her dark, heavy brows grew together over the bridge of her nose; her bite was sharp and horseshoe-shaped sinking with an angry hunger into, say, grilled cheese toast. Eating, Dutchgirl lowered her head toward her plate so her eyes went dreamy and milky as if with self-loving.

Dutchgirl's tattoo was a real tattoo, scripted into the fatty-muscular flesh of her right bicep; acquired in a tattoo parlor at Olcott Beach. It was a valentine sort of heart, purple, with a bright green snake twined around it, the words, in red, LOVE DRAKE FOREVER curled like a banner over the snake's head. Drake was serving time at Maywood and they'd broken up— "That shit," Dutchgirl called him—but still she seemed proud of the tattoo. More than once comparing it with Legs' saying how hers was real, not homemade; but curious to know what Legs' was, exactly. "Some kind of a gang? 'FOXFIRE'? Some secret?" she'd ask, "—or it's your boy friend's gang?"

Legs shrugged her off. She knew to be wary of Dutchgirl but she shrugged her off.

Legs Sadovsky's eyes too gripped, couldn't be shaken off, no-color, like beveled glass.

One morning, mid-summer after Legs had been in, and just taken out of, The Room, thus in a mood known in the facility as "hot zone" (meaning danger), Dutchgirl provoked a quarrel with Legs bullying Legs' roommate Bobbie, the three girls on kitchen duty so Legs said quietly, "Why're you crowding her?—she can't help it she's a little slow," and Dutchgirl said, "She's an asshole," and Legs said, "Watch your mouth," and Dutchgirl said, pushing closer, "A *re*tard. A cow-cunt," so Legs winced, Dutchgirl spoke so loudly, saying, "O.K. c'mon: let Bobbie alone," and Dutchgirl said jeering, "You her sweetie, Legs? That's what you do?" and Legs poked Dutchgirl in the breastbone saying, "So what if I was?"

Dutchgirl was taken off guard by this remark so she laughed, startled, rocking back on her heels. Poking Legs in the breastbone with her hard jabbing finger, saying, laughing, "Come off it, Sadovsky. *She* ain't your type."

Eight weeks, eleven . . . fifteen. Outside the twelve-foot cinderblock walls it's spring. A premature summer. Pale gummy heat falls from the sky and gets trapped inside the buildings. No time passes 'cause it's forever the same day and she doesn't have a calendar, she's the only one of these poor sad cunts not to have a calendar, she's the only one too to whom it's a profound shock that a door, any door, should be locked against her.

That, turning a knob in her unthinking fingers, she should encounter resistance adamant as Death.

NO TALKING after lights out or during count. NO TALKING in lines. NO TALKING in showers. NO TALKING when moving from cottages to meals, work area, day room, visitation, infirmary. NO LOITERING AT ANY TIME. NO SMOKING outside day room. NO personal underclothing to be washed in lavatories. NO SHOWERS outside of designated hours. NO

SHOES worn while lying in bed. NO towels, clothing, laundry, etc. hanging in room. NO latecomers for meals. NO missing any meals. NO crossing any RED LINE at formation. NO leaning against walls. NO movement out of rooms, dining hall, corridors, etc. until signal (buzzer) is given. NO borrowing or loaning ANY personal item such as clothing, shoes, toiletries, money, magazines. NO removal of food from dining hall. NO unauthorized money, items, gifts, etc. from visitors. NO food in cottages. NO more than five (5) sets of underclothing. NO more than (1) needlework or knitting project at a time. NO needlework or knitting done for another inmate. NO more than five (5) cosmetic items. NO untidy rooms—beds to be made immediately after wake-up and kept neat and orderly during the day. NO headscarves or pin curls permitted during the day. NO walking in stocking feet or barefooted. NO individual trash receptacles. NO more than two (2) visits of thirty (30) minutes per week. NO children under eighteen (18) permitted to visit. NO visits allowed from ex-inmates or persons on probation. NO written communications between inmates. NO packages permitted. NO more than four (4) pages of regulation size per letter. NO mail to be sent out except through staff P.O. NO letters sent or received without official staff inspection. NO more than five (5) snapshots, photographs, etc. in inmate's possession. NO more than three (3) such items on display in bed area. NO trading of snapshots, photographs, etc. with other inmates. NO personal contact between inmates, i.e. playing, fighting, wrestling, dancing, massaging, combing, brushing, plaiting hair, etc., assistance with clothing, washing. NO games except in day room under staff supervision. NO loud talking, shouting, etc. at ANY time. NO DISOBEDIENCE OF FACILITY REGULATIONS. VIOLATORS WILL BE PUNISHED SWIFTLY AND WILL BE SUBJECT TO EXTENSION OF SENTENCE.

* * *

Maddy, I'm so scared, I'm thinking FOXFIRE's just a dream.

She was in The Room, preferring to lie on the floor not the filthy mattress, bumping her head methodically almost gently against the wall but she was doing push-ups, sit-ups, flames licking at her face, beneath her hair at the nape of her neck as she tried to chin herself on the doorframe but her fingers slipped, her nails tore, she fell hard on her side, she shattered like a cheap clay pot.

And in the infirmary coughing up phlegm, hot sticky coin-size clots out of her lungs, it's a bronchial infection says the nurse frowning vague and worried giving her aspirin saying all you can do is wait it out it isn't *fatal.*

Skinny and snakey-agile she pushes herself through a crack between buildings, nobody's gonna believe Legs Sadovsky slipped through so narrow a space, then she's running in the open air in the dark in a sweet mild summer rain out behind the A-Cottage block she's hunched over feeling the eyes on her back, on the top of her head steeling herself for a volley of gunfire as in a prison movie but there's nothing, no one calls a warning to her, no alarm has been raised and at the wall—the wall!—she doesn't hesitate, leaps up grasping at raw blunt featureless cinderblock, leaps up like a doe shot in the heart, leaps up, up, grabbing and grasping and falling back, biting her lower lip so she'll draw blood, she's smiling thinking of how Maddy Wirtz will be astonished when she crawls into her room this time, she's thinking FOXFIRE BURNS & BURNS and FOXFIRE NEVER LOOKS BACK! till finally she's being grabbed, shouted at, walked away, half carried back squirming and fighting and one of the guards is saying damn lucky we

caught you in here, if you'd gotten over that wall it'd be six
months more for you, cold.

Maddy I cant send this letter 'cause theyd censor it but I
miss you so, all my FOXFIRE sisters I miss so I love you
I would die for you you know that dont you. Thanks
for your letters & forgive me please I dont answer except
those asshole little things its 'cause they read what we write,
I cant stand that. & if I show "bad attitude" they'll give me
marks, I already got a lot of marks, Jesus God Ill be in
here till age 18. (thats a joke—dont worry)

This craziness that comes & goes. It scares me 'cause a girl
got sent up to Milena from here, she went truly crazy tried
to kill herself swallowing stuff you use to clean toilets,
Im scared theyll send me off too but like I say it
comes & goes it isnt all the time its like a balloon drifting
and bumping against a ceiling you know stirred by air, not
predictable. So I wake up after a long time so angry I
cant talk grinding my teeth & Im stinking all sweaty but
theres a voice in my head thats calm almost like my own
voice but grownup & its saying *O.K. but youre alive.* So
I think *My God yes—I'm alive.*

Using this toilet plunger in a toilet, all stopped up & you
wouldnt believe the filth, the other day & I sort of woke
up feeling my heart beat, my muscles etc. *I'm alive* thats
the main thing.

Father Theriault says thats the miracle, not Jesus Christ
rising in his body. *Were the miracle, were alive.*

So you think my God theres so many not alive, it makes
you weak thinking it. How the earth is filling up with
the dead & theyre lost in one another, just earth. Remember that thing we saw at the museum THE TREE OF LIFE
so many animal species extinct it was sort of scarey 'cause
you wonder whats the purpose but the fact is no matter
the beginning of Time etc. how far back it was, the only
beings *alive* are *alive right now.*

One of the nasty things done to me, one of the worse insults, they had me down for "promiscuous" 'cause of my father lying the way he did, so they did these tests on me against my will, had to strap me down for whats called a pelvic DONT LET ANYBODY GIVE YOU A PELVIC EVER & took some blood so they didnt find any V.D. or anything (thought I might be pregnant too) but they did find I was a little anemic. Something missing in my blood from not eating right maybe so they give me iron tablets. *So its a fact Im getting stronger, I can feel it.*

Waking up like I said when the craziness lifts its like fog burning off the river when the sun comes up and Im surprised finding myself where I am doing what Im doing like one time, in visitation, Kathleen Connor whos my fathers ex-girl friend came to see me shes so sweet brought me some underwear, some socks & Ponds Cold Cream 'cause my hands are so bad & I started crying which is not like me & shed of hugged me except you cant get that close & I was trying to tell her, no Im not feeling bad Im crying 'cause Im happy, I cant explain. Working in the kitchen or in the yard we get to talking & laughing a lot 'specially when the trustee's not a bitch & even singing sometimes so youre in a good mood & not questioning it.

So the craziness isnt all the time, & wanting to die. Im never gonna kill myself thats for damn sure. Yesterday in the day room feeling kind of nervous & couldnt sit still, I looked & saw these strangers around me I thought *Hey you cant not know theyre your sisters too,* some of them sad & sallow & downlooking like theyre hearts are broke, bad skin from the food here & limp hair & theres Triss one of the runaways, "runaways" they call them shed just gone off from a foster home where the old man was bothering her she said & it was actually her real home she was going to but she got caught & it wasnt the first time so shes in here for eight months, they have her down for "incorrigible" like me thats on the record. & theres Marigold so shy she cant talk above a whisper, she poured

Draino in the ear of her mommas boy friend whod been
beating Marigold & her momma both & shes sorry she said
he didnt die but he was hurt pretty bad. & theres Nicky
looks a little like you Maddy, a smart girl, wears glasses,
shes in for shoplifting & runaway & sees things rushing at
her sometimes so she starts screaming & we have to quiet
her, & theres Connie Im looking at, & theres Ginger, &
Lori, theres my roommate Bobbie who got picked up
by the police for hiding stolen things for this guy she wanted
to think was her boy friend, poor Bobbie shes sort of slow
shes too trusting & unquestioning & right now shes hurt
from something I said or didnt say giving me these quick
shy glances & sucking her fingers like Rita before Rita became
our blood-sister & theres Dutchgirl yawning so you expect
her jaw to crack, theres something tight & coiled in her
like a snake, shes my enemy she thinks & I dont know
why shes all the girls' enemy reporting to the guards sometimes
she wants to be my friend & I dont give her shit & shes
watching me too, then theres Bernadette sitting by herself
staring slackmouthed, everybody avoids her 'cause the story
is she had a baby she let die just lying on the floor somewhere,
womens room in a train depot, & Im looking at these girls
in the day room & the dirty brown-green shag rug on the
floor & some Life & Ladies Home Journal & Readers Digest
magazines laying around somebody donated, & its like Im
slapped on the face waking me forgetting my own thoughts
Jesus theyre my sisters, just like me just like my FOXFIRE
sisters.

Seeing for one thing, were all poor. White girls & black here
at Red Bank.

One hot airless day they informed her there was a visitor
for her—"Your father."

Legs laughed. "Him!—what's *he* want."

Going out to visitation, though, she was trembling. Tasting
cold at the back of her mouth.

So there he was. Ab Sadovsky. Putty-colored face, a ravaged look around the eyes; that thin slippery smile and licked lips meaning he'd been drinking, probably. Out in the car, locked in the glove compartment, there'd be a paper bag, a pint bottle of Four Roses. Sure.

Seeing each other their eyes slid quickly slantwise as if greased.

"Well. H'lo honey."

"H'lo."

Why'd he come, he didn't love her or give a damn about her, she knew. Impossible not to know. Hadn't visited for four and a half months. Nor had he written—naturally.

As he'd explained before, he wasn't the type to write.

Now he cleared his throat, shifted his narrow buttocks in his chair, tried to smile. Said in a cigarette-hoarse voice, "Well Marg'ret you're looking O.K. How're you feeling?"

Legs murmured something shy, sullen.

"Huh? Can't hear you."

"—I said O.K."

"Yeah? You're looking—O.K. Looking good." A pause. He tried again to smile, you could see he meant well. Wearing an actual sports coat on this humid July afternoon, hair wetted and combed back neatly from his forehead. "You sleeping O.K.? How's the food?"

"O.K."

Legs uttered this word, this expression, such a banality of expression, *O.K.,* her lips twisting in subtle irony, the faintest of smirks.

A strange sudden anger gripped them both, father and daughter. Afterward, they'd both be exhausted.

Since he'd made the drive, made the effort, Ab Sadovsky pushed forward, an edge of reproach to his words, yes but he was trying hard too, you could see that. Talking slowly rambling and guilty-defiant, speaking of things in which Legs could have no possible interest, news of neighbors, of Lowertown, of relatives he himself knew but obliquely; news of union activities, the factory in which he worked. Father and daughter politely facing each other across a table, thirty-six inches of sticky beaverwood surface. A clock high on a wall overhead: two twenty-five. Red second hand dreamily circling. Two slack-jawed guards on duty, starched white blouses, blue skirts; a half-dozen inmates meeting with visitors along the beaverboard strip, talking quietly, now and then laughing, maybe some tears, always there are tears, you don't glance sideways, you respect privacy, jammed together like animals you learn to respect privacy that's so precious. Beside Legs and her father there was a Negro family, the girl not known to Legs by name, her mother and older sister speaking earnestly to her, and she's vehement in an undertone assuring them of something, such emotion crammed into a half-hour while Ab Sadovsky and his daughter were sitting stiff with inchoate un-defined anger blinking dry-eyed, lapsing into clumsy silence every several seconds. Legs was considering her father more directly now, her eyes narrowed, assessing. Willing the bastard to read her thoughts if he dared.

How could you. Betraying me like you did. Telling filthy lies of me in public.

As if he could read her thoughts, or interpret that look of hers, Ab Sadovsky began to speak more aggressively; with more pronounced a slur to his words. Saying he'd heard from the social worker what's-her-name that she'd been having "be-havioral problems" in Red Bank, that she'd been collecting "marks" so her sentence was being extended and he was sorry, damn sorry to be hearing such things 'cause wasn't it enough she got arrested the way she did acting so reckless the way she did for Christ's sake what was she trying to do, ruin her life completely, her own and his? And—

Legs interrupted suddenly, as if she hadn't been listening, "—Tell me about my mother. What really happened to her."

"What?"

"How she died. It had something to do with you didn't it?"

"What?"

There was a long pause. Now they were both looking at

each other, no flinching. Legs sat upright her hands gripped together in her lap, feet flat on the floor. She'd been in true control of herself lately: no isolation for the past several weeks, in fact she'd been assisting staff teaching, or trying to teach, some of the girls how to read and write. She was eating, and she was putting on weight, and she was getting stronger, she was beginning to foresee a lifetime of such strength, breathed in steadily and unresistingly as the air. Except this man, this liar this traitor this *man* said to be her father rose before her as a threat.

Carefully, just loud enough for Ab Sadovsky to hear, and no one else, Legs said, "I asked you once, and you wouldn't tell me. How could she just *die*. How could my mother just *die*. A woman thirty years old just doesn't *die*. And the things I'd hear in the neighborhood I didn't want to believe—you know how people are." Legs paused, watching her father. She felt the instinct in him, the urge to escape, stand up and walk out the door not looking back. "— *You* made her, didn't you? Have the operation?"

Weakly Ab Sadovsky said, "—Operation?"

"Abortion—wasn't it?"

Angrily, guiltily, Ab Sadovsky mumbled, " 'Abortion'! What the hell do you know about—'abortion'! You're a kid!"— fumbling with a Kleenex, wiping his mouth, his fleshy perspiring jaws. "What the hell do *you* know!"

Still quietly, fixing Ab Sadovsky with that unwavering cold stare, Legs said, "Tell me, Pa."

The word "Pa" unfamiliar in Legs' mouth as a word in a foreign language—you couldn't judge was it scornful, or wistful.

So Ab Sadovsky hesitated a long moment, then began telling Legs this story, this monologue, she'd supposed she wanted to hear; not meeting her eye, blinking, sniffing, shifting his weight in his chair, with the grudging air of a man forced against his will to speak the truth, for which he blamed the person extracting truth from him, by God if she wanted to know she'd *know.*

And Legs was leaning forward tense and tight as a bow, listening with all her concentration.

". . . gotta know this happened a long time ago . . . not when your mother died exactly, but before. You never knew what she was like *really,* when her and me, when we . . . were first going together. Yeah she changed. You bet, she changed. But in the beginning Gloria was the, the most beautiful woman I ever saw. I was crazy about her and she was crazy about me. Later on things changed, but . . . but that didn't, I mean the way it *was,* the memory of it. A kid like you, Marg'ret, look honey you're only fourteen years old is it?—or fifteen . . . O.K. fifteen. The thing is, you're just a baby throwing your life around like you think you're gonna live forever well Christ you're *not,*" laughing angrily, "you're *not.* Your old man's here to tell you honey so listen: before you were born Marg'ret your mother and me, we were crazy in love I mean real real deep in love like you smartass kids don't know shit about today, none of you, O.K. Gloria had lots of boy friends 'cause she was a damn good-looking woman with that hair of hers and her face that'd stop traffic, I'm not exaggerating, I'm serious, she was that good-looking and she knew how to carry herself like a woman should, not like some tramp or worse yet, almost worse yet some woman who's let herself go, or—doesn't give a damn how she looks, wastes her good looks, like *you*— could be a real knockout but *look*—acting like a damn boy, dressing like a boy when you could, every chance, how d'you expect any guy to give a damn about you behaving so rough, it's a weird laugh how a daughter of Gloria Mason's acts like *you,* calling yourself 'Legs' acting like a fucking guy, carrying a knife, stealing a car, oh Jesus would Gloria be ashamed, *I'm* ashamed, I'm a man and I'm ashamed, O.K. what was I saying . . . Gloria and me we were crazy in love . . . not married yet 'cause she had these other guys hot for her, and one of them had money, so she said, how much money the fucker had I never knew 'cause your mother didn't always tell the strict swear-on-a-stack-of-Bibles truth, she liked to keep men guessing but I was the one she basically loved, she admitted that, we'd go out and get drunk after some other guy'd brought her home and she got rid of him and this went on for a, a while . . . it seemed like a long time but I spose it was only a few months . . . when you're that age, in love so you almost can't stand it, you think you're gonna die if you can't have her, a week's a long time—a day! So Gloria got knocked up, O.K. let's not pull punches, O.K. we weren't married yet but living together sort of on Holly Street, upstairs over a restaurant, Diamond's, it's gone now in fact I guess the building itself's gone, O.K. by me it was a dump but anyway, your mother and me . . . I was driving a truck then, before those sons of bitches made trouble for me, took away my license . . . I mean my trucker's license not the, the other one . . . so I was gone a lot, two-three days in a row sometimes making the Pittsburgh run and back and your mother said, she said 'You can't expect me to sit home knitting can you,' she said, 'I get lonely too,' so she'd go out, I thought a few times I just couldn't take it I was gonna come back unexpected, y'know, like some guy in a movie I was gonna catch her with this hot-shit boy friend of hers that was some third-rate crook, a gambler . . . actually a bookie himself . . . so this one time, O.K. I'm home, *I am home* not on the road and we had a fight or something, I can't remember exactly but I was home I was trying to sleep and your mother was out somewhere she'd been staying with a girl friend, she said . . . 'cause we'd had this fight, she was pregnant not knowing who the father was so I said O.K. you bitch, you slut, *I* can live with that, I wouldn't be the first guy to live with that . . . 'cause secretly I knew I was the father 'cause who else's would it've been, I was keeping track better than your mother 'cause I was sober most of the time, and she wasn't. So—she's out, and unknown to me she's set this appointment up with a guy sposed to be a doctor . . . I don't know maybe he *was,* there's all kinds of doctors! So she shows up at his place, all unknown to me, she's been drinking but she's stone cold sober, scared as hell, I mean she's only a kid practically, twenty years old, and except for guys she'd been on her own since sixteen so she climbs the stairs to this place, over on Sixth Street, a place she says looks like a real doctor's office except it's sort of shabby and not too clean and there's no, whatd'yacallit, waiting room, so she goes right in and he tells her take off her clothes, she can smell his breath, he's red-eyed and scared too and swaying drunk almost but she's like she said hypnotized or paralyzed or something not thinking straight so she does what he tells her, she just takes off the lower parts of her clothes, lays down on this table and he's gonna perform it, the operation, O.K. let's not mince words, the abortion, he's gonna perform the *abortion,* without ether or anything, so your mother says she's ready, she doesn't have any choice she's ready, cold sober laying there trembling and this guy, she said he was mostly bald, with white hair around in a fringe, sort of like a Santa Claus might be, sort of chubby and, and fat and, and you'd expect him to be happy but she said he was damn scared jumping every time he'd hear some noise outside like a car door slamming or people yelling, so he's got this thing, this surgical thing, a kind of big pinchers to, uh, open you up, and a sharp thing like a razor, a straight razor, I mean a, a scalpel?—that he's gonna do the scraping with except she sees the fucker's hands are shaking and he's talking fast interrupting himself laughing wiping his face on his sleeve and he forces this thing, this pinchers inside her, she's laying there sweating praying it can't last forever, O.K. Gloria isn't using her best judgment but the guy'd been recommended to her by a girl friend she claimed and you could see by the office he was a real doctor, or had been. So he gets this sharp instrument inside her, she starts screaming it hurts so, the doctor tells her be quiet, what if the police come, but she's panicked crawling backward off the table and he's coming at her wide-eyed like he's gonna kill her, she sees there's blood on the pinchers already and on the front of his white coat so now she does go wild, kicks the bastard in the balls, she's screaming and sobbing just wanting to get out of there, so next thing she knows she's running down the stairs naked under her skirt or slip . . . she's out on the sidewalk running dripping blood and there's this friend who'd brought her waiting in his car, not the boy friend (she swore) but just a guy that's a friend, your mother had lots of friends, living alone like she'd been doing since age sixteen, and looking like she did, I mean—Gloria was the kind of woman'd look you in the eye and whatever she said you believed, *before she opened her mouth you were ready to believe,* I speak as one who knows. So: I was home, I didn't know shit that was going on 'cause she had her secrets from me, she came on up to the place and walked right in, she had a key, I was in bed and she went right to me crying like I'd never seen her, nor was she drunk either, she said, 'Oh honey hold me, hold me,' she was saying, 'Oh I love *you* nobody but *you'* so I was surprised but I was the happiest guy on earth and we got married, got married a week later and she had the baby by Christ, no more talk about who the father was 'cause Ab Sadovsky was the father, and the baby, Marg'ret the baby was *you.*"

Poor Legs!—all this while she was listening fierce with concentration, yet, at first, she didn't seem to hear. Or, hearing, she didn't comprehend. Until after a beat or two, and Ab Sadovsky staring at her with that glistening licked-lips smile, something malevolent stirring in his eyes like light behind dirty glass, she rose wordless from her chair, groping, stumbling, one of her feet caught in the rung of the chair, and Ab Sadovsky cleared his throat and said, a little louder, craning his neck like a snake angling to strike, "—Then about your mother *dying,* hell that wasn't till ten years later, in a real hospital, and her kidneys shot from alcohol, and that ain't no story for *right now.*"

Shaking her head, almost in a whisper, Legs said, "No. Oh *no.*"

Seeing her on her feet, and the expression on her face like

a child that's been forced to see some horror she can't name, the guards are alerted, advancing upon Legs, so even as she begins to scream, "No no *no* I don't believe you—liar! *murderer!*" pounding on the table top with both fists, they're preparing to seize her, subdue her, knowing how to subdue the inmate without getting struck by her mad flying fists, or bitten: they're strong husky young women, they've had plenty of practice in such outbursts.

In this way, Ab Sadovsky's second and final visit to Red Bank State Correctional Facility for Girls comes to an abrupt end.

five

Ocean Of Storms.
Sea Of Tranquility.
Lake of Dreams.
Lake of Death.

These names, I loved these names, lunar names I wrote again and again in my FOXFIRE notebook, always thinking of Legs: like maybe she was on the moon? away off in Red Bank that might have been the moon, not fifteen miles from Hammond?

The long months she was gone, stretching out beyond five months 'cause of her bad behavior, all the marks she was accumulating and there was a terror in us, in all of us Legs' FOXFIRE sisters, that she'd never come back to us. So when people asked how was Legs, how's she getting along at Red Bank, we lied and said real well, we wouldn't give FOXFIRE's enemies the satisfaction of knowing how things were.

The person you love best, you share the world with. When that person's gone the world remains but it isn't the same thing, it's at a distance.

It isn't the same world, actually. It has so little hold on you, you could just drift away: like to the moon.

I wanted to write to her OCEAN OF STORMS SEA OF TRANQUILITY LAKE OF DREAMS LAKE OF DEATH but they'd have censored such a letter for sure. When I showed Legs' letters to my friends or read them aloud, that strange flat dead voice on the page ("Things are all right here. Im making some friends here. We take classes in things like writing & hair styling & 'cosmetology' its called. I feel O.K. They feed us O.K. & work us pretty hard so were hungry") Goldie came near to snatching the letters from me to tear up, she was that upset, angry and laughing, "Shit! Listen to that! That ain't *Legs!*—It's like my cousin Mikey who was in Red Bank Boys once, the sonsabitches censor what you write."

Being on probation, also under eighteen, none of us could visit Legs at Red Bank. Which was the cruelest part. The only direct news we had of her was from Kathleen Connor who saw her maybe once a month, and was willing to take things to her from us, and there were some relatives of hers, some aunts, cousins, who saw her too, but we were shy of contacting them. Of course nobody not even Goldie wanted to talk with Ab Sadovsky, he'd see us in the street sometimes and make a spitting gesture, spoke of us as troublemakers and sluts deserving to be in the reformatory just like his daughter.

Kathleen Connor who was so fond of Legs said it broke her heart seeing Legs in prison; hearing Legs say how she was doing all right, ate O.K. and slept O.K. and was making some friends, and it had to be false, some of it at least, 'cause Legs *was* getting marks, and put in isolation, and her sentence extended, at least for a while. Of her actual misery and suffering I would not learn till she came out to tell me herself but even then (even now!) I have to invent certain things, I'm obliged to imagine, sink myself deep into Legs Sadovsky to imagine since she was the kind of girl, so much happened inside her she would never have spoken of, herself.

The way she'd laugh, embarrassed, saying, "Better not make too much of me, Maddy—it's those other girls. They're the ones seem so *stuck.*"

* * *

Nobody died, we'd all escaped Death.

That wild wild ride Legs took us on in Acey Holman's Buick, into the countryside where we'd hardly ever been but we'd never forget afterward, long as we lived.

I still dream of it sometimes. And wake up terrified, but smiling. 'Cause I'd cheated Death that once, that not everybody can claim.

It's true most of us didn't escape injury. Legs was hurt as I've stated, and was bleeding from a dozen cuts on her head and face, and Goldie lost a front tooth, and Lana broke two fingers, and Maddy and Toni LeFeber bumped heads hard so each had a swelling on her forehead that didn't go away for weeks. And poor Toby was in such a state from terror and mad yipping, he could never bark normally again—just a hoarse gravelly noise when he tried. (Toby never seemed to blame us though. Any one of us FOXFIRE girls, but especially Goldie, and Legs, Toby loved like crazy and without question. It's the way you are, dog or girl, with someone who's saved your life.)

The irony was, the only one of us hardly hurt at all was Violet Kahn.

Here she's screaming the loudest when the Buick skids off the bridge, and it turns out her face isn't even scratched.

So the highway cop that'd caused all the trouble in the first place, chasing us like he did, he comes stomping through the snow to the car that's upside-down in a snowbank, a wreck, he's shouting, "Anybody alive?—anybody alive in there?" and manages to get one of the rear doors open, and the first girl he hauls out is this beautiful black-haired girl with the big eyes and skin so white it looks poached, and he's got to be astonished seeing her, almost falling in his arms like she does, sobbing, "Oh officer! oh don't arrest us! oh it wasn't anybody's fault, I swear!—it wasn't Legs' fault! The nasty old car just kept going! Faster and faster, it wouldn't stop, it just kept *going!*"

* * *

Sure we were arrested, though. Lowertown girls especially living around Fairfax Avenue, down by the river, you can bet we were arrested. "Gang girls" the newspaper called us, like we were part of some older guys' gang, actual criminals, car thieves or something.

Those months I was on probation, and suspended from school too, it was hard for me to sleep; even to sit still long enough to read, or type, or think. Like a fire burning out of your control and even out of your awareness FOXFIRE's fame was truly spreading, there was the excitement of everybody knowing our name and talking about what we'd done, but some stories came back to us exaggerated, like Legs had drawn actual blood from Vinnie Roper's throat there in the parking lot!—that one of the other Viscount guys had gone on his knees begging not to be killed! And how Legs Sadovsky was a girl friend of Acey Holman's getting her revenge on him in the best way she knew.

Which was why, Legs instructed me, I had to record things as they truly were.

"You don't do that, and we're not careful, FOXFIRE's gonna slip away from us," Legs said.

Which is the motive I guess for anybody writing almost anything.

So Legs was sent to Red Bank. And we couldn't visit. And couldn't write any letters from the heart, nor receive any—just those strange letters of Legs', and only three of them, folded in here in the old notebook. (I looked at them just now, tried to reread them. But my eyes filled with tears and I had to put them away.)

Nightmare-tight and circumscribed as Legs' life was in prison, my life, outside, when I was barred from school and all that long summer when I was living with my great-aunt Rose Packer, was a scary loose slipping-down life, like a movie where the film is running out of control, out of focus. So I knew that if it wasn't for FOXFIRE, and missing Legs, and my job (in the kitchen of the White Eagle Hotel, where my aunt worked as housekeeper), and certain interests of mine like reading about the stars, and Time, yes I guess and typing on the old Underwood typewriter I loved, I would not have known who I was at all. Even, maybe, whether I *was.*

(I know I should explain where Momma was, what had happened to her and why. Why I stayed for a while at Goldie's, then for a while with some neighbors, then moved into Rose Packer's back room in her house on Fayette Street, I guess I know I'm avoiding certain facts but that's too bad. The hell with recounting facts I never wanted to know in the first place! Just to say: Momma wasn't living in Hammond right then, and wasn't in any condition to care about me, or anybody else. And I'm not lying when I say I did not miss her. No more than I missed my father who was dead. How can you miss somebody you never knew?)

Once, early on, we drove out into the country to Red Bank thinking we'd see Legs somehow, get within shouting distance of her. The guy who owned the car, a rusty-rattling old '47 Chevy, was a cousin of Violet's who hung out with her and Lana sometimes, and got to be friendly with FOXFIRE, the way guys, some guys at least, were starting to do. (It wasn't just the good-looking girls that attracted them, it was something in FOXFIRE itself. As long as they were *friends,* not *boy friends,* FOXFIRE had no objection.) So Mick drove us that day, Violet and Goldie and Lana and Rita, and Maddy of course, and we were drinking beer, smoking cigarettes, making a party of it, excited and scared as we were.

It was known that the state prison facilities were built deliberately out in the country to make it difficult for inmates' visitors to see them. People too poor to own their own cars, for instance. And there weren't any direct bus routes, naturally. Red Bank was between nothing and nowhere, too small to be called a town, just a settlement in the foothills of the Chautauqua Mountains. Around it the land had a raw derelict look, not a look you associate with the country, few farmhouses, the clayey red soil the color of dried blood, and acres of junked cars, and an abandoned rock quarry rising up weird and sudden as a dream, and alongside the road these tattered warning signs POSTED NO HUNTING NO FISHING NO TRAPPING NO DUMPING and finally we came to the narrow rock-gravel road leading up to the prison through a scrubby woods, there's this sign pockmarked with bullet holes

RED BANK STATE CORRECTIONAL
FACILITY FOR GIRLS
NO TRESPASSING UNDER PENALTY OF LAW
AUTHORIZED PERSONNEL AND VISITORS ONLY
IDENTIFICATION REQUIRED

and the sight was so sudden and sobering we all just sat there, even Mick, staring. Maddy jammed her fingers into her mouth, and Goldie whispered, "Shit."

Till now, we'd maybe not believed in the place, exactly.

We couldn't see the building or buildings from where we were, only the wall, and the wall was at a distance, and we decided we'd better not drive any farther, the ones of us on probation especially. So Mick turned back. And we drove another way, on a side road, not knowing where the hell we were headed but talking loud and laughing and finishing up the beer. It was nearly dusk. We were passing empty fields, scrub woods, deep ravines filling up with shadow. I said, 'cause I'd only now thought of it, "—They build these places where they do so if somebody escapes, she's got nowhere to go."

Said Violet, as if we'd been quarreling, the little bitch, "Oh no not if she's got *friends!*"

We parked the car, got out, straggled through some woods, and there again was the wall, so high, and topped with wire looking like it'd cut your bare hands to ribbons if you grabbed onto it to pull yourself up. There weren't any guard towers that we could see, the place was more like an abandoned building. Goldie cupped her hands to her mouth and called out, softly, "Shee-na!—Sheee-na!" and the others of us took up the cry, "Sheee-na! Sheeee-na!" drawing the name out long as we could. We knew not to call "Legs," to get her in trouble if anyone heard, we just walked along below the wall, maybe twenty feet away from the wall, in case there were guards, all of us except Mick calling "Sheee-na!" in soft low chanting voices sounding like a single voice. (Mick hung back in the woods, a beer bottle in his hand. He understood he wasn't welcome, even if he'd had the courage to accompany us.)

The sky darkened. We got louder, by degrees louder and more demanding, and more yearning— "*Sheee*-na! Oh *Sheeee*-na!" till suddenly some floodlights came on, and someone yelled, and we broke, and ran, ran scared as hell into the woods, we separated running not really knowing what we were doing we were so scared, but it was funny too, I ran doubled over laughing, breathless and half sobbing and laughing, twisted my ankle and fell face down and scrambled to my feet already in motion, and there was one of my FOXFIRE sisters a short distance away so we grabbed hands, Maddy and Rita, we were lost from the others for an hour or more, as was Lana, and how we ever located Mick's car again, and got together again, God knows.

Mick drove for a while without lights. We were all hunched over in the car, expecting to be stopped by a roadblock, or a spray of bullets. We were saying, "—You think Legs heard us? You think she knew it was us?" and "—Sure she heard us, sure she'd know it was us, who else would it be?" and we drove back to Hammond making plans for the next time we'd come out to Red Bank, how we'd maybe scale the wall, bring a ladder, some rope, we'd set it up by way of Kathleen Connor for an escape, for Legs, we made these plans driving back in Mick's rattly old Chevy, but we never did go back, not once.

That was May 1954. We wouldn't set eyes on Legs till June 1955.

six

Hawks

Before she woke they entered her sleep. Before she woke staggering to the window to haul herself erect to see, yes she was still alive she'd endured another night in The Room now hopeful, prayerful—

      One.
                Two.   *Three.*
          Four.
                                        Five.
            Six.   *Seven.*
Eight.   *Nine.*
                    Ten.
    Eleven.

—the sparrow hawks riding the air in the blue of morning she'd wondered would she ever see again, now staring with her one good eye, the other swollen and throbbing from a guard's mean thumb but she didn't want to think of that and of the humiliation of being half dragged half carried to The Room as her sister-inmates watched, nor would she think of

Ab Sadovsky's story, was it true, was it laced with lies like poison, What do you care of him, that man, *man*-ness, he's nothing to you as you are nothing to him not bound by ties of love or compassion or common decency and maybe not even (you heard him yourself!) by ties of blood, maybe he isn't your true father: so let him go *let him die*. Staring at the hawks actually weeping to see the hawks, those predators visible only from this place of shame her heart lifting in joy seeing their strength, their beauty, riding the air, cunning in their use of the wind, always watchful though seemingly unhurried, even languid in their graceful curving motions now rising to the top of an invisible spiral so high in the air Legs couldn't see, beyond the grudging windowframe she couldn't see craning her neck narrowing her good eye, her right eye, then the wide-winged creatures reappeared, her heart beat hard and steady making her count, like saying the beads of a rosary except the hawks lived: the hawks were real: instructing her in freedom in cunning in ceaseless watchfulness in the presence of her enemies *Make them sorry make them regret all they ever did to you and your sisters but never let them know it's* you *the strength that is in* you *the strength that is* you and suddenly she was among them her arms that ached from being twisted up behind her back were wings dark-feathered powerfully muscled wings and she ascended the air, the cinderblock wall fell away beneath her, the roofs of the squat weatherworn buildings, the land itself fell silently away but the sky! the sky was immense! she stared almost in panic seeing it was infinite lifting above her and the other hawks, these supple creatures of the air rising and dipping and rising again joyous in motion so she was allowed to know she need never return to that old life, never to that old self, now she'd been one of these creatures, knowing her secret strength.

Masters of the air. I am one of you.

seven

"Turn of Heart"

By New Year's Day 1955 Legs Sadovsky had become a trusty at Red Bank herself.

By April 1955 she'd become so model a prisoner that the superintendent of the facility cut seven weeks from her sentence, thus arranging for her release on June 1. For which Legs Sadovsky was properly grateful; gratifyingly grateful; yet managed to retain her dignity murmuring thanks, Oh thank you. Tears gathering in her eyes.

She *was* grateful, truly. Knowing at the young age of sixteen how power need never relinquish any degree of power; how those in control of our fates must be allowed to believe that not whim not caprice not cruelty turned inside-out but genuine integrity has guided their behavior.

Thanking the superintendent, smiling, animated—"I'll never forget this kindness, Miss Flagler!—never forget *you!*"

And the woman peers at her somberly, the smallest of self-satisfied smiles, dry mottled middle-aged skin and features that look as if they've been squeezed in a vise, "Well. I *hope* so, Margaret."

* * *

When, that morning, Lon Lovell the meanest of the guards came to release Legs Sadovsky from her forty-eight hours in The Room, one look at the girl told her all she needed to know—that grainy skin, the inflamed left eye, the expression of rueful resigned calm signaled a change.

"Turn of heart" the staff called it. You couldn't predict it but you could always recognize it.

Officer Lovell the brassy-haired wide-hipped hard-muscled woman in her late twenties, maybe early thirties, the kind of person you say isn't so bad really once you get to know her, she's startled and almost regretful seeing that look in poor Legs, her old adversary Legs. She reaches down to help the shaky girl to her feet, touches the swollen eye with the tip of one finger, says, "O.K. hon—you're through fucking around, eh?"

Leg steps uncertainly out into the sunshine. Giddy blinding morning of which month she couldn't have said, nor even which year. She's been sleeping like Death on that filthy mattress. Or maybe hasn't slept at all for forty-eight hours.

She wipes the mucus draining from her left eye, her sore-stippled lips crack in a rueful smile. She says, like there's a joke here, like Lovell has got the best of her and knows it, "Yeah. I'm through. Fucking around."

For a flurry of days it's the talk of Red Bank. Even among girls who hadn't known her well, but admired her, marveled at her, from a distance. How Legs Sadovsky who was always standing up to the staff, the one who'd acted almost crazy sometimes, so reckless in defiance and so protective of other, weaker girls, had changed: "turned."

It happened. It wasn't common but it wasn't unknown. Especially in the cases of young emotional girls with no strong family ties. An inmate seemingly intractable and beyond re-

pentance and beyond rehabilitation suddenly becomes, overnight, often after a sequence of rapidly escalating confrontations and punishments, tractable; reasonable; obedient; *good.*

So Dutchgirl who'd gone through the identical turn eighteen months before seeks out Legs to poke her in the ribs, lean
in close against her as if she's going to love-bite her in the
neck. She says, winking, " 'Bout time, baby."

*No one and nothing will touch me, ever again. If anybody
is to kill it will be me.*

Of course Legs Sadovsky isn't at all like Dutchgirl, she's
one of the popular trusties. Helps teach her near-illiterate sisters to read and write; helps organize softball, volleyball, bas-
ketball games; assists in the "personal hygienics" and
"cosmetology" classes; if there's an emergency, she's there.
Never informs on her sisters but will not lie on their behalf either. And is she religious?—singing in the Sunday choir, her
hoarse alto veering flat but loud, optimistic, determined.

*Maddy I'm learning, gaining in strength day by day. No-
body's ever gonna put their foot on the back of my neck again.
Never gonna take any shit from anybody again.*

It's on a chill blowy morning in early April, Palm Sunday
afternoon thus a week before Easter Sunday, that the eight
very uncomfortable girls, or are they young women, young ladies, from the United Churches of Hammond Auxiliaries come
by hired car to Red Bank to inaugurate the Big Sister–Little
Sister Christian Girls' Program.

Which is how, by chance, Legs Sadovsky meets Marianne
Kellogg.

Legs the sixteen-year-old "Little Sister," Marianne Kellogg

the nineteen-year-old "Big Sister." But a very young and inexperienced nineteen.

The inmates are ushered into the day room (the room with its familiar dreary features has been transformed, or nearly: the Auxiliaries have donated three lovely astringent-fragrant Easter lilies for the occasion) self-conscious and abashed, confronted with their eight visitors, startled-looking girls in nice Sunday clothes, stockings, patent leather pumps. Legs, who'd thought the program might be a diversion, a way of passing the time, is suddenly shy, stiff, embarrassed, wishing she hadn't agreed to participate. Should she confess she doesn't belong here?—she isn't *Christian?*

One of the staff members urges her forward, here's the girl she's been paired with, willowy-tall, fair-skinned, a plain almost-pretty girl in a red plaid woolen dress, pinkish plastic-rimmed glasses. She has a sweet uncertain smile, she's extending her hand to Legs'—"Hello! My name is Marianne Kellogg! You're—Margaret?"

Legs mumbles almost inaudibly, "Yeah—yes. 'Margaret.' " The name sounds so odd in her mouth, it's as if she has never pronounced it before.

Legs has never to her recollection shaken hands with anyone, handshaking is strictly for men, and, even then, for gentlemen in movies. What a curious custom! Legs reaches out blindly and dumbly, closes her fingers around Marianne Kellogg's cool damp fingers and releases them almost at once. With a breathy little laugh, no doubt to disguise her unease, Marianne is saying, "It's a coincidence, our names sound almost alike. I mean—they *are* almost alike."

To which Legs, in a paralysis of shyness, a sense of unreality powerful as a blow on the head, cannot think of any suitable reply.

They sit on one of the vinyl-covered sofas. They smile vaguely at each other. Marianne clears her throat, pushes her glasses primly up her nose, says, "It's a little awkward, I guess.

We're just here to introduce ourselves, to visit a little. You know—" she says brightly, hopefully, "—just to talk."

Legs touches the little scar on her chin, not knowing what she does. In Marianne Kellogg's presence she feels too starkly visible.

The visit lasts no more than forty-five minutes but it seems much, much longer. Out of the corner of her eye Legs is aware of her sister-inmates, each in conversation, seemingly Christian conversation, with a Big Sister. Coffee, hot chocolate, and chocolate chip cookies are offered, but the Red Bank girls, ordinarily voracious, eat and drink sparingly; the Big Sisters are fastidious with their napkins, but have little appetite. Marianne Kellogg is the nicest of the visitors, Legs thinks. Smooth-shiny hair, dazzling-white smile, neatly manicured fingernails with no nail polish. Marianne is talking softly of her church-affiliated work: she'd wanted, she said, to be a missionary in China, when she was a little girl; now, she's less certain. "—It can be dangerous I guess. I mean—bringing the Word of God where it isn't wanted."

Legs, unnerved by Marianne Kellogg's nearness, and by the persistence of her chatter (all the Big Sisters are persistent, querying their shy or sullen or inarticulate Little Sisters virtually nonstop) hasn't been able to concentrate; isn't sure what the girl has said. Quick as a snake's tongue, flicking in and out of consciousness, she's thinking that Marianne Kellogg for all her awkwardness is surely from a very well-to-do family: from one of those bourgeois-residential neighborhoods in north Hammond FOXFIRE invaded one Hallowe'en night.

Legs says abruptly, with a smile Marianne Kellogg can't be expected to interpret, "Yeah? It *is?*"

Part

four

one

Celebration

Who is, or was, Maddy Wirtz?—why should we trust *her?*

The closer she comes to adulthood, bearing witness with an adult's increased sense of ambiguity, and irony, and self-doubt, the less clear are her memories. (The messier the entries in the notebook.) Say there's a mirror you have trusted to give you a solid unblemished surface reflecting the world then suddenly it breaks and shatters revealing a thousand new surfaces, miniature angles of seeing that must have been there all along hidden in the mirror's bland face *but you hadn't known.*

Who *is,* who *was.*

Whoever's reading this, if anyone *is* reading it: does it matter that our old selves are lost to us as surely as the past is lost, or is it enough to know yes we lived then, and we're living now, and the connection must be there?—like a river hundreds of miles long exists both at its source and at its mouth, simultaneously?

One thing I've learned, transcribing these CONFESSIONS has taught me, we all knew a lot more at young ages than we remember knowing, later. Some kind of peculiar amnesia must set in. Some kind of reinvention of ourselves. Maybe because much of what we knew we didn't like knowing and worked to forget so if you haven't been keeping a diary or such (and nobody does, these days) you'll succeed in forgetting what's mysterious, upsetting.

Like Legs stoned at the celebration FOXFIRE had for her when she came home from Red Bank telling Maddy she'd learned one truth at Red Bank that lodged deep, it's that we do have enemies, yeah men are the enemy but not just men, the shock of it is that girls and women are our enemies too sometimes, enough like us to be our sisters but they'd suck our blood if they could more evil than Father Theriault has said 'cause there's no reason for them to hate you except they just *do.*

It was a happy time, this celebration, Maddy was stoned too (more of this later) thus didn't want to hear, exactly. And dazzled with love. Yes it's love. What else but love. That young, she'd believed it was a well tapped so deep into a subterranean spring so infinite it will go on forever and ever, oh Jesus what's your hope but that it won't drown you, and that's enough to hope.

two

Rude Surprises

What's a *surprise* but just something you didn't know replacing something you believed you did; what's a *rude surprise* but something you not only know but it affects you in some way you'd never expected.

First off was the actual fact of who drove up to Red Bank to bring Legs home; and who was invited to accompany her.

June 1, 1955—that's the date we'd all marked on our calendars, in the notebook here it's at the top of a half-dozen pages in tall red block letters. Maddy began counting the days seven weeks before, when Legs' discharge date became official, she'd divided up the weeks into days of seven solemnly X'ing them out in sequence; imagining she was in a kind of prison cell, solitary confinement, herself (which you could argue she was: that closet-size room in her aunt Rose's house, upstairs rear, over the coal shed thus unheated, and Rose Packer was sour-tempered much of the time, sarcastic, resentful, seemed to hold it against the fifteen-year-old girl that her mother was a "bad mother") and when Legs at last came home, when FOXFIRE regained its strength, Maddy too would be FREE.

(For there was the hope, which I might as well mention now, that we'd all live together in an actual house, all us FOXFIRE blood-sisters. In her last letter sent from Red Bank Legs talked of this saying we could rent a house or even buy one some day, maybe out in the country, like "true sisters of a single Family.")

The first rude surprise though was *who* brought Legs home!—not Ab Sadovsky naturally—in fact the traitor wasn't even living in Hammond any longer; not Kathleen Connor who'd been visiting Legs regularly, and had carried news back and forth between us and Legs; not any of Legs' relatives.

No it was Muriel Orvis.

Muriel!—Legs' father's girl friend Legs had always hated or said she had.

So it's a true surprise to all of us that Muriel Orvis is the one to contact us, Legs told her whom to invite to come along and Muriel's the one giving orders, like she's a sister of Legs' herself except an older sister, knows all the answers.

Muriel Orvis was so minor in our lives, I'd have thought in Legs' life too, I have not even spoken of her till now. But unknown to us Muriel had been visiting Red Bank; claimed she felt sorry for the "motherless girl"; and once she and Ab Sadovsky broke up, *and Muriel's pregnant,* she gets it into her head, God knows why, she feels some strong blood-connection with Legs, and wins her over.

(At least that's what Maddy believed. It was hard for her to believe anything else—like for instance Legs could reverse her feelings regarding Muriel, where one day it seemed she couldn't bear mention of the woman's mere name, and suddenly they're *close*.)

So early in the morning of June 1 we're driving up to Red Bank in Muriel Orvis's Ford station wagon—not hers exactly but borrowed: even four months pregnant, Muriel's one of those women never lacking for (men) friends to lend her their cars—and there's Goldie with Toby in her lap, there's Lana, there's Rita, there's Violet, there's Maddy hearing Muriel complain in her nasal, reedy voice of how luck has always run against her with men, her first husband for instance who'd beaten her, Ab Sadovsky for instance who'd revealed himself so "vicious" so "evil" when she'd loved him more than she'd ever loved any other man, so what does he do but treat her like dirt worse and worse it got him drinking like he did yes and he'd slapped her around too, then ran off leaving her pregnant the way he did, left Hammond without saying goodbye owing money to maybe a dozen people, not to mention two months' back rent on that place of his he'd about cleaned out of anything of value leaving behind only trash and his poor daughter's clothes and a few possessions, nothing more, so far as Muriel knew Ab simply got in his car that day, back in March this was, and drove south, headed for Tampa, Florida, with some new girl friend of his saying he had work promised him there, oil refinery work paying twice what he could get in Hammond—"Though everybody knows Ab Sadovsky left Hammond because he was ashamed of how he'd behaved with the only two people in the world who were close to him and should have meant something to him, I mean for Christ's sake *trusted* him—his only daughter, and me."

Muriel's listeners murmur sounds of sympathy, surprise, mild polite wonder. Rita asks shyly if being pregnant *hurts,* and Muriel startles them by saying, with a little snort of laughter, "Well actually it feels good, I'd be the happiest I've been except for that son of a bitch betraying me like he did, and breaking my heart! Last time I was up to visit I told Marg'ret I had this crazy dream, it seemed the Lord Jesus Christ himself was instructing me this baby was gonna be something special, a little girl that's *got* to be born."

To this remarkable statement not one of the FOXFIRE girls can reply.

Muriel Orvis drives the borrowed station wagon along the country highway as if she's got a grudge against it, or the highway. She's so taken up with her monologue she pays little heed to the countryside; or to cars, trucks, farm equipment lumbering along slow in the right-hand lane. Maddy, in the back seat, leaning up close behind Muriel, is consumed by a strange itchy jealousy of the woman, she doesn't know exactly why. Yes it's because of Legs, the secret connection with Legs, but that isn't all. (Maddy is also, why not admit it, fiercely jealous of Violet Kahn who has no right, to Maddy's way of thinking, to even be in this station wagon this morning; no right to be included in the special contingent of FOXFIRE sisters invited to Red Bank to bring Legs home. What does Legs see in *her.*) So she's watching Muriel close, by way of the rear view mirror, not much minding when strands of Muriel's ashy-sweetish-smelling strawberry-blond hair blow ticklish across her face. Muriel Orvis is a full-bodied woman of about thirty-five, with ruddy-healthy skin, eyes ashine with honest anger and purpose, mouth like ripe crimson fruit. She's the kind of fully mature American woman that gives a glare off her face, like an automobile's finish. Legs used to say of Muriel Orvis, when Muriel was sleeping with her father, that the bitch had a pig's snout and a rear end to balance and you could sort of see that, in the face at least, her mouth and pug nose pushing forward but she's good-looking anyway, and acts it. Right now she's had to quit her job with Ferris Plastics (the smells were making her nauseated) but a few years ago she'd had some sort of partnership in a neighborhood beauty salon so she likes to speak of herself as a "businesswoman"—her aim is to be "in business for myself."

It doesn't seem right. Those years, must have been three or four, of hard living with Ab Sadovsky, late hours, drinking, cigarettes, none of it seems to have seriously slowed Muriel Orvis down, nor did her swollen little belly, pushing up tight against her summer-knit skirt, appear to be hampering her. Maddy bites her lip thinking *This woman is pregnant! not married! showing herself bold, even proud, in public!*

At Red Bank it's Muriel, of course, who goes inside to get Legs, while the others wait impatiently outside; and when Muriel reappears, with Legs, the two of them with tear-stained faces and arms around each other's waist, Maddy sucks in her breath and says aloud, "—Oh it's 'cause Muriel's pregnant with Legs' little sister or brother that Legs is so close to her now." In the rush forward only Violet Kahn seems to hear, and she says, not to contradict but to amplify, "—Yeah Maddy but that's prob'ly not *all.*"

Then there's the surprise of Legs Sadovsky herself.

Not a rude surprise exactly, but yes a surprise.

Running to her FOXFIRE sisters, the air erupting with little screams and cries almost of hurt, and they're all sobbing suddenly, hugs and kisses and *Oh my God! my God!* and Toby the handsome silvery-haired husky is leaping against Legs, licking her hands, frantic trying to bark his hoarse hissing near-soundless bark so Legs kneels right in the gravel drive to hug *him,* and he kisses her face with his wet floppy-pink tongue, and everybody is laughing and everybody is trying to touch Legs at the same time and she's trying to touch them, more hugs, a bruising-hard kiss for Maddy that takes her breath away, and Muriel Orvis her round ruddy face streaked with tears backs off taking snapshots with her Brownie box camera.

Overhead, a lemony sun, early summer, not too warm, smelling of wet from last night's heavy rain.

The main shock is, Legs' hair has been cut.

Unless the main shock is, Legs looks *older.*

Is this Legs?—Maddy's mildly dazed, her ribs aching pleasurably from the older girl's fierce embrace. All the way home in the rear of the crowded station wagon Maddy will be watching Legs in the front seat (companionably jammed between Muriel and Goldie, Toby riding clumsy and grateful on Goldie's lap) thinking *Is* it? *is* she? since Legs appears so changed, might be twenty, twenty-one instead of only sixteen, almost-beautiful, assured. Her short-cropped hair makes the planes and angles of her face seem chiseled; the cheek bones are particularly sharp, the eyes look larger. There's even a strange squinty look to Legs' left eye, a tiny blood-speck on the iris that's new, and disorienting. Maddy wonders if Legs has been injured in that eye, if her vision has been affected.

It's a picnic on wheels!—lukewarm cola and 7-Up, lukewarm beer, bags of salty greasy potato chips, Camel cigarettes for Legs, the station wagon filled with girls' voices, raucous laughter. The radio's turned up high to a Hammond station playing popular music. Maddy murmurs a half-dozen times, in wonder, "I can't believe this—Legs is *out.*" Nobody can believe it. Legs can't believe it. Several times she bursts into tears embarrassing them then turns it into a joke, a kind of prank. Then she's leaning over the front seat urgently grabbing at Rita's, Lana's, Violet's, Maddy's hands, framing their faces between her fingers, asking repeatedly as if knowing such questions can't be answered, can't even be articulated, "How the hell are you?—oh I missed you how *are* you?" and they're in the first stages of being drunk by the time they cross the Cassadaga returning to Hammond, that city of smokestacks, church spires, industrial towers set upon hills, like gravity drawing them, the long steep hill to Lowertown, Fairfax Avenue, all they know of home. Behind the wheel Muriel Orvis herself is drunk or almost—there hasn't been a day so *happy* and so *tender* in FOXFIRE memory has there?

Through it all Maddy has been watching Legs Sadovsky jealously hiding her true feelings (which she recognizes as mean, petty, asshole kinds of feelings) not knowing what to think of this almost-stranger, her friend who has hardly written to her in fourteen months, who's been in *prison.* (You aren't supposed to think of the youth facilities as prisons but that's what they are.) It's like a lifetime, those months, an abyss between them treacherous with memories they can't share. When, clowning around, Maddy grabs Legs' hair at the nape of her neck asking, "Why did you let them do *this?*—I loved your hair the way it was," Legs bares her teeth in a forced sort of grin, pries loose Maddy's fingers, says, like her dignity's been ruffled, "I got my reasons." So Maddy can't take it as anything but a rebuff.

At which point Violet Kahn leans quickly forward to touch Legs' hair too, smoothing it back from her forehead, pursing her lips, cooing, *"I love it this new way. Legs, anything you do it's you."*

Maddy thinks, She knows things I don't know, now.

What kinds of things precisely, how cruel how brutal how intimate how carnal, Maddy doesn't want to speculate.

Here's another surprise: without telling anybody Legs invites several guests to the FOXFIRE welcome-home party who aren't in FOXFIRE and though these guests don't stay long, maybe knowing they're not welcome, it isn't what Legs' blood-sisters expected.

One of them is Muriel Orvis, so that isn't too bad, the girls have come round to liking Muriel well enough, even Maddy who's so critical of adult women so prickly-uncomfortable in the presence of pregnant women, there's the excuse in any case that Legs is staying with Muriel (temporarily: until she finds a place of her own) so it makes a kind of logic, inviting Muriel. And there's Kathleen Connor who's been so friendly to FOXFIRE too, the girls can't truly object—and it's a funny-daring thing, only possible maybe at a party like this with plenty to drink and an atmosphere of noisy gaiety, that these two ex-girl friends of Ab Sadovsky's should meet, formally meet at last, size each other up, laugh, embrace, and drift off together to exchange stories.

Ab Sadovsky, that son of a bitch!—anybody know exactly where he *is?*

But the other two guests constitute a rude surprise, at least it's so felt by the FOXFIRE girls.

Legs was saying one of them was her good, trusted friend

at Red Bank, she'd been released a few weeks ago, Legs was talking warmly about this stranger Marigold Dempster so we're reconciled to meeting her, then who comes through the door at about nine P.M.—self-conscious, sort of cringing like they're ready to back right out again—but two black girls. *Not only strangers but Negroes.*

If the record player hadn't been turned up so high the whole room would have gone hushed.

Except there's Goldie staring almost pop-eyed, so startled she spills beer on her front, exclaims aloud, "—*Niggers!*" so Maddy close beside her says reprovingly, hoping the black girls have not heard, "—*Negroes*," and Goldie manages to recover sufficiently to say, in an undertone in Maddy's ear, "—Whatever the hell you call them they're not *white.*"

Not that Marigold and Tama stay long. Hardly an hour.

Not that they're made to feel unwelcome—exactly.

The Dempster sisters are Lowertown girls too but from the black part of town; if they attend, or have attended, Perry High School, no one recalls them. Except for Rita and Maddy, and of course Legs, none of the FOXFIRE girls goes out of her way to be friendly, there's a palpable air of hurt feelings, childish resentment. How could Legs be so unfeeling!—at such a special time! It turns out that Tama is a complete stranger to Legs which makes the invitation all the more peculiar, and Marigold is painfully shy, not one of those buoyant hearty-laughing black girls who are popular at school amid the white majority, she's sweet-seeming, but plain, with a very dark skin, a flattened nose, small deep-set eyes perpetually downcast, uneasy. Even with Legs' arm slung around her and Legs' rapid-fire questions Marigold doesn't have much to say except repeating how happy she is to see Legs *out,* oh God there's nothing that matters so much as being *out,* every minute of every day Marigold gives thanks to Jesus she's *out* she's never going back *in.*

So Legs hugs Marigold tight, that ashy-blond head close behind the black girl's head, saying, "Baby you said it: they're gonna have to lay me out cold, they ever want me back *in* again."

Legs speaks so passionately, so defiantly, everybody's a little embarrassed. The FOXFIRE girls, and the Dempster sisters.

Not knowing where exactly to look.

It's late. The black girls are gone, Kathleen Connor and Muriel Orvis are gone, no one at the party except FOXFIRE no one surrounding Legs Sadovsky except FOXFIRE no cause for hurt feelings, misunderstandings, anger, confusion. Why didn't you like Marigold, yes we did like Marigold, no but you didn't like Marigold damn you you white-ass hot-shit bitches how dare you, the color of your skin's just something you got born with how dare you, but no: no disagreement really: these terrible words go unuttered.

No one remaining here in FOXFIRE's secret candlelit space except FOXFIRE these eight blood-sisters who have vowed their bond for ETERNITY Legs, and Goldie, and Lana, and Rita, and Maddy, and Violet, and Toni, and Marsha, just this secret CELEBRATION going on and on through the night and there's plenty to drink, beer in a tub of ice, and dozens of sandwiches, a three-layer devil's food cake proudly baked by Rita/"Red" and frosted by Maddy/"Monkey," rich fudge-chocolate with vanilla script WELCOME HOME LEGS! Legs declares it is the most delicious cake she's ever tasted.

Smoking marijuana too. Goldie supplied it, she's got Legs' old contacts, and Legs gets high within minutes clowning and laughing she's been fucking *deprived* for so long.

Maddy isn't used to drinking still less to smoking reefer, she falls asleep flat on the floor then wakes then sleeps then wakes and it's midnight?—it's after two A.M.?—this FOXFIRE CELEBRATION going on and on 'cause nobody wants it to stop and if a girl falls asleep she'll wake a while later, if two girls fall asleep others remain awake, the record player's turned up high the candle flames are hypnotic Maddy's dancing so wild and inspired the others are marveling at her convulsed in laughter too she's made to realize she's so *young* so *physically immature* set beside the others even the newer girls Violet, Toni, Marsha who are a year behind her in school, she's dancing to show them all and Legs is dancing with her, Legs shrieks with laughter calling her "Killer" saying she'd missed her more than anybody else—"Y'know, Maddy?—you're my *heart!*"

Then Legs is pulling Maddy away, all hushed and secret and giggling they climb the stairs to the roof, Legs is holding a candle aloft saying more serious now that Maddy's the only one who treated Marigold Dempster and her sister like human beings not like freaks and Maddy faintly protests, tries to defend the others, but Legs isn't listening—"Y'know almost I'm ashamed of FOXFIRE, making those girls feel unwelcome, I'm not gonna forget this, you wait—" but they're on the roof suddenly and the topic is forgotten as the night air washes against their heated skins, all the sky, the depth of the night sky, like a fathomless sea going on and on and on so beautiful so powerful Maddy's heart aches. She's swaying at the edge of the roof her head craned back saying, "—Ancient people, they thought the sky was so low, if you climbed up this high like we are, you'd be actually *closer.*"

Legs who's lighting one of the parchment-wrapped marijuana cigarettes says carelessly, "Yeah?—well we *are.*"

A three-quarter moon, glowering bone, with a hint of something bruised, battered, scarred. The moon has endured more than anybody can know.

And the stars—so many stars—and with a powerful telescope, you'd see more—and more and *more*—Maddy's laughing shivering to think of it except probably it can't be thought of, not truly. The cool damp night air smelling of the river briny and something sinister should soothe her but doesn't seem to, why's she so excited?—passed out an hour ago now on her feet her skin like fever and her heart racing?—this is new, Maddy is thinking, Legs is someone new, she's scared of Legs telling her in a matter-of-fact voice that in Red Bank she'd thought long and hard and come to certain "absolute" conclusions about life, Maddy doesn't want to hear anything that will scare her, not now.

Legs Sadovsky who's grown taller, five feet nine inches at least, a beautiful face, yes but she's careless of herself and her beauty isn't going to last, that sharp-boned face, that look of scrutiny, hunger, impatience, Maddy stares at her wondering what the connection is between them, and what it will be, Maddy Wirtz and this young woman with almost the body of a young man, so slender so compact in her muscles, hair cropped short and lifting from her forehead fierce as a bird's crest: Legs in a sleeveless chartreuse cotton jersey fitting tight enough so the vertebrae of her backbone and her hard little breasts with their sharp nipples are outlined, she's wearing low-slung black pants and a belt of silver medallions someone at Red Bank (one of the guards?) gave her as a going-home gift, there's something aggressive and sexual in just the way Legs stands, hip bone and pelvis tilted, stomach so flat as to be almost concave thus the mound between her legs subtly prominent, and her eyes so dilated as to be black with pupil— *They're right, she's dangerous.*

And what the hell.

Up on the roof Legs tries to talk seriously to Maddy telling her about FOXFIRE's enemies, not just men but sometimes girls too, women too like the guards at Red Bank—"Jesus Maddy, I hope *you* never find out for yourself. There's true evil, sometimes."

Maddy says, reckless she's so happy, "—I'd had my way, Legs, I'd have been up there with you. All that time."

Legs says as if she hasn't heard, or hasn't wanted to hear, "—This evil, it's enough to know it's *there*. Father Theriault thinks its 'cause of society, we can't be sisters and brothers 'cause of capitalism, and having to sell ourselves, y'know, I believe that to be true but there's something else too, like—why's a girl gotta thumb you in the eye?—somebody enough like you you could be twins, except for the face?" rubbing her left eye meditatively, not somberly but smiling, rueful, wanting to talk and needing to talk and Maddy both wants to hear and dreads hearing, she's jealous of Red Bank, of even the ugliness of Red Bank, certain experiences she has not had and cannot imagine. Legs is squatting at the edge of the roof and Maddy joins her, swaying just a little, in her laughing mood like nitrous oxide at the dentist's, Legs is saying, "Now a man, I can accept a man, a man as the Enemy, O.K. I can accept that, like at the museum there's *Homo sapiens* the one who *thinks* and one of the first fucking things he thinks of is *killing:* I mean, O.K. we all know that, if that wasn't so there wouldn't be wars, and there's always wars, we wouldn't have 'em if men didn't love 'em, I can accept that. But one of our own *kind*, the female sex, that's—unexpected."

Maddy says uncertainly, "—Did they hurt you, Legs? Your eye—"

Legs says, "Nah nobody hurt *me*. I was too smart for 'em. It came time, I escaped—turned into a hawk." She's laughing, flapping her arms, worrying Maddy she's going to fly, or fall, off the edge of the roof. "—Beautiful bird. Fucking-beautiful bird."

Maybe it's dangerous to be squatting so close to the edge of the roof but Maddy is feeling confident, sucking at the marijuana cigarette in a state of dazzled happiness, it's FOXFIRE's night of celebration LEGS IS HOME FROM RED BANK and she and Legs are hidden away from the others, maybe they're beginning to be missed and maybe time is running out so it's precious, these minutes, not far away the Cassadaga River looks like a living thing, cold wan-rippling waves, moonlit waves like shivers in flesh, and the farther shore is winking with lights, street lights, house lights, tiny stars lifting into the blackness of the foothills but you can't make out the actual hills, not even their contours, just night: Night. Like the true sky of the Universe that is a single substance revealing its nature not by day (for doesn't daylight fracture? blind? disintegrate into a multiplicity of parts, like a broken mirror?) but only by night.

Legs has been observing Maddy smoking the cigarette. Now she says, laughing, big-sisterly in exasperation, "Oh Christ, hon—you mean you've been smoking reefer like *that,* like a dumb little kid?"

So she takes the skinny cigarette from Maddy's fingers to show her how, puckers her lips as for a comical kiss and places the cigarette in the middle and sucks in deep shutting her eyes and deeper still holding the smoke for ten unhurried seconds (if this celebratory party of FOXFIRE is raided by police, what then?—if Legs Sadovsky just released from Red Bank Correctional that very day is found in possession of marijuana, what then?) and then exhales luxuriously, though in fact, oddly, very little smoke is actually exhaled. "—You gotta give it time to absorb into your lungs, I guess, and your blood," Legs says, handing the cigarette to Maddy who does exactly as Legs has instructed but something seems to go wrong, her mouth and throat begin to burn so she's coughing, almost choking, quick tears running down her cheeks, and Legs doesn't laugh, isn't derisive just waits for the attack to pass then says, "O.K. hon, take it slow, you got all night, try again nice and easy," so Maddy tries again scared she's going to explode in a spasm of coughing, Legs even holds the cigarette in place between Maddy's puckered lips and she inhales, she inhales and inhales shutting her eyes so there isn't the river and the night and her friend's face to distract her, yes and she holds the burning smoke deep in her lungs, and suddenly, unexpectedly, the top of her tight little skull gives way! moonlight enters freely! Maddy's eyes fly open as Maddy is floating Maddy is airborne Maddy-Monkey is laughing she's overcome gravity *So this is it! so easy!*

Legs seems a long way off. But no she's close. Nudging her head against Maddy's, her lean-muscled arm slung around Maddy's shoulders to hold her tight, to protect her—"Now you know why it's called 'getting high,' baby, right?"

three

The Paradox of Chronology/Dwarf-Woman

My God I was certain this morning I'd be writing about our FOXFIRE DREAM/FOXFIRE HOMESTEAD that, though it came to bitterness and grief in the end, was nonetheless, for months, a possibility of joy to us . . . but if I am to be faithful to actual chronology, to the task of setting down events not as I remember them but as they occurred, I am forced to record, here, this strange episode of the DWARF-WOMAN that took place in mid-summer 1955.

It's an ugly nasty episode of utter mystery to me (why Legs got so involved, whether in fact she *did* get so involved as she claimed), I'd forgotten completely about it except looking through the notebook I suddenly remembered—couldn't avoid remembering. And more upsetting than this ugliness and nastiness there's the *paradox of chronology* which arises when you try to record events of historical veracity; the problem of transcribing a document like this notebook is that it's a memoir or a confession where you have not the power to invent episodes, people, places, "plot," etc. but must set everything down as it occurred. Not imagination but memory is the agent but language is the instrument in all cases and can language be trusted?

If it were not for language, could we lie?

(Not that I am lying, truly I do not believe I have lied a single time in these many painful months of dredging through my FOXFIRE past. But if Truth is not always available, not always recalled accurately, or even known, isn't this *lying* of a special kind? Like the Catholic Church has dogma about *sins of omission* which are the hardest sins of all to comprehend since they lack actual existence!)

The *paradox of chronology* is hateful because you are always obliged to seek out earlier causes than what's at hand. So I must contaminate this bright coldly sunny winter morning with recollections of a DWARF-WOMAN never actually glimpsed by Maddy Wirtz tied to her bed and abused by men when I had had a hope of describing, thus remembering, and taking happiness in the memory of, the ramshackle old farmhouse FOXFIRE wanted so badly to own—FOXFIRE DREAM/ FOXFIRE HOMESTEAD, this vacated place on the Oldwick Road Legs discovered one day riding in the Parks & Recreation truck that summer, a temporary job Miss Flagler the superintendent at Red Bank arranged for her, and back beyond that (this is what I mean by hateful *chronology,* being made to know that no thing can have happened without another thing preceding it and another preceding *that* to the very beginning of Time!) how Legs spoke bemused and cynical of this Miss Flagler making so much of how she'd gone on record declaring that "Margaret Sadovsky" was one of the most trustworthy the most reliable hard-working intelligent honest totally rehabilitated inmates to have passed through the Red Bank State Correctional Facility in years, so sure Legs was grateful to her, sure Legs *was* grateful 'cause with her father gone she damn well needed a job to support herself and live independently of all adult intervention which had been her dream for years, but it's the kind of situation as Legs said, the kind of crap you're told about yourself you wind up feeling sick and ashamed and anxious about, that you'll surely let down this benefactor who has "gone on record" for you as if this very gesture, such a Christian gesture "going on record," anticipates the hour of disappointment, disillusion, betrayal!

Also, as Legs' boss on the truck crew told her, he was a pushy aggressive guy in his twenties but he'd tell the truth at least, the job Legs had with Parks & Recreation (the single job on this particular crew held by a girl since it required so much physical labor out-of-doors) wasn't any plum, hardly—paying just the minimum wage for that time, $1.00 an hour *before taxes*.

And later Legs would learn that, being a girl, she was getting less than any of the guys though she did as much, or more, of the work as any one of them did.

Which takes us far from the DWARF-WOMAN I guess. I'm sorry.

You can see how I am not a practiced writer—not leading this material but led by it, sometimes my heart fainting thinking *God knows where I will be led, what shame and sorrow.*

Legs said the "dwarf-woman" wasn't any true dwarf, that was just what people called her, being stunted as she was, and sort of misshapen, and retarded—"People have got to put a name on anything different from them," Legs said in disgust. She'd met the woman whose name was Yetta just by accident: the crew was working clearing underbrush out of the woods at the northernmost edge of Cassadaga Park, nearly in the country but a scrubby sort of countryside where there weren't real farms any longer, a lot of asphalt-sided bungalows, house trailers on concrete blocks and illegal dumping grounds—"poor white trash" the inhabitants of that area were called—and there was a tavern closed for business but a house attached, and Legs was dying of thirst so she trotted across the highway to the house thinking to ask for a drink of water, none of the guys wanted to accompany her but she didn't think anything

of that, and she knocks at the front door and nobody answers
(it's an old farmhouse, in poor repair, the yard littered with debris like nobody takes any pride in it) so she gets the idea, this
is just like Legs, she'll go around to the rear she'll help herself
to a drink of water if there's a well, and out back she sees this
person she couldn't say was it a male or a female at first sight,
then she sees it's a woman, no clear age except not young,
she's short as a dwarf or a midget about four feet five or six
inches, child-size but not child-proportioned with a long torso
and a misshapen back, and her face, not ugly exactly, but
strange, sort of twisted like her spine, and she's dressed in
men's clothes and turns around to look at Legs squinting but
already smiling as if Legs is someone she knows and likes, and
the shock of it is, the true horror, that Legs said took her a full
minute maybe to absorb, this woman is wearing a dog collar
around her neck and the collar is attached to a lightweight
chain and the chain's attached to a clothesline strung across
the yard so the woman can move about freely as far as the
chain allows . . . so Legs is standing there blinking all sweaty
herself in a T-shirt and jeans and a red-checked kerchief tied
around her head, and the woman says hello, her name's Yetta,
and she's smiling sort of hopefully at Legs in such a way Legs
can see she must be retarded.

This dwarf-woman smiling at *her* expecting something of
her like they already know each other.

The woman says again her name's Yetta, her voice is
reedy and high-pitched, one of her eyes is milky, Legs is standing there like a strange weight has fallen on her shoulders until
finally she says hello, she asks if she can have a drink of
water—it's like her brain went on functioning as she'd intended even while she herself Legs Sadovsky stood off to the
side shocked and bewildered—and the dwarf-woman leads
her over to the well close by the rear of the house and there's
a tin cup attached to the pump so Legs takes up the cup and
the dwarf-woman Yetta starts pumping bringing the handle up
high and bringing it down laughing like a child would, prim-

ing the pump to get the cold spring water up to the surface gesturing for Legs not to put the cup under the splashing water right away, to wait till it's good and cold. Which Legs does.

So she drinks a cup of water so delicious she can't believe it, nothing like our water in the city she said, she drinks not one cup but two and wipes her mouth with her hand saying thanks, she's close enough now to observe that the dwarf-woman's neck is raw and reddened from the collar but the woman doesn't seem unhappy, she's smiling at Legs just standing and waiting, and Legs tries to smile, Legs is shaken but also sort of embarrassed the way you are looking upon a person who is *human* yet not *human* in the way you know it, so she figures she can't leave without talking to somebody in the house but there doesn't seem to be anybody home, no car in sight except some junked cars in the driveway so she asks the dwarf-woman isn't it awful hot for her? out there in the sun? isn't anybody else home? *who tied her up like that?*

The dwarf-woman just giggles, staring at Legs through her fingers. It's like she can't even comprehend Legs' words.

Back on the crew Legs questions the guys, do they know anything about the woman, this poor woman?—and none of them will admit he does but they're glancing at one another with these strange little smiles, Legs figures it's a sign they do know but they're gonna play dumb, keep it a secret from her.

That night Legs makes inquiries around town. Nobody knows a thing about this "dwarf-woman" Yetta out on Mantree Road, or won't say.

But Legs can't stop thinking about what she's seen. The dog collar, the raw reddened neck. The dwarf-woman's eyes fixed on *hers*.

Friday evening she and Goldie get a ride out to Mantree with a guy Legs knows, he drops them off and leaves them at Legs' insistence though the tavern isn't open, but they see there's some activity around the house, a few cars and pick-up trucks parked in the driveway. So what do Legs and Goldie do but hide in the bushes alongside the house, to watch; and they see a sight they wished afterward they'd never seen, and hadn't ever expected to see—at the rear of the house there's a room where the dwarf-woman is kept, a single lightbulb hanging from the ceiling, a single item of furniture, a four-poster bed, and the dwarf-woman is lying on it naked, spread-eagle, a terrible sight to see her with her wrists and ankles tied to the bed's four posters so her deformed body is completely exposed and completely open . . . and one by one men come into the room. And shut the door behind them.

Clutching each other in amazement and disgust the FOXFIRE girls observe not once, not twice, but three times in the course of perhaps forty-five minutes: a man enters the back room swaying-drunk, the dwarf-woman tied to the bed begins to whimper and moan, the man drops his trousers and climbs atop her, they struggle together, thrash about together like they're drowning, the dwarf-woman's cries are high-pitched and childlike but not seemingly cries of pain . . . so Goldie says maybe they'd better get the hell out of there and Legs says they've got to *do something.*

Legs is crazy enough, and reckless enough, to go right to the front door of the house, and Goldie's trying to dissuade her, they're five miles out from Hammond without a car just two girls and how many men are on the premises?—but Legs is agitated and can't be stopped, you know Legs. She pounds on the door and a man opens it, big, bear-size, with little bright-nasty eyes and a raw-plum face, right away Legs is saying she knows what is going on in this house, she knows about Yetta and it's got to stop, there are laws prohibiting such things, abuse, forced prostitution, she's gonna notify the Hammond police, she knows people at the county welfare office she's gonna notify *them.* The guy takes all this in sort of slowly blinking at Legs but he's a mean-mouthed son of a bitch and starts telling her to get the hell home, it's none of her fucking business what people do in the privacy of their own home and if his sister Yetta's been talking to her that's none of her business either. By now there's two or three other men at the door staring at Legs and Goldie like they can't believe what they're seeing: these two young girls, out of nowhere, *here.*

So Legs and the man who acknowledges he's Yetta's brother are exchanging words. For maybe five minutes, excitable and interrupting each other.

Right away Goldie's tugging at Legs' arm, trying to draw her off. This is the most dangerous situation they've ever been in, just the two of them, on foot, and so many men, yes you'd have to call them "poor trash" if you required the most expedient means of describing them. But Legs is saying, to the guy at the door, to all of them gaping and grinning, "—Pigs! You're all filthy pigs!"

Goldie mutters, "Hon!—c'mon!" all but dragging Legs away, out toward the road. But Legs is still shouting at Yetta's brother, and he's following them outside shouting too, a big lumbering man in his forties maybe, with a dazed-wild look, rubbing his hands together, and rubbing at his belly and crotch, like he's hot to get hold of Legs, and she's taunting him, she's saying, "You better let her go! I'll tell the police, you better let her go!" and the guy says, "Yeah? Her? Go where?" and Legs says, "Give her her freedom," and the guy says, "You don't know nothing about her, you don't know shit," sneering, waving his fist, "—where's she gonna *go,* she's happy *here.*"

So this guy advances upon Legs and Goldie grinning at them, a gold filling amid his crooked and discolored front teeth like a glimmer of a thought. "Yeah," he says, "—you don't know shit, my sister's happy *here.*"

Next night, a Saturday night, Legs comes back alone—not that Goldie refused to accompany her, Legs didn't even ask—and not knowing exactly what she's going to do Legs hides again outside the house, this time at a short distance in a stand of scrub willow so she's in no danger, she thinks, of being seen. Tonight there are more cars and pickup trucks in the driveway, it looks as if (can she be certain?—maybe not) one

of the cars is a police cruiser, parked there for maybe ten minutes then driven off in a flare of flung gravel, and Legs can
make out movement in that room of Yetta's, she can even hear
Yetta's high-pitched ecstatic cries, sobbing-cries, animal cries,
of inexpressible anguish, grief, gratitude, which she doesn't
want to hear but hears nonetheless, even pressing her angry
fingers against her ears she hears just as she's been seeing that
nightmare room sleepless herself for the past twenty-four
hours, the bed, the four posts of the bed, the female body misshapen and thrashing and utterly open, wrists and ankles
bound, utter nakedness so not only the patch of furry pubic
hair is revealed but the spread lips of the vagina, and the
vulva, like a she-goat exposing her vulva, and the mouth open
too in a wide groaning O, terrible to see. One by one the
animal-men enter the room, one by one bare-assed their genitals swollen, penises stiffened into rods, mounting the dwarf-
woman, the woman-that's-a-body, one by one pumping their
life into her, evoking those cries so Legs doesn't know what to
do or if she should do anything, her threats of going to the
county welfare office or the police were mere bluffs since Legs
Sadovsky is fearful of such people, she hates them like poison
especially the cops knowing too she must not draw any un-
wanted attention to FOXFIRE any more than to herself. She's
thinking of how, once, a long time ago now, elderly Father
Theriault, defrocked priest, bum-alcoholic, sitting on his park
bench his legs so short his feet didn't quite touch the ground
was telling Legs Sadovsky who bent nervously eager to hear
that no individual can remedy injustice, the Earth upon which
we walk is comprised of the fine-ground bones of those who
have not only suffered but have suffered in silence, of both
human and animal suffering we can scarcely bear to think yet
must think, and Legs murmured, But what can we *do* and the
elderly man seemed not to hear her speaking of society of capitalism of the curse of human beings apprehending one another as commodities the tragedy is that men and women not

only use one another as things but use themselves, present themselves, sell themselves . . . as things.

But what, but what can we *do*. Tell me what can we *do*.

Legs wakes to see it's late, the moon has shifted in the sky. What has taken place tonight has taken place in her presence and cannot be undone. All but one of the cars is gone from the driveway and the lights in the old farmhouse are now out, a sleeping house, you can see there's peace and even a kind of beauty in a sleeping house but Legs Sadovsky trembling with rage leaves her hiding place slipping and sliding downhill, she makes her way by cunning into a small barn behind the house where she's alerted at once smelling kerosene: takes up a five-gallon container of kerosene: carries it to the house sprinkling the sharp-smelling liquid into the tall grasses surrounding the house, she's methodical, acts without haste, though with the motions of a sleepwalker whose directive beyond any observable action is that she must not be wakened for it is Death to be wakened, and when the container is empty of kerosene Legs sets it carefully down on the ground, and takes a box of matches out of her pocket, and strikes a match, dreamily yet deliberately strikes a match, and lets it drop, already turning, lithe as a cat, already smiling turning and running though without haste or even excitement as the first flames leap up, small teethlike flames, a necklace of flame-teeth circling both the old farmhouse and the tavern, at which Legs Sadovsky in her headlong flight does not allow herself to look for fear, another time, her heart will turn.

four

FOXFIRE DREAM/
FOXFIRE HOMESTEAD

It's true as I stated at the outset of these Confessions, FOXFIRE was an outlaw gang, and became ever more so as time passed. And we were pledged not to feel remorse—FOXFIRE NEVER LOOKS BACK!

Sure some of us were scared. We were scared of where Legs was leading us, and what was waiting. Maddy-Monkey was maybe the most scared.

Guessing what might come of outlawry. Being a *girl*-gang.

Still I believe we might have been successful, in our primary hope I mean: owning a house, living like true blood-sisters in that house, free and clear of all Others (except: if Muriel Orvis came to live with us, Muriel and her poor little weak-hearted infant daughter born five weeks premature), each paying what we could and accepting what we needed as Legs had wished. We *might* have been successful: who knows?

Had we not run too many risks.

Pledged not to feel remorse—FOXFIRE BURNS & BURNS!

* * *

Our house, the house surely meant to be ours, was on the Oldwick Road, in a semirural area, three miles south of Hammond and approximately a mile from the county fairgrounds. It was a beautiful old wood-frame farmhouse, very old, its stone foundation dated 1891, and its tall narrow stone chimney crumbling. Upstairs there were three low-ceilinged bedrooms, the wallpaper in tatters; downstairs there were four small rooms including a kitchen with an antiquated wood-burning stove and a broken refrigerator. An alcove behind the kitchen contained a crude toilet and a badly stained claw-footed bathtub. (In the back yard, maybe thirty feet away, was an old outhouse—an emergency measure for when the toilet broke down.) The veranda at the front of the house was termite-ridden and overgrown with wild rose and trumpet vine, the rotted shingles on the roof were askew, the asphalt siding was badly weatherworn; several windows were broken and "mended" with plywood panels. But: *Isn't it beautiful?* Legs demanded. When Maddy first saw the house, in a warm-blazing September sun, she began to cry it *was* so beautiful like an old noble wreck of a schooner riding the waves, lush overgrown meadows on all sides aflame with goldenrod, tiny white asters, lavender burdock flower. And everywhere wasps and bees hummed with a secret seething life!

Of the original twenty-eight acres only two and a half remained containing the farmhouse, a partly collapsed barn, some sheds. Rusted farm equipment. Drunkenly tilting fences. No one had farmed the property for years, the most recent tenants had been a welfare family with eight children who'd left by stealth one night owing months of back rent, the house looking like pigs had been living in it.

Thus the rent was low—forty-five dollars a month.

The sale price of the property itself was low—thirty-two hundred dollars, negotiable.

Lana said excitedly, why not, my God why *not*. And Rita, her warm brown eyes alight, dazed, oh yes why *not*. And Goldie who was vehement as always. And Maddy who'd em-

barrassed them by weeping. And the others, the newer FOX-
FIRE initiates: We can all help pay for it, we can live here together be happy here together oh God why *not.*

Toby the handsome silvery-haired husky, no longer a pup
but a full-grown dog of perhaps fifty pounds, clambered about
the property, in the tall grass, in and out of the barn, scaring
up birds, chasing invisible rodents, barkless yet ecstatic as if
FOXFIRE had at last brought him home.

Legs first saw the house on the Oldwick Road, and the
faded FOR SALE sign out front, riding in the Parks & Recreation
truck the day after Labor Day. Her "bad" eye—her left—was
misted over thus the farmhouse appeared hazy at first like a vision incompletely materialized or maybe Legs had been crying
her soundless raging tears so she had to blink, and stare, to
truly see the house, *our* house, she said it was like a sliver of
glass entering her heart, in that instant—"I knew it was a place
FOXFIRE could live."

So she asked the driver to please stop, she wanted to get
off (she was riding in the rear, in the open air), and when he
didn't stop, only braked a little, Legs jumped down anyway on
the side of the road already running toward the house. Behind
her the crew yelled at her, that kind of fond-nasty asshole teasing she'd had enough of through the summer, and no longer
acknowledged.

"Hey Legs!—gonna hurt your tits, jumping like that!"

"Hey Legs baby!—we ain't gonna wait around for you!"

"Where the hell ya *going?*"

Legs just kept running, through a field, stumbling and almost falling and regaining her balance, the work-boots were
clumsy for running like this, her damp T-shirt clung to her
back and her muscles ached from hours of manual labor but
she kept running, in the direction of the house. Already it was
like a sanctuary to her. Already she knew those fucking Others
could not follow.

* * *

(Why had Legs been crying on the truck?—I believe it was
because some of the guys were so crude, guys she'd thought
she could get along with, harassing her to the point of true
meanness. At the start of the summer things had been all right
most of the time: the other crew members respected Legs
Sadovsky 'cause she could almost pass for one of them, never
asked any special favors as a girl and certainly she worked as
hard, maybe harder, than any of them. Then by degrees two or
three of them began vying with the others for her attention,
making suggestive jokes, even nudging her, that kind of flirty
shit as Legs contemptuously described it—"Like they're pretending not to know who I am: I'm Legs Sadovsky I'm FOX-
FIRE *I don't fuck around with guys."*)

Legs wasted no time telephoning the realtor, made an
appointment for us to see the property. The first Sunday after
Labor Day Muriel Orvis drove us out, all of FOXFIRE, for our
first glimpse of FOXFIRE HOMESTEAD.

That sight I will recall my entire life. That sight bringing
tears at once to my eyes.

The agent from the realtor's who met us there, keys in
hand, was a pale-pasty fattish guy with glasses, not overly
bright, with a look of being the least salesman on his team,
thus assigned to this property. So Legs had no trouble convinc-
ing him we were serious.

"Maybe we can't buy the house exactly, right now," Legs
said, "—but we can rent it, maybe."

You'd have sworn Legs was twenty-one years old, at least.
Fully capable of entering into a legal contract.

The plan was: Muriel Orvis would be our intermediary.

So Legs and Muriel, they did all the talking, asked all the
questions as the real estate agent showed them around. He

was sort of apologetic and bumbling—the place was in such disrepair. As Muriel kept saying, "—Looks like *pigs* lived here!"

The rest of FOXFIRE prowled about the premises on our own. Serious at first like we needed to examine the floors, the windows, the wreck of a furnace (coal-burning), then we began to lark about, chased one another, and Toby: the stairs shuddering under our feet, the upstairs rooms filled with our laughter: and downstairs to the dank evil-smelling earthen-floor cellar—"You think somebody's buried down here?" Lana shrieked with laughter, "—sure does smell like it!" And outside into the hot giddy blazing sunshine. Tall-ticklish grasses, wasps and butterflies and bees. And in the old barn where smells of compost, and rotted hay, and bird-droppings, and decades of summer heat-decay washed over us leaving us giddy and faint. So happy! We were so happy! Knowing that Legs would bring us safely here. Knowing that *here* was FOXFIRE DESTINY.

For there wasn't a one of us who was not, and had not been for some time, at odds with her family: or what passed for "family" in our lives.

Previously I have stated that I would not speak of adults unless required. Nor any more than required. Thus I will not. Thus in fact the notebook contains little evidence of adults.

Yet I remember: Maddy Wirtz's aunt Rose Packer extracting from her every penny of what she called in her pickle-prissy tone "ROOM AND BOARD." Every penny this pauper-girl could earn at the White Eagle Hotel slaving in the steamy-hot kitchen, afterward as housemaid in the hotel, paying "ROOM AND BOARD" scrupulously week by week 'cause Maddy's mother is such a tramp (and Aunt Rose is acquainted with plenty of tramps) though you got to wonder what kind of a man would want her?—her good looks gone and half her teeth rotted out of her head and borrowing money shamelessly with no intention of ever returning it laughing in Rose Packer's face slamming the telephone receiver down in Rose Packer's ear refusing to accept responsibility for her own daughter this sullen slouch-shouldered niece of Rose Packer's the talk of the street a *gang-girl* running with a pack of notorious bitches sluts juvenile delinquents already bearing the mark of gang life that scar on her cheek like a cobweb your impulse is to wipe away but it's a true scar *it won't wipe away* and this girl has hardened her heart against God, Rose Packer has prayed and prayed to the Blessed Virgin to intercede without success thus she must take more severe measures: warning this bad girl that should she get into further trouble at school if expelled or even suspended Rose Packer will be obliged to turn her over to Juvenile Court as "incorrigible" and then she'll see!—a few months behind bars at Red Bank like that terrible Sadovsky girl and Rose Packer's niece will regret she'd ever been born.

But Maddy Wirtz whose FOXFIRE names are "Monkey" and (sometimes!) "Killer" does not regret she'd ever been born, this is a girl with happiness coiled in her heart tight and secret as a snake. She's standing there listening silently to her aunt's machine-gun voice knowing that the cold seething anger in the voice like the anger in the near-lashless eyes will exhaust itself if unchallenged: unprovoked: if the girl lowers her head, lowers her eyes, stands subdued and unresisting thinking yes but FOXFIRE IS MY HEART yes but you don't know who I am and you'll never know, you have no power to hurt me I stand here *biding my time.*

And Maddy's conviction turned out to be true, in a way.

I want to state this clearly now, so none of you need feel any pity for me, if you are so inclined. *I did escape.*

"Are you serious?"

"Sure I'm serious."

"But—so quick? So *impulsive?*"

"Who's 'impulsive'? What the hell?"

"—so hot-headed!"

"Oh shit, lay off."

"How am I s'posed to lay off, *I'm* the one's gonna sign the contract, aren't I? I got a right to my opinion."

"Look Muriel: your brains are all in your *belly*. You let me—"

"What! What kind of a thing is that to say!"

"—make my own fucking decision."

Muriel Orvis stands staring in exasperation at Legs Sadovsky, the two of them arguing quietly, in a hallway of the old farmhouse, out of earshot of the real estate agent. All Muriel wants is for Legs to think about this a little longer, overnight at least, she's appealing to the rest of us—so many repairs are needed for this place just to make it habitable, sure she can see it's an attractive property at least the idea of it, like a dream but Jesus the work somebody's gonna have to do! right away, before moving in! and what experience do you girls have keeping up a goddamn household, paying rent and utilities and setting out garbage, if there's even a garbage collection out here which probably there is not, what experience do you have shopping for food, feeding yourselves? And the plumbing's so crude, and the refrigerator's broke, and probably the furnace, and half the windows will have to be replaced, and the floorboards rebuilt where they're about rotted through, and what about cold weather, yes what about when it's a howling blizzard not a warm autumn day what *then?*—Muriel's voice lifting like a soprano's in her appeal to us but none of us is listening, we're in no state to hear.

"You know she's so hot-headed don't you?—are you all so, so—*extreme?"*

Muriel is flushed, short of breath, exasperated with us all; clumsy and maybe rueful, beginning to be frightened, in her advanced pregnancy. Her belly is so watermelon-swollen she must stand back flat on her heels to balance her weight; her shoulders back too, and even, stiffly, her head, as if she's in terror of being pitched forward suddenly. The baby is due in early November but can it wait that long?—can poor Muriel wait that long? (Muriel Orvis's pregnancy, in which Legs has been taking so keen an interest, has not been so happy an experience as Muriel had expected. Maybe, aged thirty-six, she's too old to be having her first baby? Maybe, as Ab Sadovsky, the baby's father, advised, she'd have been better off trying to get rid of it?) Now Muriel's angry to the point of tears—"You! You girls! What do you know! A house even if you're only renting can be like getting married: you want *in* then suddenly you want *out.*"

Legs laughs impatiently and says, "Thanks Muriel, but we can make up our own minds." She's brandishing her wallet, her wallet that's stuffed with bills!—mainly low-denomination bills, ones, fives, but the wallet's stuffed nonetheless. These bills Legs extracts counting out ninety dollars—enough for two months' rent, yes?—amazing her FOXFIRE sisters no less than Muriel Orvis and the real estate agent. Legs' left eye is reddened and watering but her jawline is tough, determined, nobody can doubt Legs knows exactly what she wants to do and she's going to do it. She tells Muriel, "You're nice to be so concerned, hon, but believe me I've been thinking about this for a long time."

"Oh you have? You have, have you?" Muriel demands, hands on her hips, "—just since *when,* smart-ass?"

Says Legs airily, "All my fucking life, if you want to know."

five

Escape

This American city, this Hammond, Uptown and Lowertown so bluntly divided—we'd lived in it without seeing it truly until such time as our beloved FOXFIRE HOMESTEAD became available to us.

Why do you want to leave, we were asked.

Don't you know such things are not allowed, Maddy's aunt Rose Packer demanded of her.

(But did not, as she'd threatened, turn Maddy in to the juvenile authorities. For having a niece in detention, let alone at Red Bank, would have shamed *her.*)

It's true Uptown Hammond was thriving in those years— new multistoreyed buildings on Main Street, a renovated City Hall and County Courthouse, repaved streets, sidewalks. Required to shop for household items now we were living independently, we made our way into department stores, furniture stores, specialty stores selling curtains, drapes, fabric, "appliances." We observed a treasure-trove of goods, a world of *things.* We shopped for bargains until our heads ached with the strain, our back teeth ached from grinding. The house on Oldwick Road was a luminous pit of a kind into which effort might be emptied without end—into which one might fall and fall and *fall.*

Our newest word was FINANCES. FOXFIRE FINANCES.

Maybe it was Legs' expression initially, maybe someone else's. Maybe even Maddy's since here in the notebook is an entire page given over to columns of figures, $-signs looming large, and at the top FOXFIRE FINANCES FOXFIRE FINANCES FOXFIRE FINANCES.

Till you try to live in your own household independent of outside support I guess you don't know what FINANCES means.

Yet our happiness was, we'd escaped Fairfax Avenue. We *foxes!*

Lowertown Hammond looked to be collapsing, you could see signs of its decline on all sides. The rattletrap city buses belching exhaust as they didn't seem to do, at least so bad, Uptown; the diesel trucks thundering along cobblestone streets breaking the streets to hell; cracked pavement where weeds and sapling trees were pushing up. Huron Radiator, Hammond's largest employer (as it was always boasting) had laid off one-fifth of its employees last year with the brazen intention of relocating some of its operations in West Virginia where nonunion workers could be hired, and there was a long bitter sporadically violent strike in effect against Ferris Plastics where Muriel used to work, we saw the strikers marching carrying their red-lettered A.F. OF L. STRIKE signs we saw their drawn faces, worried angry eyes the eyes of men and women who don't control their futures knowing FINANCES are the wormy heart of our civilization, can you live in dignity with such a truth?

The gauzy-gray chemical sky hung low most days but flared up gorgeous citrus colors at sunset—'cause of the polluted air I guess. The odor of old rancid blood from the slaughterhouses along the river (these slaughterhouses shut down since 1949!) permeated the air on humid days. There was a baffled percussive beat to the very air like a great heart beating beating beating invisible.

On Fairfax south of where Maddy and her mother had once lived the Collier Paper Products factory stood untenanted six years after a "suspicious" fire had put it out of business. On Fourth Street the blacktop playground of Rutherford Hayes Elementary School where we FOXFIRE girls had all gone was littered with glass and debris. The World War II tank in Memorial Park facing Father Theriault's old bench (where was the expriest?—since Red Bank, Legs never saw him) was encrusted with pigeon droppings and covered in graffiti; in fact everywhere on walls, sidewalks, even trees were ugly lurid words FUCK SHIT COCKSUCKER NIGGER and crude obscene drawings, the work of neighborhood boys effacing our FOXFIRE proverbs and torches almost completely. So you'd think a long long time had passed since we'd executed them.

Yeah it seemed like a long long time, how far we'd come.

Like we'd gone through Red Bank with Legs, we'd emerged stronger and more *knowing.*

None of these disquieting sights was a true surprise to us FOXFIRE girls preparing to leave the place we'd grown up in. For it seemed all at once Lowertown was leaving *us.*

Like Father Theriault—where'd *he* go?—Legs couldn't find out.

(Maddy'd heard a rumor the old man had died. Or had he been found unconscious on a sidewalk, taken away forcibly to a hospital, committed somewhere "for his own good"—? Maddy thought it wisest, kindest, not to say a word to Legs.)

Legs believed that, when the Revolution came, *if* there was ever a Revolution it wouldn't matter where people live— "All places would be equal, not 'rich' and 'poor.' But that's a long way away I'm beginning to see."

One of our old FOXFIRE fantasies, from the early days, we'd be in disguise in animal masks maybe running along

Main Street in full daylight smashing windows of certain luxury-consumer stores, the jewelry stores the expensive clothing stores the savings and loans companies the insurance companies the banks those sinister-captivating windows displaying silks and silky wools and furs and gossamer fabrics draped on mannequins with stick bodies, small sleek heads and perfectly composed painted faces. FOXFIRE JUSTICE FOXFIRE WRATH and how the glass shattered, how the shards flew, fell, lodged in human flesh, glittering and soundless . . .

It was just Legs and Maddy one October day pausing on Fairfax contemplating the shabby row house in which the Sadovskys had lived, inhabited now by a family of blacks whose name Legs didn't know, the two of them silent, perplexed . . . and Maddy made an uneasy joke or what she'd intended as a joke, noting trash in the gutter, not just the usual broken glass and rotted papers and leaves but the flattened corpse of a squirrel or a rat—the poor thing must have been struck by a vehicle then by subsequent vehicles for days, weeks, its once-living body pounded into the pavement till at last it was pounded flat as a piece of cardboard. So seeing this Maddy said, shivering, "—That's how a thing starts out *real* then ends up just an *idea*. If there's anybody around to think it!"

Legs was standing there hands on hips lost in a dream staring frowning at the front of the old house, the row of houses like faltering steps uphill, downhill, maybe she's thinking of her father Ab she probably loves more than she knows, maybe of her mother so long dead her name never uttered, maybe of that night she ran leaping and flying across those roofs? so it was with an air of forcing herself awake she turned to Maddy, smiled, then grinned, her insolent cheery grin, sliding an arm tight around Maddy's shoulders, saying, "Man that's how everything ends up—an *idea*. Unless it ends up *extinct.*"

* * *

That evening, in Lowertown, FOXFIRE acquired a car— baptized LIGHTNING BOLT once we got it home and painted it, all the exquisite colors of the rainbow pierced along both sides by bronze-gold lightning zigzags.

"Nobody's gonna have any choice about seeing *us* on the road," said Legs.

LIGHTNING BOLT was a 1952 Dodge in "good" condition bought from (of all people) Acey Holman for $225. The chassis swayed a little and looked sort of crooked, maybe from a collision (though Acey swore the car had never been in a collision) and the fenders and bumpers were rusted to lacework, the exhaust bellowed out like an A-bomb cloud but it was a CAR it had WHEELS thus overnight FOXFIRE took its rightful place in Hammond on the streets amid the numerous attention-drawing cars driven exclusively by guys—each gang with its "colors" car as they called it, unmistakable from a distance though the guys' cars had worked-over engines primed for drag-racing and such juvenile behavior while our LIGHTNING BOLT was more noble, dignified, and beautiful.

Also, LIGHTNING BOLT rarely traveled above sixty-three miles an hour. Racing from a dead-stop with some Hawks one night, the guys in a mufflerless roaring old Ford with some kind of fancy engine under the hood, and big wheels, LIGHTNING BOLT began to shudder and wheeze and throw off sparks from the tailpipe like firecrackers!—so that was *that*.

We accepted defeat. We let the Hawks pull away. Where you have no choice you accept defeat knowing some defeats don't matter.

five and a half

Dealing

This isn't any actual chapter just sort of a loose thread attached to the previous chapter.

Just a few words about how Legs acquired LIGHTNING BOLT from Acey Holman who everybody thought was one of the true Enemy: also a guy who hated FOXFIRE's guts for the embarrassment of the car-kidnapping, that people in the neighborhood still talked about, and laughed over.

Yeah we were surprised, nobody more than Maddy (who'd been hanging out with Legs all that day and never had a *hint*) thinking Legs Sadovsky and Acey Holman weren't on speaking terms let alone friendly terms, business terms, and there suddenly Legs is saying c'mon meet me at EMPIRE STATE NEW & USED CARS, Fairfax and Tideman at seven P.M. you're gonna be surprised!—and, sure, we *are*.

In Lowertown, white and black both, no term nastier than *pimp* and *pimp* is a word attached to Acey Holman sometimes, maybe joking and maybe not. Legs used to refer to him that

way too. So we'd thought she disliked him but now she's saying, "Oh Acey ain't bad—Acey's O.K. to deal with."

What the man's business actually was nobody knew, fully.
I guess looking back now I'd say he was a racketeer-
connected small-time crook, he had money but not like the big
guys had, and years later he was shot execution-style, in the
back of the head and his body dumped in the Cassadaga, poor
Acey. Right then in Hammond he had a flashy reputation, he
was a sharpie, the result of gambling debts owed him he had
his thumb in lots of local businesses including this car dealer-
ship EMPIRE STATE NEW & USED CARS where we, or I should
say Legs, bargained for the 1952 Dodge sedan we'd baptize
LIGHTNING BOLT.

Right off, there in the outdoor lot, plastic strips of red banners blowing and snapping overhead in the breeze, Acey
Holman with his black oily-ribbed hair, Dean Martin sleepy-
eyed swagger, expensive clothes that, on him, look cheap,
Acey and Legs start to bargain: he wants $299 for the Dodge
that's "good as new, almost" and Legs is offering $225 "tops"
and the rest of us stand around listening, looking from one to
the other like at a tennis game. Acey is one of those guys got
to touch you when they talk to you, sure enough he's laying a
hand on Legs but Legs is O.K. playing it cool for she could be
very charming when she wished. To men I mean.

I mean, Legs was *always* charming to girls and women,
that was her natural self. To men, she'd play a certain role. It
helped she was good-looking and had that hair that'd draw a
guy's eyes halfway up the block but she knew to deal with
them like she was with Acey, tough-talking trading wisecracks
but "female" too, like in the movies.

Also, Maddy sees: Violet Kahn is here too.

No reason for dumb gorgeous Violet Kahn to be included
tonight with us—that's to say Goldie, Lana, Rita, and Maddy—
except to be *visible*. Staring at Acey Holman, pouty-smiling,
big-eyed, white-powdered skin like moist bread dough and

her FOXFIRE jacket casually unzipped to reveal D-cup breasts snug in a purple cotton-knit sweater.

So Acey's shifty-shiny eyes, trailing off from Legs Sadovsky's face, have somewhere rewarding to *snag*.

Whatever the strategy, deliberate, or not, it works.

After forty minutes or so of banter-bargaining Acey Holman says, "O.K. sweetheart you win: $225 it is. Plus a free tank of gas, and a spare tire almost-new." Eyeing Legs like he's been tonguing her up and down the length of her, he just can't resist. "I can see you're the kind of modern girl means *business* when she says she does."

Legs laughs happily, there's a kind of glisten on her.

Naturally we're all happy—setting up a cheer. Climbing into the car that's now ours.

Toby, tangled in our legs, trying to bark, all frantic and hoarse and comical—Goldie hoists him up and tosses him into the back seat and there's a good deal of laughing all around.

Us FOXFIRE blood-sisters in our black jackets, crimson scarves, excited as little children at Christmas. We have a CAR. At last we have a CAR. Where Legs got the cash for it (and Acey Holman demands cash) nobody knows and nobody's asking we have a CAR.

Seeing us off a while later, leaning into the window on Legs' side and smiling at us all, with a wink for us all, Acey Holman seems amused, maybe just a little smirking if you're sharp enough to gauge it, "—Yeah I'd say you're all *modern* girls. You say *business,* you mean *business.*"

Later, some of us would figure that Acey Holman had never wanted more than Legs' price for the Dodge anyway. Seeing as how it had so many fucking things wrong with it.

But, anyway—that was later.

six

FOXFIRE FINANCES/ FOXFIRE "HOOKING"

How it began . . .

You'd have to say it began with our very happiness our
FOXFIRE HOMESTEAD bearing so sudden and so relentless a
need for FINANCES, always FINANCES sitting up late into the
night shivering in the kitchen the woodburning stove giving
off surges of heat tinged with smoke talking worrying plotting
calculating FINANCES, then wakeful in the first light of morning in our beds scattered through the chilly rooms (not beds
precisely, just mattresses laid flat on the floorboards: smelly
stained second-hand mattresses bought for four dollars apiece
at the Goodwill Shop on Myrtle Street) then continuing omi-
nous as thunder heard in the distance through the long day
though we FOXFIRE girls were all responsibly embarked upon
our separate schedules (Legs, Goldie, and Lana had jobs in
town, Maddy, Rita, and Violet were still going to school, all
rode in to Hammond together mornings in the rainbow-brazen
LIGHTNING BOLT) linked not simply by ties of blood-
sisterhood but FOXFIRE FINANCES as well for as I've stated
(and as Muriel Orvis warned us) this old farmhouse we rented
to live in together like true sisters, this FOXFIRE HOMESTEAD

we loved unceasingly was at the same time a luminous pit of a kind into which our efforts, singly and together, might be emptied without end . . . an actual pit Maddy saw in a dream into which she and the others might fall and fall . . . and *fall*.

Maddy came to wonder, those seven or eight months of her freedom from all adult interference and tyranny, whether it was not the mere fact of *adulthood,* the paralyzing burden of *adulthood,* that had rendered her mother unfit for daily life thus for LIFE: this obsession with calculating the future in terms of FINANCES calculating money brought *in* a household in terms of money going *out* and each month each season with its unnerving variations FINANCES FINANCES FINANCES now occupying pages in the FOXFIRE notebook as occupying hours of talking worrying plotting calculating the monthly rent *plus utilities* the ceaseless need for food thus for food-shopping the need for gasoline for shoes for a new second-hand refrigerator for carpets for dishware for scrub brushes for sofas for insulation for the services of a plumber for rat poison for caulking paste for disinfectant for cigarettes for beer for marijuana with which to get high: *Now you know why it's called getting high, huh?*

Another way to explain what happened to us, what made Legs so desperate thus so reckless thus so cruel or cruel-seeming . . . once you know to look with informed eyes you can never again see the WORLD like a palpable block or shape possessed of permanent dimensions, you can see only its swift shadowy MOTION. For all material things, we have learned in the twentieth century, are but the processes of invisible force-fields.

Thus what's visible is consequence not cause.

Thus you become mesmerized by what is not immediate but has dominion over the immediate, as we of FOXFIRE became so captivated by our FOXFIRE HOMESTEAD that was our paradise and our Purgatory we could think of little else.

Legs saying one night, rubbing her bad eye her mouth slack and doubting—this was the time of her brief shit-job as she called it at Mohigan Meats—"Y'know, a home is the birthplace of *memory* but I'm wondering is it too late for us, almost? How're we gonna dig out the old memories and replace them with *new?*"

About Legs' bad eye which was often inflamed and aching, that tiny blood-speck on the iris: of course we reasoned with her, Maddy in particular insisted see an eye doctor for Christ's sake what are you waiting for?—waiting to go blind?—and Legs never lacked for an answer, saying smiling sure she would go to an eye doctor as soon as she could afford it, or blunt and defiant she'd say, "Why?—look there's nothing wrong *really*, I'm in control of this with my *will.*"

It was impossible to say exactly who lived in our house as later we'd be interrogated 'cause things changed so much. I've mentioned the names of FOXFIRE sisters who rode to town together, but oftentimes there were others of us and sometimes Violet would be living at home in Hammond and several times (and these were times yielding bitter controversy, as you might imagine) girls and/or women not actual members of FOXFIRE would be invited to the house to stay for a night, for days—in the case of Agnes Dyer's older sister (Agnes Dyer was a new FOXFIRE initiate of November 1955) who was being beaten by her damn drunk of a husband and her life threatened *and* the Hammond cops wouldn't lift a finger to protect her, naturally she was made welcome and hidden away by us for as long as required for after all *this was a matter of life and death and at such extremities all women are sisters.*

(Somehow it happened that Agnes' sister's husband found out where she was hiding so one night this beefy young guy shows up pulling into our driveway and slamming on the brakes, he's staggering drunk and bawling his wife's name "Nicole! Goddamn you fuck you Nicole!" threatening to kill her if she doesn't get her ass out there and come home with him 'cause he's had enough of this shit he says, he's shamed in everybody's eyes and he isn't gonna tolerate it so he's pounding on our front door that's locked and bolted for sure then he's at the back pounding on the back door that's locked and bolted too and we've turned off the lights we're watching so he can't see us this guy in just his shirtsleeves circling the house threatening to set the house afire, and it isn't until he throws a rock through the kitchen window that at last we release Toby who's been whimpering so anxious to get outside running leaping to the attack, knocking the son of a bitch yelling on his back in the snow, and now he's begging us to call the dog off he's begging not to be killed himself and how proud FOXFIRE is of our husky guard-dog—unable to bark but growling deep in his throat like the most murderous of wild beasts, every silver-tipped hair of his beautiful coat bristling! and his sharp strong teeth bared like laughter!)

And of course there was Muriel Orvis: poor Muriel evicted from her place in town 'cause she owed back rent, and her infant daughter in the hospital, born premature, a "blue baby" as such were called requiring not one but two heart-valve operations; and when Muriel wasn't at her baby's bedside at Hammond General she stayed with us for where else in her misery was she to stay? (What a wreck of a woman Muriel Orvis was, those months. And how caught up Legs was in the situation—her own tiny sister, as Legs thought of her, so close to death for weeks after she was born; probably never to be "normal"; and my God the medical costs, the thousands of dollars . . . since Muriel had no hospital coverage or insurance, having quit her job at Ferris as she'd had to do, and that bastard Ab Sadovsky never sent her a penny of course.)

Only a black girl named Irene, a friend of Legs' from work, Legs hoped to introduce to FOXFIRE was rejected . . . I'm ashamed to say.

After maybe a week of discussion, debate, quarreling, much bitterness, Legs with three allies (one of them Maddy Wirtz) taking the stand that FOXFIRE should be open to all girls or women needful of protection, or of sisterhood in times of upset, the rest of FOXFIRE voted NO NO NO in a secret ballot. Not that they had any true prejudice against Negroes (they said) not that they were lacking in charity or generosity (they said) but *isn't it best for people to stay with their own kind, aren't they happier that way?*

(In this memoir I've vowed to tell the truth about Maddy Wirtz no less than FOXFIRE, thus let me reveal here that Maddy gloated with childish secret pleasure at Legs' anger with the others; especially the disagreement between Legs and Goldie. Most of FOXFIRE opposed Legs kind of reluctantly, but Goldie, being "Boom-Boom," had to speak her mind, and Legs being Legs spoke her mind in turn. So very quickly some harsh words were exchanged between these two friends who'd always been so tight, with rarely a secret between them. Suddenly Legs is saying, "What gives you the right to veto Irene, or anybody?—you think your ass is so lily-*white?* You're superior to any Negroes, any*where?*" and Goldie's shouting back, "Yeah, right I *am!* I happen to think I *am!* So fuck you, Sadovsky!" and Legs laughs she's so furious, "Fuck *you!*" slamming out of the house that's like a tomb as soon as she leaves . . . driving off in LIGHTNING BOLT gunning the motor and not to return till four in the morning by which time all of her FOXFIRE sisters (excepting Goldie) are in a torment that something fatal has happened to her.

How it begins.
A few days after the blow-up over Legs' black friend (which for FOXFIRE's sake Legs is determined to forget, 'cause she sure can't forgive), Legs does this brash thing without tell-

ing any of us: speaking in her smooth-modulated alto voice she makes an appointment in the city with a party named "B. J. Rucke, Ph.D." who has advertised in the newspaper he's in search of "young men between the ages of 19 and 26 with IN-TELLIGENCE, INITIATIVE, 'WINNING' PERSONALITIES & SALES POTENTIAL." Since her job with Parks & Recreation Legs has gone through several jobs, none very satisfactory and all low-paying, shit jobs she calls them, she's getting desperate.

It's FOXFIRE FINANCES gnawing at her, FINANCES FI-NANCES FINANCES and she's the one responsible, anyway the most responsible. And there's poor Muriel, and Muriel's baby Evangeline, weighing only four pounds six ounces at birth and hardly expected to live . . . who would have dreamt that any baby of Muriel Orvis' would turn out undersized, and who would have dreamt that so much *money* would be required to make things right, always *money MONEY.*

Legs feels a renewed almost a white-hot fury at her father Ab: abandoning Muriel and his own baby daughter, the fucker. Already Muriel owes more than two thousand dollars in med-ical expenses and the end (Evangeline is still in the hospital) isn't in sight.

Like Legs tells her friends it's as if her head is trapped in-side a bell. Her head *is* the bell somehow.

A deafening clamor FINANCES FINANCES FINANCES.

So Legs goes to be interviewed by "B. J. Rucke, Ph.D.," she isn't a young man but she's fed up with the kinds of jobs available in Hammond for young women with her qualifica-tions.

Anyway she's sometimes mistaken for a guy. Slick good-looking young blond guy. Dressed in men's clothes, her hair combed back and up from her forehead in a pompadour, mock-sideburns, no makeup of course and her voice gravelly-low, Legs *is* a guy, in a manner of speaking.

* * *

Legs drives LIGHTNING BOLT to the interview but is cagey enough to park the eye-catching car some distance from the beige brick residence of Mr. Rucke on Merritt Boulevard. She's in a sudden upbeat mood, hopeful, seeing that she's been asked to come to, not an office building, but a private home, a good solid expensive-looking old house on the edge of one of those exclusive residential neighborhoods she'd taken her credulous FOXFIRE sisters trick-or-treating that Hallowe'en night . . . oh Jesus seems like a lifetime ago now.

Rucke's house is on a city bus route, however. Some of the fine old houses on this stretch of the Boulevard have been converted into apartment and office buildings.

Legs' interview is scheduled for six-thirty in the evening, a weird time for an interview, it's night, damp-cold. She ascends the stone steps, rings the doorbell, peers into a dim-lighted vestibule. Though this is December, winter, Legs isn't wearing a coat, she's too vain to wear anything shabby and all she has at the moment are shabby things, she's wearing a rust-colored corduroy jacket buttoned snug against her long lean torso, cream-colored light-wool trousers with a sharp crease and a fly front. Also a white shirt, a striped green necktie Rita tied, giggling, on her; and a cream-colored suede fedora (in the rakish-glamourish style to which black guys in Lowertown are partial) on her sleek head. Leaving the house she'd been embarrassed, maybe a little flattered, that Rita and Lana and some of the others whistled after her—"No fucking around," Legs laughed, "—this is *serious.*"

All our lives that's what we wonder: is this, this-that-is-happening-to-me, *serious?* or maybe not?

If *not,* then . . . ?

As Legs waits on the stoop a young man with a blemished skin, horn-rimmed glasses leaves the house hurriedly, eyes lowered. Though he nearly collides with Legs he doesn't speak: Legs says, *"Watch it, bud."*

More and more she's feeling like a guy, easy in her skin as in her handsome clothes. She knows she's good-looking and it makes her smile not as she'd smile as a girl (for maybe she wouldn't) but just as she is, a young man presenting himself for a job interview at a dignified old place on Merritt Boulevard.

A man of about fifty appears in the doorway, big-headed, fattish-soft, inviting Legs inside. "Hello!—I'm B. J. Rucke," he says, extending his hand, and Legs says evenly, "Hello, I'm Mike Sadovsky," the name rolling smoothly off her tongue so B. J. Rucke accepts it without hesitation though he's looking at her startled, isn't he?—a nervous guy in a brown tweed sports coat with elbow patches, trousers lacking a crease. His handshake is quick, moist, and tentative.

Legs follows B. J. Rucke along a corridor hung with paintings into a handsomely furnished warm-lit room not an office nor yet, to her eye, a domestic space: it has an old-fashioned rolltop desk, chairs upholstered in taffy-colored leather, a wine-red carpet on the floor that draws the eye directly down, it's so beautiful.

Thinks Legs, MONEY.

Smiling showing her good strong white teeth with a salesman's slightly swaggering self-assurance, *he's* the one for the job.

B. J. Rucke begins at once, speaking rapidly. His product is Merritt Encyclopedias, the sales technique is door-to-door, has "Mike Sadovsky" had any experience along such lines?—meeting the public generally?—and Legs lies smoothly declaring she has been "in sales" for years; most recently in the employ of the well-known auto dealer Acey Holman of EMPIRE STATE NEW & USED CARS. "Mr. Holman promised he'd give me an A-plus recommendation," Legs says brightly.

Several volumes of the Merritt Encyclopedia are stacked on Mr. Rucke's desk, heavy volumes stamped in gilt. Legs is invited to examine these which she does, feigning interest, aware of Rucke staring at her, blinking, licking his lips . . . maybe it's rude, to have left on her hat?

B. J. Rucke, Ph.D.: face like a pudding, small close-set eyes, hairs in his nostrils, hairs in his ears. His hair a wan gray-

ing brown, thinning unevenly. Breathing audible as if he's
asthmatic. By his elbow on the desk is a fancy-looking camera
with a prominent flashbulb attachment.

Trying to speak crisply, matter-of-factly, Rucke inquires after Mike Sadovsky's background?—schooling?—where does he
live in Hammond, is he close to his family? He invites Mike
simply to "talk"—to demonstrate his "personality." So Legs
smiling her best sales smile, fixing this strange character in the
eye, chats amiably of the weather, Hammond news, the value
of a good education in the United States, the value of wisdom,
continuing with "self-improvement" all your life.

She's beginning to be uneasy, though careful not to show
it, of the way Rucke's gaze drops as if involuntarily to her feet
(long thin feet, not self-evidently feminine) then lifts slowly, it
might almost be said caressingly, to her face.

Rucke asks her a few more questions, he seems respectful
of her, or of affable Mike Sadovsky, smiling hard at her, one
eye screwed up, until, as if summoning up his courage, he
clears his throat and says, "Your hat—d'you always wear your
hat indoors, Mike? Would you like to—remove it?"

"Sure," says Legs. Careful not to disturb her ashy-blond
wavy pompadour, oiled with a fragrant hair lotion, Legs takes
off the cream-colored fedora and balances it nonchalantly on
her knee. As she does so she hears Rucke's sharp intake of
breath.

Rucke says timidly, "How old are you, Mike?"

Legs' eyes lift calmly to Rucke's and for a long moment
she doesn't answer. What is this asshole? do I have the job or
what? Legs is thinking. She says, "I think I told you I'm twenty-
five."

"But you look . . . younger."

Legs shrugs self-consciously. She feels her face warm; she
doesn't like the way Rucke is staring at her, even drawing
nearer. (He's in a swivel chair, with rollers.)

He says, "Do you shave?"

"Shave? Sure."

"Your face is so . . . remarkably smooth."

Legs shrugs again, irritated. She directs her attention back to the Merritt Encyclopedia, Volume I, A–E, leafing idly through it. Most of her life Legs Sadovsky has been too nerved-up, too restless to sit still and *read;* it's difficult for her to concentrate except on physical, crucial things like for instance the balance required to walk atop a wall or a roof, the coordination required to climb a wall, the lightning-swift dexterity required to get her switchblade knife out of her inside jacket pocket and open and raised to use . . . or, if not to use exactly, to demonstrate she means business.

The doorbell rings, sudden and harsh as a crow's caw. At first, as if entranced by her, Rucke seems not to have heard; then, unsteady on his feet, he rises slowly and distractedly from his chair. "Another interviewee! So soon! Don't worry, Mike, I'll send him away!" He touches Legs' shoulder lightly as if accidentally in passing and Legs realizes what she's been smelling without being entirely conscious of it: whiskey, under a powerful screen of Listerine.

Rucke is gone only a minute, not enough time for Legs to examine the room. She opens several desk drawers but discovers nothing of interest. Papers, documents. Loose-rattling pencils sharpened to stubs. In the center drawer there's an old, much-used leather address book stuffed with scraps of paper, even scraps of paper napkins upon which names and telephone numbers have been carefully recorded.

When Rucke returns he doesn't sit at once but hovers over Legs with an expression of profound . . . is it regret? He sighs, he tries to smile. He gives the appearance of a man whose mind has been near-forcibly changed for him.

He says, "I—I thought I'd be interviewing for days, but—"

Legs says, "You mean I have the job?"

"Well, I—"

"Is something wrong?"

"Oh no nothing is wrong! But I, I—" Rucke's eyes fall on the camera, he says quickly, "—Would you mind if I took your photograph? It's the most practical way, I've found, to—remember a face. To be attached to a file. You know."

Legs stiffens. "O.K., I guess. Do I just sit here?"

"Oh yes! Oh yes! Just—there."

Rucke fusses over the camera, takes a half-dozen blinding shots of Legs who can't help squinting, wincing. Hovering near Rucke murmurs to himself almost musically. ". . . so remarkable. So . . . beautiful."

Legs says, her contralto voice rising sharply, "Look: do I have the job, or not?"

". . . the most extraordinary ethereal *youth* I have ever . . . like a Grecian sculpted head . . ."

I don't believe this Legs thinks staring at Rucke's hand on her knee, she's nearly calm smelling the man's warm alcohol-breath, seeing the raw hope, the reluctance, the desperation in his eyes. It's as if Rucke's very soul is being bent against his will; she senses his anguish; but she isn't going to have any mercy. A man touching her!—*her!* She's so incensed she isn't even frightened as the hand, shy initially, begins to slide up her thigh, now animated, greedy.

Quick as a snake Legs shifts out of Rucke's grip, leaps away, her switchblade out of her jacket pocket as if she's practiced this maneuver many times before. As Rucke stares in astonishment Legs brings the sharp tip of the blade swiftly across his face from left to right, wielding it as if it were a straight razor.

"Oh!—oh my God—"

Rucke stands teetering, dripping blood through his fingers.

"Oh—what have you done! You—you've hurt me—"

Rucke staggers backward and half-falls into his chair. For a vertiginous moment there's the possibility that Legs, enraged, heart knocking almost happily against her ribs, is going to stick him seriously with the knife . . . but Christ no the man is harmless, the man's pathetic. Sobbing ashamed, hiding his face in his hands, saying he hadn't meant to touch only to look, to admire—"Please forgive me! Don't report me! I only wanted—"

Legs says slyly, "Yeah I'm gonna report you! Gonna call the police!"

"No please, don't be cruel—there's no need to be gratuitously cruel—"

B. J. Rucke sits defeated in his swivel chair bleeding through his fingers. He's crying as Legs has never seen an adult man cry and she finds she likes the sight, it's *wild*. If only her FOXFIRE sisters could see. Blood, and tears. *Wild.*

Rucke's murmuring he'd lost control, only for a moment he'd lost control he hadn't intended to touch, just for a moment but—now it's an eternity. Can she forgive him?—that is, can "Mike Sadovsky" forgive him? "Dear, beautiful boy—don't be cruel! You've scarred me! Isn't that enough! No one must know, my family will be—devastated! I swear I've never before—like this—"

Rucke is peering terrified, yet excited, at her; his eyes are wide and dilated; his face creased and webbed with blood. The knife's trajectory is upward from left to right across his left cheek, his upper lip, an inch or so into his right cheek, a wound like a jaunty yawn. Blood runs from it freely yet thinly, the cut isn't deep. If Legs had wanted it deep she'd have made it deep. She says, contemptuously, "You won't be scarred. Don't count on it."

Rucke reaches for his wallet, sobbing he fumbles the wallet and it falls to the floor, he's begging Legs to take all the money he has, to take his watch his ring his camera oh anything, there's more money too, he isn't sure of the sum but there's more money in one of those books on the shelf above the fireplace, in that oversized book Audubon's *Birds of North America* . . .

Deftly Legs stoops to wipe her bloodstained switchblade on the wine-red carpet. In a mocking little-boy voice she says, "Mister, sounds like you're trying to *bribe* me."

* * *

By nine P.M. Legs is back home with us in our beloved FOXFIRE HOMESTEAD, some of us are cleaning up in the kitchen when we hear the LIGHTNING BOLT in the driveway then a minute later Legs comes breezing into the kitchen, tall and lean and glowing-beautiful in her snug-fitting corduroy jacket, long long legs for which she's known and that sly hat slanted over one eye and we're staring at her wondering what in hell she's doing with a camera, big professional-looking camera with a flash, she drops a man's gold-plated wristwatch on the kitchen table, also a heavy gold ring with an onyx stone rimmed with tiny diamonds, also a plain paper bag filled and fragrant with what turns out to be marijuana (meaning Legs has made a Lowertown stop on her way home), and now knowing she has our full attention—those of us who weren't in the kitchen have come running hearing the squeals of surprise, the laughter and commotion—she drops a wad of bills mainly twenties and fifties that will add up to ONE THOUSAND ONE HUNDRED SIXTEEN DOLLARS.

We're all staring struck absolutely dumb like the breath's been knocked out of us.

Till finally: Goldie's so amazed, so in awe, her feud with Legs and her secret decision she hates Legs are immediately erased. She says, staring, "My God! Where'd you get *this?*"

Coolly, smiling, Legs says, "—Just something that got snagged on my *hook.*"

Thus, the birth of FOXFIRE HOOKING.

seven

FOXFIRE HOOKING:
A Miscellany,
Winter 1955–1956

ITEM. In the newly renovated bright-lit waiting room of the train depot, South Main Street, Hammond, New York, amid the numerous holiday travelers seated in rows of attached vinyl chairs there is an alone-looking girl of about seventeen years of age, pretty freckled face and curly red hair and she's a full-bodied girl not heavy but fleshy, solid, sweetly plump. And she's taken her compact out of her purse. And she's peering worriedly at her reflection in the little mirror. And she's putting on more lipstick, pale pink dime-store-glamor lipstick, in the hope that this will help. And this is all she is doing, she's waiting, conspicuous in her aloneness and with that curly red hair, for which train she's waiting is unclear since she entered the station and took her place in a corner of the waiting room at seven P.M. and by seven-forty she has attracted the admiring attention of a fellow traveler, seemingly this gentleman is a fellow traveler, in his mid-forties, stocky, gingery hair receding from his furrowed forehead, there's a fatherly, an avuncular look to him and he's well dressed in a camel's hair coat, we see him approach the red-haired girl before she glances up startled to see him but he's friendly, he's smiling, nothing to be frightened of, nothing to be wary of, he sits beside the girl and soon he's got her relaxed and laughing, giggling behind her fingers, we see that maybe the girl is a little too trusting of this stranger, maybe she's the kind of self-doubting self-critical girl flattered by any gesture of masculine attention, thus naive, maybe too she's desperately lonely since she's on her feet having accepted an invitation from the man to go with him somewhere, for coffee, for a drink, he's leading her out of the waiting room glancing sidelong at her as if unable to believe his good fortune, quick hungry-greedy looks the girl doesn't notice. And they're outside, in the blowy dark. And the man is steering the girl through the parking lot. To his car? Is she naive enough to go with him to his car?

It's in the parking lot we're waiting.

ITEM. In LIGHTNING BOLT six or seven of us drive forty miles to Endicott that's a suburb of Rochester on the New York State Thruway, there's the Hotel Decatur high rise and expensive and lit up like a Christmas tree, and one of us, the one with the dead-white skin and luscious lips, big sloe eyes, sleek black hair falling in curtains around her face, yes that one, you recognize that one, she's dressed in a spectacular black suede outfit, knee-high leather boots, in the lobby of the hotel she's standing searching through her handbag, gorgeous worried-looking girl of an age difficult to judge, could be nineteen? twenty-two? seventeen? and eventually the right man draws near, the first two are politely rejected but the third looks exactly right, and ripe too, taking the hook in his smug little purse of a mouth, his eyes eager, hopeful.

Afterward, speeding back home LIGHTNING BOLT filled with laughter, some of us stoned, wild like matches being struck repeatedly, and Violet Kahn is making us laugh louder telling us: ". . . What I did, I didn't do *anything*. I mean I was ready to, y'know like the last time, start undressing the son of a bitch or something y'know like just unbuttoning his shirt maybe, but it turned out I got lucky I didn't need to do even that, he got scared *I mean real scared* so fast. See, when the bellboy came up to the room with a bottle he had me hide quick in the bathroom so I timed it so I came out just as the bellboy was leaving like, y'know, I wanted help from him but he didn't see me I mean the *bell*boy didn't see me 'cause I'd timed it just right. So this poor asshole, I s'pose he gave me a false name but he said his name's 'Bradley,' poor Bradley's staring at me 'cause I'm so *changed*—in the bathroom I messed up my hair and undid my jacket so it's falling off my shoulder just about, and I'm crying loud, I'm crying so I can't hardly stop which is what happens when I start, it's like running downhill or something y'know?—once you're going it's easy, anyway Bradley says, 'Oh my God, Veronica, what's wrong?' and I'm half-screaming backing away from him saying please don't hurt me, oh please I'm only fifteen years old I don't want to be here, I said I'd run away from home that morning and the police are looking for me probably, my daddy's the kind who'd call the police he's a colonel in the U.S. Army, and Bradley's so scared I think he's gonna faint or have a heart attack or something 'cause everything changed so fast, I mean one minute I'm some kind of a dumb-ass dope coming up to the fucker's room with him, letting him push me in the bathroom and all that, then the next minute I'm crying like crazy and it's a serious situation, like with a minor, right?—so sure he buys me off, he doesn't call it that he says he never intended to touch me, 'Not so much as a hair on your head, Veronica, I hope you believe me I have a daughter myself—' so anyway he counts out this money right from his wallet his hands trembling real bad and I'm crying so hard I can't hardly make out how much it is till going down in the elevator I count it: *two hundred seventy-seven dollars.* And no fucking income tax!"

* * *

ITEM. Her name is Lori, or maybe her name is Louise. Sometimes Lulu who's fun-loving. A shapely girl with eye-catching platinum blond hair waved and curled like Marilyn Monroe's and she can pout her lips like Marilyn Monroe, do that tight-waddling walk like Marilyn Monroe teetering in spike-heeled shoes. A mature girl for her age but what's her age? She's out of school—quit her junior year. She works in Lathrup's Pharmacy. Where the men come in, the married men, the divorced men, the guys with drifting eyes, predator-eyes. Once near closing time in Lathrup's a guy strikes up a conversation with her, makes some awkward jokes and she doesn't encourage him 'cause she isn't that kind of girl in spite of her hair, her red lipstick, her shapely figure she's a good Catholic girl probably, and this guy's a good Catholic husband and father, sure you bet, a little later when she leaves the store there he's waiting in his car at the curb, the car's a true surprise and a good one, shiny-black Lincoln built like a tank, and he's smiling saying he hoped she'd be coming out how's about a ride? just to continue their conversation?

So they wind up in this town north of Hammond, a place called Tannersville. And they're in the Tannersville Inn where the bartender doesn't check ID under the right circumstances. And there's a jukebox. And Eddy Fisher's singing a love song. And Steve gets drunk. He's one of those Irishmen who'll get drunk suddenly like falling down a flight of stairs, no warning. And he's squeezing Lulu's hand, he's half crying. He's forty-seven years old he says can you believe it. He can't believe it. He has a wife, he has five children can you believe it. Lulu says sort of gently she wants to go home but Steve doesn't hear. He's so sad, touching her arm. Brushing the tip of her breast with his arm. So lonely. He says he tried sober for three years, stone cold sober but if that's the life you must live, if that's all the life granted, Jesus you might as well be dead so he's drinking again but only weekends. And they don't know it, at home. And what they don't know won't hurt them. And it's nobody's business anyway. And out in the parking lot in the car Steve tries to kiss Lulu but she slips away, she's scared and seems young now and when he gets in the car she says please drive her home please. So he starts out O.K. then a few miles out on the highway he turns off onto a smaller road. He's half crying. It's hard to distinguish his words. Saying she doesn't know who he is, she doesn't know how he'd value her. Saying he was once her age and that not long ago. Saying he bets she feels bad about her eye, her eye that's sort of out-of-focus or something, he bets young men are cruel about such things, and crude, but *he* thinks she's real pretty. *He* thinks she's beautiful.

So that's that night. And there's another night, and another, and finally Lulu lets him kiss her. But she doesn't let him touch her as he wants to touch her. And he's apologetic. He's so sorry. He's thinking of finding a room away from his house he says but he's scared, d'you know he has never lived alone? never in his life, alone? married his wife when they were just kids in high school, then the babies started coming, and he's never lived alone?—that's a fact.

Oh! is it! Lulu coos.

Lulu *is* sympathetic, bait but also hook.

Lulu *is* devious, hook but also bait.

Steve rents the room on Elmwood Street, Uptown Hammond, not in his own name but by this time Lulu knows his full name, yes and she knows his home address and his business (O'Donnell & Sons Funeral Home—Steve is one of the sons), and she knows other facts about her hopeful lover's life, as much as drunken sobbing self-pitying Steve provides her. And now it's time for money to change hands, it's a newly minted FOXFIRE principle MONEY IS MEANT TO CHANGE HANDS!

You bet.

ITEM. And then there's "Killer" not knowing from one hour to the next *is she happy so happy the happiest she's ever been* living with her FOXFIRE sisters free of the intervention and tyranny of all adults or is she *scared almost all the time scared of what they are doing scared of the police scared of what's to come.* "Killer" in the cheap-stylish fake-fur short coat that Legs bought on a shopping spree post-Christmas, and skin-tight black slacks, Violet's sexy knee-high leather boots, she's eager to prove to her blood-sisters that she's as bold as they are, as willing to take chances to improvise to bring home cash, yes to tell the truth she's excited too for there's a true pleasure in deviousness and meanness yes and in giving hurt to Others especially to men who constitute the major enemy, so one night it's "Killer" Wirtz sitting shy-conspicuous in the bustling waiting room of the Trailways Bus Line, Mount Street, Hammond: waiting for what's to come.

MONEY IS MEANT TO CHANGE HANDS!

FOXFIRE BURNS & BURNS!

In the LIGHTNING BOLT they'd been drinking beer so Maddy's feeling good, in fact she's feeling very good. Smoking a cigarette dragging the smoke deep into her lungs which she likes. It's a rainy cold April night, mid-week, a school night but what the hell, Maddy has been cutting school so much lately, she's so far behind in her work it can't make any difference if she cuts another day, or quits altogether. She's in that happy equilibrium state where you realize suddenly that NOTHING MATTERS except if you give it dominion over you to matter.

Even the burden of worry of FOXFIRE FINANCES has shifted somewhat lately. The hope of one day purchasing the house and property—the monthly bills, payments—the back debts— the several thousand dollars they hope to acquire, to pay Muriel Orvis' hospital bills: these things Legs has taken onto herself, I'll do the thinking says Legs, I'll pay the fucking bills, the rest of you just *assist* however best you can.

From each according to her abilities, to each according to her need says Legs.

A principle she'd acquired from old Father Theriault.

Whom Legs believed must be dead, he'd disappeared from Hammond and no one seemed to know where he'd gone.

Just *assist,* says Legs.

So "Killer" is in high spirits sitting in the Trailways station glancing through a newspaper discarded on a seat beside her, she's waiting, she's bait but also hook, hook but bait, except she isn't alone, several of her sisters are close by outside, she's sixteen years old now but looks younger, rather malnourished, with earnest brown eyes, wavy-kinky brown hair cut short, thin, angular, watchful, wondering. She'd heard them talking about her, her prospects. Lana saying in her superior drawl, Lana who's such a success at hooking, Oh Maddy's a sweet kid but I just don't think she's pretty enough, y'know? and Rita saying vehemently, Hell—Maddy's every bit as pretty as *me,* and I been doing O.K., haven't I? And Goldie who's more and more impatient lately, maybe 'cause she can't ever be bait, thus can't ever be hook, thus can contribute to FOXFIRE FI-NANCES solely by way of her work-wages, or outright theft, she's saying meanly, What I worry about, with Wirtz, she's a coward if it comes down to it: she's sort of not one of us, y'know?

Sort of not one of us, y'know?

Maddy had crept away, stabbed to the heart. Oh so hurt! so incredulous! Not wanting to overhear what the others said in her defense, or if they defended her at all.

Never does Maddy record in the notebook her own doubts of herself, or of FOXFIRE. How, this spring 1956, she has sense enough to know things are coming . . . swerving . . . to an end. Like LIGHTNING BOLT driven to the limit of its speed then just a little beyond so the chassis begins to shake and shudder. The newer initiates in FOXFIRE, Agnes, "V.V.," Marion, Ginny, Toy, are not girls she truly trusts nor does she even know them very well, her old blood-sisters in FOXFIRE are no longer girls she truly trusts nor does she even know them very well excepting Legs of course, always excepting Legs whom she would trust with her life. *Gang-girls, outright criminals, sluts* Rose Packer calls them all and Maddy is one of them, here she *is*.

As through our lives we discover ourselves in such spaces not able to say why, nor even how. *Here I am, I am the one who is here, and no other.*

Thus, "Killer." In the Trailways Bus station, April 8, 1956.

And within a half hour someone approaches her, she's been aware of him for some minutes not wanting to glance up, he sits beside her as if casually, by chance, then begins to chat, casually too, asking where she's going, is she in school, is she alone, isn't it rather late for her to be here alone—and she forgets how Legs has instructed her not to respond to just anyone, any man who speaks to her, the strategy is to size the man up immediately to see if he's a likely prospect, if he's likely to have money, don't for Christ's sake waste time on any deadbeats or bums, don't waste our time, but in her inexperience and confusion she forgets; has no idea how to handle the situation. It's like she's in a boat and no oar and no rudder and she's being carried rapidly downstream not even able to see where she's going.

Oh God. Scared to death.

The man is in his late forties, approximately. A quick superficial resemblance to one of Maddy's favorite teachers at the high school, one of the teachers professing concern for *her,* is further distracting. A graying crew cut, a squinty smile, veined but intelligent-appearing eyes, nicks and creases in his tanned skin. Suddenly this man she has never seen before in her life is not only sitting close beside her but trying to make conversation with her, confiding in her he's newly back north from Florida, Florida and sun so essential for physical, mental, spiritual *health.*

"Killer" stares and blinks. What comes next?

She wonders if her FOXFIRE sisters are watching through the window. She glances in that direction but can't see very clearly.

She's shivering, though the waiting room is overheated.

She's smiling, nodding, the corners of her eyes crinkle with effort. Just smile, just flirt a little, it's O.K. anything you say 'cause they're not actually listening, Legs instructed—all they're thinking about is getting you alone somewhere so they can stick their cocks in you, or some variation of that, don't *worry*.

After a few minutes the tanned man just back from Florida asks the girl in the fake-fur coat would she like a bite to eat?—she looks hungry, he says. With a fatherly-bullying smile.

She says slowly, All right I guess, her stomach clenching but already she's on her feet moving in the direction of the bus station cafeteria, but the man says no, touches her arm, says let's go somewhere else somewhere *nicer*.

So they're outside, on the street. In the damp chilly air. The girl glances around, sees no one she recognizes. Where is LIGHTNING BOLT?—not parked anywhere in sight.

The man is wearing a trench coat, good quality but not new, rumpled as if he's been sleeping in it. He's excited, just the way he blows his nose in a handkerchief is a sign.

Asking where does she live, how old is she, old enough to smoke I guess. Old enough to travel alone. Asking do her parents know where she is and this question "Killer" answers, with startling contempt, vehement as a sneeze, No they do *not!*

The perfect reply, surely.

Walking along a sidewalk, damp glistening sidewalk. Trying to keep her balance. Her companion is saying she's a pretty girl, a girl who must have lots of boy friends, right?

No I do *not!*

Somehow this is funny, hilarious: both begin to laugh.

Gulps of laughter, breath. Is she drowning?—so soon? "Killer" in sexy knee-high boots pinching her toes, blinking as the wind whips up bits of paper and grit. Overhead there's her companion the moon bright and bland tonight as a light bulb, so out of reach.

One of her FOXFIRE sisters living at the house, sharing a mattress with Maddy asked why she was reading those astronomy books, not that the girl called them "astronomy" books precisely, asked what purpose to it if it wasn't being taught in school, and Maddy thought for a moment and said, this most serious of answers she'd be giving through her life, Because the sky is always *there*.

Out of reach but *there*.

"Killer" is saying, laughing, she's hungry yes she is. She's hungry and she wants a steak, she wants french fries and ice cream for dessert. And she wants a drink.

The tanned man says he could use a drink too. Regarding her with fond-anxious interest.

Like she's a frisky unpredictable young animal, a filly about to bolt.

He's taking her to this place he knows, on the river he says, they serve first-rate steaks it's a nice place you'll like it, little girl, I promise.

I'm *hungry*.

Of course you are. And so am I.

They're descending Mount Street passing out of the commercial area, there's a darkened Lorelei's Lingerie where near-naked mannikins stand in stiff ludicrous positions, there's a darkened liquor store, a hefty grate fastened across its front window. As it turns out, the tanned man has his own pint bottle of whiskey from which he sips and which with gentlemanly courtesy he offers to the girl who wants to shove it away in disgust, and his hand too, but she hears herself say Oh yes, yes thanks.

Only wetting her lips and tongue with the scalding liquid, that's enough.

I'm Chick Mallick, says the tanned man—what's your name?

Marg'ret.

What?—couldn't hear.

MARG'RET.

Well MARG'RET you're a pretty girl, a very pretty girl.

Oh yeah?

If I say you are you *are.*

Yeah?

Glancing over her shoulder, quick and scared.

Yes there's the car. A car's headlights in any case. A half block away and moving slowly behind them, following.

Yes it must be LIGHTNING BOLT. Legs promised Maddy she wouldn't leave her out of their sight, hooking's dangerous 'cause it's *war.*

And if it's LIGHTNING BOLT: Legs is behind the wheel, the cream-colored fedora, her hooking good-luck piece, jaunty on her head. And beside her Goldie who's "Boom-Boom" tonight, you bet, grim and erect, waiting for action. And in the rear of the car two new FOXFIRE initiates, Goldie's steely-eyed protege "V.V." and Toy of whom Maddy knows little except like all the new initiates those girls are eager to show their FOXFIRE zeal.

Chick Mallick tries to restrain a belch. Saying softly, touching Marg'ret's fake-fur coat, This is real pretty, honey. Some kind of a fox?

Marg'ret tries not to shrink from him. She knows he's patronizing her. She says, laughing as if at a private joke, Huh!— *fox!*

Chick Mallick laughs too, happily. Under cover of such cheeriness he has taken captive Marg'ret's hand. His big fingers coiled and firm between hers so the absolutely mad absolutely unacceptable thought files through her brain. *Daddy.*

She's choked with indignation.

She's making an effort not to jam Chick Mallick in the gut with her elbow, and run.

Now, says Chick Mallick chuckling to himself—that's real sweet. You're a lovely girl, Marg'ret. Except: are you a runaway?

A what? No I am not a *runaway.*

Marg'ret enunciates the word with fastidious disdain as if it's a quaint obscenity.

Yes? You're sure? 'Cause if you are—

Turning off Mount Street, descending a narrower street, an alley. Can LIGHTNING BOLT follow? Has Legs seen? The wind lifts to greet them smelling of the river. River debris, river death and rot. In a butcher's shop hooks hang empty, awaiting the next day's slaughtered carcasses. The stench of meat, blood, entrails, sawdust is powerful.

Chick Mallick sighs. One of the griefs of human life is how we are *meat*. And dependent through our lives upon *meat*.

Marg'ret shivers. She'd like to crane her neck around to see if there are headlights at the mouth of the alley but she doesn't dare.

Chick Mallick adds, as if this statement followed logically from what he has just said, Y'know, I'd wanted to be a minister once. I started classes at a seminary, in Badgersville, P.A. But it was the wrong time and the wrong place for me.

Says Marg'ret with a sudden wild giggle, I want that steak you promised.

Oh yes! oh yes you're gonna get your steak: that's where we're going.

His fingers gripping hers tight and snug and fatherly, his arm sly-slipping around her waist. Suddenly clumsy, hip-bumping, their walk. His breath is audible and faintly steaming. Smelling of whiskey and something that's a deeper riper sweet, like decay.

Now they turn another time, not an alley so much as a mere passageway between buildings, and Marg'ret so strangely so unaccountably compliant; stiff but compliant. She's thinking of her mother who'd hugged her fiercely once, kissed and kissed and kissed as if to take her breath away, years ago, a mother and her very small daughter, and no words. She's thinking of her father who might be there overhead in the moon, veiled by gossamer-thin clouds.

Half resentfully Chick Mallick observes, In another few years, Marg'ret, you're gonna be a true beauty. Oh my!

The Cassadaga River is below, maybe one hundred feet

away. Is this the way to the tavern?—is this a short cut?—
Marg'ret's too shy to inquire. The two of them like companion-
able drunks, stumbling in a rubble-strewn field where once a
building stood.

Chick Mallick says suddenly, harshly, I know what you
are, I got the word on you: you're a runaway.

No.

You're a runaway, and the police are after you. 'Cause
you're a bad girl aren't you.

No.

A bad bad girl, oh aren't you.

I said *no.*

The police get their hands on you they're gonna do things
to you, little girl, says Chick Mallick, excited, out of breath—
you ain't gonna like. You know that don't you?

You better let me—

You know that don't you?

There's no path where they are, no one to hear. Headlights on the bridge some distance away, a sporadic stream of
vehicles.

Suddenly Marg'ret is crying. Now it's too late she's crying.

Chick Mallick says softly, Bad little girl like you, fucky little girl that's what you are, aren't you? Huh?

He's strong. Gripping her tight, big hands on her shoulders. Trying to kiss her, stooping panting trying to mash his
mouth against hers, force her mouth open with his tongue so
she's panicked and begins to resist, to fight. And he's *strong.*
And he's *angry.* Overpowering her, just the bulk of him, the
weight, he's wrestling with her as if it's a rough kind of play,
if she knew better she would not resist. Fucky little girl, he's
saying, groaning, oh you fucky little girls, soft and caressing
then he's making this strange choked noise *Hah-hah-hah!* he's
leaning so hard against her she loses her balance and falls, she
tries to scream, his hand is over her mouth, *Hah-hah-hah!*
moaning and tearing at her coat, at her slacks, she tries to push
him away but he's too heavy, his knee is between her thighs,

he's hurting her between the legs, looming over her grunting, unsmiling, You will will you? you will? I'll tear your head off, I'll tear your little cunt open! and his weight on her is suffocating, and the mounting pressure of his forearm against her throat. *Oh Momma help me, oh Momma where are you help me,* she's choking sobbing her nose is bleeding, blood trickling down into her mouth so she's swallowing blood, and Chick Mallick has torn her coat nearly off her shoulders, pathetic fake-fur coat considered among FOXFIRE one of their true glamor items, it serves Marg'ret right now her arms are caught in the sleeves as in a straitjacket and he's got her slacks half off as well, he's torn her white cotton underpants and his trousers are open, he's moving lunging against her, his fat cock, grunting and flailing against her like a drowning man *Hah-hah-hah!* and—

And behind him suddenly, above him suddenly and silently there's Legs Sadovsky pinch-faced with rage bringing something down hard on his bobbing head, so hard, with such skull-fracturing precision, he doesn't cry out but just *sighs:* and his weight slides off Marg'ret harmless as sand.

Yes it was unpredictable, and yes it was dangerous.

Yes we came quickly to love it. Most of us, I mean.

No we did not read the local newspapers to see how our HOOKING was being reported or if, given its special nature, it was being reported at all. Legs took it upon herself to scan the news and told us all we needed to know.

Yes we perceived our actions as justified, for so they were.

Yes we perceived ourselves in a state of UNDECLARED WAR.

MEN ARE THE ENEMY!

FOXFIRE BURNS & BURNS!

It's true there was trouble. But it was trouble mostly unrelated to hooking: a few times that winter/spring cars pulled into our driveway, shots were fired at or toward our house by angry men like the husband of Agnes Dyer's sister, who were convinced that FOXFIRE had spirited away their women; twice, officers from the county sheriff's department came to investigate—answering complaints by upset parents that their underage daughters had run away, or, again, been spirited away, to live in a "criminal commune." (When the cops came, the girls weren't to be found anywhere on our premises. Too bad!)

Yes we did fall into the pattern of menstruating at the same time each month, after a while. Those FOXFIRE sisters who lived together in the house, that is. Slept in the upstairs bedrooms on mattresses scattered and laid flat on the floor but outfitted, once we had money, with nice sheets, real woolen blankets. Even bedspreads.

eight

FOXFIRE
"FINAL SOLUTION"

Through the months of FOXFIRE HOOKING which were, over all, hit-or-miss times but mainly profitable, Legs would say, speculatively, so you couldn't gauge was she serious or not, "—Y'know, what we need is one big hook: a final solution: a million dollars, say. Then we could pay all our fucking debts. And all our bills forever. And we could buy this house and live in it forever."

Forever was a word Legs liked. A cool liquidy sound coming off her tongue.

And one of us might say, "Oh sure—a million dollars! What would we do, kidnap a millionaire?"

And Legs would laugh in that languid way of hers, stretching like a big lean cat, "Why not?"

Part

five

one

"... Never to Deny Foxfire in This World or in the Next ..."

Now as we approach the end of the FOXFIRE CONFESSIONS I find it so hard to continue.

Not just because it is THE END.

Not just because I will lose Legs Sadovsky forever.

Not just because FOXFIRE was my heart, and I have had to surrender my heart.

But because in violation of her sacred oath to FOXFIRE consecrated with her own blood Maddy Wirtz failed to behave with the utmost fidelity and loyalty when such were required of her. Because when her purported "verbal skills" were needed, in the composition of the ransom notes, and in the general orchestration of the kidnapping in, in May 1956, Maddy Wirtz refused to cooperate.

Unless "refuse" isn't the right word?—maybe just a sort of cringing-shrinking away?

When the sense of Legs' words struck home, and she realized what Legs was saying: "... The Lindbergh kidnapping was a disaster, the kidnapper, what's-his-name, was an asshole

killing that poor little baby like he did. Killing him right away!
When he should have guarded the Lindbergh baby with his
life! My theory is, a serious kidnapper must be a person of integrity. You hold the hostage until you get the ransom money,
then you release the hostage unharmed; but if the family won't
pay, or can't pay, you release the hostage anyway, unharmed.
That's to show," Legs said with a grandiloquent gesture,
"—good will. *No hard feelings!*"

Maddy just stared. Struck dumb.

". . . What's wrong? You're looking at me like . . . what?"
Legs asked. "You're thinking, a strategy like that wouldn't
work 'cause the kidnap victim's always released, whether the
ransom money is paid or not? But the idea is, of course, it only
has to work *once*—the first time. 'Cause there isn't going to be
any second time anyway, once we have our million dollars."

Maddy turned dazedly aside, pressing the tips of her fingers against her eyes. Not a word.

Legs said, beginning now to be impatient, "Look: no one's
gonna be *hurt*. No one's gonna *die*. But that would be our secret. If the family pays, or if the family doesn't pay, the hostage
will be released."

So Legs talked. Cajoled. It was sometime after three
o'clock in the morning, the others were asleep upstairs, Legs
and Maddy were alone together in the cellar, in the corner of
the cavernous earthen-floored space used for FOXFIRE
meetings.

". . . We wouldn't proceed with the first step, Maddy, if we
didn't already know the final step. Hell, we'd be in control all
the way, ahead of time, y'know?—like on some high tower
looking down so we could see things nobody else could see?
Y'know?"

This corner of the cellar was warm because of its proxim-
ity to the coal-burning furnace; because too it had a few pieces
of Salvation Army furniture, and the crude stone walls had
been hung with brilliant flame-red fabric remnants, satins,
silks, even a strip of antique crushed velvet, slightly soiled but

still beautiful. Illuminated by the flame of an old kerosene lamp this secret space had seemed to Maddy from the first, yes it must have seemed so to all her FOXFIRE sisters, the most precious of all their secret spaces.

How like the inner chambers of the heart.

Except, at this moment, stricken with dismay by her friend's words, Maddy Wirtz would have been incapable of such a thought. She was trying just to maintain her composure. Her back stiff, as if bits of ice were lodged between the vertebrae.

Legs said, ". . . You wouldn't be involved with the kidnapping itself. I don't intend that. Like taking the guy from his house, or wherever. Bringing him here. Using a gun I guess— not *you*. No you'd just help with the planning, I thought. You and me figuring everything out. The perfect ransom note to write, or maybe we'd need more than one; get them ready ahead of time, y'know? So there's no last minute panic and fuck-up."

Still Maddy did not speak. Could not speak. Thinking *No* not wanting to think *No* not daring to think *Oh Legs oh no: never!*

Legs fell silent, regarding Maddy. One of those long long moments.

". . . Hey 'Killer'? *No?*"

Laying her hand gently, not in her usual rough-playful manner, on Maddy's shoulder.

Since "Chick Mallick." Since that terrible night. I was afraid of you I guess. You saved my life but I was afraid of you having seen you hit him the way you did.

And the others. My sisters. So wild, frenzied. Striking with fists, boots. Slamming him with lengths of iron pipe, anything they could snatch up from the ground.

Like Uncle Wimpy, years ago. Except this time it's serious.

A fierce gleeful FIRE rippling through you, my sisters, but not through me.

So days later Legs when you forgave me for being so stupid, yes it could have been a fatal mistake letting "Chick Mallick" (which was not his name, as the identification in his wallet revealed) walk me off the street where you almost lost me, days later you saw in me what I could not see in myself. You saw, though I was crying, I was so grateful to you Legs for forgiving me, for loving me, as always.

You poked me in the old way, teasing, playful-hurtful your fist against my shoulder, you said, "O.K. honey—if you want to leave, if you want to quit FOXFIRE, I understand. I can make it O.K. with the others too."

But all poor scared Maddy-Monkey could say, then, crying like her heart was broken, was, "—But where would I go?"

The Plot (I)

Always there was that side to her of silence and secrecy, like a planet in part-eclipse, leading you to believe that what was *partial* was *whole;* so it should not have surprised us that, after Legs Sadovsky's "death" (I say "death" not death because her body was never recovered from the river) things came to light concerning her we had not known, we who believed ourselves her closest FOXFIRE sisters.

We who survived, I mean. Oh yes!

For instance, recall in the old days before even FOXFIRE how Legs would surprise us with small gifts and treats, taking us to the movies, several times we'd gone roller skating, and by bus "excursion" (as Legs called it) to Rochester, and such surprises were like a magician's tricks, the revelation of *something* where you'd have expected *nothing,* yes and taken *nothing* as your due. But Legs' secrecy had always to do with these revelations and with generosity springing from . . . just what, we didn't inquire.

"D'ya s'pose she's *stealing?*" Rita once asked Maddy and Lana, not in a tone of alarm or even mild disapprobation but in one of sheer childlike curiosity; and Maddy and Lana laughed, and said, "You want to know, ask her." But Rita didn't ask. Nor did Lana and Maddy, ever.

So later it came to light, by way of the testimonies of people who'd known her with no connection at all to FOXFIRE only to Fairfax Avenue and the old neighborhood, that she'd been involved in their lives, not continuously, yet faithfully, over a period of years. Like a flash of lightning Legs would appear, disappear, and appear: she'd drop by to visit, say, an elderly woman who'd been a neighbor on Fairfax, somebody's sister's mother-in-law now a widow; she would bring a plastic radio for the woman, or one of those lavish fruit baskets, or a big bouquet of roses (picked by Legs herself in a public park?), or just a gift of cash: four twenty-dollar bills, new and crisp, left inconspicuously behind on a kitchen counter. There were children, there were young wives, there were "religious" people—we'd known about the defrocked priest Theriault but we hadn't known about a nun in her sixties attached to the St. Vincent de Paul Elementary School who was a second cousin of Ab Sadovsky's thus "blood" kin to Legs herself, and this woman Legs supposedly "took guidance from in spiritual matters" (meaning what?); another nun, a sister Mary Joseph of the Sisters of Mercy, whom Legs seems to have met while both were riding a city bus years ago, believed herself an "older, spiritual sister" of Legs' as well, though she knew Legs as "Margaret Ann Mason."

Everybody in Lowertown, blacks as well as whites, seemed to have known Legs, or to have known of her. Whether to disapprove, like the parents of FOXFIRE gang-girls, or to defend her as good-hearted, generous, high-spirited. Even Acey Holman!— but what connection there was between Legs and *him,* Maddy Wirtz never cared to discover.

(After we bought LIGHTNING BOLT naturally all sorts of things began to go wrong with it. And some of us, Goldie most vocally, thought we should ask for some of our money back. But Legs said quickly, "Nah—a deal's a deal. Acey wouldn't refund us shit. What he'd say is, nobody holds a gun up to any-

body else's head to make him buy anything. That's one principle of fucking capitalism you gotta accept.")

The most unexpected connection of Legs Sadovsky's was
her friendship, unless maybe "friendship" is the wrong word,
with the rich man's daughter Marianne Kellogg.

Nobody knew a thing about it, and one day, in November
1955, when we'd just been living in the Oldwick house about
a week, Legs breezes into the kitchen, tosses down the
Hammond newspaper opened to the society page, and says, in
that teasing voice of hers you don't know whether she's serious or not, "See that 'Greek Revival mansion'?—yours truly's
been a guest there."

The newspaper photograph is of a millionaire's house,
with columns like a temple, and a caption identifying it as the
residence of the old local family the Kelloggs—this name everyone in Hammond knows, without always knowing why.
Turns out Legs knows the daughter of Whitney Kellogg, Jr.—
she'd met up with her at Red Bank!

Not as an *inmate,* as it turned out (though Legs teases us
for a while pretending this might be so) but as a *visitor* on an
errand of Christian mercy.

Legs tells us about the Big Sister–Little Sister Christian
Girls' Program; those visits to the prison, six of them in all,
from the proper young ladies of the United Churches of
Hammond Auxiliaries—how the visits quickly went sour since
even the nicest Red Bank girls, among whom Legs did not
count herself, came to resent their visitors' unquestioned as-
sumption that they were blessed with the love of Jesus Christ
and genuine knowledge of Him, as the poor Red Bank girls
were not.

But Legs and her rich girl Marianne got along like old
friends, Legs saw to *that.*

Not that she realized Marianne was *a* Kellogg, from so
prominent a family, 'cause she didn't, till later.

But: "I could see she was from some place, like some other dimension, different from mine like night and day. Just to look at her, just to *smell* her! And this sweet sort of crazy way she talked, so I could see she was a good person in her soul; and intelligent too, only not just smart. I never asked questions direct, y'know, but just sort of poked about, the way a boxer works his jab, to begin with. I figured this was the way certain kinds of rich people must be without knowing it, the ones that don't make the money themselves only grow up inhabiting it. And I could see too, in her, she's like one of those birds they found on some island in the Pacific, explorers discovered they were species that couldn't fly. Their wings were short and stunted 'cause there hadn't been any mammal-predators on the island, I guess for a thousand thousand years, so the birds hadn't *needed* wings, and they'd lost them. So any bird-eating mammal that comes along—"

Legs snaps her finger, smiling.

After Legs was released from Red Bank, Marianne Kellogg invited her to her house for a visit; and asked would she like to attend church services at Grace Episcopal Church which was Marianne's family's church. Legs accepted the first invitation, declined the second. In fact, without telling any of her FOXFIRE sisters, Legs visited the "Greek Revival mansion" owned by the Kelloggs several times: yes she'd met Mrs. Kellogg but not Mr. Whitney Kellogg, Jr. who'd made millions of dollars in some kind of steel-processing business.

Everyone has questions to ask Legs about the house and the Kelloggs but Legs loses interest in the subject suddenly, the way she does. Breaks off in the middle of a sentence, snatches up the newspaper and tosses it into the woodburning stove where it bursts into flame.

Screwing up her face like there's a bad smell in the air.

Next time we hear the name "Kellogg" it's six months later.

Legs informing us, one night at supper, that Whitney Kellogg is our man, she's figured it all out.

Says one of us, not sure she'd heard correctly, "—'Our man'?"

Says Legs, "The *X* in our plot."

Says another of us, puzzled, "—'Plot'?"

Says Legs, "FOXFIRE's 'final solution.' So, y'know, we can buy this house, and nobody can make us leave. We can live here *forever.*"

That instant, all around the table, all of us, including Maddy Wirtz, we know.

three

"Windward"

The first time Legs Sadovsky was a guest in the Kelloggs' house she'd felt herself so *young,* as if she'd shrunken in actual size. Weird!

She'd felt all her senses, every quivering nerve, alert, strained, to the point of pain.

Yes she'd wanted to come, all her cunning bade her here, but no she had dreaded coming dreading she would like it too much, but yes sure she'd wanted nothing more passionately: hadn't she as a girl of eleven or twelve, loosed to the night streets (Ab Sadovsky being out or worse yet home, drinking) wandered for hours, miles . . . drawn as if by perverse gravity to these Uptown streets, to contemplate the baronial private homes of Whitchurch Drive, Pembroke Avenue, Merritt Boulevard, Jelliff Place . . . fantasizing how she would one day enter, mysteriously empowered, maybe even invisible, to wreak such damage as she wished: or, if she wished, to wreak no damage at all.

Never had she fantasized being invited to enter, though. Being invited made her clumsy, tongue-tied. Like a guy in a movie knocking at a door and a beautiful girl answers, and he's here to say he loves her.

Seeing though that Marianne Kellogg was nervous too, winding a strand of hair around her forefinger, repeatedly licking her lips—that helped. It was Legs' thought that only one person out of a pair needed to worry, about anything.

Thus the intruder/predator's advantage.

The house, "Greek Revival mansion" belonging to Mr. and Mrs. Whitney Kellogg, Jr., 8 Jelliff Place, built atop a wooded bluff overlooking the Cassadaga River, pale pink limestone, granite, white-painted brick, four tall Doric columns that did truly suggest a place of ethereal worship, was unlike any house Legs Sadovsky had ever seen: not just because of its massive fastidiously tended lawn, and the ten-foot wrought iron fence surrounding it completely, or the fact, dazzling to Legs' hawk eye, of its sumptuous Neo-Greek furnishings and decorations, but because, so strangely, it had a *name*.

Proudly proclaimed in six-inch brass letters on one of the gate posts: "WINDWARD."

That first visit, casting about for something to talk of that wasn't Christian piety, nor had any embarrassing reference to Red Bank, Legs had inquired about the name. How open-faced how childlike in her curiosity about the name!—this reform-school girl now hoping to be, in Marianne Kellogg's kindly eyes, truly *reformed*. (She had dressed nicely for the visit. One of her FOXFIRE sisters had done her nails, ordinarily dirt-edged and uneven. Around her neck, on a thin gold chain, was a small gold cross of uncertain origin.) And Marianne Kellogg happily responded with a family tale of a kind she'd inherited, thus comfortable, even amusing in telling it, knowing how to smile and laugh with it at the forgivable pretensions of an American moneyed class, "—So 'Windward' is named for that castle, near Edinburgh, only the name really, nothing but the name, because of Daddy's family connection which isn't I guess a very close connection but mainly they called it 'Windward' because it's so windy up here, and frigid, in the winter. Oh you can't imagine, Margaret, how bitter cold, sometimes—"

Marianne Kellogg shivered, as if the wind were blowing on her right this minute.

Was there some kind of code here?—the rich man's daughter warmly dressed in a pretty white cashmere sweater and a plaid-pleated tartan skirt, the kind with the fussy little straps and buckles, white-ribbed knee socks yet she shivered so Legs Sadovsky understood: she who'd lived most of her life in slummy Lowertown, Hammond, was expected to display girlish spontaneous sympathy for the fact that somebody's daddy had inherited from his daddy a big house high upon a hill above the Cassadaga River where the wind from Lake Ontario, and beyond Lake Ontario from Canada, could sweep unimpeded over them.

Fuck you, Legs thought.

"Oh I guess I *can* imagine!" Margaret all big-eyes and fingering the little cross around her neck exclaimed.

Was there ever, in the Kelloggs' downstairs front sitting room, a Red Bank reform-girl so conspicuously so heartrendingly *reformed?*

Marianne Kellogg chattered. Spoke enthusiastically of the Big Sister–Little Sister Program they'd been told was such a success. Spoke enthusiastically of her church group, her girl friends. Spoke enthusiastically of Cassadaga Women's College where she was studying Latin and French. Spoke enthusiastically of her mother and father who believed in education for girls—that is, women. It was tricky to avoid speaking even indirectly of Red Bank but Marianne avoided some embarrassment by using the term *facility*—"Do you keep in touch, Margaret, with any of the girls you met in the facility?" And Margaret replied, quietly, just the faintest hint of surprise and rebuke, "Oh!—they don't want us to, y'know. 'Specially you're not allowed to visit or write to anybody still *in.*"

"Oh I'm sorry—I didn't know," Marianne said, blushing, adjusting her pink-plastic glasses on her nose.

Shortly after this exchange Mrs. Kellogg entered the room: professing herself eager to meet "Margaret" of whom she'd heard so much. So the awkward moment passed.

Mrs. Kellogg was a fluttery pear-shaped woman in her mid-forties, fair-skinned like her daughter but rather heavily, even coarsely made up, with elaborately styled silvery-brown hair. If this was an ordinary weekday at home for her she was strikingly dressed in black wool and wore a good deal of jewelry including sunburst gold earrings. The remainder of that day's visit consisted of Mrs. Kellogg's kindly cheerful chatter as Margaret, this most *reformed* of reform-school girls, listened gravely and respectfully; murmuring appropriate words of girlish interest, admiration, curiosity, wonderment, and assent. Oh yes? Oh really? Oh! Margaret sat primly erect, her narrow shoulders back and her chin uplifted though not too uplifted; her lips, shut, were shaped to a small attentive smile. She wore a neat tailored gray skirt and a gray-and-white striped blouse and stockings and flat-heeled patent leather shoes, like Sunday.

As Mrs. Kellogg chattered Legs looked from mother to daughter, daughter to mother. Envying them? Oh but why?—*she* would not care for such a fussy-affectionate older woman overseeing *her.*

Rich man's wife, rich man's daughter. Class enemies, they were. All unknowing—unguessing.

The three were seated in a beautiful octagonal room with a view of a steep-sloping section of the grounds. Such quiet. Too much quiet *you could go crazy hearing yourself think.* The furniture was curvy-clunky to Legs' untrained eye, what's called antique she supposed, meaning old, expensive. Much carved wood; velvets, silks, brocades; vases and figurines on the tables, in profusion. And what comical carved feet on the chairs—fans, scrolls, claws, paws, even *cloven hooves.* On a marble-topped table beside Mrs. Kellogg was a ceramic lamp with an enormous stained-glass shade of exquisite reds and blues, purples, sunbursts like true sunlight, which Mrs. Kellogg identified proudly for Margaret as an "authentic" Tiffany lamp; close by was a squat ornamental cabinet of marble, polished wood, zigzag lines and small carved heads which Mrs. Kellogg identified as an Egyptian Revival piece she'd found herself in a second-hand furniture store in Albany—selling for a fraction of its worth.

Of course, these things *were* beautiful. Even if you hated them, the idea of them, they were beautiful.

The powerful smells of furniture polish and floor wax underlay everything, though. Legs, noting the gleaming parquet floor, fell to thinking how, to have a floor like that, somebody had to get down on her hands and knees, and *wax*.

At Red Bank they'd kept the girls busy, cleaning the floors especially. Sweeping mopping scrubbing polishing where polish would take, the idea being to clean before there was dirt.

Mrs. Kellogg paused, a beringed hand raised to her throat. She'd been talking of the United Churches of Hammond Auxiliary of which, she'd modestly said, she was an officer; she'd been talking of Mr. Kellogg—"Whitney"—and his work with local youth services. She asked Margaret what were Margaret's plans for the future enunciating "plans for the future" as if the words signified a somber but respectable disease, and Margaret said murmurously, her knuckly hands clasped in her lap, her eyes discreetly lowered, that she thought oh she was thinking she'd go to business school someday when she saved up enough money from her job.

"What is your job, Margaret?" Mrs. Kellogg asked.

"—Salesgirl, in Kresge's."

"Oh on Main Street?—we go there all the time, don't we, Marianne? We *love* Kresge's for things like, you know, thread and—buttons."

"I meant Woolworth's. Down on Mount Street."

"Is it satisfying work, Margaret? Or is it just *work?*"

Margaret frowned and thought as if such a concept was new to her.

When she didn't reply Mrs. Kellogg said in a burst of feeling, the color up in her cheeks as it was in her daughter's, and her eyes shining with good intentions, "You might, you know, want to think, Margaret dear, of allowing us, I mean Whitney and me, to help you with schooling. To become, you know, trained in one or another line of—useful work. Business school is such a good idea! There is a very fine school right here in Hammond, I believe Whitney has hired a number of girls from it over the years. Secretaries, filing clerks, stenographers, oh I don't know what all—bookkeepers? He says it's a *fine* school."

Seeing an indefinable expression on her guest's face Mrs. Kellogg paused, and said hesitantly, "It *would* be a good idea, Margaret, wouldn't it? For your future?"

With her polite measured smile Margaret said, "Oh as long as it isn't charity, I mean if it's just a *loan*"—unless it was Legs who spoke, startling Mrs. Kellogg and daughter.

Which put them in their places without being insulting.

Before leaving Windward Legs used one of the guest bathrooms, a place of lime-green tessellated surfaces, spotlessly gleaming fixtures, a toilet built into a teakwood frame that flushed so silently, stirred its waters so gently, Legs worried at first it hadn't flushed at all. In a mirror with a mother-of-pearl frame her face floated annoyingly pale and insubstantial, the tiny blood-speck on her left eye glistening like a tear. She'd combed her hair girl-fashion for the visit, slantwise across her forehead and covering her ears so she didn't look so stark, so masculine. But there was her gaze, steely-cold, faintly derisive. Her high flat sharp cheekbones. "Well—fuck *you*," she whispered.

Yeah she was disappointed. The rich man's wife and the rich man's daughter had gotten the best of her, somehow.

She'd had no thought that day, none at all, of extracting money from the Kelloggs. It was true, she didn't want charity from them, or from anyone; even less would she'd have wanted a loan to attend the Hammond School of Business— *the Hammond School of Business! Legs Sadovsky!*

As for the possibility of kidnapping and ransoming one of the Kelloggs, let alone the absent Whitney Kellogg, Jr.—the thought never occurred to her at all. If it had she'd have rejected it as crazy.

She pocketed a little scallop-shaped gold thing, an ashtray?—candy dish?—her hand brushed over, on a table in the hall. She smiled thinking how they'd feel obliged to invite her back one more time at least, these Christians. To show they didn't suspect her.

Next visit, next month, no Mrs. Kellogg—"Mummy is with her hospital-volunteers group"—just Marianne Kellogg with a sweet uneasy smile, hopeful eyes. Legs perceived she was a good-hearted girl, maybe it wasn't her fault her daddy was a rich capitalist, known for his hatred of unions. Maybe someday Marianne would reject her background, come live with FOXFIRE.

What a coup that would be, Legs thought dreamily. To bring a rich girl into the gang!

But, in the Kelloggs' house, just stepping inside the front vestibule, breathing that air, Legs Sadovsky felt *young* as she felt nowhere else. Physically smaller, weak-muscled. Arms and legs atrophied like a polio victim's.

And she'd worn a dress for the visit, a cotton shirtwaist fastidiously laundered and ironed by one of her FOXFIRE sisters, yes and those same damned shoes, and stockings. How Legs detested stockings! Garter belts! The paraphernalia of femininity! Marianne Kellogg, hair bobbing in a ponytail, wore bermuda shorts, pull-over shirt, white anklet socks and sneakers.

Thus the tone of this second visit at Windward differed considerably from the first. It was as if something had taken place between the girls, in the interim. Marianne was gay, giggly, self-conscious, inspired. Leading her friend Margaret on a tour of the grounds, proudly showing her Mummy's rose garden, Mummy's "white-flower" garden, Mummy's clematis vines. (In the rose garden, a grizzle-haired hunch-backed black man was tilling the soil, glanced up smiling mumbling "H'lo Miz Kellogg" so how was the rose garden Mummy's effort exclusively?) And there on a hill behind what had been a stable was Marianne's own garden, her "victory garden" she called it, a plot measuring twenty feet by twenty-five in which tomato plants grew twining upward on stakes, and rows of carrots, cantaloupes, green beans in a profusion like grape vines on netting—"Daddy's favorite vegetable is green beans," Marianne said, as if offering her friend a secret, "—he loves them *raw*. Comes out here sometimes smoking his cigar and eats them off the *vine.*"

Margaret said, "My father too. When he was alive, I mean."

Marianne said, "Your father died in the war, you said?"

"I guess. His body was never recovered."

"And—your mother—you said—"

Margaret murmured something vague, sorrowful.

Marianne said, hesitantly, backing off from the subject, "It must be so—hard. The tests Jesus gives us, to show our faith in Him."

Margaret was combing her hair back off her forehead with her fingers, vigorously. Back behind her ears. She surprised the rich man's daughter by giving her a flare of a smile, white teeth and slitted eyes. "Nah. Not if He's in your heart all along, it's *easy.*"

Next Marianne showed Margaret her room on the second floor of the house, just the prettiest room you'd imagine all pinks, crimsons, candycane stripes. A four-poster canopied bed piled with old-fashioned pillows in embroidered pillowcases like the embroidering older women in Lowertown frequently did, those immigrant-women who still spoke Czech, Polish, Hungarian, German in preference to English—Legs was disoriented for an instant, overcome with an inexplicable rage. *How the fine handiwork of the poor, the exhaustion and deple-*

tion of their souls, slave-labor, wage-slave-labor, ends up in-eluctably in the possession of the rich, and it was Father Theriault speaking in her, it was Legs' own voice, yes she knew it was an unreasonable voice for very possibly this beautiful needlework had been done by idle rich ladies for their own pleasure, and what of that?

And if the laborer willingly even eagerly sells his labor, if nothing is to be done, after so many millenia, to transform the greedy soul of man, what of that?

Atop a white bureau were numerous photographs in gilt frames, shocking to Legs' unsentimental eye there could be so many Kellogg family members? relatives? men, women, children dear to the heart of Marianne Kellogg?—as Marianne proudly pointed out Mummy, Daddy, herself as a little girl; then Grandma Kellogg, and Grandpa Kellogg; and Grandma Croome, and Grandpa Croome; Aunt Matilda, Uncle Simon; Aunt Effie, Uncle Stephen; cousins Jill, Ethan, Mason, Bo; here a portrait of Mummy and Marianne when Marianne was ten, and here—*this* was the photograph that truly interested Legs—a portrait of Daddy, a nearly bald man with a powerful-looking head, an odd wide dimpled smile, button-shiny exuberant eyes that seemed to lift off the surface of the print. Whitney Kellogg, Jr.!—"Isn't Daddy handsome?" Marianne asked. "I mean—in his own way."

Margaret, this most *reformed* of reform-school girls, considered the touched-up studio portrait for a long solemn-admiring moment. Then said softly, "Oh yes! His soul's right there, shining in his eyes."

"I have an idea, Margaret," Marianne said excitedly, more like a girl of ten than a young woman of twenty, "—why don't we all go to church together, next Sunday? I know Daddy would *love* to meet you."

"*Next* Sunday?—I have to visit my grandmother up in Plattsburgh."

Legs spoke quickly, instinctively. She guessed she should meet Whitney Kellogg, Jr. since she should know the Enemy, but she did not want to, much; though staring contemplating the rich man's likeness she was, that day, so innocent of the wild notion of extracting money from him or by way of him she had no wish to see *him* at all.

"Maybe the Sunday following?" Marianne asked.

Said Margaret doubtfully, "Maybe."

Next, Marianne showed Margaret a guest room lavishly furnished in period antiques; then, Mummy's "sewing room"; then a balcony, and French doors, overlooking an edge of the lawn and an open swath through evergreens down to the river. Margaret, silly poor-girl, said naively, "Isn't it lucky the forest grew like that, you can see right down to the *water,*" so Marianne was obliged to explain, embarrassed, "Oh no Daddy has the trees cut like that, and trimmed. For the 'vista.' "

At the farther end of the long corridor was the elder Kelloggs' quarters, as Marianne called them: "Mummy's and Daddy's private suite, where they prefer I didn't go." Margaret said, curiously, "You mean you can't see their bedroom?" and Marianne said, "They have a suite, I've seen it hundreds of times. But it's, you know, private for them, like my room is private for me."

Margaret continued walking as if oblivious to Marianne's utterly reasonable words.

Margarét, breezy, long-legged, her ash-blond short-cropped hair back behind her ears.

Marianne followed beside her. "Margaret?—where are you going?"

"Just down here a ways."

"Oh but—like I said—this is Mummy's and Daddy's private suite and they prefer—"

"But they aren't home, are they?"

"No, but—"

"*Are* they?"

"But—"

Boldly Margaret Sadovsky opened the door and stepped inside.

So abrupt and so complete was the change in her, Marianne Kellogg could barely comprehend it, let alone respond. And what could so well-bred a girl do in such circumstances—stop her guest by force, cry for help?

It might have been then that Marianne recalled the missing scallop dish, the mystery of its absence.

The elder Kelloggs' suite consisted of an anteroom of sorts, with a lady's dressing-room attached; a bathroom; the bedroom itself, a room of graceful proportions furnished with Neo-Greek period pieces, including an enormous bed in a state of being aired; and a gentleman's dressing room, an entire wall of which was a closet, its several louvre doors partway open, as if a housemaid had been interrupted in the midst of tidying up.

Marianne was saying, begging, not quite daring to touch this intruder's arm, "Oh dear, oh Margaret, I think we'd better *go*. If Mummy knew she'd be so upset—"

Margaret, poking about in Mr. Kellogg's closets, seemed not to hear. She marveled that one of the closets was filled with woolen suits in dark shades and tweeds; another was filled with suits in lighter shades and tweeds; another consisted of shelves of sweaters and shirts neatly folded, in transparent plastic bags; yet another was shoes—dress shoes, sports shoes, slippers—arranged in pairs and rows; yet another was neckties, a spectrum of ties ranging from light to dark. So many! And such quality!

"Oh Margaret *please*—"

Atop a high shelf in one of the closets were a dozen hats with the look of hats no longer in favor. Golfing caps, fedoras, a straw boater, a black bowler—Margaret hooked the bowler on her forefinger, spun it around, smilingly placed it on her sleek blond head and went to a mirror to examine her reflection. The hat was overlarge for her but *stylish*. Yeah *nice*.

The mirror was full-length, taking the light from a pair of French doors across the room and casting it into Margaret's face. Her flat high cheekbones, her eyes. Those eyes seeking out Marianne Kellogg's in the mirror.

Marianne clapped both hands over her mouth in childish horror and glee. She gave a little scream—"Oh Marg'ret! Ohhhh!"

Margaret turned prankishly, and bounded toward her. Clapping her hands to scare. "Daddy's gonna get you, honey—WATCH OUT DADDY'S GONNA GET YOU!"

Marianne stumbled backward twisting a foot in an eiderdown bolster draped like a great snake across the bed, she squealed and laughed wildly as if tickled and ran into the adjoining room and Margaret in the black bowler hat sly and crooked over one eye pursued her, and a chair of antique cherrywood teetered drunkenly on its legs, and a table bearing a display of family photographs overturned, and a housemaid's round astonished face emerged balloonlike in a doorway, and neither girl paid the slightest heed, neither saw the face at all, as, Marianne squealing in flight and Margaret ruthless and grinning in pursuit, they ran noisily in the lady's dressing-alcove from which there was no escape, into a dead-end of rose-tinted mirrors, in an airless pocket of female fragrances— talcum powder, perfumes, hand lotions, hair sprays, deodorants—where Margaret in the bowler hat dared seize Marianne with her hair in a ponytail roughly around the waist, pretending to kiss her, and laughing losing balance tripping *did* kiss her, in any case mashed her lips and the hard damp teeth behind them forcibly against Marianne's protesting mouth.

"—Told you, didn't I?—DADDY'S GONNA GET YOU!"

four

Diversionary Tactics

The strangeness of Time. Not in its passing, which can seem infinite, like a tunnel whose end you can't see, whose beginning you've forgotten, but in the sudden realization that something finite, a piece of Time, *has* passed, and is irretrievable.

The notebook. The CONFESSIONS. Nothing but fragments and desperate scribbles for the spring of 1956. Entries that begin but break off abruptly as if the writer lost heart or was interrupted . . . Letters that begin *Legs please forgive me for letting you & FOXFIRE down* and end *Legs please DON'T do it, I know you are brave & want only what's best for us but kidnapping is serious, it's a CAPITAL CRIME.* These letters never mailed of course, nor even completed.

About the chronology of what happened and the motives behind it—Maddy Wirtz, who was expelled from the Oldwick house ("X-iled" would have been the FOXFIRE code if the girls had voted on her but Legs managed it that there was never any formal vote, just Maddy invited to leave by Legs the First-in-Command), thus living at a distance, knew only a part of what I know, now. From newspapers, testimonies, etc. From my own (adult) reasoning, years after the tragedy.

Like I said about chronology earlier, the *paradox of chronology,* things happen that don't fit in. You know you ought to speak of them 'cause they did happen; they're part of History; but they don't fit in! It's like painting a wall and there are all these cracks, bumps, hollows the paint is supposed to cover but *can't.*

So I'll list these entries Maddy Wirtz made in the notebook, on other, unrelated subjects, right up till the very night of the kidnapping (May 29, 1956) as if by being faithful to the many other things that were happening to FOXFIRE at that time Maddy could divert Fate.

ITEM. Muriel's baby.

Muriel Orvis and her baby girl Evangeline: the poor baby had to have a third heart operation that winter, in a hospital in Buffalo, that turned out O.K. the doctors said sort of guardedly so you never knew what they meant or even if they knew, themselves. But Muriel was a wreck from so much strain, she'd gained weight and looked bloated, hair falling out in patches like she was twenty years older than her age . . . saying God had turned against her, Jesus had turned against her mocking her with dreams of being special and her baby girl special, and she was living on county welfare now, renting a place in town near the hospital and naturally she'd started drinking seriously again so Legs was worried sick about her, but worried even more about the baby who was, as Legs kept saying, her *sister.*

And all the money Muriel owed! Legs wouldn't even say, finally. Lana thought it was maybe five thousand dollars.

Maddy saw the baby a few times, and, except for being so small, and not able to cry loud like other babies, Legs' little sister, strictly speaking her *half-*sister, looked O.K. What none of us knew was that Evangeline Orvis would survive, and grow up, and continue to live long after FOXFIRE was destroyed, and Legs Sadovsky died or disappeared forever! *And she wouldn't know a thing about FOXFIRE or Legs* 'cause Muriel saw to that, moving away soon as the police investigation was over, as far away as she could get from Hammond—somebody said Reno, Nevada, where she worked in one of the casinos, somebody else said Anchorage, Alaska, where she got married quick to provide a father for Evangeline and everything turned out pretty good.

But: you know what I wish? That I could meet Legs Sadovsky's half-sister. Oh God just to tell her, this woman sixteen years younger than me, how much Legs loved her, just plain *loved* her. Also so I could look in her face, in her eyes. To see what's there of Legs.

ITEM. Toby's death.

This entry, for May 8, 1956, is such a sad one I can hardly read it without starting to cry. All these years later.

Around eleven-thirty P.M. that night most of us were awake, Goldie and Marsha and "V.V." were in the kitchen and there was a noise out front, and Toby who was on the veranda where sometimes he slept got excited, we could hear him making these strange hoarse coughing-choking sounds, then there's a gunshot, and another, and another, and Toby cried out, and already Goldie's running screaming "Oh Toby! Oh God *no*" and if one of us hadn't grabbed her she'd have run right out there and maybe been shot herself. And we're all on the floor, whatever room we're in, and two more shots come, two bullets right through one of our front windows shattering the glass sending it flying all over the living room then we hear tires squealing on the road and a car driving off and we all run outside and there's Toby, poor Toby we loved so, this beautiful brave silvery-haired husky who was loyal to FOXFIRE till the moment of his death, there he was dragging himself along the driveway toward us, his hind quarters paralyzed, bleeding badly, and he'd been shot in the chest too but he was holding his head erect, eyes anxious and tawny-bright and he was panting so hard and so irregularly we knew he was dying. My God how we were all crying . . . Goldie knelt sobbing over him, hugged him in her strong arms getting blood all over her, she held him murmuring, "It's O.K. Toby, it's O.K. Toby you're safe you're gonna be O.K. Toby, Goldie's got you," and the dog was shuddering, and whimpering, and licking her face, and he lived for about ten more minutes that way and there was nothing we could do for him, he died.

Goldie was wild with grief, got drunk, saying over and over, "I gotta know who to *kill*, help me—I gotta know who to *kill*" till finally she passed out and we put her to bed.

Next day we buried Toby, in the prettiest part of the yard, by a big old apple tree. Legs made a marker for him, painted just his name TOBY on it, dignified and sad but I suppose whoever rented the property after us, or the owner himself, probably kicked it down, took it away.

Yes we wanted revenge, all of us not just Goldie. But we never got it. That was one bitterness we had to swallow.

FOXFIRE had so many enemies by the time Toby died, everyone had a different theory of who'd done the shooting. There were certain gang-boys feuding with us—the Viscounts, still, but also the Aces, and the Dukes—these fights (which FOXFIRE wasn't innocent of provoking) flared up from time to time, then died down then flared up again, who knows why. There were guys who HATED us not for gang-reasons but for personal reasons who wanted us DEAD and let us know it, guys like Agnes Dyer's sister's husband I mentioned, but there were others too, Toni LeFeber's father, Toy Bocci's ex-boy friend, these loners were in a way the most dangerous Enemies 'cause nobody except them knew when they'd strike next.

So, Toby's death. The last entry Maddy Wirtz made in her

notebook before moving out of the FOXFIRE HOMESTEAD forever.

ITEM. Rita/"Red" O'Hagan: "X-iled."

This has nothing to do with the Kellogg kidnapping either, it happened the week following Toby's death when everybody in FOXFIRE was feeling angry and vindictive and jumpy and there'd been suspicion of Rita for a while, she'd stopped living full-time in the house and only came out weekends or nights sometimes, and, at Perry, where she was still attending classes (like Maddy Wirtz: still "in" school officially but getting low grades, cutting classes and in trouble with all her teachers), she was often observed talking and laughing with Others, sometimes even avoiding her FOXFIRE blood-sisters for instance in the cafeteria, and after Maddy Wirtz left the house and was living with a relative (*not* Rose Packer) Rita was observed talking with *her* which was believed to be subversive.

Yes FOXFIRE had spies. The newer younger initiates, who were still in school, tough girls the gang-boys were afraid of, the way they'd been afraid of Legs Sadovsky and Goldie Siefried in the past.

Among these newer younger initiates was "V.V." also known as "The Enforcer." 'Cause "V.V." with her waxy-white face, skinny body (when "V.V." was tattooed, we just stared—her skeleton showed so through her skin, and her breasts weren't *there*—just nipples like tiny hard pebbles pressed in her flesh) and weird way of grinning so her eyes were just slits—"V.V." who was Goldie's special protégée believed in enforcing all FOXFIRE rules and regulations and got upset if there was a violation, however minor, and not punishment right away, at least a reprimand from one of the older girls. So "V.V." who was a sophomore at Perry, fifteen years old and just putting in time till she could quit at age sixteen, naturally made it her business to spy on Rita O'Hagan all she could.

Not that "V.V." didn't like Rita. She told Maddy she liked Rita—and her—a whole lot. Yeah she *liked* us but she *loved* FOXFIRE—"Any time I gotta die for FOXFIRE, I *will.*"

Grinning so wide her lips thinned out to practically nothing and her eyes were slits stretched at the corners.

So it happened that "V.V." caught Rita not just consorting with Enemies but *actually going out with a guy*—which was forbidden by the gang of course 'cause all FOXFIRE blood-sisters' loyalty was to FOXFIRE not to anybody else.

The guy's name was Collis Connor (no relation to Kathleen), he worked in a dairy bar near school where Rita went after school sometimes. Collis was red-haired like Rita; freckled; not fat, nor even plump, but big—heavy-set, muscular, built like a bear but *gentle*-voiced, so you almost couldn't hear what he said. He was in his early twenties, hadn't graduated from high school. Maddy thought he was a nice guy sure but not overly bright but he *was* crazy about Rita you could tell: in Corson's Dairy he'd stop dead still when she came inside alert and attentive and blushing and Rita never looked at him immediately but after a while, after she had her Coke, and lit up her cigarette, her eyes would drift casually to his where he was standing behind the counter in his white uniform and apron, and now he'd blush even harder, and Rita's face too would turn pink, never would Collis Connor approach Rita O'Hagan in any public way 'cause he knew about FOXFIRE (by now everybody knew about FOXFIRE: a lot of it crude rumor but a lot of it accurate too) but somehow the two managed to communicate since without Maddy Wirtz who was Rita's close friend knowing a thing, or even guessing a thing, Rita and Collis went out together a total of three times before she was caught—all three times to the Century Theatre where, the weekday night "V.V." trailed them, and some sappy comedy-romance starring Doris Day and Rock Hudson was playing, they would sit slouched down in the last row of seats, in the balcony, in the farthest left-hand corner of the big old theater, holding hands, Rita's head on Collis's shoulder, *kissing.*

So "V.V." reported, and Rita didn't deny it. She was sick
with guilt and regret and she cried swearing she'd never do it
again never so much as look at Collis Connor or any other guy
again, she'd just been *weak* saying yes to Collis when he asked
her out she didn't *love* him for sure it was her FOXFIRE sisters
she loved please wouldn't they believe her?—"Don't cast me
out," Rita begged, "—I'll never do it again."

But FOXFIRE voted "X-ile": a unanimous vote.

As Legs said, grim and regretful herself, Rita knew what
she was doing and how dangerous it was: this wasn't any time
to fuck around.

What "X-ile" officially meant was suspension from
FOXFIRE for a minimum of three weeks after which Rita's case
would be reexamined. During these three weeks, Rita was *invisible* to her FOXFIRE sisters should they chance to see her,
and she was forbidden to approach them or speak to them or
even look at them in any prolonged or conspicuous manner.
She was forbidden to wear FOXFIRE colors—the jacket, scarf,
etc. She was forbidden to speak of FOXFIRE to anyone or to
acknowledge that she was being disciplined and above all she
was forbidden to associate with Maddy Wirtz . . . who found
herself, not officially, but in fact, *invisible* too.

Like limbo, it was. Like the Catholic Church teaches—
limbo is the region where the souls of infants and small children who died unbaptized by the Church yet innocent of all
sin must dwell forever and ever till the end of Time deprived
of Heaven and of Jesus Christ's love, it's a politics of revenge
and life-hatred that takes your breath away, yet it's Catholic
dogma like "X-ile" was dogma in those last days of FOXFIRE
rushing to an end.

And afterward Rita would say repeatedly, oh she'd tell it
to nearly everyone reckless in her speech as she was dis-
traught in her emotions, "My God, if they hadn't voted against
me I might be dead now! I might be *dead!*"

five

The Plot (II)

"Two?—what d'you even want *one* for?"

"Self-protection, me and my girl friends."

"Oh yeah? That's it, is it? 'Self-protection'?"

"That's it."

She was such a cool blond bitch this Legs Sadovsky, fixing him that drop-dead look like she did, a man's cream-colored fedora slanted on her sleek head and her hands on her narrow hips like she wasn't the least nervous alone with him, Acey Holman had to admire her: laughed and shrugged and decided to believe her, what the hell. Also Acey's a man proud of his local connections, plenty of guys in Hammond owe him favors so he enjoyed it, the girl listening hard, observing him out of the corner of her eye as he dialed the phone, spoke quietly into it, set up the after-hours deal for her—"And no questions asked, honey"—that very night.

So Legs buys the guns. May 11, 1956.

She buys them at PITTMAN'S SPORTING GOODS, Ninth Street and Holland, at the rear of the store. Two near-identical Police Service revolvers, .38-caliber, unregistered and untraceable, guaranteed, as the seller says, to perform. The guns cost her seventy-five dollars each plus fifteen dollars for a box of bullets.

These guns, Legs Sadovsky purchases *before* it's a definite date with Marianne Kellogg, to go to church with her and her parents as Marianne had suggested, months before. That's 'cause Legs Sadovsky is so confident she just *knows* her plans are going to work out the way she envisions. She *knows!*

It's a euphoric feeling, like flying high. Better, 'cause it isn't dope it's *real.*

As once she'd said to Maddy Wirtz, "—Luck's just a combination of destiny and desire. You want something bad enough it's gotta come to you."

So, two. 38-caliber Police Service revolvers, purchased by Legs Sadovsky the evening of May 11, 1956. One of which will be the "fatal" weapon.

Margaret Sadovsky wrote a shy little note to Marianne Kellogg renewing their acquaintance, giving Marianne a telephone number (*not* the telephone at the Oldwick house) to call should she wish to call, and next day Marianne did call, saying she'd like very much to see Margaret again, would Margaret like to attend church services with Marianne and her parents next Sunday?—and Margaret expressed gratitude, and pleasure, yes she'd like to attend church services with them, yes she'd like that very much—but could she bring along a friend?—a girl friend of hers (*not* from Red Bank: just from the neighborhood) who was drawn to God but so unhappy so lonely, her mother died of cancer just last year and her father—and there was scarcely any need to continue, Marianne Kellogg was already saying, "Oh yes of course bring her, Margaret. Mummy and Daddy would be *delighted.*"

Legs Sadovsky was thinking: how lavish even reckless rich

people can be in their generosity, once you show them the way.

The trick is: you know the Enemy but the Enemy doesn't know you.

The FOXFIRE girls beg, one by one, "Take me, Legs," and "Take *me,* Legs please?" but there's no point in being jealous, resentful, muttering sullenly out of earshot 'cause of course the girl friend's going to be gorgeous Violet Kahn, for Sunday with the rich Christian Kelloggs.

"Just remember—it is 'Veronica Mason.' And your mother's dead, and your father's just plain gone."

"Oh yes!"

"And I'm 'Margaret,' not Legs. Never Legs. O.K.?"

"Oh yes Legs—*I mean Margaret!*"

Violet's so agitated, Legs gives her a hurtful poke, pulls her hair.

A playful little jungle-cat kiss, on the neck.

So, Sunday May 16, 1956, Margaret Sadovsky and her striking but rather quiet friend Veronica Mason attend the eleven o'clock service at Grace Episcopal Church in the company of Whitney Kellogg, Jr. and his wife and daughter, afterward they're taken back to the Kelloggs' home where a midday meal is served, such elegance! such bounty! such warmth such Christian charity! and the visit is a little strained but overall a happy and satisfying one, no one happier and more buoyant than Mr. Kellogg whose eye snags repeatedly on Veronica Mason, very possibly without his knowledge.

For Margaret Sadovsky's friend Veronica *is* fascinating to contemplate, like a lovely overgrown child: her sleek black hair cascading in curtains around her face; her skin a soft moist white, like flower petals; her pretty-but-melancholy mouth a muted pink, little-girl pink the very shade of Marianne Kellogg's lipstick. Her voluptuous big-breasted wide-hipped body is partly disguised in a navy blue "box" suit with a pleated skirt and a floppy white bow; it's a bargain-basement costume, but in good taste: the very costume a poor-girl would wear to church. (With white gloves and a little veiled hat.) "Remember, hon, you've suffered a great sorrow," Legs instructed her on the way to the Kelloggs', "—don't smile too much and when you do smile at *him* like he's, y'know, lit up your heart or something. *Above all don't break into a belly laugh.*"

"Oh Legs I'm not *that* stupid," Violet said, hurt.

Through the lengthy church service, through the obstacle course of the meal at the Kelloggs' table—*not* the Kelloggs' large formal dining-room table, which can seat more than twenty guests, but a medium-size table in a smaller dining room at the rear of the house—Veronica Mason does behave ideally. She *is* genuinely self-conscious in this exalted company; fumbling her silverware, her napkin, her cut-glass water goblet that's like nothing she has ever held before in her hand. Her large lovely thick-lashed eyes, the hue of licorice, brighten with an indefinable moisture when she gazes at Whitney Kellogg, Jr. who's so frequently smiling at *her.*

Mr. Kellogg is something of a surprise to both Margaret and Veronica; that's to say, to both Legs and Violet who'd expected a different sort of man—a millionaire or maybe he's a billionaire, and wouldn't he be judging them critically, cold-eyed, gruff, even hostile?—suspicious? It's hard, perceiving the Enemy at such close range, not to imagine that the Enemy perceives you . . . but Mr. Kellogg is warm, open, gregarious, wholly unsuspicious. He's a stocky thick-necked man in his late forties, bald head gleaming, more youthful than his photograph: his skin has a pinkish-bronze cast, his eyes are small, quick, and animated, he has a habit of smiling so widely that his very white teeth, or dentures, seem to take up most of his lower face. His laughter is loud and infectious, like flames crackling through wood; he's the kind of man who laughs at his own jokes. Most surprising, Mr. Kellogg is truly *fatherly—*

though his daughter Marianne is twenty years old, a college student, he treats her like a little girl, so affectionate and persistent in his teasing that Marianne finally blushes with pleasure, her linen napkin hiding half her face, and cries, "Oh Daddy *stop!*" and it's a strange suspended moment: both Margaret Sadovsky and Veronica Mason bite their lips in confused envy for of course *they're* fatherless.

As the meal concludes, over coffee and dessert, Mr. Kellogg turns somber, philosophical. Yet forceful: ". . . A human being is ordained. I mean we're *blessed* from the start. From the morning of the Creation. If we so choose. If we make our decision for Christ. If we own up to the unvarnished facts of life. If we don't shirk our responsibilities. If we don't crawl whimpering and whining casting blame on others for our own failures and sins. I realize," Mr. Kellogg says quickly, almost irritably, as if he suspects someone at the table is about to interrupt, "—there *is* Adam and Eve and the serpent and the casting-out from the Garden, I realize that but look: through the ages till this very day *some rise to the top and some do not.* Can you deny that? Can you explain that? Eh? 'God helps he who helps himself'—or do I mean 'him'—'him who helps himself'—whatever. It's a riddle, girls, isn't it? Why some *do* and some *do not;* maybe *will not.* Oh it's a riddle! If all humans are equal in God's vision, all are equal candidates for Jesus Christ's love, so why the belly-aching? Eh?"

This abrupt question, harshly uttered, and the finger-wagging that accompanies it, take Margaret and Veronica by surprise. Good girls as they are, attentive as Mr. Kellogg's own wife and daughter, they've been nodding gravely through Mr. Kellogg's impassioned little speech, though maybe not comprehending every word. What has happened? Why so suddenly? Warm genial fatherly Mr. Kellogg is frowning angrily and his eyes seem to have shrunk back into his head.

Fortunately, Mr. Kellogg doesn't expect an answer to his question, he knows the answer: "It's the Communists! The insidious Commie influence! Socialists, pinkos, whatever! Like

dry rot! Like cancer! Undermining our society! That Jew-lover
'F.D.R.' "—uttered in a tone of extreme contempt—"began it
all, opened the door to incompetence and sloth and now look!
It's a cripple's mentality! Him and Old Joe Stalin! He was
Stalin's dupe! And now look! Everywhere the Commie-backed
unions are making their moves! Like snakes in the night! Great
greedy pythons! Stuffing their bellies! Sick leave they want!
Sick *pay!* Pay 'em for being sick! Can you believe it? Eh? Pay
'em for being drunks!—falling into their machines! It's a plot to
crush us! Suck our blood! And y'know who's their dupe? Eh?
Biggest dupe of all? *Eisenhower!* Good old *'Ike'!*"

So Mr. Kellogg speaks for some tense minutes, the color
up in his face and his barrel-chest straining against his starched
white shirt front, silk necktie, tight-buttoned vest. Even as he
speaks Mr. Kellogg has been devouring his dessert, a wedge of
pineapple upside-down cake, he finishes his own piece and
wordlessly accepts half of Mrs. Kellogg's, pushed discreetly to
his place. At the table Marianne has a nervous habit of fussing
with her hair, which is rolled under, in a neat smooth page-
boy, and with her glasses, which she settles and resettles on
her nose, and Mr. Kellogg frowns at her and says, "Marianne
please," as if this is an old annoyance. But he continues to
speak, addressing his young guests, who regard him wide-
eyed and respectfully just the slightest bit fearfully which is
only to be expected in these circumstances, poor-girls at the
rich man's table, and yes it's flattering, how can it help but be
flattering even to a man accustomed to being listened to respectfully when he speaks no matter at what length and no
matter what the substance or the not-entirely-coherent emotion underlying the substance, how can it help but be im-
mensely flattering: ashy-blond Margaret Sadovsky with her
intelligent eyes, sharp features, uplifted chin and gorgeous
Veronica Mason with her enormous eyes fixed on his face as if
she's mesmerized . . . as if she has never seen or heard anyone
like Whitney Kellogg, Jr. in her entire life and maybe his
words, these very words, more passionate and more powerful

than the Episcopal priest's sermon that morning, *maybe these words have the force to change this girl's life forever?*

Like Whitney Kellogg, Jr. doesn't just speak for Jesus Christ he *is* Jesus Christ?—sort of?

The subject comes up of the girls' futures. In the case of Margaret there's some embarrassment about her past but the past's past, better to forget what you can't change Mr. Kellogg in his wisdom would surely advise. Mrs. Kellogg says, "Margaret hopes to go to business school, don't you, dear?" and Mr. Kellogg says, "Here in Hammond?—y'know I've hired many first-rate girls from the Hammond School of Business, in fact I've endowed a scholarship fund for girls in need of financial aid, did Marianne tell you?" and they talk for a while of the Hammond School of Business, yes Veronica is interested as well, yes but they need jobs right now, for personal reasons for family reasons they need jobs right now though yes they are interested in the Hammond School of Business too, both of them. Margaret says she hopes to go into business for herself someday—"It's the only way to get ahead, to be your own boss." Mr. Kellogg seems charmed by this statement, and asks, not patronizingly, but kindly, what sort of business Margaret wants to go into, and Margaret says, "Beauty. A beauty salon. A *nice* beauty salon." She pauses, smiling shyly, yet with dignity; a tall lean striking girl who might be a decade older than she is, so sharp-eyed, her forehead lightly creased as if with thought, dressed prettily for today's visit in a black and white checked "box" suit nearly identical to her friend's, and like her friend she's wearing inexpensive but tasteful patent leather shoes, stockings with neat straight seams. She says, as if confessing a secret, "I learned hair-dressing and cosmetology, some. In Red Bank. Y'know—Red Bank State Correctional."

There's a moment of embarrassment but Mr. Kellogg nods vigorously, he likes this girl this is a girl he likes, she's clearly honest, straightforward, you can trust her. "Excellent use of time," he says, "—it's the kind of program taxpayers get their money's worth out of. And you, Veronica? What do you hope to do?—I mean, between now and—getting married?"

Mr. Kellogg shifts his shoulders uneasily, as if the prospect of Veronica Mason, apart from marriage, that's to say masculine physical possession, is difficult to consider.

Veronica says softly, "Oh thank you for asking, Mr. Kellogg! I hope to work for Margaret if I can."

"Ah yes—in Margaret's beauty salon. You'd be your own most persuasive advertisement, dear."

"—In the meantime, though, I need a job. Real bad. Both of us do. Any sort of sales or office work isn't that right, Margaret?"

So smoothly does "Margaret" roll off Veronica's tongue, you would believe she's been saying it for years.

Margaret says, "Yes. That's right."

Mr. Kellogg says nothing further on the subject at the moment; but, as the girls are preparing to leave, he takes both their hands in his, and squeezes them in a gesture of paternal solicitude. For a relatively short man—he's of a height with Veronica in her high-heeled shoes, and shorter than Margaret by an inch—Mr. Kellogg has an imposing, even commanding air; he stands with his shoulders back, and his head, contemplating the world through bemused narrowed eyes. Out of earshot of Mrs. Kellogg and Marianne he says, "Well, girls. About jobs. You're both rather—young, aren't you? And inexperienced?"

Breathlessly Veronica says, "Oh no not exactly!"

Margaret says, "We both have had all kinds of experiences, Mr. Kellogg."

Mr. Kellogg says, addressing Veronica doubtfully, "Can you type, dear?"

Veronica says, "Oh I love to type!—don't I, Margaret?"

Mr. Kellogg says, still doubtfully, and in an undertone, "There *is* an opening, maybe two—for stenographers I think—in our Branch Street office."

Veronica says, in a hushed voice, touching Mr. Kellogg's coat sleeve with her fingertips, her lovely eyes large and grave and brimming with moisture, "Oh Mr. Kellogg—*I love to steno-graph!*"

In that way the May 16 visit to the Kelloggs' home on Jelliff Place ends on a congenial hopeful note: with Whitney Kellogg's promise to call Margaret Sadovsky and Veronica Mason. Soon.

Violet's eyes were puffy from crying, she said I just don't know if I can go through with it, I know it's justified like you say but I don't know if I can go through with it I mean I guess I like them, even him, I know he's evil 'cause of he's rich and a capitalist and exploiting and all that I know that Legs but I'm so sad I'm so worried not that we're gonna get caught but I sort of like them Marianne and Mrs. Kellogg they were so nice to me like almost I was their equal Legs y'know? y'know what I mean? and Legs said, Shut up.

six

The Plot (III)

Unrecorded in Maddy Wirtz's notebook there followed then a
sequence of days of euphoria and dread one/two/three/four/
five/six fucking days when "WKJ" (their code-name for him)
didn't call the sonuvabitch and Legs Sadovsky moved in a haze
of disbelief so convinced they'd hooked him, the fucker, how
he'd stared at Violet devouring her with his eyes! licking his
pulpy lips! even at Legs he'd stared as if already she was one
of his hired "girls" and he'd squeezed their hands in parting,
made his promise! So every hour of these days she waited pacing like a big caged cat smoking cigarettes and running her fingers impatiently through her hair she hated the man more
recalling what she knew what lore she'd been told of strike-
breaking tactics used by factory owners in Hammond against
the workers, her own father, her grandfather, yes their Fairfax
neighbors and it went back decades long before Legs was
born even before her father's birth and "WKJ" was of that
tainted lineage and she recalled how smiling at her he'd startled her into smiling in return and how he'd spoken to her so
kindly so patronizing her pride was like a flammable material
touched by a match and gripping her hand in his in farewell

he'd forced her to feel his strength, the unjust strength out of which his kindness flowed, she'd been forced to feel the rich man's superiority and power, the rich man's very flesh aglow in the special joy of those who move through life with advantage amidst the teeming multitudes of no advantage and to harden her heart against him she laughed how the fucker's gonna pay for the humiliation he'd caused Legs Sadovsky to suffer—not just in ONE MILLION DOLLARS but in pride.

As Legs told Muriel Orvis thoughtfully, "What's wanted from our Enemies are their *hearts,*" not noting that Muriel Orvis had no idea what she was talking of, gloating of. Not a clue.

The telephone number Margaret Sadovsky had left with Whitney Kellogg, Jr. and his daughter Marianne would be traced by Hammond police to the shabby three-room apartment on Fourth Street rented by Muriel Orvis: poor Muriel who knew literally nothing of what was being planned, not only nothing of the elaborate plot pertaining to the "final solution" as Legs envisioned it but nothing of the hooking expeditions the FOXFIRE blood-sisters had been making now for months, shrewdly and of necessity extending their territory out beyond Hammond to towns and cities within reasonable driving distance as far east as Albany and as far west as Buffalo. It's true, and Muriel would so testify to police, she understood that the girls were mysteriously involved with men, any number of men and men of all ages, not that she'd ever so much as glimpsed one of these men (she had not) but she'd formed her impression overhearing the girls talking and laughing together carelessly in her presence. Yes they shared in common a true distrust you might say an active dislike of men based not on ideology but on experience, *men are the Enemy* is no secret after all.

But Muriel Orvis aged almost thirty-seven was not a member of FOXFIRE thus not entrusted with the girls' gang-secrets, nor had she the slightest desire to be: Muriel believed they were good solid well-intentioned trustworthy girls, anyway most of them but they were girls and Muriel was an adult woman, and a mother.

Mother of a beautiful six-month baby girl who'd had to endure three heart operations since birth and protracted stays in intensive-care units in both Buffalo and Hammond. That's to say—Muriel Orvis had her own problems.

Yes she minded a little Legs Sadovsky and some of the other gang-girls using her apartment when they needed a place in town but she'd never never shut her door against them: never.

Yes she did accept money. Money, and gifts. From Legs mainly.

No she didn't know where precisely the money and gifts came from, she'd asked a few times but never got any straight answer so she'd stopped asking.

Yes she trusted Legs Sadovsky. No she never seriously questioned Legs. Yes even when she didn't exactly believe Legs.

Yes she thought maybe Legs invented things: dreamt things up, out of the air. Plans for the future. Everybody living together. That sort of thing you wanted to believe sort of but couldn't really, it wasn't *real.*

Then again, Legs had a way of surprising you with things that did turn out *real*—like renting their house, furnishing it pretty good the way they did. And that crazy car of theirs LIGHTNING BOLT.

No Muriel knew nothing about any telephone call, repeat Muriel knew NOTHING about any alleged telephone call from Whitney Kellogg Jr. to the telephone in her apartment. Not when it came nor even that it came. For certainly she didn't overhear her young friend speaking on the phone making arrangements to meet this party or any other party, Muriel Orvis isn't the kind of person to eavesdrop even in her own home.

And, as she'd said, she trusted Legs Sadovsky. *Her own baby's half-sister.*

The revolvers were tested, *did* work—at least fired when their triggers were squeezed. Whether they shot true or not it was difficult to tell.

The primary fact of gunshot is it's so loud it's deafening it takes your breath away!

They practiced, they went on disciplined target-shooting expeditions far back into the woods, miles from any human habitation. (Their Oldwick neighbors had several times called the police 'cause of gunshots fired *at* the FOXFIRE HOME-STEAD—thus they dared not risk calling further attention to themselves.) Not all the FOXFIRE sisters were selected to practice with the firearms not 'cause (as Legs explained, to each girl in turn) she didn't trust all her sisters but frankly she worried a few of them might be too soft-hearted, the *fact* of the guns would scare them.

All the FOXFIRE girls (yes even Rita, even Maddy some of the time) owned and carried knives. But a knife's a different thing from a gun, a gun's a different thing from a knife.

So they went out into the countryside deep into the woods where in season hunters shot at deer, pheasants, rabbits, anything that moved that was "sport." Six or seven of them, chosen by Legs and Goldie. "Not that we're gonna actually fire these guns when we take 'WKJ' and hold him captive," Legs said repeatedly, "—but we need them, just the fact of them. To show we mean business."

Said Goldie, grimly, but with a thin little smile, raising her pistol to shoulder height and steadying her right wrist with her left hand and sighting along the eight-inch barrel and half-shutting one eye and squeezing the trigger and CRACK!—*"I mean business."*

* * *

The telephone call from "WKJ" Legs knew must come did come finally, evening of May 28 and yes "WKJ" gave evidence in his voice of being hooked, maybe. Or maybe as he claimed he truly wanted to hire Margaret Sadovsky and Veronica Mason to work in one of his offices?

Still, Legs was suspicious: why'd the guy arrange for them to meet him after dark, nine-thirty P.M. at the rear of 2883 Branch Street?—not during the day during office hours?

"It's O.K.," Legs said excitedly. "All it does is, it speeds up our plot. We're gonna take him *sooner.*"

Said Violet, sighing, "Oh better sooner than later, Legs—I'm dying to get this over with!"

So Margaret Sadovsky and Veronica Mason, prospective office workers, nicely dressed young women in high-heeled pumps and even wearing white gloves meet Whitney Kellogg, Jr. their prospective employer at the designated place the next night, yes there he is sitting in his white Cadillac Imperial awaiting them nervously smoking a cigar and both the FOXFIRE girls are excited as ever they've been, Legs as giddy-calm as she'd be climbing a high tower or preparing to dive one of her flawless-reckless dives into deep water and Violet giggly-scared as a little girl swaying in her high heels and chewing gum in surreptitious rushes, so it's a sweet gum-fragrant breath she releases when Mr. Kellogg grips her hand in greeting, her hand more forcibly than her friend's, Mr. Kellogg saying happily, "Well hello! You did come! Hel*lo* girls!" staring at them as if he doesn't believe they are truly here, and Violet, that's to say Veronica, saying, huskily whispering, " '*Lo* Mr. Kellogg!"

What happens next is: Mr. Kellogg unlocks the front door to the small flat-roofed building, inside is an office space containing seven or eight desks, there's an inner office at the rear darkened but visible through a glass partition or window, there's a scrawny rubber plant leaning in a corner, fluorescent tubing overhead giving a yellowish-melancholy cast to the space, metal filing cabinets, telephones, stacks of paperwork on desks, watercooler dimly gleaming at the rear and Mr. Kellogg proud of ownership of AMERICAN TOOL & ASSOCIATES INC. is chattering telling his visitors facts pertaining to the "operation"—the office handles merchandising for small automotive-designed tools—facts pertaining to the "work force"—there are ten office workers here including receptionist and manager—and what the nature of their work will be if they "sign on" here.

He says, knocking ash off the tip of his cigar, "—Thought I'd show you girls the office when it's nice and quiet so we wouldn't be distracted. So you could see it *sans* a gaggle of jealous middle-aged women staring at you."

Margaret says, "So thoughtful of you, Mr. Kellogg."

Veronica says, "—*So* thoughtful!"

Margaret drifts off as Mr. Kellogg tells Veronica, clearly his favorite, about his many many operations related to steel processing and AMERICAN TOOL & ASSOCIATES is but one and Veronica exclaims *Oh!* and *Oh really!* and *Oh is that so!* her agitation giving her a sharp erotic edge while Margaret contemplates the rows of desks, old-fashioned office desks not in very good condition, scratched, battered, lives are lived out here too and might hers have been one of them?—"Margaret Sadovsky" one of the hired "girls" then one of the "middle-aged women"?—she lifts a plastic typewriter cover to peer beneath, seeing the big chunky office-model machine she thinks briefly of Maddy, Maddy-who-has-deserted-her, she lifts a telephone receiver simply to hear the dial tone, she's a tall stiff-backed blond girl with a scar on her chin, curious blood-speck on the pupil of her left eye, dark tight-belted rayon dress on her long bones and she's wearing white gloves, maybe it's a poor-girl's stratagem hoping to resemble a lady hoping to be given a job in Whitney Kellogg's employ, or maybe she doesn't want to leave any fingerprints.

Margaret casts a covert glance in the direction of Whitney Kellogg, Jr. who's talking happily with Veronica, the man's pink-bronze skin is shiny tonight, his eyes crinkling-bright, bald head so *solid*. Is Margaret feeling just slightly excluded? neglected?—gentlemanly Mr. Kellogg who after all has a daughter himself grins at her and waves her over.

"Veronica and I were just saying—"

Beyond the stink of Mr. Kellogg's cigar there is an underlying odor of alcohol: a good sign.

Meaning: the man is scared; the man is meeting Margaret and Veronica here on the sly; the man has surely told no one where he is.

Thus in a position to *disappear*.

Nothing remaining of him but the cigar-stink when, next morning, the office is unlocked?

It's nine-fifty P.M. when Mr. Kellogg switches off the fluorescent lights in the building, leads his admiring guests outside, locks the door. Makes a fuss locking the door. It's dark here at the rear of 2883 Branch Street: a single parking lot light, no street lights close by, no moon. May 29 is a cool night smelling of moist earth, damp cement, industrial fumes. (Branch Street is Uptown Hammond but this end of it, the east end, is in a neighborhood of small factories and a waste-disposal plant.) Mr. Kellogg rubs his hands together briskly saying, looking from one girl to the other, "—I thought we might go for a little drive? along the river? out toward Morganstown?—there's a nice little inn there, d'you know the Morganstown Inn? I thought we could maybe get to know one another a little better, just relax, uh just talk—?"

Margaret's rather cold eyes are firmly on Mr. Kellogg's face.

"Such a great idea, Mr. Kellogg!"

Veronica's inky-black eyes too are fixed on Mr. Kellogg's face, as if in resistance to looking elsewhere. As in a low breathy voice exuding a sweet smell of chewing gum she murmurs, "Yeah! *Such* a great idea, Mr. Kellogg!"

Following which, in the course of the next hour or so, Whitney Kellogg, Jr. *disappears*.

seven

The Plot (IV)

FOXFIRE had possession of the rich man "WKJ" for five days, no one else knowing of his whereabouts, or who had stolen him away.

Or was it that "WKJ" had possession of FOXFIRE?

Legs saying, on the second or third day, after she's over-seen him abducted at gunpoint, bound and gagged and blind-folded and brought to the Oldwick place to be tied to a beam in the cellar to await $1 MILLION ransom money to free him— "Who'd have thought, the fucker's so *real?*"

The initial part of Legs' plot went perfectly: abducting WKJ out of the parking lot at AMERICAN TOOL & ASSOCIATES.

WKJ was just opening the door for Veronica to slide into the passenger's seat of the Caddy when out of the shadows a tall burly masked figure appeared—in fact there were three masked figures, but WKJ was too panicked to even see the other two, at first—a gun in his hand, upraised, left hand steadying the wrist of the gun-holding right hand, the barrel pointed into WKJ's astonished face.

"O.K. you stop where you *are.*"

It's a low gravelly-guttural voice. A man's voice?—surely.

WKJ sees only the gun at first. The gun, and the comical-lurid mask. Maybe eyes through the eyeholes of the mask but these are no eyes he knows.

Naturally he stops. Freezes. Lifts his arms weakly. The cigar falls forgotten to the ground.

"Don't shoot—please. Take my wallet—I'll give you all the money I have. The keys to the car—"

The blood has drained out of WKJ's face, his voice is cracked and trembling. Knees quivering. Eyes pleading, damp.

Now he sees the two other figures, advancing swiftly upon him. One with a gun, the other carrying something in his arms.

One circling to WKJ's left, the other to his right.

His bowels contract. He's paralyzed, almost.

Dazed blinking panic, a quick sweat breaking out all over his body, staring at a gun barrel (is it trembling? just perceptibly?) aimed into his face, the stranger's voice and his own voice hoarse, croaking take my wallet, please don't shoot me, take my car, anything, oh please *don't shoot.* Partly aware of Margaret Sadovsky and Veronica Mason backing off innocently stricken, girls murmuring *Oh! oh! oh!* and *Please don't shoot!* backing off discreetly into the shadows leaving their companion the more vulnerable, exposed.

It requires several slow seconds before the truth of WKJ's situation sinks in—he is wanted *bodily* by these armed assailants.

Not the money in his wallet but *him.*

He's forced to his knees in the gravel, emptying his pockets as instructed. Squinting up at his tallest assailant, the only one who speaks, in that low mock-courteous voice as if he knows Whitney Kellogg, Jr. and doesn't think much of him. "O.K. man, move. You ain't gonna get hurt if you cooperate." The assailant's mask is a rubber Hallowe'en mask, a ghastly-grinning death's head, iridescent white bones crudely painted on a black background. He's approximately six feet tall, solid-bodied, in bulky layered clothing; wears gloves, a man's hat with a scarf tied around it so every strand of hair is concealed. "Man I said *move your ass.*"

They want him, not on his feet, but on his hands and knees, ignominiously crawling to the rear of the Cadillac. Why, he doesn't know. He's too terrified to protest. The two masked assailants with the guns herd him along, kicking, prodding. They're deft, efficient, excitable, probably young.

Maybe, thinks WKJ, they're *colored.*

Their plan for him, which he realizes belatedly, is to force him into his own car trunk: thus they'll drive off with him into the night. It's an abduction, a kidnapping. His life is going to be ransomed. He isn't going to be killed now but he may be killed later. "Don't," he pleads, "—have mercy on me, in the name of Jesus Christ have mercy on me," he says, his voice cracked and feeble, tears in his eyes, "—if you let me go now I won't call the police I won't tell anyone I promise I *won't.* Take my money, take the car, but please—"

"Man shut your mouth. Or I'll blow it off."

"My wife— My family—"

"C'mon man, 'Mr. Kellogg.' Put out your hands."

"—And those girls! Don't hurt—"

WKJ is unceremoniously bound, wrists and ankles, with baling wire, so tight it hurts. A rag is stuffed into his mouth and a strip of cloth is tied like a bandage around his lower face so he can't spit out the gag and can't make any sound except moans, whimpers. He's blindfolded—the last sight he sees in the open air is the cheap-glittery white death's-head, the mocking grin, the icy sexless eyes inside the eye-holes—and a canvas sack smelling of rancid potatoes is forced over his head, tied at the neck. Then he's made to topple into the trunk, it's a wide deep spacious trunk, the spare tire having been pried out and rolled away, hidden where?—in a culvert behind the building where it will be found, eventually; days later.

WKJ remembered his two girl companions belatedly but he did remember them, even in his state of shock, there's that to be said in his favor. But he's made to hear, before the trunk is slammed down, unmistakable signs of their being beaten, perhaps killed—one of them is sobbing *No oh no please!* and the other is sobbing *Please don't kill us! Oh please!* and their cries are muffled, there's the sickening sound of metal striking flesh, the butt of a gun striking flesh, a final choked cry and the sound of bodies falling to the gravel—then silence.

He'll forget about the girls, in the ordeal to come.

Those girls—already he's forgotten their names!—no he can't bear to think of them, to calculate what their (possible? probable?) fate must mean, contingent upon his own.

Legs saying, whispering, hugging her FOXFIRE sisters as they were hugging her, the five of them there in the parking lot at the rear of 2883 Branch Street, giddy, crazy-elated, half in disbelief, "—We got *him*. The rest is gonna be *easy.*"

eight

The Plot (V)

We got him. The rest of it is gonna be easy.
Oh Legs! If you'd known.

Some of it, FOXFIRE could not have known, and would not, until it was revealed in the newspapers and such, afterward: that, tied up and gagged so tight in the trunk of his own car, Whitney Kellogg, Jr. began to vomit, and choke, and knew he must die if no help came, and so in desperation he who had not (by his own admission, afterward) ever prayed in such a way before in his life now broke through at once to Jesus Christ, Who heard his appeal and promised to save him *If you will take Me in your heart;* and so by this miracle the nausea subsided, and the terrible vomiting ceased, and Whitney Kellogg, Jr. was suffused with superhuman Christian strength and courage, knowing that Jesus Christ his Savior would see him through the ordeal that lay ahead, and release him to his loved ones, unharmed.

None of this, FOXFIRE could have known.

As, resolved to confuse the kidnapped man in the trunk of the car, Legs drove in a zigzag maze through Hammond

County north and east and south and west! over bridges!
through tunnels! around hairpin turns! in dizzy circles and at
shrewd perpendicular angles! on dry pavement on skidding
gravel on rutted country lanes! for forty-five measured minutes
before returning to the open highway to Oldwick Township at
a moderate speed and so to FOXFIRE headquarters where
the kidnapped man was to be held captive until such time as
$1 MILLION RANSOM released him and altered the fortunes of
FOXFIRE forever.

Thinking, giddy and gloating in the first adrenaline-high
of success: *Nothing can stop us, now!*

"You got him?—really?"

"Sure we got him, what d'ya think?"

Unlocking the trunk of the Caddy, and all eyes springing
open in amazed stunned surprise.

Eleven-fifteen P.M. of May 29, the first telephone call was
placed from a pay phone on Fairfax, to the astonished Mrs.
Kellogg: "Don't contact the police, lady, your husband is safe
but if you contact the police he's gonna be dead: got it?" and
the first ransom note mailed at approximately that time to be
delivered to 8 Jelliff Place at noon of the following day.

By which time, unknown to FOXFIRE, Mrs. Kellogg in her
hysteria had contacted, not the Hammond Police, but the district attorney for Hammond County, who happened to be a
close family friend. Marianne's godfather, in fact.

But then there came the first of the unexpected obstacles:
the kidnapped man refused to cooperate with his captors.

Never had Legs anticipated this!—"The fucker!"

Whitney Kellogg, Jr. would not speak over the telephone
to his wife, no not even at gunpoint, blindfolded, the receiver

pressed to the left side of his head and the gun barrel to the right and the sonuvabitch is quivering with fear but *will not* speak, *will not* answer Mrs. Kellogg's desperate appeals, "Whitney?—are you there? Whitney? Hello? Are you all right? Whitney—?" and will not write a note to her assuring her he's all right *just do what's asked of you and I'll be returned to you*, nor even sign a note typed out carefully for him, not a thing!

Goldie said, white with rage, "We can starve him, then. We can torture him. Cut off one of his fingers and send it to his wife, to show we mean business!"

Legs said, slowly, almost too slowly, "—Nah he's gonna come around, you wait. I'll reason with him."

So she did. She tried. There in the earthen-floored cellar of the Oldwick house, the man bound as before, blindfolded, the sack over his head removed only occasionally and that in the presence of masked bulkily dressed figures he may still have believed were young men, even colored men, soft-inflected was Legs' voice, low, purposeful, friendly, pointing out it was to everybody's advantage, right?—for him to cooperate?—'cause he was a long long way from home a hundred miles from home and his wife must be crazy worried about him, his sons and daughters worried—this, to suggest that whoever had kidnapped him was unacquainted with the details of his family life for Marianne was the Kelloggs' only child—and what's one million dollars to somebody who's got so much?—"A rich guy like you, Mr. K'logg! Rather die than pay! Is that it!"

The word *die* didn't seem to scare him, though. Didn't make any impression at all.

It was weird. Legs couldn't figure it. She wasn't panicking but she couldn't figure it. Whitney Kellogg, Jr. who was, for Christ's sake, a businessman, dealt in money and human-beings-as-money, refusing to negotiate with her now: not responding normally, like a zombie almost. In the parking lot he'd been scared shitless now he was somewhere they couldn't reach him. Legs and Violet had witnessed him at home at church shaking hands loud-laughing and alive and zestful and energetic but now, FOXFIRE's captive, it was like he'd retreated somewhere deep inside himself.

"—Just his *bodily* self, in our possession!"

And this *bodily self,* they sure had to tend. Had to feed, or try to feed (the bastard resisted eating); had to cart away his piss, his meager watery shit.

Had to watch constantly. Day and night, two kerosene lanterns burning in the cellar. Day and night, never less than two armed guards.

Legs was down there much of the time of course. Thinking, It's like The Room again and *we're both in it.*

Day One, that's to say May 30, Toy Bocci drove out in LIGHTNING BOLT to mail, from an ordinary postal box just inside the city limits, a small neatly wrapped package to MRS. W. KELLOGG, 8 JELLIFF PLACE, HAMMOND, NEW YORK— this package containing WKJ's monogrammed white linen handkerchief, his heavy gold-and-onyx masonic ring, his driver's license. And a typewritten note of Legs'—

YOUR HUSBAND IS ALIVE & O.K. HE WILL BE SET FREE
ONLY WHEN $1 MILLION RANSOME IS PAID.
AWAIT INSTRUCTIONS!
DO NOT CONTACT POLICE!!!

On impulse, Legs cut the palm of her hand with her switchblade, smeared blood on the sheet of paper. In a rapture of assuring the Enemy, *we mean business.*

Contacting Mrs. Kellogg, though, was not so easy as Legs had expected.

Yes it was easy enough to dial her number and get an immediate answer, before the first ring was completed even, but, on the phone, Mrs. Kellogg was so *emotional*—didn't see this as a business deal at all. Didn't know, of course, that her husband was gonna be returned to her for Christ's sake no matter what.

So the poor woman's crying, can hardly speak coherently, and Legs, hoping to negotiate rationally with her, talking through a piece of cloth laid across the receiver (as she'd seen in the movies), has trouble getting a word in; starts to get anxious, sweaty-nervous, Mrs. Kellogg's stalling, so the call can be traced. So Legs hangs up the receiver like it's a snake.

Which means she has to call back, another time. And much the same thing happens.

The problem is, WKJ won't cooperate: won't talk to his wife.

This poor woman weeping, pleading, begging, you have to believe she's utterly sincere, "—How can I pay you?—if I don't even know if Whitney is alive?—how can I, how can you expect me, oh please have mercy please let me talk to him—" so Legs says, disgusted, *"He* won't talk to *you,* ma'am!"

Day Two, Day Three, Day Four . . . nobody to keep accounts, no Maddy-Monkey to type entries for the notebook . . . so it has become weird, almost sinister, the passage of Time: Each hour slow like stretching some dense resistant substance but the actual days, twenty-four-hour units, turning over rapidly. Wild! Like flying high! And each day they can't work out a deal with Mrs. Kellogg, can't get their hands on the money— each day their captive's here in the house, his big-assed Caddy hidden in the hay barn—each day's a terrible risk you almost don't want to think about.

Maddy Wirtz who'd been Legs' heart who'd broken Legs' heart, what had she said: Kidnapping's a CAPITAL CRIME.

And Legs had said scornfully: But we're not gonna kill him, and we're not gonna get *caught.*

* * *

Nothing in the Hammond newspaper about the missing millionaire, nothing on the local radio station.

A good sign? Meaning Mrs. Kellogg has obeyed the command not to contact police?

Eleven calls in all, placed to the Kelloggs' residence on Jelliff Place. Most of the calls were made from public phone booths in Hammond, or in suburban towns ringing Hammond, one or two from gas stations in the country as far away as Sandhurst, on Lake Ontario: Legs had a fear the calls were being traced, even as, with another part of her mind, and wholly logically, she reasoned that Mrs. Kellogg was acting in good faith, she wouldn't want her beloved Whitney killed would she?

Always, when Legs dialed the Kelloggs' number, and it was a number soon memorized, the telephone would be answered on the first ring: most of the time it was Mrs. Kellogg, several times it was Marianne. (Legs, stricken with guilt, regret, shame, just asked to speak to Mrs. Kellogg—she didn't want to think, nah she didn't think, that Marianne must surely know about the kidnapping, the threats—she must know her father was missing.) (Nor did Legs want to think that many people must have been aware of the absence of Whitney Kellogg, Jr. after all!—a man of business like that.) But though the telephone was readily answered and Mrs. Kellogg always, or nearly always, there, the conversations were disjointed and incoherent and unsatisfactory and covered in a cold slime of sweat Legs might cry, "I'm hanging up! Goddamn you I think you want him *dead!*"

Just the fucker's *bodily self* in FOXFIRE's possession.

That's to say, too, in their care: their responsibility.

You couldn't help but feel sorry for him, uncomplaining as he was, sure he must be scared but didn't act *scared* as if he knew (but how could he know? was he a mind-reader? picking up on unconscious stuff?) that FOXFIRE's plan was to release him anyway, after a week or so, even if the money was not delivered.

They had to remove the band tied around his lower face when they tried to feed him, had to tug out the spittle-drenched gag, kept the blindfold on, wrists and ankles tied of course, yes but he refused to eat, like a gigantic baby gripping his jaws tight refusing any and all food which just astonished them, yeah it wasn't what you'd expect, nor did he drink water, much, except a few times in a helpless spasm of muscular abandonment the poor bastard drank, drank, drank from a glass held to his lips—like he was dying of thirst, but hoped to deny it.

"C'mon, man, Mr. K'logg," Legs cajoled, exchanging looks with Lana, "—dontcha want to *survive?*"

Lana said, exasperated, disguising her voice not very successfully, "Dontcha want to *communicate?*"

But no. No he didn't. Licking his bruised puffy lips, showing his tongue that looked gray-coated, too large for his mouth. But he wouldn't utter a single word just set his mouth like concrete.

Gray-glinting hairs sprouting on his jaws, like an old rummy.

An odor as of rancid onions rising from his armpits.

Starched white shirt long since stained, filthy, torn: maybe it was fancy, high quality, but not now.

Goldie said, in the man's very earshot, "We gotta stop fucking around. Say we cut off one of his fingers, like, y'know, over the phone? So the wife hears him, so he's *got* to say something?"

Legs, white with fury, didn't answer. Upstairs though she launched into Goldie, she said, "Jesus are you *dumb*. Talking like *that*. The idea of it is, we won't hurt him: we pledged that. We can't go chopping his finger off, what's gonna come next?"

There was a strange stiff moment. Goldie sucked on her cigarette, stared at their feet. You did get the idea she'd forgotten the actual plan, THE PLOT as Legs had elaborated it, yeah they'd pledged to follow THE PLOT but maybe Goldie was forgetting?—and some of the other FOXFIRE sisters as well?

Lana said, impulsively, "What Goldie meant is—just to *scare*. We wouldn't have to cut the whole finger off, right away."

It's late at night, Legs is on guard, V.V. wordless sitting beside her, the kerosene lamps cast a queer sort of Hallowe'en light on WKJ who seems to be sleeping, or maybe just not-conscious, and it comes to Legs, who knows why, recalling the man in church, in his family pew, *his* pew, praying, head bowed, eyes shut tight, that maybe, just maybe, this weird stubborn behavior like the integrity of rock has to do with the fucker's *religion*.

That's to say, his special Christianity: Episcopal: the rich man's religion.

Like it isn't enough to own factories and mansions to have in your employ thousands of human beings this fucker has God too. Like Heaven itself is another property, he knows *he's* got a place in!

Did I make a mistake, is it too late to undo. Did I ruin everything.

She isn't thinking this, not Legs. FOXFIRE NEVER SAYS SORRY!

A girl fleeing across the rooftops, long legs flying, hair streaming in the wind. And none of you to catch her, ever. Don't even try.

* * *

Sunday June 3, the end of FOXFIRE.

And maybe they knew it would be so, some of them. The younger girls sleeping, or trying to sleep, in the upstairs dark. Teeth grinding. Skin covered in goosebumps. What is going to happen, what are we going to do, I want to go home. And Maddy miles away, her heart clenched like a fist. *Legs? Why didn't you listen to me?*

Legs, forgive me.

June 3, a long rattling day like a freight train, and by six P.M. they're not desperate but they're *serious,* yes. "We've got to get him up the stairs, into the kitchen so he can talk on the phone, okay?"

"But he won't talk."

"He *will.* He's got to."

"And if he won't?"

So they go downstairs, into that place they've come to dread, and Legs squats by that bulky monster-figure they've come to hate, saying, no she's pleading, "Look: *why* won't you talk? *Why* won't you talk? *Why* won't you cooperate? Like your poor wife she's worried sick keeps asking are you O.K. she's waiting for a word from you, hey man you gotta cooperate!"

No response except maybe the bastard's shaking his head . . . an almost imperceptible *no.*

"We're gonna call your wife now, and you better talk to her. C'mon get on your feet!"

Goldie and V.V. help tug at him, Legs pokes him in the belly with the gun barrel, but it's like he's a dead weight: won't cooperate even in his body.

Even to get some exercise.

So, panting, they let him fall back. So he's half-lying in the dirt, breathing hard, sweating, his wrists and ankles bound with baling wire it's too bad it has cut into his flesh but it's of necessity, and the blindfold is still tied around his head, poor fucker like a corpse laid out in some special way, but if Legs feels a stab of pity she feels a harsher stab of anger, rage. *You brought this onto yourself God damn you! Any time you want, you can be free!*

It's possible that, even now, Legs believes this.

So it's a matter of getting WKJ hoisted on his feet and up the stairs, for Legs, as for Goldie and V.V., the entire world has contracted to the problem at hand there's no thought for the hour beyond the next hour, certainly not to the next morning, and the morning beyond that.

So: Legs is squatting in front of the recumbent man, one of the revolvers in hand and she's prodding him with the butt, annoyed, impatient as a mother confronted with a troublesome child, prodding his knee with the butt so he feels it (*she* feels him registering the pain but as usual he gives no sign), and Goldie is hanging over Legs with the other gun in hand pointing the barrel into WKJ's face though, blindfolded, he can't see her, and V.V. is crouched behind Legs, to her right, weaponless, vigilant and alert as always, this skinny snakey-quick girl of fifteen scarcely more developed than a girl of eleven or twelve, not much is known of V.V. even by her FOXFIRE blood-sisters except she's the youngest of a family of seven children living close by the city dump, her father works as a laborer sporadically and two of her brothers are at Red Bank and her mother long ago gave up on her, let the gang-girls take her in and good luck to them, *I* can't control the little bitch but V.V.'s a fiercely loyal girl, V.V.'s a courageous girl, nerves like steel Goldie said of her, arguing for her to be admitted into FOXFIRE, she's unselfish, willing to sacrifice sleep so Legs, Goldie, Lana can sleep, so childishly grateful for cast-off clothes (the oversized jeans she's wearing, the raggedy sweater, cute white anklet socks with pink elephants embroidered on the cuffs) she embarrasses the others, snatching up their hands, kissing their hands, giggling and stammering more thanks than you're comfortable hearing so Legs has had to kid with her, calm her, look FOXFIRE's your family, from each according to what she can give, to each according to what she needs, and now, at dusk of Day Five of the kidnap-capture, Legs is trying to reason with WKJ saying, "O.K. this is serious, goddamn you you *hear?*" hollow-eyed with exhaustion she pokes the fucker's knee hard with the gun butt and as if reflexively, or maybe he's losing control too, WKJ kicks out at her with both legs, sends the revolver flying from her fingers and Legs herself stumbling, and V.V. snatches up the revolver, aims it trembling at WKJ, screams, "Fucker, don't you touch *her*"— and seeing what is going to happen Legs shoves V.V. and the gun goes off, the explosion deafening, and a .38-caliber bullet slams into WKJ's chest, pumping blood.

nine

Wild Wild Ride

V.V., the Enforcer. Hides sobbing in a corner of the barn, yanking her rat-hair in fistfuls.

She didn't mean to, yes she meant to, please Legs let me kill him all the way, now it's too late Legs let me! let me!

Legs, chalky-faced, stunned. Sick-looking as her FOXFIRE sisters have never seen her.

Legs, her eyes widened glistening like candlelight the knowledge of *the end of Foxfire* slow-coursing through her. Squatting by the unconscious man, afraid to touch him but needing to touch him, "Hey mister, hey you're not gonna die are you, hey—" her fingers coming away sticky with blood.

It wasn't a shot to the heart, a flesh wound maybe?—in the upper right corner of the man's fatty chest. Dark blood seeping through his shirt and through the clumsily wadded strips of torn sheet Legs has tried to tie around the wound, beneath WKJ's arm and over the shoulder, a stench of bowels and animal panic lifting from him. Even now the man Legs does not want to think of as Marianne's father stirs into brief consciousness, like a man waking from a dream, his lips moving, deathly pale his lips they've bared, damp with spittle, even now he's stoic in pain, will not beg, will not address his captors but murmurs *Oh Christ, oh Christ, help me oh Christ.*

Leg shouts, "It isn't fucking *Christ* gonna help you, it's *us!*"

Legs sees there is nothing to be done, now. "We'll have to call an ambulance."

"Shit, let's drag him out, somewhere!" Goldie cries. "Dump him by the road!"

"*Then* we can call an ambulance, Legs? Can't we?" Lana asks.

But Legs has made up her mind, still that sick chalky look to her face, the stunned eyes. "That might kill him. We got to *help* him. Get the rest of them ready, O.K.?"

The other girls, having heard the gun go off, are terrified, crying. Peering down the cellar stairs.

Such young girls, after all—"Legs? Legs? What are we gonna do?"

"Legs? Is he dead?"

The man in the cellar isn't dead but he's moaning, his breath comes in shudders. The force of the bullet sent him sprawling as if a violent gust of wind had blown him over and Legs contemplating him in that detachment beyond horror or even alarm sees how the Enemy is after all only a man . . . on his back, bleeding.

Legs says bitterly, "Hey, you're not gonna die. We'll get help for you, just hang on."

Upstairs she rushes about clutching the girls, hugging them to her, letting them hug her. "It's O.K. Nobody's dead. We had an accident—a change of plans. We fucked up so get out, O.K.? All of you who can, *go.*"

Meaning: those of you with homes, go *home.*

Meaning: those who weren't part of the kidnapping, hadn't been present when the gun went off, those who hadn't *seen* anything close up, thus were not to *blame,* you're safe and I'm gonna protect you if I can.

Meaning: FOXFIRE is ended.

The girls flee, crying. Through the woods, through the fields where prickly rose tears at their legs, drawing blood.

Out on the Oldwick Road there's this one girl brash and desperate and maybe too stupid to know how she is exposing herself, eager to escape anywhere, my God! that gorgeous baby-doll face streaked with tears, jet-black hair cascading in ripples to her waist, out there no more than six minutes when a passing car brakes to a skidding stop, the driver's gaping at her, then backs up the car like his life depends upon it one arm crooked around the steering wheel and the other stretched along the back of the seat and already the guy's in love, craning his head staring at this unbelievable beautiful white-skinned girl with a body not even loose-fitting disheveled-looking clothes can disguise and she's brushing her hair out of her eyes staring at him with such radiant hope so they'll boast, all their lives together, it was love at first sight— Yeah the *real thing.*

Legs gives the girls ten minutes to escape the farmhouse, no more. Sitting at the top of the cellar steps, staring down at the wounded man shuddering and groaning, unconscious now, on his back. The .38-caliber revolver in her lap as if she's guarding him, yet.

A single kerosene lantern burning now, the wick beginning to smoke.

Her life-as-Legs washing over her, wave upon wave. Insubstantial as a dream she can't quite recall.

Goldie squats beside her, massive-thighed. "What if the fucker croaks!" she whispers in Legs' ear. "Y'know—I wish he would."

"I wish he would!" It's V.V., crept out of hiding. Like a dog sidling up to Legs, cringing, fawning, yes and defiant too, daring Legs to send her away. Legs, looking at her, sees a sick, deranged girl: a mentally unbalanced girl: why hadn't she known? V.V.'s lopsided grin sets her skinny face askew, it's the kind of grin that can't help but erupt in giggles. "Then we could burn down the fucking house, huh Legs? Could we?"

Legs gives V.V. a shove, not hard; but with the butt of the revolver. "Go on, *go,*" she says. "Don't stay with me."

"I'm not going nowhere, without you!" V.V. says angrily.

"I'm not, either," Goldie says. "You know that."

"And me, neither," Lana says. She's dragging a duffel bag across the kitchen floor, crammed with her clothes. In all the commotion, she's taken the time to draw a glamorous lipstick mouth on her own sickly-pale mouth, and this mouth is smiling. "Right, Legs?"

What can Legs Sadovsky say but *yes?*

Legs clutches the telephone receiver, she's speaking rapidly in a low breathy voice, ". . . a gunshot wound, yeah! I *said!* . . . this guy's hit in the shoulder and's bleeding pretty bad, better send an ambulance . . . it was an accident, gun went off . . . Oldwick Road, three miles south of Hammond . . . mile down from the fairground . . . old farmhouse, rusty mailbox with no name on it . . . never mind who this is, you come get him, O.K.? *O.K.?"*

Goldie pulls the receiver out of Legs' fingers and slams it down into the cradle—"Let's get the fuck out of here!" They're making the call from a pay phone in the parking lot of the Mattawa Inn but still: the number might be traced.

LIGHTNING BOLT is idling close by, rackety motor running and chassis vibrating, exhaust pipe spewing blue smoke. Headlights gleaming like mad yellow eyes.

Legs and Goldie run back to the car, climb inside laughing wild as if they're being tickled. Some guys just going into the tavern stare at them, good-looking girls drunk this early in the evening?—and there's LIGHTNING BOLT all rainbow colors and zigzag lightning hardly recognizable as a mere '52 Dodge.

And two other girls inside, in the back seat?—no guys?

Next day, when the news breaks, they'll remember: FOXFIRE.

Twenty minutes later, Legs drives LIGHTNING BOLT across the Cassadaga River for the last time.

She's smart. Anyway at first. Keeping the car at a moderate speed not wanting to catch a cop's eye: *kidnapping's a capital offense, they can send you to the electric chair.*

Crossing the high windy Ferry Street bridge, that old nightmare of a bridge above the choppy-glittery Cassadaga they've grown up seeing and not seeing, the river sometimes invisible running through Hammond running through their lives so they're staring down at it for the last time and V.V. in the back seat suddenly leans halfway out the window hair whipping in the wind and fingers trailing like she's waving Goodbye! goodbye! then sighting these high-school guys in a stripped-down Chevy so V.V. yells at them and gives them the finger and there's a horn-blast retort like spraying bullets but the Chevy's headed downtown and LIGHTNING BOLT is headed north out of the city, no time for a race but this will be the last of LIGHTNING BOLT anyone in Hammond will have seen and will report having seen when news breaks next day of the kidnapping of wealthy Hammond businessman Whitney Kellogg, Jr., the wounding, or was it attempted murder, and four local teenage girls from a gang called FOXFIRE, now *fugitives from justice.*

That wild wild ride!—the crazily painted old Dodge sighted by motorists on U.S. 33 north to U.S. 104 east to U.S. 39 north and east to Plattsburgh where Legs' grandmother will take the girls in, Gramma won't call the police Gramma will hide us then we can cross the border by night into Canada into Quebec where they speak French and we can learn French where nobody's waiting and nobody *knows*.

Beyond Spragueville, sighted at about eight P.M., beyond Tintern Falls by nine, a wan opalescent-orange sky bleeding at the horizon and dusk coming fast.

Whoever's in pursuit, siren wailing, won't catch up.

Whoever, he'll have to shoot the tires out.

It's a New York State trooper who has sighted them, clocked their speed, set chase. Twelve miles south of Newton Falls in the western foothills of the Adirondacks, U.S. 39 north, a cool early-summer night, a full moon smudged with cloud: and there's this speeding rattling car clocked at twenty-two miles above the speed limit, throwing off sparks from its tail pipe, bronze-gold lightning-zigzag bolts on its sides.

In all, a nine-mile chase.

Rarely has LIGHTNING BOLT been coaxed to a speed beyond sixty-three miles an hour and now it's amazing it's surely a miracle as the red trembling speedometer needle inches beyond sixty-eight, seventy, seventy-three . . . Legs grips the wheel feeling the car's strength shuddering through its length and the hold of the tires on the blacktop highway, it's as if LIGHTNING BOLT is speeding into the night of its own volition, whoever's in pursuit will have to shoot the tires out if he wants to take her.

A curving country road, densely wooded on one side, scrubby land on the other, and damn it: the left headlight is out: but LIGHTNING BOLT isn't going to stop.

The trooper's car is close behind, the siren loud now, deafening.

Seventy-nine miles an hour, eighty . . . LIGHTNING BOLT hurtles forward filled with girls' terrified screams, only Legs Sadovsky is silent.

It's at the bridge over the Oshawa Creek that the accident occurs.

The state trooper is gaining on LIGHTNING BOLT approaching a narrow low-railing bridge over the invisible creek, and knowing the road and the danger he begins to brake, the LIGHTNING BOLT's driver seeing the backward-flying bridge begins to brake too, pumping the brake, but it looks like Death as ascending the ramp the old car skids on loose gravel, bucks and heaves and seventy feet behind, the state trooper steels himself for the terrible crash, he's appalled seeing LIGHTNING BOLT lifting at the rear, the protracted slow-motion of a nightmare as the luridly painted car unlike any car he has ever seen skids against the rusted iron railing with a screeching of metal and flies off the bridge shorn of its right rear fender but otherwise miraculously intact rocking crazily from side to side veering as if one of its tires had been shot out, and when the state trooper's front wheels hit the loose gravel his own heavy car goes into a skid, the right rear end skidding around and there's an abrupt impact and the shriek of metal too against a concrete abutment . . . and it's the state trooper who's stopped, a humiliating misjudgment amid a rain of glass and he's bleeding from his banged-up forehead dazed and fumbling radioing for help trying to describe the fugitives' car that has now disappeared.

And is never sighted again, so far as law enforcement authorities can determine.

Epilogue

Never never tell, Maddy-Monkey, it's Death if you tell. But now I have told all I know, or nearly.

Transcribing Maddy's old notebook into these FOXFIRE CONFESSIONS I've been destroying it page by page, entry by entry. Crumpling pages in my fists. In order that they might burn more readily.

My life since FOXFIRE has been a peaceful life, you would call it an ordinary American life (I was even married for a while, three years, to an astrophysicist grad student at Cal Tech) except for my line of work which is the kind that, if somebody asks, and I tell them, they look at me funny and ask, You do *what?*

I left Hammond at the age of eighteen. My heart was broken losing Legs and FOXFIRE and I was lucky getting a scholarship to a university far away where no one knew even the name FOXFIRE, nor was likely to learn of it. Yes I was interrogated for days by Hammond police and F.B.I. agents and for months made to report to "youth authorities" but no charges were ever brought against me, for Madeleine Faith Wirtz was not one of those involved, directly or indirectly, in the notorious kidnapping and ransoming of Whitney Kellogg, Jr.

Lucky for her, Maddy Wirtz had been expelled from FOXFIRE before any of it. Which was her salvation as far as the law was concerned.

I've returned to Hammond just four times. Most recently, which will be the final time I think, to visit the Hammond Public Library and the County Courthouse, to assemble out of old newspapers and records a rudimentary official account of those weeks of May–June 1956 that were the last days of FOXFIRE. Much that I never knew at the time—for instance, the police and F.B.I. had been informed immediately of the kidnapping and had believed it was a plot of "top-ranking labor union officials in league with organized crime" intended not just to extract ransom money from the Kelloggs but to intimidate and terrify other American businessmen of Mr. Kellogg's stature who had resisted union demands!—so J. Edgar Hoover was himself quoted by the media.

The very "amateur" nature of the kidnapping, the interrupted telephone contacts for instance, police interpreted as a deliberate strategy to mislead.

One of the local headlines was

KELLOGG KIDNAPPING BELIEVED
COMMUNIST PLOT

And another,

LOCAL GIRL GANG TIED TO
INTERNATIONAL RED TERRORISTS

How Legs must have laughed, if she knew!

The articles about Whitney Kellogg, Jr. and his family I skimmed over quickly, I didn't want to read of Mr. Kellogg's "conversion" to Christianity—"The *real* Christianity: Christ in our hearts"—and I didn't want to read about his daughter Marianne, how she'd "trusted" Legs Sadovsky, how she'd been "betrayed."

Feeling guilty, that sick guilt. Though Maddy Wirtz wasn't a kidnapper I'd wanted FOXFIRE to succeed.

I'd wanted the four "fugitives" to escape.

In time, police located Goldie, then Lana, living hundreds of miles apart, with no knowledge of each other's whereabouts or of Legs and V.V.: Goldie was arrested at her job pumping gas in Horseheads, New York, under a false name, Lana was arrested in Albany where she was staying with an Armenian bartender, under a false name too, hair dyed mousy brown. But police never found Legs Sadovsky, and they never found V.V. Nor LIGHTNING BOLT either.

Maybe Legs and V.V. crossed the border into Canada?— hid LIGHTNING BOLT where it was never found, and fled on foot?

Legs' grandmother denied the girls had ever come to her, and there was no proof they had. Nor any of her Plattsburgh neighbors claiming to have seen a car like LIGHTNING BOLT which you'd have to be blind not to see if it was parked in somebody's drive.

So Legs and V.V. remained fugitives from justice. The search for them was publicized for months, maybe went on for years. There were hundreds of false leads and sightings but the girls were never found and for all I know (kidnapping *is* a federal offense) they remain fugitives to this day.

"Maddy—my God is it *you?* Maddy *Wirtz?*"

And I turned and saw a pretty carroty-haired woman, a young woman my age in her late twenties with a full, fleshy body, pale freckled skin and she was pushing a stroller with a carroty-haired child in it, Rita O'Hagan it was, Rita whom I had not seen in eleven years, and maybe if I'd had warning that Rita was close by I'd have crossed to the other side of the street, maybe I'd have avoided this meeting entirely but seeing her any such thought flew out of my head and we grabbed at each other, crying right there on the sidewalk, on Fairfax, Rita's little boy gaping up at us and sucking his fingers.

Like long-lost sisters you'd think, seeing us.

So Rita insisted I come back with her to her place, her older kids were in school and Collis wouldn't be back till six, we had a lot of catching up to do Rita said, so many years since I'd left Hammond!

She and Collis Connor were married and living in a new apartment building on Ferry Street. He had a job in an appliance store, sales-and-repairs. I knew she'd married Collis didn't I?—right after the trouble?

By "trouble" meaning the breakup of FOXFIRE, the arrests, the scandal.

Up in the Connors' apartment in their living room Rita offered me coffee, then a bottle of beer, we sat, drank, exchanged news. Mainly it was Rita talking—she seemed happy to talk, excited to be talking to me—several times leaning over to touch my arm as if to make sure I was real, saying, with an edge of sisterly reproach, "I almost didn't recognize you, Maddy—you look so different."

I laughed self-consciously. Not wanting to ask in what way did I look different.

Rita added, with a sigh, "—I s'pose we all look different. Or should."

It was June 1968. I'd returned to Hammond for a brief visit. Not intending to look any of my old FOXFIRE sisters up, no not even to scan the telephone directory seeking certain names.

I believed I was not a sentimental person any longer. I believed I had hardened my heart against hurt.

In the work that I find myself doing, you might call it the contemplation and quantification of rock-debris, it seems natural you *would* harden your heart, doesn't it?—or, your heart would harden by degrees, without your knowing it.

Maddy, you're my heart.

No one has ever said that to me again.

No one has ever been given reason to say that to me, again.

Rita inquired, curious, yet tactful, where was I living now?—meaning was I married, did I have a family, had I turned out "normal" like her. I explained yes I'd been married but only for a brief while—"It just didn't work out, lucky we didn't have children"—not wanting to see Rita's look of pity, for, to a mother, what is more meaningful more precious more soul-defining than children, "—I live in Quincy, New Mexico, I work at the observatory there, I love my work but it's lonely, and I guess I'm a little lonely, sometimes. But I'm happy, too."

"Oh Maddy, I'm so glad to hear that." And it seemed Rita was glad, and this surprised me. "—Of all of us, except . . ." her voice trailing off and her gaze slipping quick to one side, so we could both supply the name and need not utter it, ". . . you were the one the most . . . different."

Recalling how once I'd overheard Goldie saying *Maddy's sort of not one of us,* how those words cut me to the bone.

Quick then I changed the subject. Asked about our former sisters and Rita gave a rapid recitation of all she knew, which was a good deal, most of it passing by me swift as a scene blurred outside the window of a speeding vehicle, but I took note of Violet Kahn—"Oh for sure *she* did O.K.," Rita said, shrugging, "—married this guy that's with his father and uncles in some big construction outfit, none of them even finished high school but they're rich and guess where Violet's got a house?—on Meridian." It took only a second for this to sink in: Meridian Boulevard intersects Jelliff.

This brought us to the point where Rita asked, almost shyly, "And you've never heard from—her?"

Quickly I said, "No. Have you?"

"No. Not a word." Rita paused, with a wistful little smile. "Nor a word *of* her, either. Except . . ." Again a pause that was a gentle inhalation of breath, a glance at me gentle too and conspiratorial as between old, former lovers.

We'd been talking by now over an hour, finishing our second glasses of beer, not so uneasy with each other as at the start. A carroty-haired little boy prattled happily to himself in a playpen a few feet away, it made me sad but wanting to smile too, the maudlin thought that Rita's son would never know of FOXFIRE, never a glimmer of knowledge of Legs Sadovsky who had changed his mother's life when she'd been a girl, yes had made *his* life possible. Rita murmured, excited as a young girl, "Uh—I got something to show you, Maddy, to tell you— not many people know about."

Seeing the look in her eyes I quickly set down my glass, I felt weak.

All this time, neither of us had spoken her name and I could not bring myself to whisper, *Legs?*

Rita hurried out of the room, and returned with a much-folded newspaper clipping. She smoothed it out on the sofa cushion beside me, saying, "Jesus, Maddy!—one night I happened to see this in the paper, years ago it was, such a coincidence 'cause I never pay any attention to politics and that sort of thing but I saw this on the front page of the paper, I thought oh God it's *her,*" showing me the clipping as if it were something precious, fragile, "—Maddy it's *her* isn't it?"

I stared at the newspaper photograph. There was a stiff bearded military figure, Fidel Castro, on a raised platform addressing a large crowd gathered in a square in Havana, Cuba; the dateline at the top was April 22, 1961, which made it shortly after the failed invasion of the Bay of Pigs. And there far to one side nearly out of the frame was a figure distinctly American, tall, slender, blond, male? female? wearing a shirt and trousers, swept up in the mood of the crowd of raptly listening angry spectators: Legs Sadovsky.

Or someone resembling her closely as a twin.

"Maddy—? It *is,* isn't it?"

I could not answer. I went to a window, holding the clipping to the light, to examine it more clearly.

Rita chattered nervously, laughing, emptying the remains

of a bottle of beer into both our glasses, "—I showed it to some of the girls, we don't see each other much any more, but I showed them and it turned out that Toni LeFeber—remember Toni?—she's married to Richie Wright—Toni'd seen it in the paper too, she recognized Legs but was scared to say anything to anybody, thinking, y'know, the F.B.I. might show up and arrest her! (You think they would, after all these years?) Collis, now—I never breathed a word of it to *him*. He'd have ripped it into pieces, he hated Legs so."

Then, reconsidering, quickly, "—He's real sweet, though. Just about the sweetest guy I ever met, he practically saved my life after all that ugliness came out. Like you guys did, when I was a little kid."

I was thinking if only a microscope, if only a microscope could magnify a newspaper photograph but it can't, don't be absurd, of course it can't: magnify the tiny dots and you magnify the space between them.

Rita said, musing, "It was smart of Goldie and Lana to plead guilty, I guess—that's what people said. You heard, they're both out, by now? But not living anywhere around here . . ." Her voice trailed off. She sipped from her glass of beer. She said, mildly anxious, "What d'you think Maddy?—you're awful quiet. It is *her* isn't it?"

My eyes were so damp, I couldn't see the photograph any longer.

My voice quavered, "Oh Rita, hon—I just don't *know.*"

Rita's laugh came sharp, disappointed. "Well, shit—*I* know!"

That wasn't my last visit to Hammond, New York. But it was the last visit that I saw anyone I knew.

And of the remainder of that visit I recall almost nothing, for once you're gone from a place, once you're expelled from it, all visits back dissolve into one, and that, in time, into a blur teasing and elusive as a dream.

Out of which I can recall vividly only the clipping from
the Hammond paper, the old brittle much-folded clipping, I
think probably yes it was Legs Sadovsky, who else so distinct,
that way she had of standing so straight so taut it was as if her
whole body were listening, every sense alert, unless I am
imagining it, inventing it out of my deep yearning, like Rita
O'Hagan inventing, yearning, staring at those minute pinpricks
of newsprint those atoms of light coalescing to produce a human figure, a face, features you somehow recognize, or believe you recognize: know, in an instant: a neurological trick,
or miracle, of the human brain: how, seeing, we *know*.

And if that had been Legs, in Havana, Cuba, on April 22,
1961, where is she *now?*

My days are almost entirely spent, I should explain, scan-
ning photographs through a microscope. Not hazy newspaper
photographs but elaborately detailed solar photographs; not
ordinary microscopes but stereo microscopes powerful enough
to allow me to see through the plane of the solar system, deep
into space and back into time. Sometimes I grow vertiginous,
flying through space and time: my skies are white skies, pho-
tographic negatives, against which stars are black specks, frozen in space, yet in motion, as I move film back and forth,
back and forth, examining black dots, blurs smears smudges
starry clouds, with an eye for discovering (if without the
power to avert) impending catastrophes: asteroids of unstable orbit, potential "earth-crossers" flying like wayward celestial thoughts out of the main asteroid belt floating
between the orbits of Jupiter and Mars.

Not that I'm an astronomer—I am not. I have only a B.A.
degree from the University of Iowa. But I am an astronomer's
assistant, one of those trusted, much-appreciated if modestly
paid assistants at the Mt. Quincy Observatory in New Mexico,
and I take my work seriously, such methodical work, such silent work, there's an element of mysticism in it I suppose,
looking for motion in films of identical parts of the sky set side

by side: an eye for light, for negative-light, for imminent dreamy disorder, for catastrophic rock-debris.

If there is some connection between my life now and my life as a girl I do not know what it is, and I do not want to know. Human motives have come to interest me less, through the years, than human actions, *being*. The stars have no motives after all, even their death-plunges are pure, in the service of *being*.

Maddy Wirtz was a smart girl for Fairfax Avenue but she'd been mistaken believing the stars were permanent, telling herself the stars are *there* in the sky no matter how things change on earth—soon coming to learn of course the stars aren't permanent nor are they even *there,* that's the most ironic fact of all. The heavenly light you admire is fossil-light, it's the unfathomably distant past you gaze into, stars long extinct.

Even our own sun, our domestic star, is eight minutes into the past. *Look-back time* it's called, such tricks of light and Time, such paradoxes, best not to think of it. I mean—not to think of it with any emotion, not a shred.

So assembling these FOXFIRE CONFESSIONS these past several months turned out to be a true effort for me, all I haven't felt or wanted to feel, for years. Undertaken now because I am fifty years old—*Maddy-Monkey fifty years old!* Undertaken now because I have the proper telescopic instrument for examining *look-back time,* that I hadn't had before.

Now the CONFESSIONS are finished, Maddy's old notebook destroyed, I guess I'm in no time at all.

And Legs Sadovsky—what kind of time is she in?

Is she—*are* you, Legs—in any Time at all?

There was a conversation we'd had once, in the early FOXFIRE days, both of us living at home then, in our separate homes, Legs with her father and me with my mother and the subject was one of those exciting-disturbing ones you have at that age, things we used to talk about when we were alone to-

gether and nobody to overhear: Legs said she sure didn't believe in God and all that crap, or the "immortality of the soul,"
it didn't figure Legs said that we were all that important, and I
said, trying to hide how shaky I felt, "—So you don't believe
we have souls I guess?" and Legs laughed and said, "Yeah
probably we do but why's that mean we're gonna last forever?
Like a flame is real enough, isn't it, while it's burning?—even
if there's a time it goes out?"